Edward Backhouse Eastwick

# Venezuela

Sketches of life in a South American republic - with the history of the loan of 1864

Edward Backhouse Eastwick

**Venezuela**

*Sketches of life in a South American republic - with the history of the loan of 1864*

ISBN/EAN: 9783337313586

Printed in Europe, USA, Canada, Australia, Japan

Cover: Foto ©Andreas Hilbeck / pixelio.de

More available books at **www.hansebooks.com**

# VENEZUELA.

# VENEZUELA:

OR,

## SKETCHES OF LIFE IN A SOUTH-AMERICAN REPUBLIC;

WITH THE

## HISTORY OF THE LOAN OF 1864.

BY

## EDWARD B. EASTWICK, C.B., F.R.S.,

LATE SECRETARY OF LEGATION AT THE COURT OF PERSIA; AND
COMMISSIONER FOR THE VENEZUELAN LOAN OF 1864.

AUTHOR OF "MURRAY'S HANDBOOK OF INDIA," "THE JOURNAL OF A DIPLOMATE," ETC., ETC.

WITH A MAP.

LONDON:

CHAPMAN & HALL, 193, PICCADILLY.

1868.

TO

# PHILIP ROSE, ESQ.,

OF RAYNERS, BUCKS.

—•—

My dear Rose,

To you I owe my pleasant visit to Venezuela.  To you, therefore, if to anyone, these pages ought to be inscribed ; and I am so glad of an opportunity to thank you publicly for many acts of friendship, that I dedicate my book to you, without allowing myself to consider how much your name may lose, as mine must gain, by the association.

Ever yours,

EDWARD B. EASTWICK.

38, Thurloe Square,
1868.

# PREFACE.

On the 7th of June, 1864, I was asked to go to Venezuela as Financial Commissioner for the General Credit Company. The appointment was offered, in the first instance, to Lord Hobart, and on his declining it, to me. The terms were liberal. All my expenses were to be paid, and I was to receive one thousand pounds for three months, reckoning from the day of embarkation. But the pleasure of seeing a new country, and learning a new language, and the experience of financial transactions I should gain in such a mission, were to me still stronger inducements to accept it. Besides, curiously enough, Mr. Cobden had been talking to me on the 2nd of June, the last time I ever saw him, about a certain matter, and, after expressing his sympathy, had ended by saying, " Why don't you go to the City ? They will treat you better there." So, taking his words as a *Sors Virgiliana*, I accepted the Commissionership at once, purchased a pile of Spanish books, imbibed a draught of the pure *Castilian* stream daily, in the shape of a lesson from Dr. Altschul, glanced at, and put aside for complete deglutition on board the steamer, a huge *liasse* of papers, and on the 17th of June found myself *en route* for St. Thomas, in the "Atrato," commanded by the ill-fated Captain Woolley.

I returned the same year, in the last days of October. In 1865, and the beginning of 1866, I wrote for Mr. Dickens some of the chapters which follow, and they appeared in "All the Year Round." In those light sketches my object was only to give a general idea of Venezuela and its people, so that what I have there written is not always to be taken *au pied de la lettre.* It is otherwise in the grave part of the book, which refers to the business of my mission. I have there striven to be as accurate as possible, my aim being to pilot others who may go out on similar missions with as little experience as myself, and who might, perhaps, be shipwrecked amongst dangers which have never been properly buoyed.

# CONTENTS.

## CHAPTER I.

### TO VENEZUELA.



## CHAPTER II.



## CHAPTER III.



## CHAPTER IV.

## CHAPTER V.



## CHAPTER VI.



## CHAPTER VII.



## CHAPTER VIII.



## CHAPTER IX.



## CHAPTER X.

# CHAPTER XI.



# CHAPTER XII.



# CHAPTER XIII.



# CHAPTER XIV.

# ERRATA.

At p. 126, lines 6, 18, and 29 ; and p. 127, lines 5 and 7 ; also at p. 128, lines 5 and 12—for Engelckye, *read* Engelke.

# VENEZUELA:

## OR,

## SKETCHES OF LIFE IN A SOUTH-AMERICAN REPUBLIC.

## CHAPTER I.

### TO VENEZUELA.

Sailing on a Friday—Juan—The Royal Mail Company—The Story interrupted—Hat Island—Harbour of St. Thomas—A Battle with the Sharks —The Virgin Islands—A Cruise among the Cemeteries—Blockade-runners—Voyage to La Guaira—The Death at Sea—Aves Islands— At Anchor.

"NEEDLES indeed! they look more like Grinders; and, à propos of that, if this confounded wind continues dead in our teeth, we shall pitch bows under as soon as we get outside." I uttered these words without addressing myself to any person in particular, for I knew no one on board, and, in fact, there was no one near enough to hear me, but my servant, who, like myself, was leaning over the taffrail, watching the pilot drop astern. I looked at my watch; it was seven minutes past seven, on the 17th of June (I like seven, it is a lucky number); we were off the Needles; the pilot had just left us; there was a strong breeze right ahead, and the weather did not look altogether so propitious

B

as it should do on a midsummer evening. My servant, Juan, was a fine specimen of a Santa Cruz man. He stood six feet five inches in his boots, was an excellent valet, never drank, smoked, nor swore, spoke Spanish and English, loved England with all his heart, and, like most natives of Santa Cruz and Saint Thomas, fully considered himself an Englishman. I knew little of Juan, who had been in my service only a few days, and was now to learn one of his peculiarities. He was subject to an extraordinary flow of spirits on the occurrence of anything which others regarded as depressing. A simple contretemps put him in a good humour; but a disaster made him jocular, and the graver the case the more he was elated. On hearing my exclamation he turned round approvingly, and said, "Yes, no fears, sir, but we'll have a rough night of it; I never hur-red no good of sailing on a Friday." "Pooh, pooh, Juan," said I, "that's a mere prejudice. Why, on Friday, the 9th of August, 1492, no less a man than Christóval Colon sailed from Lagos to discover the New World, these very West Indies to which we are now going, and on Friday, the 12th of October, he did discover San Salvador, not so very far from where you were born; and on Friday, the 1st of March, 1493, he saw land on his return—that is, he ought to have seen it if the weather had not been rather thick." I said the last words with some hesitation, for, in fact, I recollected that Colon, on his homeward voyage, encountered a regular tormenta off Portugal, and was near foundering; so that the third Friday was rather against me. Juan, however, as became a man of his inches, was not to be beaten from his opinion, and said: "I don't know nothing about Columbus, sir, but my father, who was a better man, leastways made more voyages 'tween 'Merica and Europe—for he was a ship's steward, and spoke English as well as I do—said he never hur-red no good of sailing on a Friday." So saying, and laying a peculiarly grating emphasis on the word hur-red, Juan stalked off.

"Confound the fellow!" said I to myself, "it's absurd, but he makes me melancholy with his forebodings. Yet, imagine anything like risk in a grand vessel of three thousand tons and upwards! Why, the wretched carvel in which Columbus made his voyages, was hardly so large as the long-boat there. It is no exaggeration to say that she would scarcely have carried the admiral's potted meats, which the steward tells me weigh over twenty tons. It is true, however, that though the voyage from Lagos to Guanahari was three thousand and forty miles—nearly as long as from Southampton to Saint Thomas, which is but one hundred and forty-seven more—yet, as Humboldt says, 'A voyage from the coast of Spain, and thence to South America, is scarcely attended with any event which deserves attention, especially when undertaken in summer. The navigation is often less dangerous than crossing one of the great lakes of Switzerland.' Whereas in our voyage there is that odious Bay of Biscay to be crossed, and a still worse sea on the homeward passage ; and steamers, however grand, have risks of their own. Well, who knows! Juan's forebodings may be justified." So, after finishing my reverie, I went to smoke a cigar in the allowable place before the funnel, and next to arrange my cabin, and so, in due course, to bed.

I was awoke in the morning by a hideous jabber of several small voices crying all at once, " Steward ! steward !

for vy I say call I you many times? Vy you by your own selves not ask me vat I vant?" This reminded me of Trollope's grinning Frenchman and his rotten walnut; and incontinently I laughed somewhat loudly, which had the effect of shaming my neighbours and stilling the clamour. On leaving my cabin I was astonished to see outside the next cabin door four such Lilliputian pairs of half-boots that I could not but come to the conclusion that my neighbours must be all children, and yet their voices were the voices of middle age. Afterwards I discovered that the Spanish Creoles have feet as tiny as those of Chinese ladies, but of a natural tininess, and without deformity.

Travelling per steamer is a trite affair. People think little more of crossing the Atlantic in one of the gigantic vessels of the Royal Mail Steam Packet Company, or of the Cunard line, than of passing a river on a bridge. "The river," says the old Sanscrit proverb, "is crossed, and the bridge is forgotten." Fourteen days, or so, of short whist and long flirtations, of bad cigars and pleasant yarns, of hot calms and cold gales, a transfer of cash and billets, and the voyage is over. But the utility, wealth, and importance of such an association as the Royal Mail Company, the admirable system organised for the performance of the duties of every individual serving under it, and the consequent safety with which so many voyages, at all seasons, are performed, deserve more consideration than is usually given to the subject. In my first lounging fit I took up the prospectus and the book of regulations of the company, which dates from 1830; and setting myself to calculate, found that this one company now owns a fleet of twenty-three steamers, of forty-five thousand eight hundred and four tons, and eleven thousand four hundred and seventy horse-power. These vessels, I calculated, convey on an average some thirty-five thousand passengers yearly, and over twenty million of dollars in specie, besides other valuable cargo. There are prizes in such a service. The superintendents make from one thousand five hundred to two thousand pounds a year. The senior captain draws one thousand two hundred in cash, and has his living and lodging free. The other captains, with like advantages in other respects, get one thousand per annum. The junior officers are proportionably well paid. There is a home for them at Southampton, where they live at free quarters. In the large steamers there are four or five officers besides the captain, and their duties are strictly defined. The chief officer keeps the log, the second has charge of the treasure, and accompanies the Admiralty's agent on shore with the mails, the third and fourth stow the cargo. A junior officer is never left in charge of the ship at night. There is a goodly crew. On board the vessel in which I was passenger were fifty-three seamen, fifty-four engineers, and twenty-three servants. One might well feel at ease in a vessel so provided.

I soon became acquainted with most of the passengers. There were several naval officers of rank, a handsome admiral with a fine bold nose, a baronet with a romantic name, a captain of the race of England's naval demi-gods, several West Indian planters, and not a few pretty planters' daughters, some, too, without chaperones; a shabby Columbian general, a few lively Frenchmen, and a score of Creole nondescripts. I passed my time in playing chess and learning Spanish. Unfortunately, there were no señoras or señoritas of whom to be taught. There was, however, a young aide-de-camp to the President of Peru, who possessed so much patience and amiability, that he would talk to me in pure Castillano by the hour, though at first I did not comprehend more than one word in a hundred. Nevertheless, by the time we reached the Azores, I had made some progress, and had even once asked publicly at the dinner-table, in Spanish, for the mustard. It was the 23rd of June, at 4 A.M., that we passed the islands, and sighted two of the group. They lie directly in the course out, but homeward, a very great circuit is made to the west. The outward bound captains like to see the islands, for the currents in the Atlantic are so strong and so various that no reckoning can be perfectly true. There is an equinoctial current from east to west, and there is the Gulf Stream, which is a hot current, from west to east; and there are local currents and abnormal currents, and a great-circuit-current, compounded of all these, which has a periphery of three thousand eight hundred leagues, and a log of wood dropped into the sea opposite Senegal would go, as many other sticks do, " on circuit," and return to its starting-place in two years and ten months.

We passed, I say, the Azores on the 23rd of June, and forthwith the weather waxed hot. We had not yet caught the trade-winds, and, though there were occasional squalls, on the whole it was sultry, with a rather lurid sky at night. On the 25th it was particularly close and oppressive. I had been playing chess all the morning. It was 2 P.M., and I was lazily talking to my late antagonist, a good-looking Frenchman, who, though he was, he informed me, thirty-five, looked like a mere youth, owing to an entire absence of beard, whiskers, and moustache. Groups of

people, some reading, others playing chess or draughts, sat
or lounged around us. It was a dead calm, and the polished
mirror of the sea gave back the sun's rays with interest.
"Monsieur voyage pour son plaisir ou pour les affaires?"
I inquired. "Pour mon plaisir?" repeated the Frenchman, with some surprise, "du tout, du tout, monsieur. Je
suis médecin, monsieur, et j'ai aussi une fabrique de bottes
à Lima." "Quoi, monsieur," said I, raising myself a little
on my elbow, "médecin et marchand de bottes à la fois—
vous plaisantez!" The Frenchman opened his lips to
reply, but just at that moment there was a tremendously
loud crash, followed by a strange whizzing noise, and almost
immediately afterwards by a succession of terrific thuds, as
if some Cyclops had suddenly commenced hammering in
the engine-room. At the same time showers of splinters
came flying from the starboard paddle-box, and a dense
cloud of steam and smoke burst all along the deck, so as
almost to hide the funnel from sight. Great confusion of
course ensued. Chess-tables and chairs were overset;
screams of ladies, questions of men shouted in various lan-
guages, rushes of sailors amid the cloud of steam, oaths
and scuffling, added to the din. It was curious to see in
that moment of terrible uncertainty, when an explosion, or
some other catastrophe was expected by all, how some of
the foreigners who had been sneering at religion all the way
out, suddenly betook themselves to prayer. For myself, I
felt exactly as I did some years ago in a railway accident.
In both cases I expected every moment to be killed, and
yet the most trivial circumstances did not escape me, while
my general thought was, as I looked at the bright sun
and quiet sleep of Nature, that a violent death was all the

more shocking with everything around so quiet and peaceable.

Half a minute, perhaps, had passed, but it seemed a long time, and I was rushing forward to see what really had happened, when I felt myself stopped by a powerful arm, and the huge figure of Juan blocked the way. "Best stop here," he said, with a grin; "I have got finely scalded myself, without being of no use. Now the engines are stopped, the captain will soon put matters to rights, if any one can; but, Caramba! this all comes of sailing on a Friday. I never hur-red of no good from sailing on a Friday." Destiny, however, was for this time to let us off with only a fright. The thundering blows ceased with the stoppage of the engines, the steam and smoke gradually cleared away, and the hubbub abated. It was then we learned that the great shaft which connects the paddle-wheels with the machinery had suddenly snapped, and, starting up like a snag, had caught some ponderous gear, which it whirled round with each revolution of the engines, smashing the paddle-box and everything near it. In the confusion there had been an upset of hot coals and an escape of steam, which scalded several men, and drove the others out of the engine-room.

The danger of the late accident was soon forgotten, and some of those who had been most alarmed were unmercifully quizzed. About one short fat Creole in particular the jokes were never ending. He was in his cabin when the crash took place, and fancying from the smoke and steam which entered his quarters that the ship was on fire, he actually contrived to thrust his corpulent body through the round window, though one would have thought it too small for the passage of a fat rabbit. From the window he somehow scrambled on deck, and made his appearance, steaming with perspiration, with one sleeve of his coat torn off, and with a face and figure, as every one declared, considerably elongated by his squeeze through the bull's-eye.

How the damages were repaired I know not, but, in a few hours, we were going on much as usual; so much so, indeed, that the Frenchman, who had told me he was doctor and bootmaker at once, could now finish his story and explain himself. "When I commenced my career," said he, "I found that no one would trust me to prescribe, on account of my juvenile appearance. In despair, I consulted a friend, who said to me, ' My dear fellow, with that child's face of yours, you will never have a patient. But stay! I know a certain college in which a Greek professor is wanted. You shall be the Greek professor; you shall have the place!' In vain I protested that I knew nothing of Greek. 'I make it entirely my business,' replied my friend; 'you shall have the place.' Accordingly, I found myself at the college, with a letter of introduction to the lecturer, who had been temporarily discharging the duties of the defunct professor of Greek. I had counted on several days to prepare myself, but, on handing him the letter, he said, in a sharp voice, ' Charmed to see you, and to resign my functions. The students will be ready for you in ten minutes. I will send a man to show you the lecture-room.' At that moment I felt my knees tremble under me, and my uneasiness was so great, that I almost resolved to jump into an omnibus I saw pass, drive to the station, and return to Paris. Somehow, I found myself at the lecture-room, and just then a lucky thought occurred to me. ' Range yourselves,' I said to the students, 'as you ranked at the last examination. Now,' I continued, when they had done so, 'let the lowest read first.' When he had finished, I said to the next, 'What mistakes has he made, and how do you correct them?' He mentioned one or two blunders, and I then put the same question to others, till no one had anything left to say. The reading and the corrections occupied a long time, at the end of which I said, 'That will do for the first lecture; at the next I shall have more to say to you.' In fact, when the next séance came, I had, by great industry, prepared myself a little, and managed to deliver a discourse, and, in the meantime, I had the satisfaction of hearing that my fame was great among the students, who were tickled with the novelty of my system, insomuch that my senior colleague congratulated me on abandoning the career of a physician, and assured me that I was born to be a professor! I longed, however, to return to my original employment, and, as I did not see my way in France, I went out to Lima, where I married a Creole, fell ill of dysentery, and, as I could not recover my health in Peru, I opened a shoe-shop, left my wife in charge of it, and returned to Paris, and I am now going out to bring home my daughter to be educated."

Next day we arrived within the influence of the trade-winds. We had now frequent squalls and thunder and lightning till the 30th, on which day, at seven P.M., we made, as the sailors say, the little island of Sombrero, or "Hat Island." It is only three-quarters of a mile long and nine hundred feet broad; is a perfectly flat rock, about twenty feet above the level of the sea; and derives its name from its fancied resemblance to a cardinal's hat. In 1850 it was uninhabited, except by sea-fowl and black lizards: the only place of landing was at a bight on the west side: and getting on shore was what Yankees would term a caution to snakes. "Under very favourable circumstances," says a nautical writer, "by watching an opportunity, you may jump on to a flat ledge to the cliff, and with some difficulty ascend to the summit." The almighty dollar, however, would make a landing anywhere, and as there was abundance of guano on the rock, the Americans had taken possession of it, and we saw them hard at work with cranes and carts loading vessels with the precious deposit.

At 3 P.M. on the 1st of July we anchored in the harbour of St. Thomas. I looked in vain for the little steamer which I expected would be ready to convey me to La Guaira. Instead of it I was shown a schooner of about eighty tons, which was to sail next day for that place. Viewed from the decks of the gigantic Royal Mail Steamer, she looked like a cockle-shell. Spite of the heat, I landed at once, and went straight to the store of a young merchant, whose family I knew. He was a handsome fellow of about two-and-twenty, with bright blue eyes and curly hair, and with such an overpowering share of good nature that all his other qualities seemed absorbed by it. He produced some excellent brandy, and still better cigars, and we began to discuss how I should amuse myself till the schooner was ready to start. Of course I had a list of commissions, all of which it was agreed should be executed at a cooler hour next morning. Then we began to talk about the harbour, and I happened to ask if there were many sharks in it? Hereupon my host brightened up, and said : "If you would like to see a few, I'll show you some. A horse of mine was taken ill last night, and is just dead.  We'll tow the carcase off with a boat to the mouth of the harbour, take a couple of rifles and a harpoon, and it's odd if we don't have some sport."  No sooner said than done.  Orders were at once given to drag the dead horse to the water's edge, and my host, followed by myself and a big negro, who carried the rifles and the harpoon, walked down to the boat.  It was a large boat, with four rowers and an awning, and as the boatmen, notwithstanding the heat, pulled with a will, we made way rapidly, and before long had got past the steamers, and were nearing the mouth of the harbour.  As yet I had seen nothing, and was becoming rather impatient.  "Why," said I, "I don't believe there are any sharks.  I have not seen a single back fin above water."  In reply, my host checked the rowers for a moment, when, as the surge we made subsided, several dark lines showed themselves just astern of the horse.  "Give way," said he to the boatmen; "we have not yet reached the place where we can fire safely, and if we stop another half-minute the horse will be torn to ribbons."  When the boat had gone a few hundred yards further, he said to me, "Now cock your rifle, and look out! The instant we stop, the sharks will rise, and the first that turns to seize the horse, fire right into his belly.  I'll give him both barrels, too, and four conical pills should settle him.  Are you ready?"  "Quite ready," I replied, and the boat stopped.

In an instant the dark lines were visible again, but this time they came rapidly up to the surface, and five monstrous sharks showed themselves.  The apparition was so sudden, and the sharks were so huge, so much larger than any I had seen before, that I started, and, had I cocked my rifle as I

had been told to do, there is no knowing where I might have
sent my random shot. But it has always been my practice
not to cock till I see the object; and this has prevented my
making many a bad miss. In a moment I recovered myself,
and, as the foremost shark turned on his back and darted at
the carcase, I took good aim, and fired nearly at the same
moment with my friend. All our four balls told: one of
them, as we afterwards found, going right through the heart.
The smoke came full across my eyes, but there was a
tremendous splash, and I caught an indistinct glimpse of
the monster as he sprang half out of the water and fell back.
Almost at the same instant, the big negro who had the
harpoon sent it into the shark just below the lower jaw with
such force, that, had he had more life in him than remained,
he would hardly have escaped. Meantime, the other sharks,
who sank for a moment when we fired, had risen again to the
surface, and one of them had already torn a great bit out of
the horse, giving such a violent jerk to the boat, that one
of the niggers took fright, and before we could see what he
was about, undid the rope by which the carcase was being
towed, and it was immediately jerked into the water as the
other sharks fastened on the prey. This they did in such
numbers, and with such right good will, that before we could
reload and prepare for another shot, they had dragged the
carcase under water, and we could only tell by the bubbles
and bloody foam what a worry was going on below. However, we had got one monster safe, and returned towing him
in triumph. When we reached the landing-place there was
quite a crowd to receive us. It took eight or ten men to
drag the shark on shore, and we found he measured over
sixteen feet long, and nearly six feet in circumference. His

stomach was quite empty, which accounted for his being ravenous.

I was glad of a bath and a change of toilet, after which my friend drove me in his carriage round the west part of the island, of which some description may be acceptable. To begin then with the beginning, be it known that, between the eighteenth and nineteenth degrees of north latitude, a little to the east of Porto Rico, in an almost continuous cluster, lie the Virgin Islands, so called by Columbus from the eleven thousand of sainted memory, with whom in number these islets seemed to vie. Exactly in the centre of the group is St Thomas, and next to it, on the east, is St. John. All the islands to the east of St. John belong to the English, and all to the west belong to the Danes. You may tell the English possessions by the roughness of the nomenclature and the utter want of high-flown titles. There is, for example, Salt Island, followed by Ginger, Cooper's, and Beef Island. Next we come to Camanoe, Scrub, Guano, and Jost-van-Dykes Isles. Then there is Anegada, or "Drowned Island," famous or infamous for wrecks, where many a gallant seaman has gone to his rest beneath the waters. It is a curious place that Anegada. It lies all awash with the sea, and when the mist comes up, as it does very often, one would fancy the waves were rolling clean over it. Anegada is ten miles long, and has a reef to the south-east of nine miles more, and upon this reef many scores of vessels have gone to pieces. But to the west there is good anchorage, and abundance of funnel-shaped wells, full of fresh water, in which, curiously enough, the fresh water rises with the salt tide. The bays there in the old time swarmed with buccaneers. When they were gone,

came gangs of wreckers and colonised the island, and reared
stock, and grew cotton ; but their true market-day was when
a vessel struck on the reef, and many a rich prize they got,
and perhaps do get even now. A curious proof of the strong
westerly current in the Atlantic is to be seen at Anegada,
where the fishermen find sufficient cork drifted to them, from
the coast of Spain, to supply their nets. Bottles, too,
launched in the River Gambia, have been picked up in the
Virgin Islands. Between these islands themselves, the
currents are in many places most violent. To row from
island to island is a most dangerous and almost impossible
undertaking. Many boats have been swept away, and their
crews drowned, in the attempt. Between the eastern part of
St. Thomas and the Island of St. John, in particular, there
is a furious current, and the waves rise in huge surges.
When the southern tide is in its strength, it would be
impossible for any small vessel to encounter that terrible
sea.

Twelve miles to the west of Anegada is Virgin Gorda, or
" Fat Virgin " Island, nine miles long and a mile broad,
with some ten thousand inhabitants, who export sugar, rum,
and tobacco. On the north-east is a good harbour, called
Gorda Sound, and another to the north-west, called West
Bay, and a third, Thomas's Bay, to the south. Three
miles west of Virgin Gorda, is Tortola, nine miles long and
three broad, with a population of eleven thousand, and a
good harbour at Road Town, the capital. Moreover, here,
with Tortola to the north, St. John's to the west, Virgin
Gorda to the east, and a dozen little islands to the south,
nature has formed a magnificent basin, fifteen miles long
and three and a half broad, land-locked and sheltered from

every wind, where all the navies of England might ride in safety. Why not choose Tortola as the station for the Royal Mail Company's vessels? Why go to St. Thomas,* that nest of yellow fever, where fresh water is hard to get, and which belongs to a foreign power?

Not being able to answer this same why, I return to St. Thomas. The island is twelve miles long from east to west, and three broad; and across the whole length of it runs a range of hills, the highest point of which may be eight hundred feet above the sea. These hills were once covered with woods, and the island was then watered by rivulets; but the improvident Danes cut down the woods, the streams dried up, and the inhabitants now suffer from drought, insomuch that the captains of steamers are enjoined to husband their fresh water, lest none should be procurable at St. Thomas. Charlotte Amalia, the capital and harbour of St. Thomas, lies on the south coast, and opens to the south, so that vessels coming from Europe or North America have to make a half-circle to enter it. The approach is not without its dangers. There is, first of all, a rock called Frenchman's Cap, seven miles from the harbour's mouth, and four miles further on there is Buck Island. Between these you steer, but in mid-channel is a danger called "Scorpion Rock," with only twenty-one feet of water on it. Having cleared that (and there is a buoy on it to help you), you enter the harbour: having on your right, at its mouth, the lighthouse, the red light of which, being ninety-five feet above the sea, can be seen fifteen miles off. Near it is a fort called Mohlenfel's Battery. On the left are Prince

* This was written more than a year before the last great hurricane at St. Thomas.

Frederick's Battery, and the Great Carenage, where vessels can be moored during hurricanes. At the very entrance, however, are three other dangers. There is, first, on the west, a shoal which juts out the length of a cable from Frederick's Point; and then, a little east of the mid-channel, is Prince Rupert's Rock; and further east, and close to Mohlenfel's Battery, are the rocks called the Triangles. Lastly, there are coral rocks in the harbour itself.

The panorama of the harbour of St. Thomas has been extolled by a well-known writer, and with justice. The port itself is of a horse-shoe shape, and, having entered, the town is right before you, rising in three triangles, with a glittering white building to crown each apex. In the background rise hills of the brightest green, rendered more dazzling by the clearness of the atmosphere. To the left, the harbour runs out into a long creek, too shallow to be crossed except by boats. On the right of the town is Christiana Fort, garrisoned by half a regiment of Danes, and some artillerymen. Above, on the hills, is a tower, where in the good old times lived a notable buccaneer. Close by the fort are the King's Wharf and a hotel, and all about and around are such lovely bunches of flowering shrubs and trees, as almost to make one in love with the " white man's grave."

I had been amused with my expedition against the sharks in the afternoon, but now it was over my spirits went down. There is something fearfully depressing in St. Thomas and its associations. Sharks and yellow fever in the harbour, yellow fever and grinning black men in the town, the heat stifling, and the smells unbearable—this is the programme; and the talk is all of so-and-so who died on yester-night, and such a one who is like to die to-morrow. Our drive was not exhilarating. On the left was the shallow stagnant creek, with a row of miserable huts, interspersed with shambles at the water's edge. On the right, were more huts and many cemeteries. There was the Moravian Cemetery, with all the slabs of exactly the same height and size; and there was the Jews' Cemetery, and the Catholic Cemetery, and what might be called the Omnibus Cemetery, for what the well-known writer before referred to irreverently terms the Hispano-Dano-Yankee-doodle-niggery-population-in-general. My host, the best of good fellows, who was never hipped himself, had no idea of comforting a man who was in low spirits. On my asking, out of the gloominess of my heart, "Is there any yellow fever here just now?" he replied, "Well, the yellow fever is always here. Just at present, however, we are considered rather clear. It is true there have been a few scattered cases—there have been five, for instance, in the house next mine—but only three died, and, for myself, I have no sort of apprehension, for I am a born St. Thomas man, and natives seldom suffer. In general, it is the new comers who get in for it." I could only mutter, "Consolatory, certainly!" and change the subject. I asked about the state of the colony. "Well," he said, "the American war has been pumpkins to us. Our house alone has cleared upwards of fifty thousand pounds since it began, and two or three other houses have been doing nearly as well. It's pretty, too, to see the blockade runners lying under the very noses of the Northern men-of-war. They see 'em load, up anchor, and off, and they mustn't chase 'em for four-and-twenty hours, though they know, if they've a good start there's no chance of taking them.

The times have been lively, too, with the sailors. The crews
of the Confederate vessels have had so many fights with the
Federal men, and the English have joined in with such jolly
good-will, first on one side, and then on the other, that now
the Danes won't let any Americans land." "And pray,"
said I, " besides these rows, how do you amuse yourselves
here ?" "Well," was the reply, "we *don't* amuse ourselves.
We trade."

After our drive we dined at the hotel. The dinner consisted of all the most indigestible dishes conceivable, and at
St. Thomas it is *de rigueur* to eat of them all. I went to
bed with a racking headache, and in a state highly favourable for yellow fever. Morning came at last, however,
without an attack, and released me from the tender mercies
of the mosquitoes. I went round with my friend to several
shops to make my purchases, posted my letters to England,
and by noon was sailing for La Guaira in the schooner
Isabel. Juan came on board at the last moment, having
deserted me all the time I was at St. Thomas. He merely
said, " Friends on shore, sir; you'll excuse my being late."
I said, " Of course ;" and begged him to release me from
the importunity of the negro boatman who brought me on
board, and who asked two pounds for the job, though the
legal charge was only one dollar and eighty-two cents. We
got rid of him at last for three dollars.

We ran out of St. Thomas's harbour on the 23rd of July
with a fine breeze. The crew of the Isabel consisted of a
captain, five men, and a boy, each blacker than the other,
and all of an extremely hang-dog look. As I had thirty
thousand sovereigns on board, it seems a miracle that they
did not tumble me quietly into the water when I was asleep.

The crew of the Isabel, however, were pirates only in look, and I lost among them nothing more important than a gold pencil-case. We slept on deck in a sort of hencoop, in which were not more vermin than are usually in hencoops. Our meals, over which the captain presided in his shirt-sleeves, were principally of land-tortoise, hard sour cheese, pickles, dried fish, pastels filled with nameless ingredients, and quimbombo: an excellent vegetable, and almost the only thing I could eat. It is the okro hibiscus, has somewhat the look of a young cucumber, and is full of a cold gluten, very pleasant in a hot climate. There was a Creole lady, with two or three small children, who lived in the cabin or hold of the vessel, and never made her appearance on deck throughout the whole passage. Once or twice, during a squall, I descended to this cabin, and found it full of ants, cock-roaches, and rats. The Creole, half undressed, lay gasping with the heat, while her children, in a state of perfect nudity, scrambled over her. Besides this lady, myself, Juan, and an American doctor, there was also another passenger: a thin feeble old man, who was brought on board with great care. I heard him ask his servant for a cigar, which turned out to be stramonium, for the man was too ill to smoke tobacco; and to say this of a Spanish Creole, is saying a good deal.

About 5 p.m. we were passing the island of Santa Cruz, belonging to the Danes. The governor of St. Thomas shows his appreciation of the healthiness of his own island by living at Santa Cruz, which is thirty-two miles south of St. Thomas. Santa Cruz is nineteen miles long and five broad, and contains a population of fifty thousand souls. In general it is much flatter than St. Thomas; but there is one hill, Mount Eagle, which rises to one thousand one hundred and sixty-two feet above the sea, and another near it, called Blue Mountain, which is but sixty feet lower. There are two towns, Christiansted to the east, and Fredericksted to the west. At the former there is a harbour very difficult of access, but safe enough when once entered. The island is well cultivated. We passed Santa Cruz; the sun set; and after smoking a last cigar, I turned into my hencoop and slept soundly, except for a few minutes about midnight, when I soon went to sleep again with an indistinct idea of something disagreeable going on. The red horns of the sun were just showing above the horizon, when Juan came up and woke me, under pretence of asking me if I would bathe; but I could see by the grin on his features that there was something wrong. Presently not being able to contain himself any longer, he exploded into a chuckle, and said, "There's a dead man on board, sir."

"Indeed?" replied I, by no means gratified. "And pray who may he be, and what does he come on board for, if he's dead?"

"Well, sir," said Juan, "it's the old man, the passenger who seemed so ill. About midnight he got worse, and called the captain, and asked to be thrown overboard, he was in such pain. The captain said he could not accommodate him in that way, but he would get some hot fomentations, and see if that would ease the pain in his chest. 'It's no matter,' says the passenger. 'Whereabouts is the moon?' When the captain had showed him where the moon was, he said very quietly, 'When the moon goes down I shall die.' And so he did, sir. You would hardly believe it, but at the very moment the moon went down, the old man died."

" Did he ask for the doctor ? " I inquired.

" Ask for the doctor !  I should think not," said Juan, in high disdain.  " Why, all the doctors in New York couldn't have saved him ; nor they couldn't have done him much harm neither.  He was too far gone for that."

I walked forward to bathe, and there I saw a sad bundle which told its own tale.  It was the corpse sewn up in a hammock, with some six-pound shot, belonging to the one gun of the schooner, attached, to sink it.  An hour afterwards, a short prayer was said by the captain, and the body was launched into the sea.  I watched it go down.  It went fast—so fast that it was gone before a dolphin that had been playing about the bows, and darted out to see what the splash meant, could reach the spot.

The incident was a painful one, and conjured up melancholy reflections.  There were only about a dozen of us in the schooner, reckoning crew and passengers together, and one was gone.  I could not help thinking how wretched it would be to lie ill on board that little vessel, with nothing but a hencoop to rest on, and only the American doctor for a medical attendant.  The heat was overpowering, and, considering where we came from, it would have been no great wonder if we had had a visit from the yellow fever. Right glad was I, then, when at 2 P.M. on the 4th we passed the rock of Ochilla, one of the Aves Islands, which lies only eighty miles to the north of La Guaira.  Ochilla is about ten miles in length, and a very dangerous reef projects from it for two miles in an easterly direction.  Twenty miles off is a sunken rock, not given in the maps, on which a small vessel was totally lost about a year before we passed. Her crew had scarcely time to take to the boats when she

foundered. There are from two hundred to three hundred
tons of guano on Ochilla, which may be worth twelve pounds
a ton. The place had some interest for me, for one of the
claims I was going out to settle was called the Aves Island
claim. The Americans had gone to a rock of that name,
nearer St. Thomas, to collect guano, and had been stopped
by the Venezuelans, who maintain that the Aves Islands
belong to them. For the loss caused by this demurrer, the
Americans now claimed one hundred and fifty-five thousand
dollars of the Venezuelan government: a sum sufficient
to have plated the whole rock with silver instead of
guano.

Two hours after passing Ochilla, we saw the great mountain called La Silla, or "The Saddle," which overhangs La
Guaira. The Silla is eight thousand six hundred feet high,
and we saw it at seventy miles' distance. As the sun set,
we discerned the lights at La Guaira, but the wind now fell,
or came only in fitful gusts. At one moment we were
running at the rate of nine knots an hour, straight, as it
seemed, on shore; for the land, being overshadowed by this
stupendous mountain, appeared much nearer than it was.
The next instant we were becalmed, with all sail set, and
flapping so heavily as to banish sleep from my eyes. The
nigger captain and his crew, however, being used to it, lay
like logs, and we might have drifted on shore for all they
seemed to care. Morning came at last, and with it a
gentle breeze, which carried us to our anchorage at La
Guaira.

# CHAPTER II.



ANCHORING in a harbour usually implies rest. It is not so at La Guaira. In fact, La Guaira is no port, but an open roadstead, where, though it seldom blows very heavily, there is ever a high swell, so high that landing is always difficult, and often dangerous. With the wind at north, the shore is directly to leeward, and a general smash among the shipping is then inevitable. Luckily, such winds are most rare; but some time before the arrival of the Isabel there was one, and every vessel at La Guaira was stranded. Even with other winds the danger is sometimes great, and then a cannon is fired from the fort as a signal that the rollers are setting in. Forthwith, all anchors are weighed, and the ships run out to sea till the swell moderates. Indeed, it is one of the inscrutable things that no one can understand, why La Guaira should be made the port for Carácas at all, when a mile or two to the west, on the other side of the next promontory, Cabo Blanco, there is the snug harbour of Catia, whence an easier road to Carácas might be made than that from La Guaira. But no; in spite of the swell which has caused the loss of so many vessels, which makes communication with the shore so troublesome, and which stirs up the sand in a fashion that renders it necessary to weigh anchors every eight days, lest the ships should become sand-locked; in spite of the ravages of the barnacles, the teredo navalis, la broma, as the Spaniards call them, more destructive at La Guaira than anywhere else in the world, commerce, which seems to be the only conservative thing in America, still keeps to its old route.

"So this is Venezuela, Little Venice," thought I to myself, as we lay tossing; "can't say I see much resemblance to Venice in these great mountains, that look as if they had been piled up by Titans to scale a city in the clouds!" Nor is there, through all the vast region now called Venezuela, much to remind one of the city of the doges. But it is at La Guaira that the unlikeness comes out most forcibly. It happens, though no one seems to have remarked it, that La Guaira is the very ὄμφαλος of the Venezuelan coast; for it lies half way between Cape Paria, on the extreme east, and Chichibocoa, on the extreme west, and just at La Guaira towers up La Silla, the tallest mountain between the Andes and the Atlantic; so that, instead of thinking of Venice, one cries out with Humboldt, "The Pyrenees or the Alps stripped of their snows, have risen from the bosom of the waters." Venezuela is a misnomer. The first Spaniards who came to the American coast, the Conquistadores, found the Indians of Maracaibo living in huts on piles in the lake, and so called that locality Venezuela; and the misnomer spread and spread till a region four times the size of Prussia came to be styled "Little Venice"—a name which now comprehends a forest larger than France, steppes like those of Gobi, and mountain tracts which it would take many Switzerlands to match.

But for the abominable saltatory movements of the Isabel, I could have passed hours very contentedly with a fragrant cigar in my mouth, gazing from the sea at La Guaira, which is one of the most picturesque places in the world. Humboldt says there is nothing like it, save Santa Cruz, at the island of Teneriffe, where, as at La Guaira, the town, perched on a little rim of shore, at the foot of a tremendous peak, seems like a world's finger-post pointing to the littleness of man and the greatness of nature. Once landed, much of the effect is lost. There is then no more such startling contrast between the strip of white building at the sea's level, and the huge blue, black, and green masses of rock and earth heaped up into the very clouds; and it is no longer so easy to trace the long line of fortification mounting from height to height. Moreover, a mountain that starts up all at once, eight thousand feet from the sea, into the clouds, is a wondrous sight, and I looked and mused long. But my reverie was interrupted by those common-place, matter-of-fact fellows, the custom-house officers, who came on board punctually at 6 A.M., and showed at once that they had more of the Paul Pry than the poet in their natures. As nearly the whole revenues of the country,. and the whole of their salaries (report says, something more than the whole), are drawn from the custom-house, there was some excuse for their energetic proceedings, which would, no doubt, have terminated in a rigid scrutiny of my numerous boxes, had I not been armed with the name of commissioner and a diplomatic passport. At sight of that document, the official tartness of their aspect sweetened to a smile, and they invited me to go ashore in their large comfortable boat : no slight favour at such a place as La Guaira.

Watching the auspicious moment when the frolicsome surge pitched the bow of the boat up within a foot of the landing-place on the pier, I made a spring, and was effectually prevented from falling back by half a dozen arms and hands, which snatched at every accessible part of me; one fellow, whose civility outran his discretion, giving me a sharp pinch as he clutched hold of my trousers. I was safe, however; I had landed; I stood for the first time on American ground, and I felt myself in a glow—but less, perhaps, from enthusiasm than from the intense heat consequent on the exertion of jumping from that tossing boat. There was, in reality, no great room for enthusiasm. Some dingy buildings now shut out the view of the mountains, and the atmosphere was so close, and so impregnated with the odour of decaying fish and other things still worse, that no enthusiasm could have withstood it. It would be well if the Venezuelans, so proud as they are of their country, so sensitive to the remarks of strangers, would prepare a cleanlier landing-place for their visitors. In other countries, foreigners who are to be propitiated are presented with bouquets of flowers. Columbia welcomes the traveller with a bouquet of a different kind. They were working away at the wharf and breakwater, which had already, they said, cost one hundred thousand pounds, though I suppose a tenth of that sum would have more than covered the outlay in England. Earth was coming down in buckets, which travelled on long ropes fastened at a considerable incline to posts at an eminence across the road, where the men were at work. These buckets came along with an impetus sufficient, had they struck a passer-by, to knock his brains out; an accident which might easily have happened, for the ropes were stretched just at the height of a man, and no one gave any warning of their approach. On the left of the wharf was the harbour-master's house, and a nondescript building—something between an office and a fort, where a lot of Creole clerks were idling. In front, was the custom-house, and to the left of it the town. To the right, rose a long straggling line of filthy huts, swarming with naked darkie children.

We walked straight to the custom-house, a strong useful building, but not picturesque. The superintendent, an official of no little rank, for the appointment is the usual stepping-stone to the portfolio of finance, received me in his shirt-sleeves, with the inevitable cigarette in his mouth, and on reading the letter of introduction I had brought from General Guzman Blanco, shook hands, and told me he had been the general's A.D.C. in the war just concluded. The sun was already disagreeably hot, and I was glad to hurry on a few hundred yards up the principal of the two streets —which, with a branch or two climbing the mountain's base, form La Guaira—and take refuge in the hospitable house of the merchants to whom I was accredited. Having heard not a little of the wealth of the La Guaira merchants, I could not help venting my astonishment in a hearty *caramba*, when I entered the house. A huge outer door opened into a square court-yard, smelling strongly of turmeric, and half filled with bales of merchandise. The house was two-storied, the lower storey containing a set of dingy offices, while the upper was divided into bed-rooms, but the whole building looked so dirty and dilapidated, that I asked myself, " Can this be the residence of a merchant prince ? " One of the partners, in whose apartment I found a piano, books, and some neat furniture, explained the mystery.

There are only three or four tolerable houses in La Guaira, and he had been in vain trying to get one. This was simply a warehouse, and the other partners lived at Carácas. Juan, a mulatto servant, and a nigger boy, now set to work to get the spare room ready for me, and raised such clouds of dust as choked off for a time the mosquitoes, of which the atmosphere was full. They are a peculiarly sharp-stinging sort at La Guaira: small, speckled, and insatiable.

I was now fairly installed. The first thing that struck me was the intense heat. I had not then read Humboldt's Table, in which he compares the climates of Guaira, Cairo, Habana, Vera Cruz, Madras, and Abushahr, but without his assistance I arrived at his conclusion, that I was now in the hottest place in the whole world. Perhaps the best way of conveying to a European an idea of the heat, is to say that the mean temperature at La Guaira, in the coldest month, is four degrees of centigrade higher than that of the hottest month in Paris. If it be added that there are no appliances whatever to make things bearable—no good houses, no ice, no cold water, no shade, and no breeze, it will be possible to arrive at a faint notion of the reality. I was peculiarly well situated for promptly realising a just idea of the climate, for my room had but one small window, and when I opened it, there came in a perfume which obliged me to close it again instantly. The locality was, indeed, not very agreeable. The house almost abutted on the mountain, which of course kept off every breath of air. On one side was a boys' school, from which arose an incessant jabber, and on the ridge above us was a long building of very forbidding appearance.

"What place is that?" said I to Juan.

" That, sir ? " replied he, with a beaming countenance. " That is the Small-pox Hospital, but there ain't no great number of cases there at present."

It was some alleviation of our misery that we took our meals in a building much higher up the hill, and, consequently, cooler than the warehouse in which we slept. The cuisine was tolerable, the poverty of the native supplies being eked out with European stores. The wine was hot ; but there were good Clicquot and Rhenish wines in abundance, and intense thirst made us undiscriminating.

There are no Englishmen at La Guaira, and, consequently, no out-of-door amusements. No one walks, rides, rows, or sails, for pleasure. The Europeans, who are chiefly Germans from Hamburg, confine themselves strictly to smoking, drinking, playing whist and billiards. It would be quite easy to have a good place for driving and riding by the sea-shore, but everybody tries to make the approach to the sea as inaccessible as possible.

In my first walk I took a look at the hotel, and saw ample reason for congratulating myself that I had found other quarters. It was a very poor posada indeed, and the reek of garlic made me quite giddy. Garlic, by-the-by, is as dear to a Venezuelan as the shamrock to an Irishman, and one feels surprised that it is not adopted as the national emblem. I was assured by a traveller that he had exhausted his inventive powers in devising means to escape eating of dishes flavoured with this herb, but all in vain. As a *dernier ressort*, and when half starved, he determined to live on eggs, but the fatal fragrance pursued him still, much to his astonishment as well as disgust. At last, on carefully examining an egg before attempting to eat it, he found that the small end had been perforated, and some of the favourite herb introduced by the innkeeper, who was resolved that the national taste should be vindicated, and that, too, ab ovo and in extremis. From the inn I went to make my first purchase, one naturally suggested to me by my visit to the posada. I went to buy some medicine at a botica, or apothecary's shop. As my Spanish was not very profound, I was glad to find a German in the shop, and to him I explained that I wanted a blue pill. Hereupon he took down a book of prescriptions, and set to work to find out how to make it. After some search, he began compounding the pills with pestle and mortar. As I had no great faith in his knowledge, I thought I would take a peep at the book, which was in Spanish, for, to quote a certain advertisement, "I could read and write Spanish, though I could not yet speak it." What was my horror, when I discovered that the apothecary was making me up a pill for leprosy! "Oh!" I exclaimed, "by-the-by, I think I won't trouble you to compound that pill for me;" and, snatching up a box, labelled "Brandreth's Pills," I paid him for it, and walked off, too glad to escape. This German had, no doubt, failed in some other *métier*, and had taken up a trade in drugs without knowing much about them. Before I left America I saw empirics more than enough.

After experiencing the disagreeables of the sea-shore promenade at La Guaira, I took to climbing the mountain for a constitutional. So disinclined are the Venezuelans to exercise, that I had the greatest difficulty in persuading a friend to accompany me. He was a very handsome, tall, well-made fellow, and the son of an Englishman, but, having been born in the country, had much of the Creole indolence in his nature. We used to ascend about twelve hundred feet, and for that distance there was a succession of forts; one of these, the Cerro Colorado, completely commanded the town. These forts now lie in ruins, having been taken by the revolutionary forces in 1859. They had three columns of one thousand men each, and came down from the heights to the attack. About one hundred and fifty men were killed on both sides, and the dead were all buried in one common grave. The man who fought best in the whole force engaged, was a gigantic negro artilleryman, on the side of the aristocrats, who occupied the forts. He did a good deal of execution with his gun, which, even after he was wounded in many places, he continued to fire. At last he was struck on the back by a large ball from a swivel-gun, while he was in the act of re-loading his cannon. When they came to collect the corpses for interment he was found still breathing, and was taken to a doctor, from whom I heard the whole story, and who assured me that, though tetanus supervened, the negro recovered from his wounds. " This," said the medico, " was the only case of recovery from lock-jaw that I have ever witnessed."

After toiling up the mountain by a steep zig-zag path, we used to descend a ravine, in which flows a rivulet dignified by the name of the Rio de la Guaira. This stream is usually about ten inches deep, but sometimes is swelled by the rains into a formidable torrent. Thus, in 1810, it swelled suddenly, after a heavy rain in the mountains, to a stream ten feet deep, and swept away property to the value of half a million of dollars, as well as many persons, of whom forty were drowned. There is a sickly yellow-feverish smell in this ravine; nevertheless, numbers of people bathe

in the pools it forms at every broad ledge of rock. One
of these pools is called the Consul's Bath, owing to a piece
of scandal in which an English Lurline was concerned. Of
the three routes to Carácas from La Guaira, the shortest,
but most difficult and dangerous, passes for some distance
up this ravine. It is called the Indian's Path, and is actually
that which was used by the Indians before the Spanish conquest. Between it and the present coach-road is the road
which was in use when Humboldt visited the country. I
was anxious to make trial of all three, but being invited to
breakfast at the Rincon, or Corner, a pretty country-seat
beyond Maquetia, I determined to go by that road first.

It was 9 A.M., on the 10th of July, when I left La
Guaira, accompanied by my friend and Juan. The sun was
terrifically hot, but the prospect of being jolted over the
chaotic road to Maquetia being more terrible still, we resolved to walk to the Rincon, and let the coach, which we
had engaged for our exclusive use, pick us up there. The
said coach appeared to be considerably smaller than the
smallest four-wheeled cab in London, and was so vamped
up, and moved so heavily, and with such a flapping of
doors, that I quite agreed with Juan, when he, unconscious
of a pun, called out to the driver to get on with his vampiro. We walked, as I have said, to Maquetia, and turned
gladly out of its dirty streets up a lane bursting with
flowering shrubs, which led to the Rincon. Presently, we
were aware of two female figures ahead of us, the figures
evidently of two young and well-shaped Creole ladies.
Before long, one of them dropped a kerchief and a prayer-
book, which I picked up, and found they belonged to la
Senorita Trinidad Smith. Not being used to Spanish

nomenclature, Trinity struck me as a curious Christian name, but my friend told me it was nothing to what I should meet with. Thus Dolores, or Pangs, is a most favourite baptismal appellation; and even Dolores Fuertes, Strong Pangs, is not uncommon. These strange Christian appellations sometimes yield a curious sense when added to certain proper names. C. gave me, as an instance, the case of a lady christened Dolores Fuertes, who married a gentleman named Battiga; thus the whole name stood Strong Pangs of the Stomach.

The Rincon is a pretty little country-house, very like an Indian bangla, at the foot of a deep ravine in the mountain. All around were trees and shrubs in profusion, so that it was really " life in the bush." On my proposing to take a walk in the garden, the lady of the house said, very naively, that there were a great many snakes there, particularly rattlesnakes : an observation which rather damped my ardour. The breakfast-party was large; there were ourselves, several Creole ladies and gentlemen, two French officers, and five children. Among the things at table with which I was not familiar, were a párga fish weighing fifteen pounds, the alligator, or, as it ought to be called, advocate's pear, and the fruit of the passion-flower creeper, which is as big as a pumpkin, and not less insipid. The párga might be called the sea-perch for its colour, shape, and taste. It is common enough, and I had seen it before, but never of such a size. The alligator pear has been often described, and it is said that a good deal of practice in eating it is needed before a relish for it can be acquired. To me its flavour seemed to be a compound of the tastes of pumpkin, melon, and very mouldy Stilton cheese.

At 2 P.M., our shambling equipage, the vampiro, came flapping up to the door, drawn by three rat-like ponies, who, however, soon proved that they had some mettle in them. The road, which is about twenty-five feet broad, and not an intolerably bad one after fairly quitting Maquetia, skirts, in a perpetual zigzag, the eastern side of the great ravine called Quebráda de Tipe. The western side of this ravine, which is a mile or two broad, leads directly from Carácas to the Bay of Catia, already mentioned as a desirable harbour. Along this side of the ravine, surveys for a railroad were made by Stephenson, which have been repeated by a gentleman who arrived at Carácas at the same time as myself. The difficulties of this route for locomotives are, perhaps, not insurmountable, but they seem at least to be greater than any that have yet been overcome elsewhere.

For the first thousand feet of elevation our progress was slow, as the clouds of red dust were literally suffocating, and the heat so great that even the case-hardened driver was fain to take things quietly. Besides, no little management was required in order to pass safely the strings of cattle, asses, and pedestrians, and the numerous carts we met or overtook. When once we had reached the elevation of a thousand feet, we perceived a marked change in the temperature, and began to be repaid for our previous sufferings by a fine view over the Quebráda, the narrow line of coast and the ocean. The whole distance between Maquetia and Carácas by this road, is about twenty miles, while, as the crow flies, from La Guaira to Carácas is not more than nine miles. Here and there we came to a venta, or poor inn, where the carters, carriers, and coachmen get a drink of aguardiente, or fire-water, as rum is here called, while their wretched animals take a·few minutes' rest, if rest that can be called which is robbed of its solace by the swarms of flies. At one place our coachman, an Italian (it is curious that the principal Jehus on this road are Italians), requested us to hold our noses, at the same time applying the lash vigorously to his ponies. As we galloped by, a flock of zamuros, or small vultures, rose from the body of a horse, which might very easily have been pitched over the precipice by its owner; but no South American would ever think of giving himself a little trouble to oblige the public. We stopped at a venta half way, and changed horses. Three or four rough-looking fellows, with guns and dogs, were smoking there. They said they had been out all day, and had killed four quail, and *seen* a few partridges. We had now ascended about five thousand feet, and it was comparatively quite cold. The road, too, was less steep, and we started with our fresh horses at great speed. This rate of travelling is not so pleasant on such a road to those who cross it for the first time. The turns were so abrupt as to be quite invisible while one was approaching the precipice, from which they diverged almost at right angles. We seemed to be galloping straight into the abyss, and we did reach its very brink, and then swept round by a turn in the road, which only at that moment showed itself. Until habit deadens sensation, one cannot but feel a little nervous at such charioteering, and the more so as dreadful accidents have actually occurred. There are similar roads over the mountains in Peru, and it is said that a late President of that country got so alarmed on one occasion, that he shouted out to the youth who was driving, to stop. The mozo, however, rather enjoying the joke, drove on faster than ever, till the President, drawing out a pistol, called to him that he would shoot him dead unless he pulled up instantly. This was a hint not to be disregarded, so the youth obeyed, but turned round and said, with the usual freedom or impudence of the country, "Truly you're a fine fellow to be President of Peru, if you are afraid at such a trifle as this!"

Two miles from the place of changing horses, the road begins to descend, and we went on with increasing speed. The road now grew narrower and narrower at every turn, and the view more confined. At length, about half-past 5 P.M., we came suddenly in sight of Carácas, which is not seen from any distance by this route. About fifty students, wandering in cap and gown along the road, were the first sign of our approaching the capital. We next plunged into some dirty lanes, and then suddenly emerged into the paved streets of the city. Along these, Francisco, our driver, urged his ponies with all the speed they could muster, at the same time cracking his whip with reports like those of a pistol, to announce his arrival. The result of all this energy was, that we were pitched against one another, and up to the roof of the coach, in a way that nearly dislocated our necks, and utterly destroyed any dignity that we might otherwise have assumed. The streets were full of holes, over which we bounded in the most unpleasant fashion, till we pulled up dead, with a jerk that nearly sent us out of the windows, at the door of St. Amande's Hotel, where the Brazilian minister's rooms had been engaged for me.

# CHAPTER III.



THE hotel was a square house of two stories, close to the market-place, and not far from the centre of the city. All the rooms on the ground-floor were bedrooms. On the floor above was my apartment, a very large room divided into three by partitions, and overlooking the street. On the side opposite my room was another very large one, where the table d'hôte was held. To the left were three rooms occupied by the landlord and his family, and on the right were some more bedrooms for travellers. The concierge was a huge negro, who, having been a custom-house officer, gave himself all the airs of a government official, and had grown so fat that he quite blocked up the doorway. The landlord had come to the country as a savant, to collect articles for some museum, but, having married an English lady's-maid, condescended to allow her to make *his* fortune by keeping this hotel. He was the most silent man possible, and all the time I was there I never heard him say but two words, "Mon Dieu!" An unmarried daughter lived in the house, and played the piano at a great rate. The establishment consisted of two Indian waitresses, and a mulatto stable-boy.

There was also a cook, so enormously fat that I put her down as the wife of the fat concierge. I was glad that I encountered her only once, and that at my departure, as I should never have been able to relish my dinner after seeing by whom it was cooked. I found my apartment very neatly furnished, and beautifully clean, and congratulated myself on having so comfortable a lodging. That night I dined at C.'s, and was agreeably surprised at the elegance of his ménage. His house was but one story high, but there were many fine rooms in it. The drawing-room, for example, was about sixty feet long and twenty-five broad, and furnished like a first-class saloon in Paris. In the centre of the court, round which the rooms were built, was a garden full of beautiful flowers, and a fountain of clear water.

I have said I was well pleased with my apartment, and I ensconced myself in my mosquito curtains about midnight, anticipating a long and pleasant slumber. However, about half-past three, I woke in the midst of a dream, in which I fancied myself in a belfry, with the bells playing triple bob-majors. On my awaking, sure enough bells were ringing furiously all round. The sound seemed to come from every direction. What could it be? "Perhaps," thought I, "this is the way the Caraquénians announce a fire or an earthquake, or is it a popular émeute? Oh, bother them! I wish they would have their revolutions in the daytime, like reasonable people." Still the bells rang on, and presently there was a great noise of people passing in the street, and then a sound of firing and of rockets being let off. I should have gone to the window to reconnoitre, but a salutary awe of the mosquitos and the penetrating* fleas kept me where I was

* The *pulex penetrans* is a flea that burrows in the flesh where it lays its eggs.

until the day dawned, when I got up to discover the reason of the hubbub. I then perceived that on the other side of the street there was a large convent, in which, although not a soul was to be seen, the bells were ringing in a way, that reminded me of the Devil and the Old Woman of Berkeley. Further down the street than the convent was a small square, and on one side of it a church, where again the bells were ringing at least as obstreperously. In the direction of this church, which was brilliantly lighted up, there was quite a crowd of people coming and going, and from among them rockets shot up from time to time. On inquiry, I found it was the fiesta of the Isleños, or people from the Canary Islands, of whom there is quite a colony at Carácas. In South America every one has his patron saint, and the Isleños have theirs, and in honour of their saint sleep was made to fly from the eyelids of all in the quarter of the city where I was, while our nerves were harassed throughout the day by a continued hubbub of bells, fireworks, processions, and bull-fights. But even fiestas must come to an end, and I found solace in the hope that quiet would at length be restored. Alas! the Catholic year at Carácas is made up of feasts and fasts, and, fasting or feasting, the inhabitants are for ever ringing bells, discharging holy squibs and rockets, and walking in tumultuous processions. I lived weeks amid this din, and never could get accustomed to it, nor enjoy that hearty sound slumber which Sancho apostrophises as the best of wrappers. But, in fairness, it must be added that fiestas have their attractions for strangers as well as their disagreeables. On these days, especially on notable holidays, such as that of Nuestra Señora de la Merced, the fair sex come forth in their gayest attire, and walk in bevies to the churches. It is then, if you are an impartial Paris, that you will resolve to bestow your golden apple on the Creole Venus in preference to all other beauties, so lovely are the faces that shine upon you from under the coquettish mantilla, and so graceful the figures that undulate along the streets. There may, indeed, be rosier cheeks and fairer skins elsewhere, but not such large black eyes, teeth of such dazzling whiteness, such taper waists, and faultless feet and ankles, as belong to the Venezuelan ladies. As for any devout feeling, that, of course, is entirely out of the question. The women come forth to be looked at, and the men stand in groups on the church steps, or cluster inside, to look at them. All round the churches are pictures, usually sad daubs, and a profusion of wax dolls, representing the Virgin at various periods of her life. Anything more contrary to common sense, to say nothing of good taste and devotional feeling, than these images, it is impossible to conceive. Among the absurd groups of dolls I was particularly struck with one at the Merced fiesta, in which the Virgin, dressed in all the frippery imaginable, was kneeling beside a gigantic crucifix, while a six-year-old angel fluttered above the cross, dressed in silver-embroidered trunk-hose and tartan leggings of the royal Stuart pattern. About the middle of the day, when the heat is most trying, there is generally a procession, and the image or picture of the saint is carried about, amid a train of ecclesiastics, and with a body of soldiers as a guard of honour. Every now and then the host is elevated, and down go the people on their knees, and anon guns and rockets are discharged, and the use even of squibs and crackers is sanctified on such occasions.

On seeing all this, my recollection went back to India, and the processions of Durgá and Krishnah. Indeed, the yátrotsavahs of Hindustan, and the fiestas of South America, have a common origin. They are the resource of an idle people, and an excuse for putting on best clothes, loitering, gaming, and love-making. I was assured that at the grand fiesta at Santiago, the Virgin receives some thirty thousand letters from the girls of the city and its environs. Some ask for husbands and lovers, others for ball-dresses and pianos, and, incredible as it may appear, the petitions are answered, and, where it is thought politic, granted. As for such trifles as husbands and lovers, one knows from Herodotus that such matters are easily arranged, but even a piano is occasionally sent. At Carácas, absurdity is not carried so far, but even there fiestas are no doubt the busiest days at Cupid's post-office.

The site of Carácas is one to please an Oriental sovereign. It is at about the same elevation above the sea as Tehrán, the capital of Persia, and resembles it in accessibility. With a few batteries judiciously placed, the approach to Carácas from the coast might be completely closed against an enemy, excepting, of course, English sailors, to whom all things are practicable that imply prize-money and a fight. In the beginning of June, 1595, the renowned Corsair Dracke, as the Spanish historians call him, or Francis Drake, stood in with his squadron towards the coast of Venezuela, till he arrived within about half a league from La Guaira, when he embarked five hundred men in boats, and landed. The inhabitants of La Guaira fled without resistance, and carried to Carácas the news of the terrible Englishman's descent on the coast. Then did the valiant alcaldes, Garci-Gonzalez and Francisco Rebolledo, assembling all the men who would and could bear arms, march out to repel and chastise the invader. They marched with banners displayed along the royal road leading from Carácas to La Guaira, leaving ambuscades in the less frequented passes of the mountains, where the thick trees and rough ground favoured such strategy. But Drake had found at Guaicamaento a Spaniard named Villalpando, who was willing to sell his country, and who led the corsair by an unfrequented route, perhaps that which is now called the Indian's Path, to Carácas. So, while the valiant alcaldes were marching down to the sea, and their gallant men in ambush were lying ensconced in the dank grass, the Englishman was hanging Villalpando, for whom he had no further use, on a tree, and packing up, with great care and very much at his ease, all the valuables he could find in Carácas. Now, who can adequately describe the fury of the alcaldes when they heard that, while they were guarding the stable-door, the steed had been already stolen! So they marched back again to the capital, resolved to make a pastel of Drake and his merry men, and hoping to catch them with their pikes and their hangers and their arquebuses laid aside, and their hands full of plunder. But Drake was cautious as well as bold, and had turned the municipal hall and the church near it into little fortresses, and the Spaniards had a presentiment that there was no taking these strong places without bloodshed, so they surrounded the city at a safe distance, and prepared to put every Englishman to death, who, not content with the booty he had already got, should go out to the villages round about to look for more. But one old hidalgo named Alonso Andrea de Ledesma, who was, perhaps, a native of La Mancha, mounted his steed, and put his lance in rest, and an old target on his arm, and rode forth alone to drive out the English. The chivalry of the old don moved Drake's compassion, and he bade his men not to harm him; nor would they, had he not charged them at full speed, and tried to do mischief with his spear. Thereupon they killed him as gently as they could, and carried his body to a grave in the city, and interred it with all honour. So, when eight days were passed, Drake and his five hundred moved out of Carácas with their booty; and, after burning all the houses that they had not knocked down already, marched merrily away to their ships, and embarked without the loss of a single man.

Carácas is, as has been said, very inaccessible from the north—that is, from the side towards La Guaira and the sea; but, in the opposite direction, the slopes are easier. In order to form a correct notion of the site on which the city is built, one must keep in mind the direction of the mountain ranges of the country. The Andes alone run north and south, dividing South America like a backbone, but into two very unequal parts—the part parallel to the Pacific being infinitely narrow compared with the eastern portion that extends to the Atlantic. A number of cordilleras descend from the Andes, and run from west to east, and that cordillera which skirts the Caribbean Sea forms quite an angle at La Guaira and Macuto, approaching there almost to the sea, and ending in a huge clump, the highest part of which is La Silla, a great double-peaked mountain, that towers up two miles to the east of Carácas. La Silla is, consequently, nearly opposite to Macuto, while the ridge which separates Carácas from La Guaira is called

Cerro de Avila. This ridge appears to swell on without a break until it terminates in La Silla, but it is in reality separated from it by the deep ravine of Tocume. On the south side, then, of Avila and La Silla is a plain, called the plain of Chacao, with a steep slope from N.N.W. to S.S.E. —that is, from the mountains just mentioned to La Guaira, a stream which flows with a south-easterly course into the Tuy. The latter river falls into the Caribbean Sea, sixty miles to the east of the town of La Guaira. The plain of Chacao, which is a lateral branch of the far larger valley of the Tuy, is about ten miles long from west to east, and seven broad from north to south, and at its western extremity, where it is narrowest, stands Carácas.

Some authors have pronounced it to be matter of regret that Carácas was not built further to the east, near the village of Chacao, where the plain is widest. There is no doubt that Francisco Fajardo, who, in 1560, first built on the site which the capital of Venezuela now occupies, was led to choose the spot as being nearest to the coast, and also to the mines of Los Teques, which were the attractions that brought him into a locality then swarming with hostile Indians. In 1567, Don Diego Losada, who wished to make a permanent conquest where Fajardo had been little more than an explorer, founded a city on the site chosen by the latter, and called it Santiago de Leon de Carácas—thus giving it his own name Santiago, or Diego, the name of the Governor de Leon, and that of the Indians of the district, Carácas, which last alone survives. Losada, of course, little imagined that his new city would ever become the capital of a great country, and in selecting the site he was probably guided by the accident that Fajardo had chosen it before him. In fact, if advantages of site were to decide the position of the capital, the government of Venezuela would be transferred from Carácas to Valencia, a city which has the richest soil and the best seaport in all South America. In the meantime, the Caraquénians are very proud of their native town, and boast much of its climate; but the question of its title to rank first among Venezuelan cities is decided in the negative by Humboldt, who says: "From the position of the provinces Carácas can never exert any powerful political influence over the countries of which it is the capital."

I soon came to know Carácas and its environs well, for fresh horses were lent me every day, and I rode somewhere or other every morning and evening. The horses of Venezuela, be it said, *en passant*, though spirited and well shaped, are so small that one would certainly snub them as ponies, but for their self-assertion and haughty little ways, which, it must be owned, are at times supported by worthy deeds in carrying their riders bravely into battle, and in aiding in the slaughter of furious bulls twice as big as themselves. They do not understand high jumping, but they go very well at ditches, however broad and deep. Their favourite pace is the pase-trote, a sort of quick amble, and they know very well that they are to go that way if the reins are held rather high, and the mouth is felt pretty strongly. Trotting is not fashionable, and, altogether, the English style of riding does not seem to be admired, for it is usual to say of a bad rider "he rides like an Englishman." The Creoles ride with excessively long stirrups, so as just to touch them with the toe, and the ambling pace of their horses is well suited for that kind of seat, as well as for the paved streets of Carácas, for neither rider nor animal is shaken by it.

My first ride was to the east of the city to Petaré, a large village about seven miles from Carácas. In a few minutes after leaving St. Amande's Hotel, I found myself in La Gran Plaza, the principal square, where the daily market is held. It is about the size of Portman-square, but looks larger, the buildings round it being all very low, except the Government House, which is on the western side, and the cathedral, which stands at the south-eastern angle. Both these buildings survived the great earthquake of 1812. I found nothing in the cathedral, either externally or internally, worth noticing, except the tomb of Bolivar, which is of white marble, and tastefully executed. The Liberator is represented standing in his general's uniform, and below are three female figures, intended, I suppose, for the three States who owe their freedom to him. The inscription is: "Simonis Bolivar cineres hic condit, honorat, grata et memor patria. 1852." Somehow, on looking at this monument, a certain sentence would recur to my mind: "He asked for bread, and they gave him a stone." Bolivar, whose ashes are here so honoured in the cathedral of his native town, died far away, starving, and an exile.

A little way from the cathedral is the theatre. Juxta-position seems to be the rule as regards these edifices in Venezuela. At La Guaira, the theatre stands next a church. Things have so far changed for the better since the time of Humboldt, that the theatre at Carácas, which was then open to the sky, is now roofed. During my stay there was no operatic troupe, and the pieces played were generally dull tragedies, in which all the characters were killed in succession, apparently to the great satisfaction of the audience.

At about half a mile from the cathedral, I came to a bridge over a stream which falls into the Guaira, and which bounds the town on this side. Here are two fine coffee plantations, and a mile further is another still finer, notable for being the point at which Humboldt commenced his ascent of La Silla. The scenery here is very beautiful, the valley being a mass of cultivation, while from no point inland does the great mountain look so imposing. However, that which interested me most was the Ferro-Carril d'Este, or " Eastern Railway," the terminus of which is just beyond the bridge already mentioned. I dismounted to inspect the station, and as it was quite deserted, I was obliged to clamber over a gate fifteen feet high to get into it. 1 found that the rails had been laid down for about half a mile, but the grass and weeds were growing over them. There were engines and carriages, and piles of wood for sleepers, sad emblems of the slumber into which the whole concern has fallen, and from which it seems doubtful whether it will ever awake. I found the posada at Petaré full of people smoking and playing billiards, and the whole place had a more thriving, bustling appearance than I expected. There are about five hundred houses in the village, and some fine estates near it. Still there never could be sufficient traffic to repay the expense of a railway, unless the line were continued to Valencia.

My next expedition was to the north of the town, and to the slope beyond lying immediately under the Cerro d'Avila. The city of Carácas, as may be seen from this slope, is in figure a great square, with long parallel streets crossing it from north to south, and with the principal square of the market-place in the centre. But at the north-east angle there has been a suburb, through which the old road to La Guaira passes. The "Indian Path," already mentioned, branches off from that road. I was astonished to see the destruction that the great earthquake of 1812 caused in this direction. Not a house seems to have escaped, and though a few have been restored, the marks of the disaster are apparent everywhere, and whole lines of ruins still remain. In fact, the nearer the mountain, the greater seemed to me to have been the shock. I was confirmed in this opinion afterwards by the narrative of an eye-witness, Major M., who still lives, and who was in official employment in Carácas when the earthquake happened. Major M. was writing in his office with his clerk at 4 p.m., on the 26th of March, in that year. It was intensely hot, and no rain had fallen for a considerable time. Being Holy Thursday, the churches were crowded with ladies, dressed in their gayest attire. The chapels of the convents were filled with nuns, and the streets, as is usual on holidays, with people who had come in from the neighbouring villages. At the barracks of San Carlos, a regiment of six hundred men were mustering under the walls. There was not a cloud in the sky, not a thought of danger in the heart of any one. All of a sudden the earth seemed to move upwards, the church bells tolled, and a tremendous subterranean noise was heard. The perpendicular motion lasted four seconds, and was instantly succeeded by a violent undulatory movement, which continued six seconds more. In those ten seconds that great city, with fifty thousand inhabitants, had become a heap of blood-stained ruins. The churches of Alta Gracia and Trinidad, with towers one hundred and fifty feet high, were so completely levelled, that in their place only shapeless mounds remained, spread out to a great distance, but not more than five feet high. Every convent was destroyed, and of the inmates scarcely one escaped. The barrack of San Carlos was hurled forward from its base, and of the six hundred soldiers mustering below its walls not a man was left alive. At the first shock, Major M. started from his seat and rushed towards the door, followed by his clerk. M. sprang into the street, but his clerk was too late, and was crushed to death by the falling house. The major had seen many terrific sights in his long residence in these regions of the volcano and the earthquake, and had been in many battles both by sea and land, but he declared that the spectacle which Caracas presented at the moment of the great earthquake, was the most terrible of all. A vast cloud of dust rose up to heaven, and with it ascended the shrieks of more than twenty thousand human beings dying or wounded in the ruins. Great rocks came thundering down from the mountains, and at intervals explosions, like the discharge of innumerable pieces of artillery, were heard beneath the earth. Major M. fled down to the river La Guaira, and remained there without food till the next day. Even then it was difficult to procure the means of satisfying hunger, for the houses were all fallen, and the streets were so encumbered with ruins, that it was difficult to pass. So for many days the sad sights were renewed of digging out the wounded and the dead.

Men's minds were so affected with terror, that for a long time they could not return to their ordinary occupations, but were continually absorbed with prayer and religious ceremonies. Then were many marriages performed between those who had for years been living together without that .tie, and men who had defrauded others made restitution, appalled by the horrors of that tremendous day, and apprehensive of their recurrence.

At a few places in the Cerro d'Avila, I observed houses perched up at an elevation of several hundred feet, and among them one belonging to the Dutch minister. Below it is a country-house, called the Paraiso, once the property of an English minister, and which passed from him to a famous Creole beauty. But that which interested me most in this direction was the Catholic cemetery, said to be the finest in all South America, and well worth a visit. It stands on very high ground, and the view is magnificent. The singularity of the place is, that the inner side of the very high walls by which it is surrounded is lined with a sort of gigantic pigeon-holes. They are eight feet deep, and three feet wide and high, and are used as receptacles for coffins. Persons who can afford to pay a fee of thirty-five dollars are allowed the privilege of placing the coffin of a deceased relative in one of these receptacles for three years. The name of the deceased person is printed over the recess, and the coffin can be brought out at any time if required. Of course, it is thus preserved from destruction, being quite dry, and sheltered from the weather, and also safe from the attacks of insects, especially the formidable black ant, which is three-quarters of an inch in length, and devours everything it can get at. At the expiration of three years coffins are taken down, and the remains of the deceased person are, if the family wish it, handed over to them. Otherwise, they are thrown into a large pit, called a carnero. Poor people, and those who do not choose to pay for the three years' lodgment in the pigeon-holes, are buried at once in the grounds of the cemetery. I observed the words Calentura Amarilla in many of the epitaphs, which told plainly of the ravages of the yellow fever. Humboldt mentions that this disease had been known at La Guaira only two years before his arrival, and says nothing of its having appeared at Carácas.

After I had ridden past the cemetery a few hundred yards, I came to a mound about one hundred and fifty feet in length, and was told that this marked the spot where the persons who died in the great outbreak of cholera a few years ago, were buried. The victims were so numerous that it was quite impossible to inter them separately, so a very long deep trench was dug, and the dead were brought in carts and cast into it. The English burial-ground and the German are on the southern outskirts of the city, and are very poor places as compared with the Catholic cemetery. They are both covered with weeds, but, in the British burial-ground, the rank grass is so tall that it is impossible to see the graves, and the whole place is full of ant-hills several feet high. There is a chapel, with an inscription to say it was built by Robert Ker Porter at his sole expense. I felt interested in seeing the name of a man who, like myself, had come from the Caspian Gates to this distant country of the West.

North of the city, I found only one other place worth a visit. This is the Toma, or reservoir, which supplies Carácas with water. It is situated in a thickly-wooded ravine, and a very narrow path among the bushes leads to it. It is necessary to tread with caution here, as, on account of the dense thickets, and the place being so little frequented, snakes abound in incredible numbers. I was assured that, on a little rocky terrace where the shrubs will not grow, sometimes forty or fifty rattlesnakes and other serpents might be seen basking in the sun. With such protectors a human guard might seem unnecessary. There is, however, a superintendent, and, on entering his cottage, I found his wife, a native of the Canary Islands, working with her daughter at making sandals. She said they could make two dozen a day, and got six and a half dollars, or about a pound sterling, a dozen. This is only one instance of many I saw of the enormously high rates at which labour is paid in Venezuela.

Westward of the city I did not ride. In this direction there is only the road to La Guaira, along which I had come by coach. I took, however, a walk to the Calvario, a hill on which the stations at Calvary ought to be marked by crosses, but I observed none. The hill, which being some hundred feet high, commands a good view over the city, is remarkable for a very severe action fought there on the 23rd of June, 1821, between Colonel Pereira, the Spanish commandant at Carácas, and General José Francisco Bermudez, of the patriot army. Bermudez, who had only fifteen hundred men, attacked with great fury the Spanish forces, though far outnumbering his column, and advantageously posted on the high ground, and was so completely defeated that he had great difficulty in escaping to Rodea with two hundred men.

To the south there is a fine road, made by a European engineer, which leads to Los Teques, a village about twenty-five miles from Carácas, where there were gold mines once worked by the Spaniards, and which, in fact, were the glittering bait that lured them into the province. The first station on this road, at about six miles from the city, is the pleasant village of Antemano, where Caraquénian beauties go to bathe and ruralise during the heats of summer. There is also a road more directly south, which leads across the river La Guaira into the hills, and so to the valley of the Tuy. There is a beautiful estate in this direction, belonging to Señor Espino, whose income from land may be about twenty thousand dollars a year. With a visit to his property I closed my survey of the environs of Carácas, and came to the conclusion that, were it not for earthquakes, epidemics, insect plagues, triennial revolutions, and bell-ringing, there would be few more desirable localities for a residence.

# CHAPTER IV.



"Why, Juan," said I, as I sat examining my first week's accounts at Carácas, "things are exorbitantly dear in this land of liberty. There's that dinner I gave the day before yesterday. It was a very plain dinner to thirteen, and they have charged twenty-three pounds for it! That's a charge one might expect in London with real turtle, ten kinds of fish, and as many courses; but here we have had nothing very much beyond the usual *table d'hôte* fare, except, indeed, a turkey—yes, there was a turkey, and——"

"Things *are* dear, sir, interrupted Juan, "and if they weren't so in a general way they would be to us. Why, there is not a man, woman, or child in the whole city that doesn't know we brought two boxes of gold to La Guaira, and that you are a comisionado."

"And what difference does that make ? The gold was for the government, as everybody knows. And if any man ought to be careful of money, and to examine well into accounts, it should be a financial commissioner."

"Well, sir," replied Juan, "that's one view, and I'm not

a going to say that it's a wrong one; but it's not a Creole view.  Sir, it's of no manner of use being too honest out here, for no one gets the credit of it.  As for government business, there's, perhaps more cheating in that than in anything, for it's a kind of proverb, 'La mejor hacienda es el Gobierno mal administrado'—'The best estate is the government ill administered.'  So, no offence, sir, but if you would really like to know what is thought, I'll be bound the general opinion is, that being a very sensible man, you won't part with those boxes of gold without keeping a cuartillo for yourself out of every real; and of course they think that when you have such a lot of money you ought to leave some of it behind for the good of the country.  As for the bill, the rules for marketing here is, 'get all you can, and make him who has most, pay most.'"

So saying, Juan walked off with the intention of passing the morning at various friends' houses.  In the evening, at my dinner-hour, he would show himself again for a short time, after which I should see nothing of him till next day.  This free and easy style of service is regarded as quite the correct thing in Venezuela: a country which might, indeed, be called the paradise of servants, were the name of servant applicable at all to the vagrant gentlemen and ladies who pay you short visits to replenish their purses and wardrobes, leave you without notice, and severely repress any attempt to communicate with them as to your domestic arrangements.  But you may talk with them on general topics, such as the weather or the theatre, and on politics you may be as expansive as you please, for where any one may become a general or a president in a few days that subject is universally interesting.  The doctrine of perfect

equality is so well carried out, that, in one of the best
houses where I was a guest, the gentleman who cleaned the
boots always came into my room with his hat on and a cigar
in his mouth ; and another gentleman whom I had engaged
to assist Juan, left me the day after his arrival, on being
refused the custody of my keys and purse, which he candidly
stated was the only duty he felt equal to.  At dances, as soon
as the music strikes up in the drawing-room, the servants
begin to waltz in the passages and ante-rooms, and as en-
tertainments are almost always on the ground floor, and
generally in rooms looking into the streets, the great " unwashed " thrust their naked arms and greasy faces between
the bars of the windows and criticise the dancing with much
spirit.  I have seen a gentleman in rags leaning into a
window from the streets with his bare arms almost touching
those of a beautifully dressed lady, while his most sweet
breath fanned her tresses.  On another occasion I was talking to some ladies at an evening party, when a worthy sans-
culotte jerked in his head so suddenly to listen to our conversation, that I stopped, on which he called out, " Oh, these
are the aristocrats we have here, who won't talk to any one
but their own set ! "  On my sitting down to play chess with
the wife of the president of one of the states, half a dozen
female servants, of every shade, from tawny twilight to black
night, surrounded the table and began to watch the game.
The first time I went to a tailor, I was accompanied by a
Creole friend, who undertook to show me the best place. We
had to wait some time before the gentleman of the shop
appeared.  When he did, he came in with the inevitable
cigar in his mouth.  He raised his hat politely to my friend,
walked straight up to me, shook hands, and asked me how

I did. He then sat down on the counter, put various questions to me regarding my coming to Venezuela, talked on general subjects, and at the end of about a quarter of an hour intimated that he was ready to oblige me if I wanted a coat. This tailor was an officer of rank in the army, and he was wearing his uniform and spurs when he came in to measure a friend of mine.

Juan was an excellent valet, but he would have lost caste had he been too attentive to his duties in Venezuela. So he walked off, as I have said, to amuse himself, and left me to think over the difficulties of the business entrusted to me. I had no experience in South American affairs, so my first measure had been to secure a coadjutor, who was thoroughly *au fait* in them. C., the son of an Englishman, had all the integrity characteristic of his race, and being a Creole by birth, that is, born in Venezuela, knew all about the country. He chanced to come in just as Juan left the room, and seeing that he had taken a cigar and settled himself for a chat, I said: " Now, tell me, C., how is it that this country is so wretchedly poor, and so eternally borrowing money? For my part, I can't make it out. You haven't a particle of show. Your Government House looks like an East Indian godown, your great men make no display, and as for your soldiers, one would think that the last successful campaign had been against the fripiers, and that the victors were carrying off the plunder on their backs. It is evident that you Venezuelans are not extravagant, and it is plain that you have great resources if you knew how to use them. Your soil is the richest in the world, and has never been trodden by an invader since the Spaniard was driven out. Then what is the reason that you are always borrowing

from other countries ?   How is it, too, that while the United
States of North America have made such progress, the population in your republic is all but stationary, the seas and
rivers without steamers, the country without roads, and
commerce languishing ? "   C. knocked the ashes from the
end of his cigar, assisted thought by perching his legs
conveniently on the top of a chair, and finally replied as
follows : " You see, in the first place, there's a difference
in the breed.   The Yankees are a go-a-head lot, there's no
mistake about that.   There's plenty of quicksilver in English
blood, but fog and damp keep it down in England.   At
New York it rises to fever heat, and to the boiling point down
South.   Besides, long before Lexington and Bunker-hill,
the North Americans were ripe for self-government.   In
South America things were very different.   The Spaniards
kept their American subjects in profound ignorance.   Four-
fifths of the population could not even read, for there were
no schools.   Even at Carácas, the capital, there was no
printing-office till 1816, when one was set up by the Frenchman, Delpeche.   The illiberality of the Spaniards went so
far, that, after Isabella's death, nothing was done to introduce the cultivation of any plant, or improve farming.   The
culture of the vine and olive was prohibited, and that of
tobacco was made a crown monopoly.   Emigration, too, was
all but entirely prevented, and, in the total absence of
vivyfying power, the wonder rather is that Venezuela should
ever have become free, than that it should have made so
little progress.

" Then as to the poverty of the government and its
constant borrowing, there are several reasons for that.   In
the first place, the Creoles of South America, though they

have many good qualities, are very averse to physical labour. They won't go to work in a new country, like Englishmen —clear away timber, stub up, and drain. Their wits are sharp, and they do well for superintendents; but as to work that tries the sinews, it is my belief that all the haciendas in the country would go to ruin, if it were not for the Indians and the mixed breeds. Again, the taxes levied by the Spaniards—the alcabala, or excise, the armada and corso, or coast taxes, the medias anatas, or deductions from salaries, the monopolies of salt, cards, cane-liquor, and tobacco, and numerous other imposts, were all so odious to the Columbians, that as soon as they declared themselves independent, they made a clean sweep of them, leaving only the customs to supply a revenue to the government. Now, it is in the customs that it is most easy to peculate and defraud the state. With a coast line of two thousand miles, how is it possible to keep down smuggling? To give you an idea of the extent of the contraband trade, I may mention that a finance minister of Venezuela has proved that of the two hundred million dollars' worth of goods imported into the country during the first sixteen years of independence, one hundred and twenty-nine and a half millions' worth were smuggled! But, besides that, the venality and corruption of the custom-house officers is such, that, as Señors Brandt and Iribarren have shown, the defalcations of revenue from the Aduánas up to 1852, amounted to no less than one hundred and one and a half millions of dollars. At present, the annual loss to government by contrabands and frauds of various kinds, is reckoned at six millions. But don't suppose that this calculation is based on information furnished by the accounts kept here. If other countries—

France and the United States, for example—did not publish the amount of their exports to Venezuela, no one would know what is really brought into this country. It is only by comparing foreign statistics with home fictions that we come to know the extent to which the government is cheated. Indeed, one would not be wrong in saying that the incessant revolutions which distract this unhappy country, all commence at the custom-houses. Owing to the frauds of the officials, the revenue falls short; to make up the deficiency, the customs are raised until the necessaries of life are too dear for men of small means. Thus discontent is sown broadcast, and discontent leads to conspiracies. Yet, great as the evil is, one cannot help laughing at the impudence of some of the frauds. According to the published returns, the people here must be the dirtiest in the world with any pretensions to civilisation, since it is officially made out that a quarter of an ounce of soap in a week is all that each person uses. We know that the province of Carácas alone consumes a hundred barrels of flour a day, whereas, according to the custom-house returns, the daily consumption of all Venezuela does not reach sixty-nine barrels. Under such circumstances, it is no wonder that the public treasury is empty, that the revenues of the Aduánas are all more or less mortgaged, and that there are no remittances to the capital except from La Guaira and Puerto Cabello. Of course the only resource is to borrow in foreign markets, and hence," said C., throwing away the end of his cigar, " I have the pleasure of meeting you here. Apropos of which, as there is a bull-fight to-day, and you have never seen one, let us stroll down to the Corrida."

Before we could reach the eastern outskirt of the town,

where the building stands in which the bull-fights are held, a mass of clouds came drifting from the Avila, and a light rain began, in earnest of a more pelting shower. Looking about for shelter, and seeing at a window some ladies whom we knew slightly, we went in to talk to them. I said to one of them, a slim girl with immense dark eyes, and singularly long eyelashes, "We are going to the Corrida; does the señorita ever go ?"

"No, señor, I never go. The ladies of Venezuela think bull-fights very barbarous. As for me, I cannot understand how any one can take pleasure in such odious cruelty."

"Indeed!" said I, rather astonished. "But surely in Spain ladies think differently. At Madrid it is quite the fashion for them to attend."

"That may be; we do not follow the fashions of Spain. Perhaps we are more tender-hearted here."

After this dialogue, I was not surprised, on entering the Cirque in which the bull-fight was to be held, to find that the spectators were nearly all men, and that the few women who were present were of the lower orders. The building was of wood, open to the sky in the centre, and anything but substantial. Several tiers of seats, each a foot or so higher than the other, had been erected round a circular area about a hundred and twenty feet in diameter. These seats accommodated perhaps fifteen hundred people, and there seemed but little room to spare. In front of the lowest seat, which was not much raised from the ground, were strong palisades, between which a man could slip with ease, and thus they afforded the toreros a secure retreat from the fury of the bulls. Close to where I took my place there was a large gate, which was thrown open to admit the bulls one by one. First of all, however, a squeaking band struck up, and eight toreros, or pedestrian bull-fighters, entered, and saluted some person of note who sat opposite the large gate. Just at that moment, the thunder-shower which had been gathering descended in torrents, and the people shouted to the toreros, "No moja se "— "Don't get wet!" on which they slipped in between the palisades, and so put themselves under cover. They were very well-made active fellows, with extremely good legs, which were seen to advantage, as they wore white silk stockings and knee-breeches embroidered with gold.

As soon as the rain stopped there was a loud shout, and presently the large gate opened and in rushed a bull. He was a dark animal, almost black, and had evidently been goaded to madness, for he came charging in, tossing his head, and with his tail erect. I could see, however, that the sharp points of his horns had been sawn off. One of the toreros now ran nimbly up to the bull and threw his red cloak on the ground before him, on which the animal made a furious charge, attempting to gore—not the man, of whom he at first took no notice, but the cloak. The torero dragged this along rapidly, and adroitly whisking it from side to side, fatigued the bull by causing him to make fruitless rushes, now in this direction, now in that. This was repeated again and again, until the animal seemed quite tired. The most active of the toreros then advanced with a banderilla, or javelin entwined with fireworks in one hand, and his cloak in the other. He came so close to the bull that the animal charged him headlong. In a moment the torero glided to one side, and drove the dart into the bull, pinning the wretched animal's ear to his neck. Immediately the fireworks around the dart began to explode, and the terrified bull turned and rushed madly across the arena. In half a minute or so the fire had reached the flesh, and began to burn into it. The bull then reared straight up, bellowing piteously, while its poor flanks heaved with the torture. Anon it dashed its head against the ground, driving the dart further into its flesh, and so continued to gallop round the ring in a succession of rearings and plungings. This seemed to be a moment of exquisite delight to the spectators, who yelled out applause, and some in their excitement stood up clapping and shouting. I was heartily disgusted, and would have gone out at once had it been possible, but I was too tightly wedged in. Meantime, the large gate opened again, and the poor bull fled through it, to be slaughtered and sold with all despatch. After ten minutes' pause another bull was admitted, and was similarly tortured. And so it fared with four more bulls.

The sixth bull was a very tall gaunt animal, whose tactics were quite different from those of the others. He came in without a rush, looked warily about, and could hardly be induced to follow the torero. In short, he was so sluggish, that the people, enraged at his showing so little sport, shouted for a matador to kill him in the arena. Hereupon, one of the toreros darted up to stick a banderilla into the sluggard. But the bull, being quite fresh, not only defeated this attempt by a tremendous sweep of his horns, but almost struck down his assailant, who was taken by surprise at this unlooked-for vigour on the part of an animal which seemed spiritless. However, by a desperate effort the torero escaped for a moment, but the bull followed him like lightning, and, as ill luck would have it, before the man could reach the shelter of the palisades his foot slipped in a puddle and he fell back. Expecting that the charge would end as all previous ones had ended, I had got up with the intention of leaving, and I was thus able to see more clearly what followed. As the man fell backward, the bull struck him on the lower part of the spine with such force that the blow sounded all over the building. The unfortunate torero was hurled into the air, and came down with his head against the palisades, and there lay, apparently dead, in a pool of blood. A sickening feeling of horror crept over me; the bull was rushing upon the poor fellow again, and would no doubt have crushed him as he lay motionless, but, just in the nick of time, one of the toreros threw his cloak so cleverly that it fell exactly over the bull's head and blinded him. While the brute was trampling and tossing to free himself, the matador came up and drove a short sword into the vertebræ of his neck, and down he went headlong. At one moment full of mad fury, the next he was a quivering mass of lifeless flesh. A few minutes more, and the dead bull, and seemingly lifeless man, were removed from the arena, and another bull was called for. I, however, had witnessed enough, and gladly made my exit.

It wanted still several days to that appointed for my meeting the ministers, and I determined to spend them in visiting the few buildings of interest in the city. My first expedition was to the Municipal Hall, and indeed I had but a little way to go, as it is close to the Gran Plaza. This hall is one of the oldest buildings in Carácas, and externally is not only plain, but almost shabby. Inside, however, there is a very respectable council chamber, with handsome gilt arm-chairs for the president and eleven members, who impose the town dues, and discharge the ordinary functions of civic authorities. Round the room are hung some very tolerable portraits. Among these are that of the ecclesiastic who filled the archiepiscopal chair of Carácas in 1813, and those of President Monagas and his brother. There are also portraits of Bolivar, of Count Tovar, and Generals Miranda and Urdaneta, and one remarkable picture of the reading of the Act of Independence, with likenesses of the leaders in the revolution. The mob are represented compelling the Spanish general to take off his hat and salute. As a pendant to this picture hangs a framed copy of the Act of Independence. But the great curiosity of all is the flag of Pizarro, sent from Peru in 1837, and enshrined in a case. All the silk and velvet are eaten off, but the gold wire remains, with the device of a lion, and the word Carlos. The flag is about five feet long and three broad, and being folded double in the frame, only half is seen, and they will not allow it to be taken out. There are also two flags of Carlos the Fourth, taken from the Spaniards, and the original MSS. of the Act of Independence, and other important documents, bound up together.

A day or two after, I went to see the university of Carácas, which, with the House of Assembly, the National Library, and a church, forms one great block of buildings. The National Library does not contain more than ten thousand volumes, and in that of the university there are about three thousand five hundred. The department of divinity seemed best represented ; but there was no great evidence of the books being cared for. The professors of the university were most obliging, and showed me all there was to be seen in the college, which is massive and not ill suited for its present purpose, though originally it was a convent of Carmelite friars. The departments of chemistry and medicine seemed the best organised. I concluded my inspection with a visit to the dissecting-room, and that for anatomical preparations. Among other things I was shown the skull of a man whose bones had turned to chalk. The skull was from an inch to an inch and a half thick, and if a piece of it had been broken off and shown separately, no unscientific person would have guessed it to be, or to have ever been, a human bone. One of the professors then went with me to the Hall of Congress, where also are pictures of Bolivar, and of the meeting at which the Act of Independence was settled. The locality seemed to inspire my cicerone, for, though I, and a man who sat there reading, and who never raised his head, were his sole audience, he delivered with the greatest animation an eloquent harangue on the subject of liberty. If it be true that still waters are the deepest, I should fear that the republicanism of South America is somewhat shallow, it does so babble as it runs. However, I was glad to hear the orator express himself with great warmth as regards England, saying that she was the only power that had assisted them in their great struggle with the Spaniards, and that without her they would hardly have secured their independence.

The time had now come for my interview with the ministers on the business I had in hand. C. came for me at 11 A.M. on the appointed day, and we walked together to Government House. As we were very busy conversing, I did not notice the sentry, and indeed he was such a mite of a man, that I might have been pardoned for overlooking him. It seems that in Venezuela " such divinity doth hedge " a sentinel that no passer-by must come within a yard of him. Having approached within the limits, the small warrior soon convinced me that his dignity was not to be so offended with impunity. In the twinkling of an eye he brought down his musket with a terrible rattle to the charge, and very nearly wounded me a little above the knee, at the same time snarling out some unintelligible words. It is a curious fact that the Venezuelans are, generally speaking, a very civil race, until they put on uniform (a red uniform, by-the-by, like the English), when their whole nature seems to be soured. " Don't go near that sentry," was a caution I often received, and I once heard it suggested that a mat with Cave canem ! should be laid down in front of every soldier on duty. Very different is the demeanour of the civilians. One day, for instance, I was walking with a friend on the northern outskirts of the city, when we met a gardener with a store of fresh fruit. " Now is your time," said my friend, " to try your Spanish. See how you can manage a bargain with the gardener." So, for the mere sake of talking, we detained the poor man a long time, and looked at his fruit, and tumbled it about, until I was ashamed, and would have bought a quantity of it. Then he asked where I was living, and when I told him, as it was a very long way off, he said it would not pay him to send so far. " Well, then," I said, " I fear there is nothing to be done, for I should not know how to direct my servant to come to you." " That's true," said he, " but I should like you to taste this fruit, which is really very fine, so you must accept a few specimens." With these words he insisted on my taking some of the best mangoes and other fruit he had, and positively refused to be paid for it.

Escaping from the surly little sentry, we entered the Government House, and were received by the official whose duty it is to usher in those who come to pay their respects to the ministers. This official, whose name is Godoy, is a negro of the negroes, and is a genius in his way. Many of his bon-mots are current at Carácas. On one occasion, when government had suddenly changed hands, a conceited official, who had just got into power, said to Godoy, " You here still? How is it that you have not been turned out with the rest?" " I," said Godoy, with an affectation of humility, but casting a significant glance at his interrogator, " never ascend, and consequently never descend." His questioner was soon enabled to appreciate the philosophy of the remark, for he descended from Government House as suddenly as he ascended, being turned out by another change. Another time, during the late troubles, a number of young men, chiefly students from the university, collected in a threatening manner near Government House, and began shouting out various seditious cries. Godoy, and one of the generals on the side of the party in power, came out on the balcony to see what was the matter: on which stones were thrown at Godoy, and the mob shouted: " Down with the negroes!" " Down with the brigands!" " Do you hear what they say?" asked the general, sneeringly, of Godoy. " Your excellency," he replied, " I hear. They are calling out, ' Down with the negroes!' meaning, of course, me; and ' Down with the brigands!' which, as no one else is present, must refer, I suppose, to your excellency."

We were ushered by Godoy into the council-room, a handsome apartment, looking on the Gran Plaza. It contains the inevitable picture of Bolivar. There is also his sash, but I do not remember to have seen his sword anywhere. We entered and found a suffocating atmosphere, for the rooms at Government House are open only during the day, and the doors and windows are kept closed from sunset till the hour when business commences, which is generally about eleven o'clock. There are, besides, no verandahs, so that the public rooms at Carácas are hotter than those at Madras. However, as the ministers, with the acting president at their head, were already assembled, there was nothing for it but to go forward and take our seats. The meeting was one of vital importance to every one present. Not only were the exigencies of the government most urgent, but each individual supporter of it knew that on the satisfactory termination of that meeting depended his hopes of indemnity for losses, and the settlement of his claims, whatever they might be. The public tranquillity, too, was at stake, because the greater part of the army, after five years' incessant fighting, had no other reimbursement to look to for all their toils and dangers, but what might be allotted to them if this conference passed off well. Nay more; at the very moment that we were seated there, an extensive conspiracy was on foot, in which a minister and several other persons of rank were said to be engaged, and which, if some of the conspirators had not turned informers, might have been successful. Yet so great was the command of countenance possessed by the ministers there assembled, and so complete the absence of all appearance of excitement, that no one would have supposed the business under discussion to have been more than an every-day matter. War is a sharp teacher, and in troublous times political students learn in months what it takes years to acquire in peace. The men who sat there as ministers had been, not very long before, one a clerk, another a cattle-farmer, and so on. And now they were governing a country twice as large as France, and had learned so much from the experience of the late struggle, that they were by no means unfitted for the task of government.

After a long discussion, our business, for the time at least, was satisfactorily concluded. C. and I then took leave, having received several invitations to breakfast from the ministers; for at Carácas it does not seem to be the fashion to give dinners. These invitations we accepted, and walked back to the hotel. On the way we heard a good deal of shouting, mingled with laughter, and presently we met a big wild-looking man, who seemed to be in a perfect frenzy, stopping from time to time and imprecating the most dreadful curses on all about him. He was followed by a number of people who were jeering and throwing stones, which he returned with interest, picking up flints as large as one's fist, and throwing them with a force that would have shattered the skull of any one but a negro. He was, in fact, a madman; in general, they said, tolerably quiet; but on this occasion goaded to fury by his persecutors. I said to C., "This is a very disgraceful scene. In any European city the police would interfere, and prevent this poor maniac from being tormented. Have you no madhouse in Venezuela to which this wretched man might be sent?" "Well," said C., "as to the police, you yourself must admit that, though our streets are not patrolled in the daytime, disturbances are rarer here than in European towns. With regard to mad people, I never heard of any serious accident from their being allowed to go about as they choose; and so I don't see the use of madhouses here. But you will have more opportunities before you leave Venezuela of forming an opinion on this subject. Our lunatics are, in general, very quiet. What you see to-day is an unusual occurrence."

By this time we had reached the hotel, and I parted with C., having first accepted an invitation to dine with him next day. I went to his house accordingly about 7 P.M., and found no one but himself and the ladies of the family. In the middle of dinner, a gentleman whom I had not seen before, entered and walked straight up to the hostess, as I thought, to apologise, but he said nothing, and, after looking at her strangely for a moment or two, moved across the room to a picture, which he began to examine. I thought this rather curious conduct, but supposed he was some intimate friend or relation, who did not stand on ceremony. As to our conversation the day before, de lunatico inquirendo, I had forgotten all about it. When, however, the new comer began to walk round and round the table, murmuring broken sentences, I began to understand the state of the case. Presently the madman, for such he was, went up to the buffet, and began fumbling with the things there. "If he takes up a knife, and makes a rush at some one," thought I, "it will not be pleasant." However, as no one took any notice of the intruder, I too said nothing about him, and went on talking to the lady who sat next me, and eating my dinner. In a minute or two my eyes wandered back to the gentleman at the sideboard, when, to my consternation, I perceived that he had indeed got hold of a knife, with which he had already cut himself pretty severely, for the blood was trickling from his wrist. He was muttering, too, faster than ever, and his eyes glittered like sparks, though he did not seem to be looking at us, but had his gaze fixed on the wall. I tried to attract C.'s notice, but, failing to do so, said in a low voice, "Look out, or there will be mischief directly!" C. glanced quickly at the man, and, with great presence of mind, filled a glass of wine, and rose and offered it to him. He looked at C. for a moment in a way that was not agreeable, then very quietly put down the knife, and walked out of the room without saying a word. C. resumed his seat with the greatest composure, and said: "Poor fellow, he was one of the best scholars in Carácas, and would certainly have distinguished himself; but the girl he was engaged to fell in love with his brother, and married him. He has been insane ever since."

I went away, wondering whether it was by peculiar infelicity that so soon after my arrival at Carácas I should have witnessed a visit of this kind, or whether such incidents were common. I had not long to wait before learning that they were by no means rare. I went one evening to a musical entertainment at the house of a person high in office. The lady of the house was singing "Il Bacio" very charmingly, and a group had been formed round her, near to which I had taken a seat with my face towards the door. Presently I saw a man enter, whose peculiar look immediately reminded me of the gentleman with the knife at the buffet. The new comer, like his predecessor, walked straight up to the lady of the house, and in a hoarse voice commenced a muttering accompaniment, which jarred strangely with the music and the sweet tones of the singer. Everybody looked annoyed, but no one spoke to the intruder; only, the group near the piano gradually melted away, leaving him standing by himself. At last, he went closer to the lady, who continued to sing with marvellous self-possession, and leaning over her, began to strike chords on the piano. This was too much even for her aplomb—she stopped and walked down the room; and the stranger, after addressing some incoherent remarks to the people near him, followed her. I was too far off to see what took place then, but there was a bustle, and I heard the intruder talking in a loud angry voice, after which he suddenly went off, and the party broke up. This man, I was subsequently informed, was intoxicated as well as insane, yet no attempt was made to remove him, nor was he even told to go.

On the following Sunday I went to breakfast at the house of the minister of public works. It was a sumptuous entertainment, with very beautiful fruits and flowers displayed on the table, and many more dishes than guests, for of the latter there were only sixteen. The place of honour fell to my lot, opposite to the acting president of the republic : an old general with an iron constitution, who, unhappily for me, supposing all men to be equally vigorous, plied me at every pause in the collation with fruits pleasant to the eye, and of tolerable flavour, but to the last degree pernicious to a person of weak digestive powers. Owing to these flattering attentions, the order of my meal ran something in this style. A brimming plateful of turtle-soup, good in quality, overpowering in quantity, and indifferently cooked ; a large fruit of the custard apple genus; prawns, párga fish, and oysters ; several fruits of the cactus, called here tuna, selected for their size by the general; turkey, prepared in a fashion peculiar to the country, boned, and the inside filled with a kind of stuffing redolent of garlic; a plate of cherries; a fricandeau of some unknown meat; several slices of pine-apple; a dish, name unknown, the chief ingredient being the flesh of the land tortoise; grapes of various kinds; and an infinite series of other trifles. No speeches were made; indeed, the meal was too severe for any but the most languid conversation. The longest meal must, however, come to an end, and at last, after a wind-up of coffee and cigars of exquisite flavour, we separated. The Sunday following, the scene was repeated, but on this occasion it was the acting president who gave the breakfast. Having determined not to risk my life any more by undue complaisance, I refused all offers of fruit, and ate more moderately. At last the meal reached its termination, and the president, filling his glass, looked round the table, and then at me, and said, "Brindo al señor qui nos ha llevado treinte mil libras."—"I drink to the gentleman who has brought us thirty thousand pounds." I was somewhat disconcerted by the wording of the toast, and thinking that it spoke for itself, judged it unnecessary to rise to respond. Presently, filling his glass again, the old general said, "I drink now to the English government, which has always been the protector of Venezuela, and has set the best example for free states to follow." This, of course, compelled me to reply, and I expressed the pleasure I had had in visiting that beautiful country, in which Nature had been so lavish of her gifts, and whose inhabitants, by their gallant struggle for liberty, had shown themselves worthy of such a fair inheritance. England, I said, was the friend of all free nations, and would no doubt support the Venezuelans in maintaining their independence, as warmly as she had aided them in acquiring it. These, and many other things, I was obliged to say in English, not having sufficient Spanish at command for an oration. A friend, however, translated what I had said into pure Castilian, and his version seemed to give great satisfaction, more particularly as he compressed my harangue into very small compass. Nothing, however, seemed to please the company so much as my happening to say "Viva la Amarilla!"—"Hurrah for the yellow!" which I did when a flower of that colour was given me, though I had no idea that yellow was the colour of the party in power. The next speech was the health of the ministers, proposed by a red-hot republican, who discoursed with immense fluency on the rights of man. Among other things, he assured us that, as all obstacles to perfect freedom were at length removed, Venezuela would now enjoy permanent tranquillity, during which all the blessings of the golden age would be restored. Ten days afterwards, one of the ministers and a number of leading men were arrested and thrown into prison, while, at the same time, an insurrection with which it was supposed they were connected, broke out in several of the provinces.

# CHAPTER V.



"MISTAKE! my dear sir," said the major, "faith! it's no mistake at all, at all. No, no, divil a bit of mistake in it; but I'll jist go and settle it for you. Wait here a bit till I come back."

"But, major," I exclaimed, trying to detain him, "you must tell me what course you mean to take."

He put aside my hand, and was gone in a moment, in spite of my attempts to stop him.

"Confound it!" I muttered; "am I never to get this affair explained? Here this Spaniard comes mixing up French and Spanish in such a way that I can't understand what he means, except that it is pistols and coffee for two; and when I tell the major that I have got into a quarrel, without knowing how, and that I think there's some mistake, he won't listen to a word I have to say, but goes off to settle it without knowing what it is. Well, I suppose I must wait here till he returns, or I get a message from the Spaniard."

With these words half aloud to myself, I turned to the window of the refreshment-room, into which I had lounged

from my place in the theatre.   It was full moon, and everything in the streets of Carácas was as visible as at noonday.
I gazed for a long time, and was beginning to think of
going away, when I saw a company of soldiers turn the
corner of the street, and advance to the entrance of the
theatre.

" Rather an unusual number of men for relieving a sentry,"
said I to myself; " what can they want ? "

The soldiers ascended the steps and halted in the lobby.
Their officer in command entered the box from which I had
just issued, and the door of which faced the open door of
the saloon where I was.   He returned immediately, with a
tall dark man who had been sitting near me, and who I knew
was the minister of war.   The soldiers advanced; the
minister of war was placed between their files and marched
off to prison.

" Egad ! " thought I, " this is a pleasant country, where
one goes from the opera to prison :—or is this, perhaps, another mistake ? "

I was still, as orientals say, biting the finger of surprise at
the arrest I had just witnessed, when back came the major.
With him was the handsome young Spaniard, who had
accused me of saying something which was not polite.   He
was looking quite satisfied now ; but his right arm was in a
sling, a circumstance I certainly had not observed when
he spoke to me before.   His face wore a bland smile,
however, and, taking off his hat with his left hand, he
said,—

" Monsieur, I learn there has been a mistake.   It appears that I deceived myself.   Monsieur had no intention——"

"Monsieur," said I, interrupting him, "I could have had no intention of doing or saying anything disagreeable to a gentleman who is, I believe, an entire stranger to me."

Thereupon the Spaniard bowed, and replaced his hat. We both then bowed, and he withdrew, with the air of one who had had a most gratifying interview.

"There's the end of the affair, I suppose," said I to the major; "and now it's over, I hope, as you seem to know, you will tell me what the deuce it is all about."

"Well, you see," said the major, "I heard it all from a friend, before I met you in the refreshment-room. When you crossed over to the box where Iñez was sitting, Enriquez—that's the Spaniard's name—followed you. He won't let any one have a *tête-à-tête* with Iñez, you know. Well, he asked you how you liked Venezuela, and you said —I forget what you said; but I know I have had a man out for less."

"But, since Enriquez is a Spaniard, what did it matter to him what I thought about Venezuela? It must be a mistake, after all."

"No, faith!" cried the major, impatiently; "it is true enough. But I know you didn't mane to offend Enriquez, and so I told him, or you wouldn't have forgotten all about it. But he said you did mane it, so I told him I'd prove it to him you didn't, if he'd step across the street to the house of a friend where we could find a couple of rapiers and some one to see fair play. We went, and at the first pass I ran him through the sword-arm, and then we tied up his arm, and I said, as he couldn't fight any more, he'd better come and make it up with you; and so he did, and that's all about it. And here we are at my quarters, so come along; and mind the dog, or you'll find him mighty playful with the calves of your legs as you mount the staircase."

Paying due regard to the major's caution, I managed with my cane to keep off the attentions of a stout terrier who followed us into the smoking-room, and then seeing me take my seat like an honest man, ceased to snuff at imaginary rascals in my legs, and bestowed himself under the table.

Meantime, his master had taken a pipe and filled it carefully with some of that cave tobacco which is the boast of Venezuela, sold in boxes, with *De cueva Luz* inscribed on them. For a man who had just been engaged in a duel, the major's countenance wore a most serene expression. But the exceeding calmness of his look was one of his characteristics, and it never altered under any circumstances. Another peculiarity of his was the mellifluous tone of his voice, which remained unchanged even when he chose to utter, as he sometimes did, most despiteful words. Snow-white hair, too, added to his peaceful appearance; but he was a man of iron build, with the chest, shoulders, and arms of a gladiator, and a complexion of bronze. He was a renowned duellist, and had been out with every kind of weapon, and so very often, that he sometimes confused the incidents of his encounters, and would shake his head and heave a regretful sigh after speaking of a man whose affair had ended in a miss and a shot in the air, while in another case, in which his antagonist had been mortally wounded, he would close his reminiscences with a smile and a joyous " Faith, sir, I'm glad it ended as it did ! "

"Now, major," said I, "for the story you promised me. In your case there was a mistake, I suppose ? "

" You may say that," responded the major, settling himself in his easy chair, and opening correspondence with a fragrant glass of rum-and-water which he had just mixed for himself. " A mistake there was, and so I tould O'Halloran, but he wouldn't believe it, worse luck to him, poor fellow."

" It was a very long time ago ; let me see now, yes, faith, as long back as April, 1821, that I landed at Angostura—Ciudad Bolivar they call it now—to join the British Legion under the liberator : that's Bolivar, you know. I was a smart boy then, with fair hair and rosy cheeks, just come from serving in one of the Duke's crack regiments, full of life, and ready for anything, from a fight to a fandango, from stealing a kiss to taking a battery. There were many like me on board the ship that brought us over from Europe, but all our high spirits could not make our first impression of the country we had come to free, an agreeable one. The northern coast of Venezuela woos the voyager to land with many a glorious bit of scenery, but Guiana, at whose capital we were about to disembark, is anything but inviting. A swampy forest as big as France and Spain put together, with a huge muddy drain running through the middle of it, that's Guiana and the Orinoco. Yet Raleigh cruised about in search of palaces of gold in this vast howling wilderness, full of snakes, jaguars, and alligators, with a sprinkling of wretched human savages, who think ant-paste a luxury. ' Pat, my boy,' I said to a friend, who, like myself, was leaning over the bulwarks looking at the town, ' what think ye of El Dorado ? '   ' Faith, I think,' said he, ' that its only virtue

G

is that it tells the truth; for it says, as plain as can be, that Yellow Jack is always in command of the garrison here, and that he'll give half of us permanent quarters on the ground-floor.'

"With this pleasant prophecy ringing in my ear, I landed on the muddy quay, and, as the smell at this point was anything but agreeable, and the sun piping hot, I made tracks for my quarters as fast as possible. I found I was billeted on a Señor Rivas, who lived at some distance from the river; and I might have had a difficulty in finding my way, but that the adjutant, who spoke Spanish, was quartered there, too, and I had but to put myself under his guidance. Mighty glad was I to get under shelter, and to take in succession a cup of good coffee, a cigar, and a siesta. But that which pleased me most was that the señor had two pretty daughters, Luisa and Helena.

"'Come along, my boy,' said Power, the adjutant, shaking me as I still lay snoring. 'It's cool now, and I'm going to see the recruits land. Are you ready for a walk?'

"'I'm ready, all that's left of me; bedad, I think the mosquitoes have eaten off both my ears,' said I, rubbing the injured parts.

"Off we started, and were down at the quay in half the time we took to come from it. It was just as well we got there, for the men were in bad humour at being kept on board for some hours after the officers landed, though there was a good reason for it, to save them, namely, from exposure to the sun in the heat of the day.

"However, the boys, as Donnelly, the orderly-sergeant, called them, soon showed their ill-humour. Among the natives who were helping to get their kits out of the boats, was a huge negro.  He stood six feet five at the least, and had lots of sinew, and a head like that of a bonassus.  He picked up the heaviest box like a feather, and walked away with it; but, in trying to get hold of too many things at once, he let one man's kit fall into the water.  It was quickly fished out again, but with plenty of black mud sticking to it.

"'Tare and 'ounds,' said the man to whom it belonged, 'you great murthering villain! is that the way you wash clothes in your counthrey, with mud for soap, to make 'em as black as your own ugly face?  Take that, thin!'

"With these words he struck the giant a blow on the head as he was leaning over to get hold of some more boxes.  It was a hard knock, and sounded as if one had struck a paving-stone with a heavy mallet, but it made no more impression on the African than it would have done on a buffalo.  It roused his fury, however, which he showed very much as a buffalo would have done.  He shook his great head, and glared about him like a demon, then went back a few paces, and, putting his head down, ran at poor Paddy, who was squaring away, not expecting that sort of combat, and struck him full amidships, sending him flying a dozen yards at least, and knocking all the breath out of his body.  As flesh and blood cannot see a comrade mauled, without coming to the rescue, there was soon a ring of fellows round the nigger, all wanting to revenge Paddy's disaster.  But one down, and another come on, blackey was a match for them all; and one after another down they went, none of them knowing what to do with an antagonist who came on like a ram.

" Things were looking 'entirely onpleasant,' as poor Paddy, who had begun the fight, and who was now sitting up again, coughing, observed, when Donnelly stepped up to the adjutant, and, touching his cap, said :

" ' By yer honour's lave ? '

" ' Oh ! of course, Donnelly, of course,' replied Power; and, turning to me, he added, ' Now you'll see some fun.'

" In a trice the sergeant had stripped, stepped into the ring, and confronted the African. He was a small man, compared with his antagonist, and rather too handsome for a gladiator ; but he was young, muscular, active as a deer, and his fine clear blue eyes were bright with confidence. There was no need of a challenge. In love and war gestures are everything, and no sooner did Donnelly present himself than the negro retreated, as before, a few paces, lowered his head, and came thundering at him with fifty-bull power. But this time the issue was very different from that of the preceding encounters. Just as the negro was almost upon him Donnelly made a side spring at him, and struck him a tremendous blow in the face with his knee, at the same time planting a right-hander behind his ear that would have stunned an ox. The effect of this judicious appeal to the knowledge-box of the African was to drive him obliquely headlong to the ground, the blood streaming from his nose and mouth. One would have thought that his late defeat would have taught him caution, and that he would have changed his tactics ; but no—he rose, lowered his head once more, and rushed upon Donnelly, like a thunderbolt. Again he was met, and his rush turned aside, by a fearful blow from Donnelly's knee, of such force that the negro turned a complete somersault, and then lay extended flat on his back, and this time without power to rise.

" 'Faith, sergeant, you have killed the black baste this time entirely,' was the exclamation that greeted the victor. Power and I, afraid that the man was dead, made them lift him up, and give him some brandy. After a time he revived.

" Night fell before our labours in superintending the landing of the men were over, and we were glad to get back to our quarters without any further rambling about the town. The miasmatic influences at Angostura are increased tenfold after the sun goes down, and, to say nothing of the mosquitoes, all sorts of noxious insects and reptiles get abroad, for which reasons, or for others as good, that I don't know, people there soon make for their beds."

" I don't wonder at that, major," said I, interrupting him, "if what the consul in Guiana related to me as having happened to him be a common occurrence. He said he was somewhere in the environs of Angostura, and had gone to sleep in his hammock, with his slippers on the ground within easy reach. Being an unconscionably early riser, he essayed to get up at the first faint streak of light, and before he could well see ; so putting his foot out of the hammock, he felt with his great toe for his slipper, and, having found it, was about to thrust his foot into it when he found it was full of something odiously cold and slimy. Snatching back his foot, he made the same attempt at the other slipper, and with the same result, on which he was fain to ensconce himself under the clothes again till it was light, when, to his horror, he discovered a small rattlesnake curled up in each slipper ! "

"Your example is *un peu fort*," quoth the major, "but still queer things do happen in Guiana. It is a fact that when the river has been in flood, people have been taken away from their own doors in Angostura by alligators. But, to return to my story, a day sufficed to exhaust the lions of the town. Well! when all other amusements had been used up, no resource was left me but to fall in love with one of the señoritas in whose father's house I was living. The family of Señor Rivas consisted only of these two daughters, of whom the elder was nearly nineteen, the younger seventeen, and of one son, Francisco, who went by the familiar name of Panchíto, a little boy of seven, a regular pickle, who, as the manner is in Venezuela, was generally running about naked. After a few weeks I picked up enough Spanish to let the tongue assist the eyes in tender expressions to the girls. The opportunities, however, of saying sweet things were rare, for in Venezuela the ladies of a family keep so much together, that, to use a sporting phrase, there is no getting single shots at them, For some time, too, I was in doubt as to which of the two sisters was to have my heart. Luisa was very fair, quiet, with brown hair, an unusual thing among Spanish Creoles. Helena was bright, sparkling, roguish, a very pretty brunette, and, altogether, very charming. Upon the whole, my thoughts rather inclined to Luisa, and on one occasion, having caught her for a moment unguarded by the maternal dragon, I went so far as to ask if she would grant me an interview alone. She said she was never left by herself, and I had only just time to say I hoped I might have one kiss before I left Angostura, and to hear her reply in the shape of an intimation, accompanied by a faint blush, that it was not the custom in Venezuela, when her mother rejoined us. Meantime, Power, though he was so busy with drill and the other duties of an adjutant, did not fail to observe what was going on, and took me to task more than once about it.

"'Charley, my boy,' said he, 'what on earth are you after with those girls? If you don't mean to marry one of them it's not fair to the old Don, who has been so hospitable to us, to give one of his little beauties a sore heart. And as for marriage, it's out of the question. We may get the route to-morrow, and have to join Bolivar, and who knows how many of us will come back? Besides, you have no cash, and at all events I hope you don't mean to settle down here and turn cane-planter.'

"I said that several officers who had been in the country before our arrival had married, and seemed to be very happy; and I instanced O'Halloran, who had been made a captain in our corps.

"'Pooh! nonsense, Charley,' replied Power, 'where's the happiness of having to leave your wife for months in places which are just as likely as not to fall into the enemy's hands? And as for O'Halloran, his example proves my case. O'Halloran has married a very pretty woman, who is about the most spiteful little devil I ever met, and gives him no end of trouble.'

"Power's remarks made an impression on me, and for some weeks I rather shunned than sought the ladies. But living in the same house with them, and being young, idle, and impulsive, it was not easy to be on cool terms with two young beauties, whose looks showed they were vexed at my assumed indifference. My self-imposed restraint increased the warmth of the feelings it concealed. In short, my liking for Luisa was fast ripening into love, when one morning Power came hurriedly into the room where I was sitting, and slapping me on the shoulder, cried out:

"'Hurra! the route has come, my boy! We are to join Bolivar in the Apúre. We march in ten days, and in less than a month we shall see, I expect, what the Spaniards are made of.'

"This glorious news made me jump up and shout, 'Viva el liberator!' at the same time that I threw the book I was reading up to the ceiling. The report soon spread, and now all was bustle and excitement in place of the ennui that reigned before. We all set to work to buy horses and mules, and to prepare for the expedition, while the principal inhabitants vied with one another in entertaining us. In particular, the commandant of the garrison sent out invitations to every officer in the place to a ball for the night but one before our departure. Rumour said this entertainment was to be on a scale quite unique for Angostura. The only difficulty was to find a place large enough to hold the numbers invited, for even the town-hall was too small; but, by dint of certain contrivances in the shape of temporary pavilions, this was got over.

"Meantime, what with the gaieties going on in all directions, preparations for the march, and the anticipations of a first campaign, my pulse was up to fever heat. All my good resolutions went off to the place where good resolutions have been going for so many ages. Fortune generally favours the audacious, and my excitement seemed to make me worthy of the smiles of the fickle goddess. I resolved, therefore, somehow or other, to have a stolen interview with Luisa, and I thought only of the pleasure of a conversation with her alone, without caring for the result, or prescribing to myself any rules for what I should do or say on the occasion. It was no easy matter, however, even to let Luisa know what I was scheming. I made several fruitless attempts, and was at last fain to have recourse to the old expedient of bribing the lady's maid. Terésa, who waited on the señoritas in that capacity, was an Indian girl, not quite thirteen years old, but with a discretion beyond her years. She was a light brunette, with well-chiselled features, a very fairy in the symmetry of her tiny figure. She soon understood that I wanted to talk with her, so, under pretence of bringing me a cup of coffee, slipped into my room. I broke ground by giving her a couple of reals, and then produced a note I had written to Luisa; but, before entrusting her with it, I began to sound her as to the possibility of obtaining a *tête-à-tête* with her mistress. She was in the act of suggesting a plan to me when we heard steps coming along the corridor. The slow, heavy tread assured me it was my host. Terésa ejaculated, 'El amo,' 'My master,' skipped behind a mampára, or screen, which hid my washing-apparatus, and so turned my bed-room into a sitting-room; for as for the hammock, that is used as much in the day as at night by South Americans.

"'You did not come to breakfast this morning. Out buying mules, I suppose?" said Rivas, entering. 'Well, I have come to smoke a cigar with you, and to give you a little advice for your march. You may trust me, for I have had some experience. I marched with Bolivar from Ocaña in 1813, and have been out with Paez in the Apúre more than once.' With these words the worthy señor seated himself, and went on, interminably as it seemed to me, recounting his adventures, smoking, and prosing to an extent that wound up my feelings to a pitch of desperation. At last I interrupted a long story by declaring that I was obliged to go out to look at a horse I thought of buying. It was an unlucky excuse, for Rivas declared he would walk with me.

"'Panchíto,' he called to the urchin who just then ran past my door, 'tell your mother I want to speak to her for a moment.'

"'The madre has gone over the way to the Señora Ochoa's,' said Panchíto, arresting his steps and coming into the room.

"'Well, then, where is Terésa?  I will send her with a message.'

"'Terésa is here,' replied the *enfant terrible*.  'I saw her bring the Ingles some coffee half-an-hour ago.'

"'And has the Ingles swallowed her along with the coffee? or has he put her in his pocket?' said my host, laughing, and rapping his son slightly on the head with his cane.

"'Perhaps he has hidden her behind the screen,' retorted Panchíto, and the little wretch made a dart to get behind it.  I caught him, but too late to prevent him laying hold of the screen, and down it came with the pull.

" 'Terésa!' exclaimed the old Don, staring at the girl and starting back, while his yellow face assumed a cadaverous hue with surprise and annoyance, 'por mi fé! you shall pay for this.'  Then turning to me, he added, 'Señor, I have been giving you some hints for campaigning; let me conclude by advising you never to make a foray in a friend's hacienda.' With these words Señor Rivas made me a stiff bow and quitted the room, and was followed by Terésa and Panchito, the latter ruefully rubbing his head, which had been bruised by the falling screen.

"Left to myself, I could not help laughing at what had occurred, though I was excessively vexed at the *contre-temps*. I reflected, too, that Rivas would probably tell his wife, and that so the affair would become known to Luisa, by which my position with her would, I thought, hardly be improved. It turned out that I was wrong, however, in this part of my supposition. The next time I met the Señora and her daughters, the former indeed showed that she was displeased by her stiff behaviour. But I saw by the half-timid, half-arch glances of the girls, and by an undefinable something in their manner, that they knew what had taken place, and were by no means offended. The fact, no doubt, was, as my greater experience of life now convinces me, that Terésa made each señorita believe that I was in love with her, and each was too conscious of her own charms to feel any jealousy of Terésa, or to doubt that she came to my room for any purpose but what she really did. Opportunity for explanation there was none, but I consoled myself with the knowledge that we should meet at the ball, and I was determined to tell Luisa then all about it.

"Parties begin at an early hour in Venezuela. At 9 P.M., the night after my adventure with Terésa, I found myself dancing with Luisa at the commandant's ball. The room was crammed to suffocation, and the most jealous chaperone could hardly in such a crowd maintain a successful espionage on the doings of the girls under her charge. I gave Luisa my version of the affair with Terésa; and after we had laughed over it sufficiently, I obtained her hand for the next dance. I danced with her and Helena repeatedly. My spirits rose, I took Luisa to supper, I drank glass after glass of wine, and began to commit sundry extravagances. Luisa offered me a guayába. I refused it unless she would bite it first. I then devoured it like a maniac. In short, I lost control of myself, and ended by an offer of marriage, couched in the wildest terms of extravagant devotion. I was accepted, and my ardour would, perhaps, have made me too demonstrative, had not Luisa just then, perceiving her mother enter the supper-room, suddenly quitted my side with the remark, ' Mamma will be so glad to hear this; she has wished for this so much ! '

"Impulsive persons are subject to violent reaction. I have outlived all that," continued the major; "but I was then particularly subject to such revulsions of feeling. Luisa's remark somehow disturbed me, and I stood for a moment thinking over it. In the midst of my reverie a hand was laid on my shoulder, and a well-known voice said, ' Don't lose your time in thinking, Charlie, but go back to the ball-room. We shan't have any more dancing till we enter Carácas.' It was Power, and I could not help saying, ' Perhaps it would have been better had I thought a little more, especially before acting.' Something in my manner struck Power, who knew my character thoroughly. He had seen me dancing with Luisa, and my short speech having excited his suspicions, he said at once, ' Why, Charlie, you have not been making yourself a fool with one of those girls ? ' ' Indeed, but I have though,' I replied. ' I have proposed to Luisa, and she has accepted me.' 'Then I forbid the banns,' said Power. 'You shall not make yourself such a blockhead. Aye! there they are,' he added, looking round and seeing Luisa with her mother. 'I'll bet the old woman is rejoicing at having hooked you.' In another mood I should have quarrelled with Power for this speech : but Luisa's parting remark had created a disagreeable feeling in my mind, which was heightened by this sneer. Seeing his advantage, Power set himself to improve the opportunity at once. 'Be a reasonable fellow, Charlie,' he said. 'We march the day after to-morrow. You surely don't mean to apply for leave of absence just when we are going to meet the enemy! Then as for engaging yourself, who the deuce can tell how long the campaign is going to last, or how it will end? Take my advice, and break it off at once.' 'It's all very well to say break it off,' I replied, ' but how am I to do it? Can I go and tell Luisa, ten minutes after proposing to her, that I meant nothing?' Power thought a moment with rather a serious face, and then resuming his usual bright look, exclaimed, 'I have it, Charley. You sha'n't have the pain of speaking to Luisa, and, moreover, I won't trust your courage in that quarter. Take another bottle of champagne, and then go and pop the question to her sister. Depend on't, after that you'll hear no more of the matter.' With these words Power filled me a tumbler of champagne. I drank it, and made up my mind to follow his advice.

"Now it so happened that Helena was dressed that night rather peculiarly. She wore a pink silk bodice and a white muslin skirt with very deep flounces of Venezuelan lace, and I remembered saying to her that it was a good costume for a ball, as a partner in search of her could tell her colours a long way off. 'I shall soon find her,' said I to myself, 'but how shall I account for having neglected her for so many dances, and then coming all at once and proposing to her? Let me see; perhaps I had better slip a note in her hand, and then vanish. I have promised Power to do what he said, but I don't half like the thing, and least said, soonest mended.' Acting on this idea, I walked off into one of the retiring-rooms, got pencil and paper, and wrote, 'Dearest, I have in vain tried to conceal my feelings; but now that I am on the eve of leaving you, I can no longer restrain them. Though I have appeared to be engrossed in another quarter, this has only been a mask to allow me to follow you with my eyes, and assure myself that your love is not given to another. I see now, or I think I see, that you are free; suffer me then to offer you my heart, which indeed has long been yours.' Having signed this effusion, I returned to the refreshment-room, and, fortifying myself with several additional bumpers, I proceeded in search of Helena. But the great quantity of wine I had taken, the heat and excitement I felt, had their effect on my brain. The room seemed to turn round, as well as the dancers; I came, somehow or other, into collision with several people, and made excuses in a thick voice, which sounded oddly even to myself. I was conscious of my condition, and felt I must get out into the air, or make an unpleasant exhibition of myself. Just at that moment I came on the pink bodice. The wearer was not dancing, but leaning against an open window with one white arm, while the other hung beside her. I slipped my note into the open hand, and the fingers, as if experienced in the reception of such missives, tightened on it. I turned and made off through the crowd; but as I did so, she turned too. I half caught her look, and the features seemed to me strangely unlike those of Helena.

"In what manner I returned to the house of Señor Rivas I know not. The open air, instead of sobering me, seemed to make me worse; but the first thing I distinctly recognized was a horribly cold sensation in my left hand. On drawing it towards me, a squelch of falling water followed, and I found I had been lying with my hand in the ewer, out of which I suppose I had been drinking. Getting up with a splitting headache, I dressed slowly, and had scarce refreshed myself with a cup of coffee, when somebody knocked at the door. I called out 'Entrate,' and, to my surprise, in stepped an Irish officer I knew by sight only, who, without a word of preface, handed me a challenge from O'Halloran.

"After reading the epistle twice, and looking a third time at the address, to make sure I was the party intended, I turned to Kelly—that was the name of the officer—and said: 'Will you have the goodness to explain what this means? I think there must be some mistake.'

"'Mistake, sir,' said Kelly; 'you're mighty fond, sir, of that word "mistake." Ye said it was a mistake last night; but, faith, sir, it's a mistake that there's only one way of clearing up.' Then putting his hand into his pocket and producing another note, he handed it to me with great ceremony, saying, 'Do you call that a mistake, sir?'

"What was my surprise, on opening the note, to find it was the same I had written to Helena. I held it for several minutes without saying a word, while I endeavoured to recall the incidents of the preceding night. By degrees I came to the conclusion that I must somehow have mistaken O'Halloran's wife for Helena, and this idea became certainty when Kelly, who was an old hand at duelling, said impatiently: 'Pshaw, sir! a man of honour never makes mistakes in affairs of this kind. Mention your friend, sir, at once, and have done with it.'

"Stung with his words and manner, I exclaimed: 'My friend, sir, is Lieutenant Power. His room is close by, so no time need be wasted; and, excuse me, if I say the sooner you relieve me of your presence the better.'

"'You're polite, sir,' retorted Kelly, frowning, and rising from his chair, 'and, maybe, I'll ask you to explain those words; but one mistake at a time. Good morning, sir.'

"Ten minutes afterwards Power entered my room with a grave air.

"'Milligan,' he said, 'this is a serious business. Of course, it was a horrid mistake. I know that well enough; but there is no explaining matters of this sort to a fellow like Kelly. Then O'Halloran is mad with jealousy, and perfectly unreasonable; besides, I hear he tried to strike you, and that you knocked him down. They say he wanted to have it out over a handkerchief on the spot, and that, seeing how tipsy you were, they forced him away with great difficulty. Blenkens of ours says he literally foamed at the mouth, and kept shouting, "I'll not wait till morning. Blood and 'ouns, I'll not wait." I've arranged that the affair shall come off at 5 P.M., with pistols. I don't think you have a pair with hair triggers. I have; and I know by experience that they shoot straight. If you have anything to settle I advise you to do it at once, for O'Halloran is a good shot when he is cool, but I hope his fury will make him miss.

Anyhow, you must not try to miss him or fire into the air, for he will certainly hit you, if he can. The only good thing is that this has broken off your affair with Luisa. The old señora has heard of your giving a note to Madame O'Halloran, and vows her daughter shall have nothing to do with you.'

" ' I'll be ready, Power,' I said, ' and I'll just put down a few things I want you to do, if anything happens to me. After which, I shall turn in again and have a sleep ; for I feel tired, and I should like to come to the ground cool and comfortable.'

" I said this more to be left to myself than for anything else, but after penning my memorandum, and drinking some of the delicious sherbet they make in Guiana from the juice of the pomegranate, I did really go to sleep for several hours. Looking at my watch when I awoke, I found it was half-past three, so I took a cold bath and prepared to accompany Power. At a quarter-past four he came to my room, we walked out into the street, and started off at a brisk rate into the country. About two miles out of the town we came to a ruined garden-house, where Kelly and O'Halloran were waiting for us. Power and Kelly saluted each other, but to my cold bow O'Halloran only returned a ferocious stare. Kelly then led the way through the garden to a lane between walls, and not more than ten feet broad, when he stopped short, saying, ' This is the place ; the sun won't be in their eyes here.'

" I must confess I was a good deal surprised at the choice of such a spot for the encounter, where, when we were placed, we should not be more than eight feet from one another, and where the wall would assist one so much in taking aim. But my blood was up. I was quite prepared to fight even across a handkerchief. Power, however, did not take the matter so coolly. He spoke a few words in a low voice to Kelly, but his manner convinced me he was much exasperated. Kelly, however, was obstinate, and after a short parley O'Halloran and myself were placed opposite to one another, but with our faces to the wall. Kelly then said, 'Now, gentlemen, I shall ask you, "Are you ready?" and at the last word you will turn round and fire. Gentlemen,' he continued, 'are you——' Before he could get out the word 'ready' there was an explosion, a bullet whizzed past my left ear, grazing it slightly, and by an involuntary impulse I wheeled round and fired. O'Halloran leaped up several feet from the ground and fell forward. The ball had passed through his heart. I threw myself on my knees and raised the fallen man. His eyes were fixed, a thin jet of blood issued from his mouth; he was quite dead.

"'He fired a moment too soon,' said Kelly; 'but, by the powers, he has paid for his mistake.' ·

"That word reminded me of the absurd origin of the quarrel. I was in no mood, as you may imagine, to allow the hateful blunder to produce any more mischief, so I frankly told Kelly at once by what accident the note had come into the possession of O'Halloran's wife, and Power corroborated my statement.

"'Well,' said Kelly, 'it's a pity, so it is, but it can't be helped now. You have behaved like a man of honour, and I see, after all, that it was a mistake!'"

With these words the major concluded his story. I

had finished my fourth cigar. " Good night, major,"
I said. " I am glad that my mistake ended better than
yours."

" Oh, faith, my dear sir," said he, " you know it was no
mistake at all with you ; but, anyhow, I'm glad it ended as
it did."

# CHAPTER VI.



So far this narrative has been carried on without any distinct account of the business of my mission. I must now give, as concisely as possible, the history of the loan for which I was commissioner. Were that untold the moral of my story would be wanting. But for the benefit of those who may have similar business to transact with a modern republic, or who may desire to invest their money in one of those numerous financial operations in which the surplus capital of London is continually disappearing for the benefit of foreign states, I register what took place. Those who are disposed to place faith in the solemn assurances of Republican governments, and risk their fortunes by lending them on such guarantees, will do well to study carefully this chapter, not omitting any part of it. Contracts and Powers of Attorney are dry reading, but they must be read by those who would understand the subject.

The history of the last Loan to Venezuela, then, commences in July, 1863, when General Falcon and his partisans, the most conspicuous and popular of whom was General Guzman Blanco, gained a complete triumph over the so-called oligarchs, and overthrew the government of Pedro José Rojas. That able, but unsuccessful man, who, a short time before, had obtained a loan of a million sterling through the house of the Barings, fled to Europe, leaving Venezuela under the absolute sway of Falcon and his army. The new government found the treasury empty. The revenue, which consists mainly of the export and import duties levied at the custom-houses, was weighed down by debts, of which some were owed to private individuals, others were loans contracted by former governments. Besides these liabilities there were the arrears of pay due to the Federal army. This last claim was the most pressing of all, for creditors with arms in their hands take no denial, and where money is concerned patriots are quite as troublesome as mercenaries. What was to be done! There were several ways of dealing with the difficulty. For instance, large sums might be obtained from the foreign merchants by granting them a liberal discount for cash in advance for payments of dues on cargoes yet to be shipped. The State might have recourse to the granting of assignats, or money might be raised by putting up to auction in the home and foreign markets the waste lands, of which there was ample store. If by any such means the immediate exigencies of the government could have been met, an honest and frugal encouragement of the State's resources would soon have filled the exchequer to overflowing.

But the easiest expedient for getting money was to borrow it from England. General Falcon, therefore, decided on obtaining a loan from the merchants of London, and his first step to this end was to constitute General Guzman Blanco his representative. Let the following document testify to the solemnity with which the honour of General Falcon and the good name of the Republic of Venezuela were pledged in this preliminary to the loan.

Juan C. Falcon, General in Chief of the Federal Armies, Provisional President of the Confederacy of Venezuela, &c., &c., &c.

In the name of the Republic and exercising the powers with which I am invested, I hereby appoint General Antonio Guzman Blanco, Vice-President of the Republic, and my present Minister of Finance and for Foreign Affairs, to be Fiscal Commissioner for the Republic, with the special charge to contract in London, or in any other emporium of Europe or America, a Loan, which is not to exceed Two Millions of Pounds sterling, at the most favourable rate of interest, and on the best terms that he can obtain, authorising him to mortgage especially and particularly the unincumbered portion of the Import Duties of the Custom-houses of La Guaira and Puerto Cabello or the whole of the Duties of the other Custom-houses of the Republic; or the Export Duties of some or of all the Custom-houses of the Country, with power also to give as a Guarantee any other property or estates belonging to the Nation for payment of the Interest as well as for Redemption of the Capital, pledging as I do from this moment the Public Faith for the fulfilment of the obligations, which he may by virtue of this authority contract with the lenders. And for this object I confer upon him all such powers as may be necessary to execute the same and to bind the Republic as effectually, as I myself, he being empowered to receive the amount of the Loan, make arrangements for its transmission to this city, give receipts and discharges, countersign the bonds that may be issued, and settle the periods and the manner of their payments. I fully authorize General Guzman Blanco to effect all these operations, should he consider it expedient, by means of a confidential agent, whose acts shall be as binding on my Government and have its approval in the same way as if they had been performed by the principal Commissioner. And finally, I authorize him to apply part or the whole of the Loan, which he may contract, in any financial operation that he may consider advantageous to the interests of the Republic, he being empowered to act therein with his most ample and free will without any restriction whatever, as also he may freely negotiate in the name of my Government with the present Creditors of the Republic in London, and make with them any arrangement, which they may mutually consider most satisfactory for the future interests of the State. In witness of all which I have delivered these presents at the.palace of the Government in Carácas on the sixth of August, one thousand eight hundred and sixty three, under the Seal of the Republic and countersigned by my Secretary of State.

(L. S.)     J. C. FALCON.

Countersigned.

The Secretary ad interim for Foreign Affairs,

GUILL : TELL VILLEGAS.

Countersigned.

The Secretary delegated by the Minister of Finance,

GUILL : IRIBARREN.

The Secretary for War and the Navy.

M. E. BRUZUAL.

Armed with such powers, General Guzman Blanco, Vice-President of the Republic of Venezuela and its Minister of Finance and of Foreign Affairs, arrived in London as Commissioner to contract the loan. He was at the same time accredited as Envoy from Venezuela to the Court of St. James's, so that nothing was wanting to render his contract a national engagement. Under such circumstances it cannot be matter of surprise that, at a time when investments were being largely made in far more speculative operations, the General Credit and Finance Company of London should have been willing to negotiate the loan to Venezuela. The Government, of which Pedro José Rojas, the opponent of General Falcon, was the head, had been able, as has been mentioned, to obtain a million of money from Messrs. Baring, and the interest of that debt continued to be paid regularly. It might, therefore, fairly be argued, that since General Falcon respected the engagements made by an adversary, he would certainly be still more conscientious in observing his own. Even those who had little confidence in the good faith of the South American Republics, thought that so long as the chiefs of the present dominant Venezuelan faction continued in power they would be led by prudential motives and a regard to their own interest, if not from a sense of honour, to observe the conditions of any contract with English capitalists into which they might enter. Impelled by such considerations, the acute Mr. Laing, and his brother directors of the General Credit Company, entered into the following contract with the Venezuelan Minister and Envoy.

Agreement entered into the 3rd day of October, 1863,

between General Guzman Blanco, Vice-President of the Republic of Venezuela and Minister of Finance and of Foreign Affairs, Fiscal Commissioner of the Republic, of the one part, and The General Credit and Finance Company of London (Limited) (hereinafter called the General Credit Company), of the other part.

Whereas His Excellency, General Juan C. Falcon, General-in-Chief of the Federal Armies, Provisional* President of the Venezuelan Federation, by a writing, by him signed, bearing date the 6th day of August, 1863, and countersigned by Guillélmo Tell Villegas, the Interim Secretary of Foreign Affairs, Guillélmo Iribarren, the Secretary charged with the Ministry of Finance, and M. E. Bruzual, the Secretary of War and Marine, in the name of the Republic, and in the exercise of the unlimited powers with which he was invested, did nominate and specially charge General Guzman Blanco, Vice-President of the Republic, and his present Minister of Finance and of Foreign Affairs, the Fiscal Commissioner of the Republic, to contract a Loan in London, or in any other mercantile city in Europe or in America, which should not exceed Two Millions of pounds sterling, at an interest and upon conditions the most favourable he could obtain, authorizing him to hypothecate specially and specifically the unincumbered portion of the Import Duties of the Custom-houses of La Guaira and Puerto Cabello, or the whole of the Import Duties of all the other Custom-houses of the

---

* Provisional only until the vote of Congress could be obtained, but by that vote now, and since his election, President and Grand Marshal, or Commander-in-chief of the Republic.

Republic; or the Export Duties of some, or of all the Custom-houses of the country, with power also to give as a guarantee any other property or estates belonging to the nation for payment of the interest as well as for redemption of the capital, pledging the public faith for the fulfilment of the obligations which he might contract with the lenders in virtue of this authority, and did confer on him all the powers which might be necessary to seal it and to bind the Republic, the same as if he, the said President, had done it himself, enabling him, the said General Guzman Blanco, to receive the proceeds of the Loan, to arrange its remittance to the city of Carácas, to give receipts in full discharge, to authorize the bonds, which may be issued, with his signature, and to fix the terms and mode of payment.

And Whereas the General Credit Company at the request of General Guzman Blanco, and in consequence of the authorization unto him given, have agreed to negotiate for the Government of Venezuela, a Loan of the nominal value of One Million five hundred thousand pounds sterling on the terms and subject to the stipulations hereinafter stated —wherefore the following has been agreed upon :—

Article 1. The loan shall be raised by issuing bonds to bearer for £500, £200, and £100 respectively, each one bearing interest from the 1st day of October, 1863, at the rate of £6 per cent. per annum, the interest thereon to be paid half yearly, on the 1st day of October, and the 1st day of April, of each year, until the full payment, or redemption of the Bonds, at the office of the General Credit Company in London, in sterling, and at the office of Messrs Saloman Oppenheim, Junior and Company, in Cologne, in Thalers, at the Exchange of the day.

Article 2. The said Bonds shall be in such form as the General Credit Company may require, and they shall be signed by General Guzman Blanco, in the name of the Republic, or any other Fiscal Agent, properly authorized by the Venezuelan Government.

Article 3. The sum of £60 shall be accepted in full for every £100 of the Loan, that is to say, a Bond shall be issued for £100, and so in proportion for every £100 subscribed, so that the sum really required, will be that of £900,000 sterling, and the General Credit Company are hereby authorized to accept from the subscribers each portion of £60 at the dates following, that is to say, a deposit of £5 on the application for the subscription, a first instalment of £10, in thirty days after the ratification of the Loan has been received in London; a second instalment of £15, a month after the first; a third instalment of £15, two months after the second; and a final instalment of £15, a month after the third, in payments for each bond, which shall bear full interest from the date before mentioned, in like manner as though the total sum had been paid in on the 1st of October, 1863.

Article 4. At least 2 per cent. of the said Bonds shall be redeemed or paid off by the Government every year, requiring for that purpose the sum of £30,000, which shall be provided in manner hereinafter expressed. If the price the said bonds may bear on the Exchange at London should be at par, or below par, and sufficient can be purchased on the Exchange at London for completing the sum of £30,000 the said bonds shall be purchased. But if they should bear on the Exchange a price above par, or being at par, or less, a sufficient quantity cannot be purchased there in order to make up the said sum of £30,000, then the bonds that are to be redeemed or paid off upon the terms above mentioned shall be selected by lot in the usual manner.

Article 5. In addition to the public faith and general credit of the Venezuelan Republic, which is hereby pledged, the following duties are specially and specifically hypothecated and mortgaged for the payment of the interest and sinking fund in this Loan (which interest and sinking fund amount together to £120,000 a year), and for the commission payable to the General Credit Company, as hereinafter mentioned—viz., 1st, the whole of the Export duties or Customs Revenues at the ports of Là Guaira, Puerto Cabello, Máracaibo, and Ciudad Bolivar:

The said General Guzman Blanco hereby guaranteeing, in the name of the Government of Venezuela, that the said Export duties, which are or will be wholly uncharged, have hitherto produced, and will continue to produce, more than the requisite sum of £120,000 a year; and that if from any cause they should ever fall below that sum, the deficiency shall be immediately made up from the Import duties or balance of Import duties at the Custom-houses of all the ports of Venezuela.

Proof that the said Export duties are wholly uncharged shall be given to the General Credit Company or its Agents simultaneously with the ratification of the Loan, or if any claims exist, the General Credit Company may retain a sufficient amount of the deposits on the Loan to settle them, so that the security for the Loan may be a clear first charge on the said Export duties.

Article 6. The said Export duties or Revenues of the Customs shall be paid over periodically once in every week

by the competent authorities of the said ports to the British
Vice-Consul, or other Agent or Agents, to be specially named
for that purpose by the General Credit Company, for him
or them to remit the same, or so much as may be requisite
for the payments specified in this Agreement, to the said
Company, and every facility or information shall be afforded
to the said Vice-Consul, Agent, or Agents, that they may
require for ascertaining the accuracy of the sum that may
have been paid to them, or having reference to this particular, and such Vice-Consul, Agent, or Agents, shall be paid
for their trouble a commission of $\frac{1}{4}$ per cent. by the Government of Venezuela, which shall be included in the amount
handed over to them. If more be received from the said
Export duties than is sufficient for the full and punctual
payment of the interest, sinking fund, and commissions of
this Loan, the balance shall be returned by the Vice-Consul
or Agent at La Guaira, as soon as the collections for the
current year have amounted to a sum sufficient to pay the
said interest and sinking fund of £120,000, and the sums
required for commissions, to the Government, and if such
Export duties should prove deficient, such a percentage of
the Import duties shall be paid over to the said Vice-Consul,
Agent, or Agents, by the competent authorities, out of the
weekly receipts of Customs, as will suffice to make good the
deficiency.

Article 7. The said sum of £900,000, or such other sum
as the Company may receive in subscriptions to the said
Loan, shall be employed by them in manner following—
that is to say, in the first place, the General Credit Company shall retain thereout the sum for commission and
brokerage on the negotiation of the Loan and for stamps,

and all and every other expenses connected therewith. In the second place, they are to retain the sum of £45,000 for payment of the first half year's interest that will fall due on the said Loan, and they are to pay over the residue of the Loan to the Government or its order.

Article 8. The General Credit Company are to apply the sums to be received from the Export duties, or other sources above-mentioned, or so much as they shall from time to time receive in respect thereof, in manner following—that is to say, in the first place, they are to set apart thereout the sum of £90,000 per annum for the purpose of paying periodically the interest on the Loan of £1,500,000, or on such portion thereof as may remain unpaid. In the second place, they are to set apart thereout the sum of £30,000 per annum, and apply the same periodically towards the redemption or payment in full of the bonds, in manner mentioned in Article 4; and they are also to apply the overplus that may remain of the said sum of £90,000, after payment of the interest then due, periodically adding the same to that of £30,000 per annum, to the redemption or payment in full of the bonds. In the third place, they are to retain thereout their Commission of one per cent. on all the dividends or interests they may pay, and one-half per cent. on the sums employed in the redemption of the bonds, the General Guzman Blanco hereby guaranteeing, in the name of his Government, that a sufficient sum to cover such Commission shall be collected and remitted, together with the sums due for interest and sinking fund.

Article 9. It is expressly understood and agreed that, if this Contract be not ratified by the Constituent Assembly of Venezuela to the satisfaction of the said General Credit

Company, and the ratification be not received in London before the 15th day of March next, the General Credit Company shall be at liberty to withdraw the Loan and to cancel whatever may have been done in respect thereof, and to return to the Subscribers the amount of their deposits. But the General Credit Company shall be at liberty to extend this term if requested by the Venezuelan Government to do so.

Article 10. It is furthermore expressly agreed by the said General Guzman Blanco, on behalf of the Venezuelan Government, that, in the event contemplated in the last Article, the said Government shall remit such a sum of money to the General Credit Company, on or before the said 15th day of March next, as will enable the said Company to pay Interest at the rate of 6 per cent. per annum to the Subscribers to the Loan, upon the total amount of their deposits from the time they were received until they are repaid, and a Commission of £3000 as a compensation to the Company for their trouble and their expenses, and in such case the General Credit Company shall be at liberty to return the money to the Subscribers in such manner and at such dates as they may deem suitable, and the Loan, as well as the whole of the negotiations relative thereto, shall in consequence be considered withdrawn and cancelled.

Article 11. It is further agreed that the Loan is to be brought out at the time when the said General Blanco, or other duly authorised Agent, on behalf of the Venezuelan Government on the one part, and the said General Credit Company on the other part, believe the moment favourable to open the public subscription.

Article 12, and last. Lastly, it is also understood and

expressly agreed that the General Credit Company do not incur any responsibility, neither do they furnish any Guarantee in respect of the points expressed, or any of them.

In Witness whereof, the said General Guzman Blanco hath hereunto affixed his hand and seal, and the said General and Finance Company has hereunto affixed its corporate seal, this 3rd day of October, 1863.

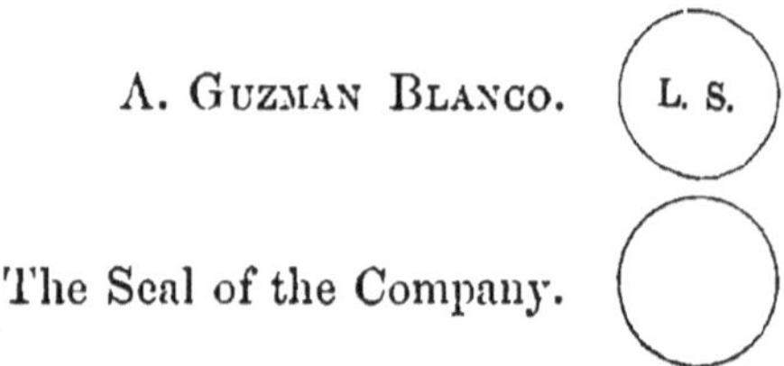

A. Guzman Blanco. ( L. S.

The Seal of the Company.

Signed, sealed, and delivered by the within-named General A. Guzman Blanco, and sealed by the General Credit and Finance Company of London (Limited), in the presence of

F. H. Hemming,
Consul-General for Venezuela.
James Macdonald,
General Manager of the General Credit and
Finance Company of London (Limited).

The first remark that it is requisite to make with regard to this contract is that, considering the credit of the Venezuelan Government on the Stock Exchange at the time, the terms were very favourable. Messrs. Baring's loan of 1862 was brought out at 63, but its price when the prospectus of the 1864 loan was issued had fallen to $55\frac{1}{4}$ ex div. It must also be especially remembered that in June, 1863, Messrs.

Matheson & Co.* had brought out a Venezuelan 6 per cent. loan at 60, which was less advantageous to Venezuela than that of 1864, inasmuch as a portion of the bonds were redeemable at par, to which it was, of course, absurd to expect them to rise in the market until, perhaps, the last year of paying off. Messrs. Matheson's loan, however, was a failure, which in itself was a circumstance unfavourable to Venezuelan credit. Moreover, a comparison of the terms accorded to Venezuela by the contract of 1864, with those obtained by other governments, who entered the London market as borrowers about the same time as Venezuela, will prove the favourable character of the former. Thus the last great French Loan was brought out in 1864 at $66\frac{2}{10}$. It is true that the interest is only 3 per cent., but then the difference between the credit of France and that of Venezuela is that between absolute security and the opposite extreme. The Imperial Ottoman 5 per cent. Loan of March 1865 was issued at $47\frac{1}{2}$, and the Turkish 6 per cent. of 1862 stood in April 1864 at $71\frac{1}{2}$. And to take the cases of countries more akin to Venezuela, we find that Spanish 3 per cent. Bonds, which in 1864 stood at $53\frac{3}{4}$, stand now at $35\frac{1}{2}$, while the Portuguese 3 per cent. Loan of 1867 was issued at 37; besides which, the present market prices of the public debt of Italy, Egypt, and Austria, indicate that these countries would have to borrow on terms at the least as unfavourable as Venezuela.

It may, perhaps, not be out of place to observe here that there seems but little sense in the custom adopted by foreign Governments of introducing nominal values into the loans borrowed by them. For instance, the Venezuelan

* See the Prospectus in Appendix A.

Government in 1864 obtained a loan for the nominal value of one million and a half at £60 for the £100, and consequently for the real value of £900,000. By that transaction the said Goverment added a million and a half to the national debt, and an annual charge *for interest* of £90,000 —that is, they borrowed at 10 per cent. Now, if instead of borrowing a nominal amount of £1,500,000 at 60, and paying 6 per cent. on each £100 of the nominal amount, they had borrowed £900,000 at 10 per cent., they would have paid no more interest, and saved £600,000 in the nominal amount of their debt. As to the terms at which they did borrow, they would have been onerous had they been bound to pay off the debt at par; but they had the option to redeem by purchases in the market, and the probabilities were that they would be able to purchase on the same terms as they borrowed. In point of fact, what they did redeem of the debt they bought *considerably* under the price at which it had been issued.*

It was expressly stipulated by Article 9 that, unless the Constituent Assembly of Venezuela ratified the Loan, the General Credit Company should be at liberty to withdraw from the transaction, and that the money subscribed by the bond-holders should be refunded to them. Now, as if expressly to take away all pretext for future cavil regarding the Loan, or any of its conditions, on the part of Venezuela, the Great Parliament of the country not only did ratify the Loan, but empowered the National Representative, General Blanco, to increase its amount to three millions! The solemn declaration in which the ratification is expressed is couched in the following terms :—

* See the prices of the Venezuelan Loans in Appendix A.

GOD AND THE CONFEDERACY!
THE CONSTITUENT ASSEMBLY
OF THE
UNITED STATES OF VENEZUELA
DECREES.

In the name of the Republic is ratified the contract made on the third day of October last by the Citizen General Antonio Guzman Blanco, with the General Credit Company of London, for raising a loan of a million and a half of pounds, and, in consequence, the Executive Power of the United States of Venezuela is fully authorised to arrange any difficulties which may arise in its execution, and to make all arrangements which it may consider most advantageous to the Public Exchequer. Also, in like manner, it is authorised to increase the amount of this Loan to three millions of pounds; this Assembly reserving to itself by a subsequent Decree to determine the application of the additional million and a half of pounds, or of the surplus, which may be contracted for upon the basis of the Contract of the third of October aforesaid.

Given in Carácas in the Hall of the Sessions of the Constituent Assembly of the United States of Venezuela, on the 14th of January, 1864.

The President                     The Deputed Secretary
J. G. OCHOA.            JOSÉ MA. ORTEGA MARTINEZ.

This ratification completely exonerated the lenders of the loan from any imputation of undue rigour. The borrowers not only declared themselves content, but stated their willingness to borrow as much again on the same conditions.

It now only remained for the General Credit Company to send out a commissioner, who should ascertain that the duties, which were to be hypothecated for the payment of the Interest and Sinking Fund, were free from valid claims, and who should then ratify the loan on the part of the Company, take charge of the custom-houses, and appoint agents for the receipt of the duties. This, then, was my business, and I have now to relate how I performed it.

I must premise that before the date of my departure from England, the 17th of June, 1864, a number of persons had advanced claims upon the export duties, notwithstanding the declaration of General Blanco that they were not chargeable, and in spite of his assertion that he was entitled to offer them as security for the loan. The exact amount of all these claims was unknown to the General Credit Company, but they were aware of the following sums :—

Claim of certain creditors represented by the Chevalier Jacques Servadio, Consul at Venezuela for the King of Italy . . . . . . . . . . . £100,000

1. Claim of S<sup>r</sup>. Manuel Camacho of Carácas . . . 52,000
2. Claim of Mr. Richard Thornton $109,800 / 6½ years Interest on the same $ 35,685 } $145,485   22,382
3. Claim of Mr. Aaron Goodrich, called the Aves Island Claim } $155,000 .   23,846
4. Claim of the Colonial Bank    $134,676 .   20,719
5. Claim of Messrs. Moron & Co. of St. Thomas . .   37,723

Total      £256,670

My instructions were to leave the Venezuelan Government to decide on the validity of these claims, with the exception of the first, which had been paid in scrip of the loan by General Blanco. On my arrival in Venezuela I was to bring the claims 1, 2, 3, 4, 5, to the notice of the Government, and if it should decline to recognise them, and solemnly declare the export duties free of charge, and hand them over to the agents appointed by me for collection, I was to consider that fact and the declaration, as being that of a Sovereign State, as sufficient proof of there being no valid charges on the said duties.

According to the strict letter of my instructions, nothing more than attention to the said points could be required of me. Nevertheless, I thought it right to investigate, as far as practicable, each claim, and report upon it to the General Credit Company; and in their interest, and in the interest of the Government, I did all I could in a quiet way to get what appeared rightful claims settled. Thus the claim of the Colonial Bank, whatever its merits, having been taken up by the British representative, I gave him my support and obtained its recognition and settlement. I lent what aid I could to the American Minister also, with reference to the Aves Island claim, and that, too, was adjusted.

The first thing, however, which I had to do on arrival was to persuade Messrs. Boulton & Co. to become agents for the loan. This was a point on which great stress was laid in my instructions, and I at once saw its importance. Messrs. Boulton & Co. were incontestably the most respectable house in Venezuela, and I felt that if I could secure their assistance I should be safe from the mistakes into which any stranger, though much more *au fait* at business than myself, would very likely have fallen. But Mr. Boulton was extremely indisposed to accept the agency for the loan, and his partner at La Guaira was still more averse to such a step, though a third partner, a Venezuelan by birth, had attended General Blanco's conferences with the General Credit Company, and had aided in nego-

tiating the Loan, a fact of which I was quite unaware.
I had to combat their objections, and after long argument succeeded in overcoming their reluctance. This
was a great success, and an important result immediately
followed. I discovered that the export duties, which
General Blanco offered as security for the loan, were
encumbered with debts to most of the principal merchants
at La Guaira and Carácas, amounting to more than a
million dollars. These debts had been incurred by the
Government for the discharge of what they owed to soldiers
and others, who had suffered in their cause during the war
with the faction of Paez and Rojas. But besides these
incontestable debts there were other claims made by the
Spanish, Dutch, and French Ministers after my arrival, and
some brought forward by the English *chargé d'affaires* on
behalf of British subjects, of which I had no cognizance till
I reached Carácas. An abyss of liabilities had opened
under my feet, and when I surveyed its insatiable maw and
then glanced at the two chests of sovereigns, which were all
I had to throw into it, I could not help thinking of the
Cavern of the Winds in Persia, into which if you cast a
pebble it is said that a heterogeneous mass of projectiles is
vomited forth with prodigious sound and fury, and sweeps
away all before it.

Now that my responsibilities are over I cannot forbear
smiling, when I recall the confusion worse confounded than
that " of King Agramante's camp," in which I lived during
those days of conflicting claims and *hydra*-headed creditors.
No sooner have I done breakfast than a Representative is
announced. He burns so to get his business settled that,
in spite of polite attempts to conceal his impatience, his

very body seems to radiate importunities. He soon comes
to the point. "Has Monsieur placed before the Ministers
the matter of the Agostino billetes?" "Be assured, Excellency!" I reply, "I have done my best, but the Ministers
acquaint me that the claim is not recognised." "How! not
recognised? Is it possible that they can seek to evade the
most just, the most clear, enfin les obligations les plus
sacrées?" "Pardon me, Excellency; I am chagrined
beyond measure, but one can do no more than represent the
matter; the decision rests with the Government." "Then,
Monsieur, I must bring to your notice that I have already
warned the squadron to be prepared to sail for La Guaira.
I have the honour to prévenir Monsieur que l'affaire est
grave, très grave." In vain at this moment I renew
assurances; in vain I press upon him fragrant cigars,
symbolical of the calumet of peace, and typical of those
graceful wreaths, in which I know the menaces of armed
intervention are sure to end. The affair remains grave, and
the Minister departs with decidedly less cordial empressement towards myself than he showed on entering. I am
scarce reseated when a long despatch from the Spanish
Minister arrives, containing an interminable correspondence
about the claim of one of his protégés, the immediate settlement of which he thinks I am bound to accomplish, if for
no other reason than because it has already been fruitlessly
discussed for a dozen years and has wearied out every
Minister in succession during that period. In the middle
of reading it I am disturbed by a visit from the American
Minister, who comes about the Aves Island claim, and then
by the ———— chargé d'affaires, who also utters what I
know to be a most innocuous threat as to a naval demon-

stration. In short, it seems to be the object of every power represented at Carácas to invest me, in a certain sense, with the order of the Golden Fleece; an honour which I do my best to elude.

Nor was the current of my intercourse with the Venezuelan Ministers altogether without checks. They were, indeed, extremely polite; and, personally, I had not the slightest cause to be dissatisfied with their behaviour. But I think that, in reply to my letter of the 6th of July, in which, immediately after my landing, I requested the President of the Republic in making over to me the collection of the export duties, to furnish me with proof that they were free from charge, it would have been more candid to have stated at once that there were claims on the duties to such an amount, for monies borrowed from the principal merchants, and to have assured me that those claims would be satisfied by drafts on the proceeds of the loan, which drafts the President would direct General Blanco to see duly honoured. Instead of that, a serious responsibility was thrown upon me, and but for the stand I made, and the firmness of the General Credit Company, it is a question whether the claims of the merchants would have been settled to this very day. Having ascertained, however, in the first instance, through Mr. Boulton, the nature of these debts, I was resolved not to report in favour of concluding the loan until they were liquidated, and having seen that the Venezuelan Government drew bills to pay them off, I wrote to the General Credit Company as follows:—" In advising the transmission of these bills, it is my imperative duty to state that I have agreed to ratify the loan, with the distinct understanding and on the sole condition that all these bills, including those for the British claims, are honoured and paid before the Venezuelan Government avails itself of the proceeds of the loan for any other purpose. The same remark applies to the settlement of the 'Aves Island' claim, which, though it has been referred to General Blanco, must be settled before the funds of the loan become available for the general purposes of the Venezuelan Government."

With regard to the British claims referred to in the above paragraph another very serious difficulty arose. Major Matheson, the British *chargé d'affaires*, was determined to have them settled, and said he could not allow them to be discussed, as the orders from Lord Russell were peremptory regarding them. I felt bound to support him. Claims from the subjects of other Governments I, according to the letter of my instructions, left to the decision of the Venezuelan Ministers, but I could hardly take up a similar position with regard to the claims which my own Government declared must be paid. Besides Lord Russell had given me a letter to the English *chargé d'affaires*, calling on him to assist me to the extent of his power, and I could hardly do less than reciprocate. On the 18th of July the Ministers yielded, but on the 19th General Ochoa, the Acting-Minister for Foreign Affairs, having arrived in Carácas from the provinces, the aspect of affairs changed. On that day the Ministers gave an audience to the English *chargé d'affaires*, Mr. Boulton, and myself, in the Government House. General Ochoa then said that with the exception of that of the Colonial Bank the claims had not been recognised, and some of them were made by parties who were not even British subjects. Supposing, he added, their claims to be just, it did not follow that they were to be paid out of the loan—that was a question for the Venezuelan Government to decide. There were many other claims, French, Dutch, and Spanish, and the funds of the loan would not suffice to pay all of them. To this I replied that the claims had been recognised by the British Government, and by former Governments of Venezuela, and Lord Russell had given peremptory orders to his Minister to get three of them settled. England would not allow her claims to be mixed up with those of other powers. The answer to those powers was as regards the loan that, as it had been raised in England, British claims ought to be settled first. "When Venezuela could borrow money in Paris by all means let the French claims be first settled with the sum so raised, and similarly with regard to the other powers." General Ochoa rejoined that the loan was not in any way an affair of the English Government. It was contracted with a private company. My business, he said, was to see that the duties were clear, and after that I could not refuse to ratify the loan. I answered that it was impossible for me to report that the duties were clear, when the representative of my own Government, who had been fifty years in the country, declared they were not. At all events it would be impossible for me to report by the next packet, and the delay would be a greater loss to Venezuela than the settlement of the claims, even if they were open to question. The debate continued for hours, and would have ended unsatisfactorily had it not been for Mr. Boulton, who persuaded Major Matheson to agree to half the claims being settled at once, and the rest by securities on the 25 per cent. extra import duties.

This arrangement was made on the 19th and 20th of July, and on the latter day I received a letter from her Majesty's *chargé d'affaires*, in which he officially stated that " the arrangements made for the settlement of the recognised claims at her Majesty's Legation are quite satisfactory." On the 22nd of July the Finance Minister, in reply to my request that he would state " briefly and explicitly that the duties made over are free of charge," addressed to me a despatch which ran as follows :—" In reply to your letter, dated this day, I have the honour to assure you, categorically, that the export duties of the custom-houses of La Guaira, Puerto Cabello, Maracaibo, and Ciudad Bolivar are free of all charge ; and that, as I have informed you in previous letters, you may proceed to collect what is realisable in them under that head." In accordance with this letter the collection of the export duties was, on the 23rd of July, placed in the hands of Messrs. Boulton & Co., whom I had appointed agents for the loan. On the same day bills to the amount of £209,848. 0s. 7d., drawn on General Blanco by the Venezuelan Government, in liquidation of the recognised liabilities of the export duties, were forwarded to England by the steamer.

It may be supposed, therefore, that my anxieties were at an end ; but that was far from being the case. The bills, indeed, were drawn, but I felt uncertain whether they would be honoured. I knew that General Blanco would be mortified at having such an enormous sum as the bills represented taken from the amount he was to receive in cash ; and knowing the claims he had to settle in London and Paris were very large, I was not sure that there would be a balance quite sufficient to meet the bills. Still, in a position of immense difficulty, I had done my best. I could not have conscientiously stated that the duties were clear until I had ascertained, to the best of my power, that every claim which the Government could not but recognise was provided for. Having done so, and having called upon the General Credit Company, in the strongest terms, not to consider the loan ratified until the creditors were paid, I had now only to wait patiently for the result. In the meantime what I heard of the management of the revenues of Venezuela, and the loose way in which people talked of public and private obligations, was not encouraging.

The great pressure of work being over I had time to reflect on the means of rendering the contract for the loan as binding as possible on the Government. I took care, in the first place, to have every document connected with the loan registered in the British Legation, and I tried to impress upon every one in authority that any infraction of the conditions of the contract would strike a fatal blow at the national credit. I exerted myself to show that, with so many unrecognised claims still to be examined and laid to rest, with such large demands upon the revenue on account of the loans, and with such a troublesome spirit of faction still existing, it behoved the Government to practise the most rigid economy, and look into the abuses, which were only too notorious, in the management of the public finances.

Among other things it occurred to me that I ought to have a personal interview with the President. Without entering into the question of how far it may be good or bad policy for the President of a Republic to be always absent from the capital, the plain fact may be stated that General

Falcon did so absent himself and, leaving the conduct of affairs to ministers appointed by his own decree, lived for the most part in a distant province difficult of access. In order that it might not be said that the General was not cognizant of the arrangements I had made, or that he was dissatisfied with any part of them, I resolved to see him myself, and I worked hard at Spanish that there might be no necessity for an interpreter. An account of the interview will be found in another chapter. On my return from it I was chagrined, but not very much surprised, to hear that General Blanco had dishonoured the bills drawn on him by his Government. Had he persisted in that impolitic proceeding, all my labour would have been thrown away and a disastrous complication would have ensued. After a struggle, however, the bills were paid, and I left Venezuela with the satisfaction of knowing that the most pressing debts of the Government were settled, and that with proper economy the national credit might be maintained, and the revenue gradually augmented. Mr. Boulton informed me that the Constituent Assembly would probably vote me their thanks, and though that expectation proved to be illusory, I had the gratification of receiving the thanks of the General Credit Company, and of knowing that I had relieved the Foreign Office of some troublesome claims.

And here, in order to finish the history of the loan, I must go on to relate what has happened with reference to it up to the present moment. In 1865, under various pretences, the Venezuelan Government stopped paying the interest on Messrs. Barings' loan. That loan had been negociated by the party opposed to General Falcon, and had enabled them to continue the war when they were *in extremis*. The faction now in power in Venezuela could not be expected to regard such a loan with much favour, and that they should endeavour to impugn its validity, though inexcusable, was not very surprising. But it was not long before symptoms of further change appeared. On the 30th of January, 1866, a Mr. Engelke, a German long resident in Venezuela, and much engaged in the intrigues of parties there, arrived in England and called upon me. He asked for an introduction to the manager of the General Credit Company, and he then unfolded to me that in his opinion the only way of extricating Venezuela from its financial difficulties was to unify the debt, pay a small interest upon it, and apply the balance of the revenue to the construction of railroads and other public works. On these becoming profitable the Government would be enabled to increase the rate of interest payable to the bondholders, and in the end, perhaps, liquidate the debt itself. On hearing this proposal I distinctly told Mr. Engelke that the Government could not with any fairness adopt such a scheme. I reminded him that General Falcon and the ministers now in office had negociated the loan of 1864, that it had been protected by the observance of every possible formality, and that no excuse had ever been alleged for infringing the contract. I pointed out that on the 3rd of January, 1865, General Blanco had submitted the report of his proceedings as regards the loan to the Constituent Assembly, and that all he had done had been finally ratified. As for myself, I said, I had not words strong enough for condemning his scheme.

But Mr. Engelke, being a German naturalized in Venezuela, viewed matters very differently from an Englishman. My arguments made not the slightest impression on him.

He called upon the manager of the General Credit Company and paraded his scheme with a *sang-froid* worthy of a better cause. His suggestions were received by the manager with as little favour as by me. This, however, made no difference to Mr. Engelbkye, who returned to Venezuela with unshaken purpose. On my mind his visit made a deep impression. I knew that Mr. Engelbkye was an intimate friend and the confidential adviser of General Falcon. Directly I heard his scheme I inwardly exclaimed " *Actum est*," and I urged those interested in the loan to put out all their power to avert the coming storm. On the 2nd of July, 1866, payment of interest on the loan of 1864 was suspended, renewed in the beginning of December in that year, and finally stopped in March, 1867.

Since that date deputations from the General Credit Company and the bondholders have had interviews with Lord Stanley on the subject of this scandalous breach of faith on the part of Venezuela. On one of those occasions I was present and spoke. The nature of my views, particularly as regards the ability of Venezuela to pay, and of England to enforce payment, will appear in subsequent chapters. It is only necessary here to add that, in one respect, the bondholders seem to me to have placed themselves in the wrong. The Venezuelan Government asserting its inability to pay, called on the bondholders to send out a commissioner to confer with the ministers at Carácas. It is the opinion of the agents for the loan that, had I gone out, supported by the Foreign Office, all difficulties might have been removed. At all events such a measure would have deprived the Venezuelans of the only excuse now left to them. As it is, they can say that they made a proposal which has been refused.

It only remains to add that the mole which has been so long burrowing under the mound of the national debt has at length worked its way to the surface. The last mail from Venezuela (February, 1868), brings intelligence that Mr. Engelke has been appointed Minister of Finance. That announcement is accompanied by various indefinite statements, which seem to be made with a view of encouraging the bondholders. Let those be taken for what they are worth. On the other hand it is no doubt the fact that German interests are in one sense antagonistic to English in Venezuela. The Germans have completely extinguished the trade of England with that country. Mr. Engelke is a German—it is to be hoped that his aim is not the alienation of the two countries of England and Venezuela. In the meantime there is reason to fear that, unless the *deus ex machinâ*, in the shape of a special commissioner from the British Foreign Office interposes, the claims of England on Venezuela will soon pass into utter oblivion.

Having thus briefly sketched the history * of the loan, I return to chit-chat, leaving the questions of the solvency of Venezuela, and the means of compelling her to fulfil her obligations, for consideration in the two concluding chapters.

* The statement regarding the Loan of 1864, furnished by the General Credit Company, with the documents connected with it, will be found in Appendix A.

# CHAPTER VII.



HAVING made up my mind to see Valencia, I resolved to
go from Carácas by the hot sea-route, recruit in the moderate climate of Valencia, and return by Aráguas, along the
shores of the celebrated Lake of Tacarigua. When I had
selected my route, and persuaded my friend C. to be my
companion, at least as far as Puerto Cabello, the next
thing was to fix the date of our departure. We had
just heard of a European dying of yellow fever at La
Guaira, having caught the disease at Puerto Cabello, and
as to the intensity of the heat, we had the evidence of our
own senses, it being, in fact, the hottest and most unhealthy
time of the year. However, as I was very anxious to meet
the President, General Falcon, whose arrival at Valencia
was expected, we determined to start immediately. In the
hope of getting the ride to La Guaira over before the sun
grew fierce, I rose on the 8th of August at 4 A.M., and
walked over to C.'s house. I and he were to go by the
short cut over the mountains called the Indian Path, and
my servant was to follow with the *impedimenta* by the coach
road. But the course of travel never did run smooth, and
the first annoyance was, that the mules we were to ride did

K

not come at the appointed time, and when they made their appearance, the sun had already cleared off the mists that descend at night upon Carácas from the Avila. Two very diminutive animals they were, these mules, a brown and a white one, and were both equipped with that invention of the Evil One, the South American saddle, which has a huge sharp peak rising up in front, and another in rear, so that to lift the leg over them requires the lissomness of youth, or the natural suppleness of Creole joints. My temper had been somewhat ruffled by the delay of the muleteer, and I cast rather a sour look at his mules as I asked him which I was to ride.

"Señor," said the man, very civilly, "this white one is little, but he knows the road well; he is for you."

"Little but old, like the pig in the story," I muttered, as, putting my left toe into one stirrup, I carelessly threw up my right leg with the intention of seating myself on the white mule's back. But it was not for nothing that the snows of age had descended on that subtle animal, who, with all his outward solemnity, had learned more tricks than a monkey. The instant my right leg went up, he jumped back with a sudden violence that transferred my foot to his ears instead of the place intended for it, and I was sent toppling over into the arms of my tall servant, whose expansive mouth opened with a grin of exquisite enjoyment. Seeing how much he and the other servants, as also the rascal of a muleteer, relished my discomfiture, I ordered a man to stand on each side of the mule and keep his head fast, and, laying firm hold of the high pommel, made a second careful and most resolute attempt to seat myself. But the aged animal was too skilful a strategist, and the instant I threw up my leg he also threw up his hinder quarters, and that too with such agility, that so far from bestriding him I only kicked him in the stomach, and was again sent back into the arms of my servant, who this time fairly broke out into a loud laugh, in which even C. joined. I held my peace, and made several other efforts to mount the brute, but all in vain. So at last I had the Spanish saddle taken off and replaced by an English one, and then, in spite of the venerable creature's tricks, succeeded in mounting him. Once on his back, I gave him the taste of a very sharp pair of spurs, to which he responded with a series of kicks, but went on at a quick pace. We passed rapidly through the streets to the north-eastern angle of the city, and skirting the Toma, or city reservoir, we began to ascend the ancient military road over the mountains. "C.," said I, after riding for some time rather sulkily, "I shan't forgive you for letting them bring me such a troublesome brute as this." "Don't be angry, amigo mio!" replied C., who had hardly yet done laughing; "that mule is called ' El Bailarin,' ' the dancer,' on account of his capers, and many a fellow has been spilt in trying to mount him; but when once you are on him, you are sure to like him, for he has the best paces of any animal on the road. Let me tell you, too, we shall come to places presently where you will not be sorry to have a sure-footed beast under you."

By this time the ascent was becoming very steep, and turned incessantly in a sharp zig-zag, and at every turn beautiful views broke upon us. In front, on the right hand and on the left, were the mountains, with deep precipitous ravines, in which the trees grew so thickly that no eye could

spy a single glitter of the waters that brawled along beneath
their branches. Behind us were the city of Carácas and
the rich valley of Chacao, at the furthest end of which a
mass of light vaporous clouds were floating, while in the
distance towered the mountains of Higuerota. We stopped
more than once to gaze at the scenery, but our mules were
so good that in thirty minutes we had gained the crest of
the mountain. Here we passed the ruins of a chapel,
which was thrown down by the earthquake of 1812. "What
a view," said I to C., "there must have been from this spot
of the falling city, of the descending rocks, and the other
horrors of the earthquake!" "Why, yes," replied C.,
"if you could have kept your feet to look, but it is my
opinion that you would have been knocked down by the
shock. There was one man up here at the chapel, but he did
not see much, for the walls fell upon him and crushed him."

We now turned our backs on Carácas, and saw no more
of it, and in another half-hour we reached a posada, a mile
beyond which we turned off from the broad military road
by which we had hitherto been travelling (and the making
of which does the Spaniards no little credit), into the far-
famed Indian Path. This winds along the mountain, at a
height of some six thousand feet, through thick low woods,
varied by patches of coffee plantations and other cultiva-
tions. In places there is a sheer precipice, and in others,
where there is only a steep slope, some hardy adventurers
have built cottages, and planted coffee and the ubiquitous
yuca and plantain. Storms of wind are luckily not very
common in this locality, or these huts and their owners
would, perchance, go a visiting in the valley below. It
happened, however, that the night before we started had

been very tempestuous, and we now saw many traces of the mischief wrought by the storm. In some places we came upon long avenues made in the wood, in which the trees had been uprooted or smashed by the wind, and some had fallen so as almost to block the path, and put us to no little difficulty in passing them. However, I was determined not to dismount, having a wholesome dread of the Bailarin's capering performances on such a ticklish stage as the Indian Path. At last we came to a place where a cottage had been blown down, and the débris lay right athwart our way, and here I made up my mind to be stopped altogether. The mule, however, having more of the female than of the male nature, in that it is *rarium et mutabile semper*, does ordinarily baffle calculation in its proceedings. My cunning old animal knowing, perhaps, that the place we were at was more than half way to La Guaira, and that, consequently, it would get its provender sooner by going on than by returning, scrambled over the ruins like a monkey.

From the place where we had turned off into the Indian Path to the ruined cottage—that is, for about four miles—we had constantly been looking over wooded ravines to Cape Blanco, and beyond that to the sea. Far to the westward, also, our eyes travelled over the Tierra Caliente, or "hot land," as the coast is called, with an horizon, which, according to Humboldt, has a radius of sixty-six miles. But our prospect to the east was cut short by the jutting of the mountain, which continually advanced with and beyond us, bold and high towards the sea. We now at last turned its flank, and, looking eastward, were repaid with a very noble view over the gorges that run down from the Silla to Macuto. The path grew narrower, and the precipice so sheer, that it seemed as if a bound would carry us, if we leaped from the mountain, over the slender strip of coast into the sea. We now began to see below us Maquetia and La Guaira, with the vessels at anchor, and so much was the distance apparently diminished by the height at which we were, that I fancied I could have thrown a stone upon the roofs of the houses.

Humboldt seems not to have gone by the Indian Path, for though he dwells very much on the beauty of the view to the west, which he prefers to that from the mountains of Mexico between Las Trancas and Xalapa, he says nothing of the eastern view over La Guaira and Macuto, which struck me as far more wonderful. The view to the west he could have seen, though not quite to such advantage as we did, from the military road : the yellow line of which we occasionally noticed, at the distance of a mile or so, cropping out from the woods below us.

It was now past 8 A.M., and the heat of the sun was so fierce that the coast and the sea seemed to shimmer in its rays ; but up to this point we had been quite protected by the mountain, which rose in some places nearly one thousand feet above our heads. No sooner did we turn to the east, however, but we met the sun face to face, and the encounter made me quite giddy. It was with some uneasiness that I descried, ahead of us, a place where the rain of the previous night had almost entirely washed away the path, leaving only a ledge about a foot broad. "C.," said I, "how are we to pass that place? I think I must get off, even if I should have to walk all the rest of the way in this broiling sun." "Best trust to the mule," he answered. "You may slip, but he won't, I'll bet ten to one." "It's of no use betting," I said, "when I am to be killed if I win; but I'll take your advice, and chance it on the mule; so here goes." With these words, I let my bridle drop on the mule's neck, feeling sure that if he slipped, it would be of no use trying to save him, and thinking I might do harm by holding him too tight. The animal seemed to know the danger, for he put his head down and sniffed, then walked steadily over the ledge, and was followed by C.'s mule, and then by that of the muleteer, who carried our cloaks. I was just ejaculating "All right," when the career of the latter individual was nearly brought to a close. The last bit of the ledge consisted of a great stone, which had perhaps been loosened by the successive pressure of the mules. At all events, when the last animal had got his hind legs upon it, it gave way, and down it went with a shower of earth, crashing among the bushes, until, gathering velocity, it made a huge bound into the abyss, and we saw no more of it. As for the muleteer, it was well for him that his mule had got its fore legs firmly planted on the path beyond the ledge, and that the spurs, which in his fright he drove up to the rowels into the mule's side, were sharp, for it was only by a desperate effort that the poor beast saved itself from falling back. The fellow, though used to rough work, so lost his nerve at the narrowness of his escape, that he got off, and leaned against the rock for a minute or two, with a face which terror had blanched to a whity-brown.

"Do you know," said C., "that at this very place, which before last night's rain was three times as broad as it is now, a rather disagreeable accident once occurred? It was about eight years ago. We had made up a party to take advantage of the full moon and ride down to La Guaira at night. A Frenchman, partner in one of the houses at La Guaira, whom you may have seen there, had been persuaded to join us. He was exceedingly nervous, and rather short-sighted, and we quizzed him unmercifully as we rode along in high spirits, and with rather more champagne on board than was desirable on such an occasion. When we arrived at this place, which was even then the worst bit on the road, a cloud came over the moon, and some one called out in joke to the Frenchman, who was riding a white horse, to go first, as he would be better seen by any one coming the other way, and so a *rencontre* would be avoided where the path was too narrow for two riders to pass. He unfortunately took the request in earnest, and made an attempt to get first. There being a bush beside the precipice, his horse mistook it for terra firma, stepped on it, and went down like a shot. The poor Frenchman uttered a cry of horror, which was succeeded by a loud crashing among branches and a rattle of falling stones, and, after a moment's pause, by a tremendous thud, as the horse struck the rocks many feet down, and bounded off into the abyss. We stood aghast at the loss of our poor friend, but, as it was impossible even to see down the precipice, we had no alternative but to go on to La Guaira, leaving two of our number to watch at the spot where he had fallen. I was one of those who went on, and as soon as I reached the town I got together ten or a dozen men, and having procured some long ropes, set off, just as the dawn was breaking, to the precipice, intending to lower some one down to see whether there was any chance of recovering the body. What was my astonishment, on nearing the place, to hear the sound of laughter and loud talking! This levity seemed so ill-timed, that I intended to remonstrate with my friends who had been left to watch. My anger, however, was soon turned into joy, for I found the laughers bending over the precipice, and addressing jokes to the bushy head of a stumpy tree which grew from the side of the mountain, some fifteen feet below the path, and in which the Frenchman had providentially alighted, while his horse had been dashed to pieces. Of course we soon pulled our friend up. We found he was unhurt, except by a few scratches, though fear had at first so paralysed him, that for a good quarter of an hour after his fall he had been unable to utter one word. Even now, at this length of time, he has not completely recovered his nerve, and will not cross the mountain, even by the coach road, on horseback."

This story took so long to tell, that we had reached the grass-grown walls of the Fort of St. Carlos, just above the Quebrada, which runs into La Guaira, before it was done. The sun was now terrifically hot, and we pushed on with all speed to C.'s house, which we reached at half-past 9 A.M., having been about three hours in coming the whole way. My only business at La Guaira was to inspect the custom-house, of which I might now be said to be joint proprietor with the government, as my agents had assumed the collection of the export duties. On going over the building, I found the lower story divided into six long stores—which together might contain about two thousand five hundred tons of merchandise—and one square store, capable of holding as much as the other six. Perhaps five thousand tons in all could be warehoused at one time in the building, but it being the dull season, there were not above six hundred tons at the time of my visit. The timber of the custom-house is almost black, and as hard as iron, and of a kind that no insect can make any impression on. Of the three stories, the lower, as has been said, consists of warehouses. In the second, sit the accountants, whose books I examined carefully. At 5 P.M. I had embarked with C. on board a brig of two hundred tons, and was soon sailing with a light breeze from La Guaira to Puerto Cabello. At night, the wind fell, and I who was below, among colonies of industrious ants, fleas, and cock-roaches, all doing their best to carry me away piecemeal, passed the dark hours in wondering whether I should melt away before I was eaten up, or should be eaten up before I could melt away.

In the morning, we found ourselves sweltering in a dead calm, abreast of the mountains of Ocumare, and about twenty-six miles from Puerto Cabello. The heat went on increasing until noon, when it became so intolerable, that we could do nothing but lie down panting in our shirts, and dab our heads and hands with wet towels. The sea was like glass; I looked in vain for even a cat's-paw anywhere on its surface. Not a bird or a fish was to be seen, except one dolphin: a beautiful creature of a golden green, with silver fins and tail, which kept darting about under our bows, as if in mockery of our inability to move. The mate, a huge surly, swarthy fellow, whose natural ill-humour was increased by the heat, swore at the fish, and tried to kill it with the grains, but only struck off a few glittering scales, after which it sank out of harm's way. At half-past 4, in spite of the sun, I went up the rigging to spy for a breeze, thinking I should hardly live over the heat of such another twenty-four hours. My reconnoitring seemed to bring good luck, for the wind sprang up almost immediately, and we ran before it at the rate of eight or nine knots an hour, towards our destination. In a short time we were able, with our glasses, to make out the Mirador of Solano, or Castle of Puerto Cabello, which stands on a rock five hundred feet high, about a quarter of a league to the south-east of the harbour.

We now began to hug the shore, and passed first the Bay of Turiamo, nine miles east of Puerto Cabello, and then those of Patanemo and Burburata. Here the coast is lined by narrow strips of low land, covered with bushes, called the Islands, on which the sea breaks very heavily. I observed that from these the coast runs in a great curve to the north-west and north, making much more of a semicircle than appears from the maps. By this curve of the coast is formed a great bay called the Golfo Triste, which lugubrious title it well deserves, the coast being, perhaps, the most unhealthy in the world. At a quarter past 7 we were rounding a spit of land which runs out about half a mile from the coast in a north-westerly direction. Having rounded the spit, at the extremity of which stands a lighthouse, extremely well built, but which has never once been used, we entered a bay between the spit and the mainland, which is thus protected from all winds, on the east, north, and south, and found ourselves in the far-famed harbour of Puerto Cabello. It only required a glance to see that the port was secured from storms on the west also, partly by islands, and partly by the curve of the mainland. In short, there is perhaps no harbour in the world where the sea is at all times so calm as at Puerto Cabello. This being the case, it is surprising that the Spaniards should in the first instance have made Burburata, which is three miles to the east, their chief port, it being in every respect inferior.

Night in the tropics, when once the sun has set, soon veils everything : so I had no time on arrival to do more than cast a hasty glance around. The brig anchored abreast of the fort, which is on the spit of land already mentioned, and we had only a hundred yards or so to pull to the shore. On landing, we walked about a quarter of a mile to the house of one of C.'s partners, where we were to pass the night. I had heard much of the unhealthiness of Puerto Cabello ; but if I had not, I should have formed a bad opinion of the place from its lying so low, and being encircled with jungle, and still more from the peculiar smell which the night air brought to my nostrils from the swamps, and which made me shiver. I had smelt the same odour in what are called the barrier jungles in India, and in some parts of China, and I knew very well what it betokened—fever and cholera. I made up my mind at once as to what I should do. In the first place, I asked my host for mosquito curtains, which are a protection, though but a slight one, against malaria.

" Mosquito curtains ! " said my friend, with an air of surprise ; " there are no mosquitoes here."

" Well, of course you know best," I replied ; " but, if there are none, what means that hum ? "

" Oh," he answered, " there may be a few, just one or two, but we never use curtains. I advise you to adopt the plan of General A. You know, when Bolivar was in Guiana, he sent for General A., who was the only person who had curtains in camp, and said he must borrow them. The general brought them accordingly. The next morning

Bolivar asked him how he had slept without his curtains. ' Excellency, I slept very well,' was the answer, ' for I always take with me a second pair; ' at the same time producing an immense liquor-flask, quite empty, which he had drained as a substitute."

Not admiring this plan, I adopted another of my own, and as soon as I entered my bedroom, I closed all the doors and windows, and wrapped myself up tight in a blanket. As the temperature of the room was one hundred and ten degrees Fahrenheit, the effect resembled that of a Turkish bath, and I streamed with perspiration at every pore. Of course, while this lasted, there was no chance of fever, and I slept soundly till 2 A.M., when I struck a light and descried an immense spider just over my head, and a scorpion of a pale yellow colour ascending the wall near the door. After that pleasing discovery I thought it as well to keep my light burning until dawn.

My first visit in the morning was to the custom-house, which I found under the superintendence of the brother of the Secretary of State for Finance : a small, taciturn man, who replied to all remarks that were not direct questions by a violent puff of his cigarette, and a very slight inclination of his head. The custom-house has but two stores, which will hold only one-sixth of the amount of goods that can be warehoused at La Guaira. The trade of Puerto Cabello is chiefly in exports, the imports being comparatively insignificant, while the reverse is the case at La Guaira. I was now able, with the help of daylight, to appreciate the excellence of the harbour, which is said to be the best in America. Not only is it landlocked in the way already described, and at the same time easy of access, but the water is so deep that ships can lie alongside the wharf and take in cargo direct from the shore. The custom-house, too, is conveniently situated, being but a few yards from the wharf, and the road to Valencia passes straight from it through the town into the country. It has been suggested that the pentagonal fort, on the spit of ground to the east of the harbour, should be pulled down, and the site turned into docks. Indeed, if a battery, which has been constructed opposite what are called the reefs of Punta Brava, at the entrance of the harbour, were mounted with guns of the largest size, no other defence would be needed. The castle, or mirador, on the high rock to the south-east, would not be of much use against a foreign invasion, but it has ever proved a great obstacle to troops advancing against Puerto Cabello from the interior; for, being compelled, in order to take it, to camp in the jungle, they have always suffered terribly from yellow fever, and in some cases have been quite destroyed by this fearful scourge. Some idea of its ravages may be formed from the fact that M. Julien, principal surgeon of Puerto Cabello, at the time of Humboldt's visit, told that traveller that in seven years he had had eight thousand cases of yellow fever in his hospital alone. Previous to that, things had been even worse; for in 1793, when Admiral Ariztizabel's fleet lay in the harbour, every third man died of the disease. Subsequently, during the War of Independence, a European regiment that was sent down to besiege the castle, died almost to a man, and more recently there have been instances of the entire crews of ships in the harbour perishing, so that the authorities have had to take charge of the deserted vessels. Some good has been done lately by cutting down the mangroves, which filled the port with decaying vegetation, but until the swampy jungle for miles round shall have been drained and cleared, pestilence will always hold its head-quarters at Puerto Cabello.

After walking round the wharves, and throwing various things into the sluggish waters, in the vain hope of getting a rise out of the monstrous ground-sharks that swarm at the bottom, I paid a visit to the largest private store in the town. It was about a hundred and fifty feet long, and contained all sorts of European imports, from calicoes to pen-knives and pale ale. But there was one article in immense quantities, which rather surprised me—Chinese crackers. " Good Heavens," I said, " what gluttons the children here must be for squibs ; why, English boys are moderate in comparison ! " " It is not the children," replied C., smiling, " that have such an appetite for fireworks, but the saints. All these crackers will be used up at the holy ceremonies during the fiestas of the next few months." Behind this building was a coffee store, in which heaps of the shining berry were being packed for exportation. The coffee is brought down from the interior on mules. Every mule carries two bags, containing each a quintal, or hundred-weight, worth, at the time of my visit, sixteen dollars. The native bags, of which I saw forty-two thousand lying in the store, are not stout enough for stowing aboard ship, and much time is lost in transferring the coffee from them into strong canvas bags. The coffee is judged of by the smell, and according to the evenness of size of the berries. I was told that the proprietor of this store, an Englishman, who had resided about twenty years at Puerto Cabello, was just going home with a fortune of seventy thousand pounds. From the store, I went to look at the aqueduct, which supplies the town with excellent water from the Rio Estéban, a distance of about three miles. It is a useful work, but there is nothing remarkable in its construction. The village of Estéban is a favourite resort of the Cabellians for picnics; for they are a pleasure-loving race, in spite of earthquakes, intense heat, and yellow fever.

The next thing was to settle whether I should proceed south to Valencia, or west to San Felipe, a town about forty miles from Puerto Cabello, where it was said that General Falcon had promised to attend at the consecration of a church. On inquiry I found that the route to Felipe lay through a treeless waste, where, if I went by day, I should be exposed to a sun that no European could encounter with impunity, while at night I should infallibly be stricken down by the fever, for which the coast of the Golfo Triste is infamous. Of two European engineers, who had been out on this route a few weeks before, one had died of sun-stroke, and the other was lying at the point of death from fever at Puerto Cabello. Besides, General Falcon's movements were so uncertain, that I thought it likely he might not come after all; and so, in fact, it turned out. On the other hand, if I went to San Felipe, I could easily go on to the copper-mines of Aroa, which I was desirous of visiting. These mines were worked for a time under the superintendence of Englishmen with good results; but unfortunately one fine day the native miners took it into their heads that they had a grievance against the foreigners, so they fell on them suddenly, split their skulls with hatchets, and decamped with their property. For this cruel and cowardly deed some of the guilty parties were afterwards executed, but the mines were for a time abandoned, and the working of them had only lately been resumed. After some consideration I resolved to send a courier with a letter to General Falcon, and proceed myself to Valencia, whence, if requisite, I could go by a less unhealthy route to San Felipe.

At 4 P.M. on the 12th of August, I took leave of C. and my kind host, and started with a friend and my servant Juan for Valencia. Just before we left, a Creole, who wished to curry favour with C., rode up to us upon a magnificent mule, and said that he too was going to Valencia, that he observed I was indifferently mounted, and that he would, therefore, be very glad to accompany us, and lend me his mule whenever I got tired of my own. Having made the wished-for impression on C., this rusé individual started with us, but remained in our company for only about half a mile, and then set off over the heavy sandy road at a speed which our poor beasts could not rival. I found that my mule stumbled abominably, and I inwardly resolved to exchange animals with the polite Creole, for a mile or two at least, on the first opportunity. We rode on, under a terrible sun, for five miles, through a dense swampy jungle, full of blue land-crabs and snakes, to Palato, where there is a miserable hovel to represent a village, and where the sea reappears, not sluggish and sleeping, as at Puerto Cabello, but breaking on a wild coast in foaming surges. Here we sat down and smoked, and discussed the prospects of the railway from Puerto Cabello to San Felipe, the first station of which we knew would be at Palato, while from the same village another line would diverge to Valencia. Thus far we had gone west, but we now turned south, and began to ascend from the coast, rejoicing to emerge from the dense low jungle, through which we had hitherto been plodding. On our left, was a ravine, at the bottom of which flowed a small stream called the Rio del Ultimo Paso, or "Ne Plus Ultra River." About a mile to the east of Palato is the mouth of the Rio Agua Caliente, "Hot-water River," in which, according to Humboldt, the alligators are of uncommon size and ferocity. It is curious how these disgusting animals thrive in thermal springs, as at the Magar Talao in Lower Sindh, and other places in India.

After going a mile or two we came to a posada, and here whom should we see smoking indolently with his feet up on a bench, but our friend the Creole, owner of the fine mule. As I was heartily sick of my own animal, and did not understand that Creole promises meant nothing, I reminded him of his proposal, and said, "I should like to exchange mules for a mile or two." "With all my heart, señor," replied he, "but I have a little affair to settle with the landlord here. I will overtake you, before you have advanced a couple of miles; we will then not only exchange mules, but you shall, if you like, ride mine all the rest of the way to Valencia." As I rather misdoubted this arrangement, and was determined not to ride my own animal any more, I mounted Juan's, in spite of his assuring me that I should lose by the change. After about half an hour we spied the courteous Creole coming up at a great pace, and of course expected he would stop when he reached us. Instead of that, he had the effrontery to pass us like a flash of lightning, seeming not to hear our calls to him to pull up, but leaving for our benefit a cloud of dust, which drove directly in our faces, and which was the sole advantage that accrued to us from our interview with this polite individual at Puerto Cabello, and the courteous promises he there made to us. Even

Juan, though used to the country, was rather scandalised at his behaviour, and could not refrain from shouting after him "Picaron! Embustero!" "Rogue, humbug," and other angry expressions, which no doubt afforded the Creole immense amusement.

As we left the coast behind us the soil grew firmer, the pestilential smell ceased, and the jungle waxed higher and higher. Many lofty and beautiful trees now attracted our attention, especially palms, as the sago palm and the cocurito. Juan also pointed out to me the bread-fruit-tree —which looks in the distance as if some one had been hanging human heads on it—and the famous Palo de Vaca, or "cow-tree," which supplies a milk exactly like that of animals. There were also many fruits and flowers, very beautiful to look at, but some of them most poisonous, as the manzanilla, which resembles in appearance and pernicious effects a certain fruit that "brought death into the world and all our woe." The sun set, but a bright moon rose, and we jogged on pleasantly, though very slowly. A little after 8 p.m. we saw, not quite a mile off, the lights of the village of Camburé, which is only seven miles from Palato, so tardy had been our progress, and so often had we stopped to smoke, to look at flowers and trees, and to discuss the proper line for the railway to Valencia. Seeing the village so near, I lagged behind to light another cigar: not an easy matter with the bad matches of the country. While I was absorbed in this undertaking, my mule gave a violent start, which almost sent me off my equilibrium, and began to run at a pace of which I had not before thought it capable. Pulling at the reins with both hands, I looked over my shoulder, and saw a large animal leap into the road behind me, stand for a moment or two, and then pass into the thicket on the other side. Presently a savage roar from the jungle about fifty yards to my right, told me what sort of animal it was, and set my mule galloping on towards the village, at a speed which I now did not attempt to check. In a minute or two I was met by Juan, who came hurrying back to meet me. "Did you hear anything?" I asked. "Yes, yes," replied Juan, "I heard. It's a tiger, sure enough. They don't often attack men, but this one must be hungry, or he would not come so near the village ; so we had better get to the posada as soon as possible." We pushed on accordingly, but before we reached the village we heard the jaguar, for such it was, roar repeatedly in the jungle behind us, and, to judge by the sound, he seemed to be following in our wake.

Camburé is a village of about forty houses, or rather hovels, in the midst of a very dense jungle, and with a deep ravine to the east. At the bottom of this ravine runs a stream, in which there are alligators, for Humboldt saw one nine feet long near the village. Once or twice while *en route*, I had been intending to go down to this stream for a drink, not suspecting there could be alligators in such a mere brook, but I learned afterwards that the saurians of this particular rivulet are singularly large and ferocious. On the night of our arrival the place happened to be quite full of people, some on their way to Valencia, and others, chiefly natives of St. Thomas, who had come out from Puerto Cabello for a drinking-bout. Up to the hour of our arrival, these merry folks had been bringing themselves up to the right pitch of excitement, and being now thoroughly intoxicated, they began to dance furiously to music which strongly reminded me of the Indian tom-toms. I stood for some time looking at their performances, while Juan was bargaining for a room with the landlord of the posada, whose house was already crammed, but who, at the sight of a handful of dollars, unceremoniously ejected some of his guests for our accommodation. As for the merry-makers, whose proceedings I was watching, two of them would stand up at a time and dance frantically a sort of jig, with the perspiration streaming from their faces, until they were quite exhausted, when they sat, or rather tumbled down, and were succeeded by two others, who imitated their example. When I was tired of this, and of looking at some very pretty Creole ladies who sat outside the door of one of the houses, dressed in white, as if for a ball, I entered the posada, which I found alive with fleas, and reeking with garlic. After a miserable dinner I turned into my hammock, but not being used to that kind of bed, I was almost immediately deposited on the floor on the other side, to the great delight of Juan, who, however, instructed me how to conduct myself so as to avoid such an ignominious ejectment for the future.

Next morning we were up by 4 A.M., and after I had packed, and paid eight dollars for our miserable fare, and had got myself covered with black ants, which bit furiously, we started. The road continued to ascend, and the hills on either side grew higher and higher, and the ravines deeper, till we came to Trincheras, or "The Trenches," a village so called, because some French freebooters, who sacked Valencia in 1677, halted there and entrenched themselves. It was twenty minutes past eight before we reached Trincheras, though it is but six miles from Camburé, and there we stopped and smoked, and I chatted with some women, who received my remarks with most extraordinary *empressement*, for which I was quite at a loss to account. Close to Trincheras are some very celebrated thermal springs, said by Humboldt to be the second hottest in the world. Of course we inquired about them at the posada, but strange to say, the people could not tell us exactly where the springs were. At last, a man who was going to Valencia volunteered to guide us to them, and we set off. After riding a few hundred yards we came to two or three cottages, all the inmates of which issued forth, and went down on their knees to me. I was petrified by this extraordinary procedure, but Juan irreverently bursting into a peal of laughter, called out, "Do you see that? May I be hanged if they don't take you, sir, for the archbishop, who is expected here on his way to consecrate the church at San Felipe! It is your hat with the turban round it, a head-dress they have never seen before, which they take to be part of an archbishop's travelling costume." I now began to understand why the women at the posada had been so deferential, and was not a little dismayed at finding myself figuring as the head of the orthodox church in Venezuela.

Our volunteer guide to the hot springs, soon after we had passed these cottages, bade us alight and follow him into the jungle, which we did; but after struggling through thorns and thick bushes, and wading in muddy pools to no purpose, we had to return to the road, without being able to find the springs, minus parts of our garments, and plus pounds' weight of mud, which no effort could dislodge from our boots. This failure was several times repeated, and it really seemed that, having come thousands of miles to

Trincheras, we should have to quit the spot without seeing what we had heard so much about. At last a man arrived from the neighbouring cottages, and led us down to the place we wanted to see, which is but fifty yards from the road ; but the jungle is so thick, that without a guide no one would be able to discover it ; and it would be well if some mark to show where it is, were set up for the convenience of travellers. The springs are situated in a hollow of about one hundred yards diameter, which has evidently once been the crater of a volcano. Through this hollow flows a rivulet, two feet deep, and never less than eighteen feet wide in the greatest drought. Steam ascends from the surface of the water, the temperature of which, according to Humboldt, is above ninety degrees. In some places it must be very much above that point, for the guide stepped with his bare feet into one part that was so hot as to make him skip out again with surprising agility and a doleful countenance, swearing that he had been scalded by it. The bed of the stream is coarse-grained granite, but there is a good deal of mud. The vegetation grows quite rankly all around this Stygian water, and clusias, mimosas, and arums especially thrive in it. At forty feet from the hot stream is a rivulet of cold water. Altogether it is a very curious place, and worthy of a more lengthened visit than we were able to pay it.

From Trincheras the road continues to ascend through a lovely forest, bright with fruits and flowers. The turns are in places very sharp, overlooking deep ravines. After three miles, we arrived at what is called the Entrada, or " entrance," which is the highest point between Puerto Cabello and Valencia, being probably about eighteen hundred feet above the sea. Half a mile beyond, the jungle ends, and the road enters a beautiful salubrious valley, about twenty miles broad, with grass and trees, as in England, but without jungle. Here we put up some fine coveys of quails. Two miles further on, we came to the village of Nagua Nagua, and, as it was half-past ten, and the sun terribly hot, we were glad to take refuge in the posada. In the room into which they showed us, there were three very rough sofas, whereon we gladly threw ourselves, and were rather astonished, on going away, to find that we were charged for three beds, though we did but lie down for a few hours in the daytime. As for rest, that was out of the question, for the flies covered our faces and hands in countless numbers, and effectually barred sleep. At 1 P.M. we were called to dinner, and sat down with a goodly company of drovers and others, who were doing the journey to Valencia on foot.

As for myself, the smell of the garlic was quite enough, and I retreated, without tasting a morsel, to my sofa. Even there I was not left in peace, for fowls, dogs, and even pigs, kept wandering into the room; and in my sorties to drive out these intruders, I discovered the cause of the immense number of flies. All along the verandah in rear of the apartments, the worthy posadero had hung up in rows joints of meat, some of which were quite black. The odour of these pieces of flesh overpowered even that of the adjoining stable-yard, and brought all the insects of the neighbourhood to the spot. I should have left the place without eating, had not a Creole woman offered me a large sweet-meat made of *membrillo*, or "quince," which I greedily devoured. Our bill was seven dollars, or about two-and-twenty shillings, for the use of the room and the abominable food, which Juan had the courage to masticate, but the very smell of which I could not endure. At 3 P.M. a rumbling coach drove up, and took away the shoemaker's wife who had given me the quince, and her family; and as the road was blocked up for a bull-fight, they had to make a *détour* over such rough ground as to threaten the old vehicle with destruction at every moment. We soon followed, and rode the five miles that remained to Valencia in an hour.

The country was lovely with the richest natural vegetation, and, here and there, coffee estates and sugar plantations. There are so many trees and gardens round Valencia, that the city is almost concealed from view until it is entered. However, long before we reached the streets, we passed bevies of pretty Creole ladies, promenading or sitting in the open air, in front of posadas resembling tea-gardens in England. Among these groups my hat with the turban still continued to create a sensation, and though they were too civilised to take me for an archbishop, the mistakes they made about me, as I afterwards heard, were scarcely less ridiculous. On arriving in Valencia, we made our way to the Gran Plaza, and alighted at a posada called La Belle Alliance, which had no upper story, and no comfortable room of any kind. I was shown into a gloomy apartment without a window, and with one great folding-door. When this door was closed, I was obliged to light a candle, but it was impossible to keep the door shut long, without being stifled. We had to wait several hours before the dinner we had ordered could be got ready, and when it did appear, although our appetites were keen, we could not induce ourselves to touch anything, except some boxes of sardines and a dish of potatoes. On going to bed, I found it impossible to sleep, from the suffocating closeness of my room, and I passed the night in vowing that as soon as morning came, I would cease to be a member of La Belle Alliance.

# CHAPTER VIII.



THE posada of La Belle Alliance, at Valencia, is situated in the centre of the eastern side of the Gran Plaza : a square which is as large as any in London, and which looks larger from the surrounding buildings, except the cathedral, being only one story high. On the left of the posada is an enormous mansion belonging to Señor A., who was once secretary to the Venezuelan Government, and is something of a poet, philosopher, and statesman. The south side of the square is entirely taken up by public offices and the Government House of Carabobo, of which State Valencia is the capital. Business is conducted in true republican style. The council meet in the plainest of rooms, with not one superfluous article of furniture, and the great " unwashed " lean on the window-sills, and stare irreverently at the debaters. " What are they discussing ? " I asked a long lank fellow, one of those who, cigar in mouth, were leaning against the window. " Nothing of any consequence," quoth he, with a grin and an expectoration; " only whether we shall go to war with Russia." Not satisfied with this reply, I made further inquiries, and learned that the matter really in hand was no less than the ratification of the new constitution. Even on such an occasion the assembly seemed to me to be much less animated than a London parish vestry, and certainly not a whit more dignified in appearance—which is saying about as little for its dignity as need be said.

On the west side of the plaza is the house of General Uslar, an old Hanoverian soldier, who served under Wellington in the German Legion, and was one of the duke's orderlies at the battle of Waterloo. When the war was over he entered Bolivar's army, and having been taken prisoner by the Spaniards, was made to work in chains among the labourers employed in making the bridge over the river of Valencia. He had his revenge, however; for, having been exchanged for some Spanish officer, he commanded Bolivar's body-guards at the crowning victory of Carabobo. The northern side of the square is made up of some private houses and the cathedral, beside which passes a long street, which leads northward to a good bridge over the river, the identical bridge at which General Uslar worked. Thence the road passes on to the Lake of Valencia and the valleys of Araguas.

If my room at the posada had had a window—if there had been any privacy and quiet in the place—any food besides pork and sardines—I would not have migrated, for the Gran Plaza at Valencia is really a charming place to live in. It is dry and healthy, and there is always a breeze from one of the long streets which stretch away from the corners of the square to the hills. There are beautiful views, too, of the mountains and lake, not to mention the strings of pretty Creoles who are always passing to and from the cathedral.

But as I had no fancy for undergoing a process of etiolation
in the den without light that had been assigned to me, I
determined to quit the posada forthwith. It happened that
the first person who paid me a visit was a Señor Colon, or
Columbus, a name extremely *apropos* for a voyage of discovery in South America; so I resolved to put myself under
his pilotage, and at once go in quest of a new lodging. I
soon found one: a house belonging to Señor A., above
mentioned, perfectly clean, being only just finished, and
with an upper story commanding an enchanting view
of the lake.

It was Sunday morning when I entered my new abode.
A very pretty Indian girl, about fourteen years of age, with
bare feet, and such feet!—Cinderella's were clubs in comparison—came and arranged the few articles of furniture
that a friend had sent for my room. My hammock from the
Rio Negro, which, with its gay flowers of feather-work, was
of itself a sight worth seeing, was suspended by Juan so judiciously, that as I lay I could descry the lake glittering some
nine miles off, beyond innumerable plantations which stretch
all the way from the city to its shores. I thought myself
fortunate in having such a view; but there were other good
things in store for me. On going to the windows looking
into the street, I beheld two lovely Creoles, beautifully
dressed, coming home from mass, enter the house opposite
mine, and afterwards take their seats at the window on the
ground-floor in front of me. From the garden, too, behind
my house, came the musical laughter of girls. Unluckily,
the window in this direction was so high from the floor that
it was only at rare intervals, and with great caution, that I
could reconnoitre, lest I should be caught in the undignified

attitude of a peeper. It was quite evident, however, that there was more than one Eve in the paradise to which I was now translated.

I had resolved to stop a whole month at Valencia, but I thought it as well to commence lionising as soon as possible. Accordingly, in spite of the heat, which was not less than that of a bright day in summer at Naples, I sallied out before noon to inspect the cathedral. This edifice, styled " a very pretty structure " in the guide-book to Venezuela, published in 1822, is, in point of fact, a perfectly plain building of stone, with two towers in front, about eighty feet high. These towers are exactly alike, even to the extent of injury they have suffered during the two centuries which have elapsed since they were built. In attempting to ascend them, I was brought to a stand-still at exactly the same place in each—that is to say, about half way up the second story. There are four stories—the three lower ones square, and that at top octagonal, with a cupola roof. Descending into the body of the church, I found a congregation of, say a hundred women and five or six men, with a mumbling priest and a discordant choir. Several mangy curs had also put in an appearance, and ran about among the rows of worshippers, behaving altogether more like heathens than good Catholics. One pertinacious individual, of a foxy red, ran three times under the nose of a kneeling Spaniard, a tall, lean man, of a grave aspect, whose bile was so moved by the annoyance that he at last bestowed a violent cuff on the offender. This produced a dismal howl, which agreed ill with the music, and caused a slight titter amongst some of the younger women. I came away anything but favourably impressed with the cathedral service.

The bells, however, are worthy of any church, having a noble sound, clear, ringing, deep.

From the cathedral I went to the church of Nuestra Señora de la Candelaria, which is one cuadra to the south of the Gran Plaza, and was built in 1802. It is a very small building, not capable of containing more than three hundred persons, and I found it crammed from end to end. As usual, there were at least twenty women to one man, many of them very beautiful women, and one astonishingly so. I passed next to the Franciscan monastery, where there is a neat chapel, which was nearly empty at the time of my visit.

There is no dust at Valencia, and water-carts are never needed. Nature does the business of watering the streets gratis. I had a specimen of her performance in this line on my return from visiting the churches. The sun was shining brightly when I entered the Franciscan monastery, and I stopped there only a few minutes; but on my coming out the scene was changed. In a minute or two, with scarcely any warning, clouds came drifting over the hills; there was a sound of very subdued thunder, a sharp shower for about a quarter of an hour, and out came the sun again. This process happens daily, sometimes twice a day, in this delightful climate, where the temperature never varies more than four degrees of Fahrenheit—from 78° to 82°. In this respect Valencia resembles, but excels, Singapore. Yet, the sun being vertical, it is not safe to be exposed to its rays between 10 A.M. and 4 P.M. One day Don Manuel M., a native of the country, paid me a visit, with his face literally flayed. "It's all from riding about in the sun," said he; "so you, who are a stranger, must not attempt it. A young American, who came to Valencia last year, thought to harden himself, and was continually in the sun; but he died mad, just after he had told us that he had got the better of the climate."

The people of Valencia (except the posaderos, or inn-keepers, who seem by some strange monopoly of evil qualities to be in general ugly, dirty, and avaricious) are the handsomest, kindest, most hospitable race imaginable. I am bound to speak well of them, for I never received more kindness anywhere. Among other attentions, I had a continual succession of fresh horses sent me to ride. I took my first gallop that Sunday evening on a handsome grey, not unlike an Arab. I rode five or six miles on the way to the lake, and coming home saw a wild animal of the leopard or tiger-cat species. Leopards are extremely numerous all over Venezuela, and the puma, or American lion, is not uncommon near Valencia. I saw one that was killed in the garden of General Uslar's country-house, which was about five feet long.

Next day, August the 15th, a European, who had been long in the country, came to take me to a bull-fight at Nagua, a village five miles west of Valencia. I was rather surprised, and not much gratified, at the appearance of the vehicle which was to convey us to the spectacle. It was a common cart of the coarsest description; yet in that identical cart the President of the Republic, at the conclusion of the last war, made his triumphant entry into Valencia. Our driver, a rough fellow three parts tipsy, drove us at a furious pace over stones, holes, and furrows in the road, so that conversation could be carried on only by jerks. On arriving at Nagua, we found there was to be no corrida, as the bulls were not forthcoming; but *en revanche*, abundant entertainment was provided, in the shape of gaming, swearing, and tippling, to say nothing of a little stabbing and not a little debauchery. But a bull-fight had been intended, for about two hundred and fifty yards of the principal street was palisaded at either end, and in the space between, sundry caballeros were galloping up and down, and showing what they would have done had there been any bulls to encounter.

The houses on each side of the street were full of roisterers. We entered one of them, and were introduced to a general: a very handsome, powerfully built man, standing about five feet eleven: with large bright eyes, a hooked nose, and a pink and olive complexion. Among the company were ten or a dozen men, whose thews and stature would have recommended them to the Blues. One of these, a negro, was at least six feet three inches high, and looked like a man who would have been a dangerous antagonist to King or Mace. On being introduced to the company, we drank tumblers of bitter ale in a very solemn manner with every individual near us: a ceremony which completely relieved me of any inclination to touch more liquid for the rest of the day. A short, thickset personage, who was evidently the orator of the assembly, now put himself to the fore, and addressed a string of sententious remarks to me, of so prosaic a nature as to depress my spirits far below the point above which they had been elevated by the ale. He spoke at great length in praise of his government, and of his countrymen, something after this fashion: "In what country but this, after a war of unprecedented character, which rolled its destructive course during five long revolving years, would you, a stranger, be able to move about unarmed, with, doubtless, a considerable sum in your possession, and yet safe, secure, and even unapprehensive?" &c. &c. At the expiration of the harangue, I was forced to pledge the orator in two more tumblers of bitter ale. To escape from this persecution, I made a rush to the gaming-table and pretended to be immensely interested in the play. A handsome bold-looking fellow, who was, they said, an American colonel, but who had probably assumed that character for the nonce, and who seemed to be master of the concern, immediately began to explain the game to me, and assured me that a gentleman, a friend of his, had won a large sum that morning. Hereupon a tall, dirty Yankee-looking individual, with an ominous obliquity of vision, interposed, saying: "Guess you're talking, stranger, of the gentleman that won the seven hundred dollars, and began with nothing. Guess I'll fix you gratis, if you'd like to try his line of play, for I saw how he done it." My new friends soon found their allurements thrown away upon me, so they left me alone; and, indeed, their attention was presently fully occupied. A brawny peasant, who had been playing at the end of the table farthest from me, suddenly started to his feet, and, drawing his machete, made a rush at the colonel, his face distorted and his eyes blazing with rage. His spring was so sudden and so violent, that he overthrew five or six persons, who cursed and belaboured one another on the floor, each imagining that the man next him was the cause of his upset. But long experience had taught the confederate gamesters what to do. One of them, who had evidently been watching the poor losing wretch, clutched hold of his shoulders, and another, seizing his wrist, twisted the machete out of his hand, while the tall colonel himself, rising up and putting one hand into his breast, where he had, no doubt, a revolver or a bowie-knife ready, called out: "What's the matter, friend? Take care." "Curses on you," shouted the peasant; "I have lost all: I will have my revenge!" But by this time he was pulled back by half a dozen strong arms, and in spite of his struggles and threats was soon summarily ejected from the house. These outbreaks are common enough, and often end in stabs, sometimes in loss of life. The South Americans are inveterate gamblers, and a man will pass a whole year in patient saving, and then lose all his earnings in a single night at the gaming-table.

After this we walked through the village, and my free-and-easy friend spoke to every pretty girl he saw. At half-past five I insisted on going home, though I was assured that the fun was only just beginning, and would go on waxing more and more furious until the small hours. Our driver, who was three parts tipsy at starting, was now unmanageably drunk. Seeing a huge trolloping negress, not ill-favoured, but slatternly and shameless, on her way back to Valencia on foot,—looking in her white dress, as the Spanish proverb has it, like a mushroom in cream,—he stopped, and made her get up beside him on the box, and the two together then carried on such a fire of rough jokes with all and singular who came in our way as created quite a sensation. I protested against travelling under the tutelage of this nymph; but the driver was past reasoning with, and I had to put up with the annoyance as far as the out-skirts of Valencia, where, just as I had made up my mind to get down rather than enter the city under such auspices, the sable beauty herself took it into her head to descend, and, kissing to us a hand of the size and colour of an ordinary coal-shovel, struck into a back lane and disappeared. I was horribly scandalized by this adventure, but still more so on overhearing that same evening the barber at a shop nearly opposite my house, who could speak a little English, bawl out to Juan, no doubt with a gesture indicating my whereabout in the upper room: " Hear bad thing of him!" "Ay!" said Juan, delightedly, thrusting his head out of the window, " what's that ? " " Hear he came home from the corrida——" The last words were lost in the rattling of a cart which went by at the moment, but I heard Juan, with an obstreperous peal of laughter, bawl out in reply, " That's a lie!" A low chuckling conversation followed, which was interrupted by a squall of thunder and lightning, during which I fell fast asleep in my easy-chair, and awoke well-punished by the mosquitoes, and with a splitting headache.

Next morning I started with three companions to ride up the Morro : a steep, rocky, semi-isolated hill eight hundred feet high, situated about half a mile to the north-east of the city. A meadow of tall grass skirts the foot of the hill, and over this we trotted very pleasantly; but as soon as we began to ascend the slope on the west, from which quarter alone the Morro is accessible to a man on horseback, we found we were in for a severe struggle. The path was only about a foot broad, and led sometimes between rocks which pinched our legs, and made us go through evolutions worthy of a *cirque*, to save ourselves from being dragged off; sometimes through thickets, whose thorns made sad havoc of our thin clothes. One of the party, who led the way, and was mounted on a mule, got on very

well, but we who had horses could hardly keep them on
their legs. At last we emerged from the thorns and the
narrow path, but only to land on slippery sheets of rock
at a steep incline, which were even more difficult to cross.
However, when we reached the top, the view well repaid
us. The hill had a double summit. On the first peak, a
cross had been erected; then there was a steep ascent; and
an equally steep ascent to the other top, which was covered
with great boulders and brushwood, and seemed to be an
uncommonly likely place for snakes. At our feet, on the
south side of the hill, lay the city of Valencia, in a thickly-
wooded valley three or four miles broad, the city itself
being full of gardens. Between us and the town flowed a
stream, which bears the same name, and is from fifteen to
twenty yards broad, with a general depth of three feet, but
with pools at intervals. This valley, in which Valencia
lies, is formed by two sierras, the S. Diego to the north-
east, and the Guataparo to the south-west, and comes
curving from the mountains of the coast, which I had
crossed from Puerto Cabello, but runs almost due west and
east for the five miles from Nagua to Valencia. The Morro
is, as it were, the boundary-stone of this valley, and stands
where it debouches into one much broader, and running at
right angles to it; that is, from north-east to south. On
turning to the north-east, my eyes were delighted with the
beautiful view of the lake. I could see some of the islands
in it, but its expanse stretched far beyond my vision for
miles and miles into the Golden Valley of Araguas. When
I had done gazing in this direction, my eyes found new
beauties as they travelled eastward and southward over a
park-like country to the famous battle-field of Carabobo.

The soil in the immediate neighbourhood of Valencia, up to the borders of the lake, is, perhaps, the richest in the world. It is said that an iron rod has been passed down uninterruptedly for upwards of sixty feet through this black soil, the quality of which may be judged of from the fact that sugar-cane plantations will here yield twenty successive harvests without requiring a renewal of the plants. This extreme depth and richness will appear less surprising when it is remembered that all this ground was within the last century covered with the waters of the lake, into which many streams discharged themselves; the principal of them, the Pao, being really worthy to be called a river. These streams brought down a rich deposit of slime, which has now been laid bare by the rapid shrinking and diminution of the lake. When it is considered that the annual evaporation at Valencia amounts to one hundred and thirty inches, it will not appear extraordinary that the waters of the lake have rapidly decreased since it first became known to the Spaniards. But other circumstances have within the last one hundred and fifty years immensely accelerated the desiccation of this body of water. About the beginning of the last century the Pao was turned by a planter southward into the river Portuguesa; and thus a most important feeder was cut off from the lake. Subsequently, the woods by which it was everywhere fringed were cut down, to allow of cultivation being extended. The result has been that, while from the time of Oviedo to the close of the eighteenth century the waters retired only a mile and a half, in the last fifty years they have receded nearly five miles from the vicinity of the city. Thus, in 1810, Valencia, we are told, was three miles to the west of the lake; but it is now nearly eight miles from it, for the distance from the nearest part of its shores to the Gran Plaza is exactly eight miles and a quarter, as measured for the railway. Again, whereas Humboldt makes the entire length of the lake over thirty miles, it is now only twenty-three; and to the list of islets given by him seven new ones are to be added, so that the waters must have sunk so much as to lay bare seven places which they covered half a century ago. The rapid evaporation and the exposure of new land do not appear to have affected the climate of Valencia, which is still one of the most salubrious in the world. Immunity from fever the city no doubt owes to its being not only eight miles distant from the lake, but also one hundred and ninety-five feet above it, or thirteen hundred and sixty-four feet above the sea-level, while the lake is about eleven hundred and sixty-nine. However, the old proverb, that "no one ever dies at Valencia," is now so far altered that they say, "no one dies there unless he calls in a physician!"

As I gazed at the city, and reckoned up its advantages of a healthy and beautiful site, a soil unmatched for fertility, a position on one of the great high roads of South American commerce, and near the unrivalled harbour of Puerto Cabello, I could not help asking myself how it was that in three centuries it had made so little progress in wealth, population, and importance. It was in 1555 that Don Alonzo Dias Moreno founded this western capital of Venezuela, and in 1578 it was strong enough to withstand the attack of the Great Carib tribe, who came up in thousands to surprise it. The savages were the tallest and bravest of the Indians, and had fought many battles with Europeans, both in the West Indies and in Venezuela; but they failed in their enterprise against Valencia, and were driven off with immense loss by Garcia Gonzalez. They retreated, as they had come, by boats down the river Guarico, and so into the Orinoco—a proof how easy it would be to establish water-communication between Valencia and Guaiana. From that time to this, Valencia has never suffered from any great calamity. A few years after, Carácas was sacked by Drake, and again in 1679 by the French; and in 1812 it was almost entirely destroyed by the great earthquake, as were Cumaná, Barquisimeto, and other towns. But neither earthquake nor the sword of the enemy has ever devastated Valencia. Even the cruel tyrant, Lope de Aguirre, spared it; and though it changed masters more than once in the war between the patriots and the Spaniards, it suffered injury from neither party. In spite of this, the city has made no progress, there is little or no money circulated in it, and the population has not advanced much beyond the figure of six thousand assigned to it by Humboldt; whereas Carácas has risen with increased strength from its overthrow, and is ten times as populous as Valencia. What, then, I asked myself as I stood gazing from the Morro, is the spell that keeps this city stationary, and how is it that Nature has been so lavish of her gifts in vain? Perhaps the climate is the true key to the paradox. Perhaps the Valencianos will slumber on, and their sleep will not be broken until some more energetic race takes possession of the land, and the snort of the iron horse disturbs the profound repose of the sunny valleys.

Opposite to the Morro, the sierra of Guataparo, which lies south of Valencia, terminates in a round hill. Beyond this a mile or so, is the Mountain of the Caves, so called from a cavern which excited the wonder of Humboldt. I resolved that my next expedition should be to that cavern, so I asked my friend Colon to pilot me. Though a native of Valencia, he had never visited it, and was obliged to look out for a guide. As it is a Creole peculiarity to undertake anything, a guide was soon found, and we started very early, when the first ripples of light began to come above the horizon. There were four of us—Colon, myself, Pedro, the so-called guide, and a man to look after the horses. It struck me as curious that Pedro would give us no distinct account of the place we were to visit. To all my questions he replied with a " tal vez," " perhaps," or " asi asi," " so so ; " with which I was obliged to be content.

After riding about a mile, we came to a cemetery: a veritable Elysée. The most luxuriant grass and flowering shrubs grew round it. On three sides the ground was level, while to the west a gentle slope swelled gradually into the mountains of the Sierra, the ravines of which were thickly wooded. Opposite to us we could see shining streaks in the crest of the mountain, which we took to be the caves we were in search of; the rather as Pedro nodded his head with great gravity when I asked him if that were the place. Resolving to inspect the cemetery, I dismounted, and knocked at the gate, at first gently, but gradually louder and louder, until the echoes answered me. As that was the only answer I got, we then began to walk round the enclosure (which, except in front, was of wood), to see if we could find an entrance. Fortune favoured us unexpectedly. There happened to be a herd of half-wild cattle grazing close to the place, and one of them, taking fright, charged the enclosure, and broke down enough of it to get through.

Hereupon the great gate was suddenly flung open, and the bullock was driven out again by two men, who had been digging a grave, and who would, it seemed, have dug on for ever without caring a straw for our appeals to be admitted. Out came the bullock, charging with his head down, and out rushed the men after him, flinging stones at him as big as one's fist. We stood meekly by, to let this whirlwind pass, and then quietly walked in. Back came the grave-diggers, banged the door, and went on digging their grave without vouchsafing us a word. The first thing we saw on entering was about forty baskets full of skulls and bones. There was a receptacle in the middle of the cemetery, and into it all these remains would be cast, as belonging to those whose families were not rich enough to pay double fees. In Venezuela even the dead must pay for a single bed, and those who cannot, or will not, will be dug up at the end of the year and chucked into an omnium gatherum. I counted about a hundred tombs of mark, some of them bearing the names of the most illustrious families in the republic. Among them was, I remember, one inscribed to the memory of Catalina Cunningham de Oldenburg!

We remounted and rode straight to the mountain. In a few minutes, we got among low jungle, which grew more and more impervious, until we had to alight, and, leaving our horses with the groom, pushed our way through the jungle on foot. This was not very pleasant, but worse things were coming; the bushes were so thick that we could not see where we were stepping; and presently all three of us descended, with a crash, into a precipitous ravine. As soon as I could recover my equilibrium, I shouted in great wrath to the guide, " Is this the way to the cavern?" My temper was not improved when the confounded fellow made his eternal reply, "tal vez," "perhaps." I have no doubt the delectable place we were in was full of snakes, but I caught a glimpse of only one, and that a very small one; small as it was, however, I knew it to be a *coral*, the bite of which proves mortal in an hour or two. The sight of this creature seemed to lend me wings, and in spite of my great riding-boots, I emerged on the other side of the ravine almost as quickly as I had descended. We now got upon a very steep bit, covered with grass, in which lurked innumerable pieces of rock, and over these we stumbled in a way that very soon relieved us of the little breath we had left. Thinking, however, that the caves were straight above us, we struggled frantically on until we got to the height of about a thousand feet, when I called out to Colon that I was completely exhausted and must sit down. "Well," said he, "don't sit down where you are, unless you want to be picked as clean as those bones we saw in the cemetery." At this I looked about me, and saw that the whole place was swarming with ants; and, indeed, close to me lay the skeleton of a large bird, which looked as if it had been prepared for an anatomical museum, so well was it cleared. I had to creep some distance under the scarp of the mountain before I found a place where I could rest my weary limbs. The view was enchanting, but my satisfaction was somewhat marred by the uncomfortable idea that a slip would send me headlong down the side of the hill, which, where I was sitting, was almost perpendicular.

Meantime Pedro the guide had been trying at various points to clamber up the scarped crest of the mountain, to find the cave he had undertaken to show us. "Are you certain that you have brought us to the right place?" "I am certain," said he, with a rueful look, "that the cave *was* here; but where it is now, the blessed Virgin alone knows!" In short, after nearly breaking our necks, we were forced to come to the disagreeable conclusion that our friend Pedro knew nothing at all about the cave, and that the best thing we could do was to return to Valencia and make another attempt under better guidance.

On telling our failure that night to some German friends, G., a fine active young fellow who had been a sailor, undertook to pilot me to the cave next day, though he said he had not been there for years. This time I resolved to take Juan with me; and, with a lively recollection of the dense jungle we had gone through in our late expedition, I made up my mind to carry my revolver, by way of a " caution to snakes."

We started next day, long before the sun was up, and soon got past the cemetery, and turned our horses towards the mountains, but struck along the side of a ravine nearer the town than the ravine we had before visited. Here, the jungle was thinner, and we got on fast, until, finding the ground growing steep and rocky, we dismounted and clambered up about two hundred feet, when we suddenly beheld the cavern yawning above. Its mouth was at least thirty feet in diameter, with a very scarped and slippery entrance, after surmounting which we found ourselves on a sort of platform. This portal of the cave was like a great room, which had, on the right as we entered, a huge window, from which there was a lovely view of the valley up to the lake. To the left of the entrance was another platform, ten feet above that on which we stood, while facing the entrance was a long gallery or tunnel in the rock, very lofty, but narrow, and sloping upward at an angle of thirty degrees. At the end of this gallery, the light appeared, and we could see the festoons of creepers that hung down over the outlet. But in the centre part the gallery was dark. Its dimness and narrowness made it seem of immense length, though probably it did not much exceed a hundred feet.

After resting and smoking our cigars, I told Juan, as he had much the longest reach of the party, to try to mount the second platform, and see what was to be seen. After two or three attempts, in which he bruised his shins considerably, Juan gave up the enterprise, observing that he was too tall to play the monkey, and too heavy to go up a rock, birds'-nesting. G., who was as light and agile as a cat, soon clambered to the top, and reported that there was nothing to see. He then sprang down to us, and, in spite of the slipperiness of the rock, and the depth of the jump, kept his footing. Of course we praised him immensely for his activity; and to give us a new proof of it, he volunteered to explore the tunnel, and tell us what there was on the other side. This, however, was no such easy matter. In the first place, the entrance to it was six feet above our platform, and this rise was absolutely perpendicular, with a hard, smooth surface, and nothing on which to place hand or foot. Then the gallery was very dark within, and the floor of it was horribly rough. Somehow or other, G. managed to get up, but he had no sooner advanced a few yards into the interior than a prodigious number of bats and other night-birds came swooping out, with such a dust and noise as to half blind, suffocate, and deafen, our adventurous pioneer. We could not help laughing loud and long to see him reappear powdered all over like a miller, rubbing his eyes, and swearing energetically in excellent Spanish and German.

"Don't be frightened, señor," said Juan, taking off his hat with mock politeness, but grinning all the time like an ogre; "the birds won't hurt you, and they're not worth killing, or you could shoot as many as you like with our revolvers."

"Caramba!" said G., "whether they are worth shooting or not, I'll have a shot into the gallery before I go in again; for I would rather be shot myself, than smothered with this filth."

Juan handed up a revolver to G., who forthwith discharged several barrels into the tunnel. The explosion brought out a fresh flock of birds, and, until the dust they made had subsided, we could see nothing.

"Come, G.," I said, laughing, "look about for the game. I want a specimen of a vampire to take home. I hope you have killed something."

Hereupon Juan, whose height gave him an advantage over me in reconnoitering, exclaimed,—

"Blest if I can tell what's been killed; but I think the shots have made something alive, for I can see what looks like the stem of a great creeper moving up and down like a live eel in a frying-pan."

"Stem of a great creeper!" shouted G., who had now again entered the tunnel; "by Heavens! it's a snake, and the biggest I ever saw."

With these words, he discharged the remaining barrels of his pistol, and then bolted back to the mouth of the gallery, ready to drop down to us, in case the brute turned in our direction. Luckily it made off the other way. G., who saw it best, declared it was sixteen or eighteen feet long. After this, none of us felt inclined to explore any further, and we unanimously agreed that we had seen all that was worth seeing, and that the place was a very nice place for a picnic—barring the bats and the serpents !

" It's a queer spot," said G., as we descended the steep path to regain our horses, " and some curious things have been done in it. In the last war, a famous robber, named Hernando Maza, lived here, and committed many atrocities before they found out his den. No one thought of looking for him in the cave. At last they sent for bloodhounds and tracked him to it, and then he died there, sword in hand, like a brave man."

" More like a snake in a hole," said Juan, who did not care for romantic histories, and was rather disgusted with the day's proceedings. " I shall be very glad to get back to Valencia, and I don't care if *I* never see no more caves, nor serpents neither, as long as *I* live."

# CHAPTER IX.



I HAD met at Puerto Cabello a young Englishman whose appearance interested me. He was only in his twenty-third year, overflowing with spirits and good nature, and so very handsome that it did one good to look at him. He was six feet and one inch high, perfectly well made, and as for his strength, I have seen him lift four hundred-weight with the greatest ease. His hair was dark brown, and curled naturally; he had a pink and white complexion, a slightly aquiline nose, and dark-blue eyes with black eyelashes. The black, brown, and yellow visages of the Creoles made his face look all the handsomer from the contrast; and when one saw him in company with some of the cadaverous natives, it was impossible to help exclaiming, " What a superb fellow !" But Mr. George Hayward—for that was his name—had a weakness for which personal advantages are a very insufficient compensation. He was extremely extravagant, and, consequently, not very scrupulous in settling his liabilities, and had already spent so much money that his friends had been very glad to get him out to South America as a clerk in a commercial house, with the prospect of becoming a junior partner—in time. When I was introduced to him at Puerto Cabello, finding that he had been at Oxford, and that he was an agreeable companion, I inquired no further into his antecedents, but asked him to pay me a visit at Valencia, when I had got a little settled there. He had been some time on the coast, and spoke Spanish fluently; but he had never visited the interior, and was very glad to accept my invitation. After about a fortnight I wrote to remind him of his promise, and he returned me answer that he would come immediately, and begged me to send a fresh horse to meet him at Nágua, as he should ride the whole distance on the night of the 26th of August, so as to be at my house by sunrise.

The day begins early in South America, and although it wanted a quarter to five when I got out of bed to look out for my visitor, there were already signs that Valencia was wakening up. The bells of the cathedral and of the convents had been at work for a good hour. A group of Indian and mulatto women were coming up the Calle de la Constitucion, in which I was living. They were going to market, and were making such a merry chattering and clattering that you would have fancied a dozen pair of castanets were in motion besides their jaws. Further off, several parties of women were crossing the street into side-lanes which led down to the river, for this was the time when modest people went to bathe. The lazy barber opposite my lodgings, cigar in mouth, was just beginning to open his shutters. Suddenly he stretched out his head, as I did, to see who it was whose approach was being heralded by a loud smacking of whips, and a noise of laughter and swearing that broke all at once upon our ears.

"It's Hayward, of course!" I exclaimed. "But what has he got in front of him? It looks as if he were driving before him a mule with a dead man on it!"

In another minute up came Hayward and his servant, mounted on a couple of horses, driving before them a mule; on which was the baggage; and strapped on the top of it lay the muleteer, a negro, so drunk that even the violent jolting he had gone through had failed to rouse him. Juan undid him in a trice, and pitching him like a log on to some straw that lay in the yard, said, "There let him lie, and if the ants don't sober him before the evening, I'll pay for a first-class surprise ticket—that's all!"

Next, I myself ordered the horses at 4 P.M., and as I was impatient to show off my handsome visitor, and to see what sort of impression he would make on the Creole beauties, I went to him half an hour before that time, and called out, "Come along, Hayward, and make yourself as great a swell as possible. I am going to present you to some of the prettiest girls in Valencia."

"Oh! there are some pretty girls, then?" said he, looking up from a book he was reading. "I was afraid, from the specimens I saw as I rode up the street, that all the Valencianas were of the colour of the King of Dahomey's body-guard." To this comparison I objected.

The Calle de la Constitucion is one of the central streets that run from the Gran Plaza at Valencia, as straight as a die, on and on, till the houses begin to be interpolated with gardens and orchards, and at last cease altogether, and one finds oneself in the green valley which bounds Valencia to the east. At the opposite or south-western angle of the plaza there is another long straight street, which runs on till it merges in the road to Nágua. The houses in each of these streets near the square are large and fashionable, and they grow smaller and smaller as one approaches the outskirts of the town. It was not, however, the houses that interested us; for, indeed, nothing can be uglier or less attractive than the outside of a Venezuelan house, with its low one-story-high façade of plain brick. But at this hour every window was open, and in every window sat the ladies of the house, some lovely, all more or less good looking, for the plain and antiquated keep in the background on these occasions. "I always wonder," said I to Hayward, "what becomes of the men at this time of day at Valencia. It may be true, as I have heard said, that there are five women in the place to one man; but still, what becomes of that one? He is nowhere to be seen. Whether it is that the men are riding, or walking, or congregating to smoke, I know not; but whatever the reason, the fact remains that the women are left all alone, and can indulge in any amount of flirtation they like. Now, mark me; the white Creoles live at this end of the street, near the Plaza; lower down we shall come to the trigueñas, or ' brunettes ; ' and beyond these we shall find mulattas and mestizas, and we shall finish up with some beauties of a downright black, who are not so much to be despised as you would imagine. Now mind, I am not going, like a Yankee pedlar, to keep my best wares to the last, in the hope of fixing you with a Number Two or Three article. I mean to show you one of the prettiest girls in Valencia straight off at once. You see the large house on the right hand, with the two little maidens seated at the first window? They are the younger sisters. We will ride up and speak to them, and Erminia will be sure to show herself at the next window, with her second sister, Camila, who is almost as handsome as Erminia herself."

With these words I was turning my horse towards the window I had pointed out, when a boy, about ten years old, a brother of the girls, suddenly jumped on to the window-sill, and sat down between them without a particle of clothes on.

I was not much surprised, for it is one of the peculiarities of Valencia that the boys, even of the best families, think nothing of stripping themselves and running about in *puris naturalibus*, so that I had often seen a naked urchin leaning out of a window between elegantly dressed women. But, somehow or other, I did not like to choose exactly that moment for introducing my friend, so we rode by, and as we passed, Erminia came to the window, bowed, and smiled. She was just eighteen, a little above the middle height, but looked taller, from her perfect symmetry; a cloud of shining black ringlets fell on her ivory shoulders. Her face was oval, her complexion fair, a little too colourless, perhaps, but, in revenge, her lips were red and pouting, and disclosed, when she smiled, teeth of such dazzling whiteness that they seemed to flash like gems; but the most attractive feature of her face was her immense black eyes, fringed with long silky eyelashes.

"I have seen enough," exclaimed Hayward; "I don't want to go a step beyond that house. I don't believe there is such another beauty here or anywhere. If I can but win that girl, I am content."

"On my word," I said, "that's very well for a beginning; but I came out to show you the lionesses, so I must finish my undertaking. Turn your eyes to that next house on the right. Don Fernando, the proprietor, has ten children, and the three eldest girls, grand, queen-like beauties, are already married. The fourth daughter, Olympia, the handsomest of all, sits there, as you see. She is magnificent; not so very much shorter than you are yourself, and modelled like a statue. But what is the use of looking?—she is engaged; so come along, I see Felipa Hernandez in that small house on the left. She is a dark brunette, but she is very accomplished, sings charmingly, and is the best dancer in Valencia. She also teases most agreeably."

So saying, I presented Hayward to the señorita at the window, and being forthwith invited to enter the house, we spent half an hour in chatting and smoking cigarettes. We then mounted, and after talking at one or two other windows, finished our ride by a gallop outside the town. On our return, though it was nearly dark, I introduced Hayward to Erminia, who seemed more than usually shy. A few compliments passed, and we rode home to dinner.

As we sat talking after our meal, I was amused with Hayward's indirect attempts to find out all he could about Erminia, and punished him by giving the most laconic answers possible; but seeing that at last he was getting quite vexed, I told him all I knew about her.

" Her father," I said, " is a man of good family, who has always sympathised with the oligarchical party; consequently his estates, which are large, have been laid waste, and now bring in very little. Erminia's mother is dead. She was the eldest of three daughters, and inherited her father's estate, which has now passed to Erminia, who has, by-the-bye, a step-mother in her mother's third sister. By this second marriage there are several children, while Erminia has no full brother or sister. It is an odd thing that Erminia does not marry, for last year she was acknowledged to be the beauty of Valencia, and she has an estate which, if properly cultivated, would bring in six thousand dollars per annum. I believe the fact to be that her mother's second sister, who is in a convent, and is a most bigoted religieuse, wishes Erminia to take the veil and bestow her property on the convent. I am told this good lady has been the means of breaking off more than one engagement into which Erminia had entered, and it is not unlikely that she will be equally successful in putting an end to any future love affair that her niece may have."

Hayward made no reply to this speech, but flung the end of his cigar rather viciously out of the window, and, by way of changing the conversation, asked if Valencia was not famous for its lace manufactory, and where the best specimens could be procured. "To-morrow," I said, "you shall see the place where the finest things are made. It is at the principal ladies' school. I have been there once already, under the guidance of a Spanish gentleman, who will be very glad to accompany us to-morrow. We can also, while we are out, pay a visit to the house of the celebrated General Paez, which I myself have not yet seen. The walls are covered with paintings of his victories.*  To-morrow, at 11, we will start."

---

* Round the walls of the court-yard of the house are delineated the most signal victories gained by Paez over the Spaniards. The following are the battles depicted :—

Batalla de la Mata de la Miel, 16 de Febréro, 1816.

Accion de Yagual, 8 de Octúbre, 1816.

Combate de Guyabal, 18 de Diciembre, 1816.

Batalla de Las Mucuritas, 30 de Enero, 1817.

Toma de San Fernando de Apure, 7 de Mayo, 1818.

Accordingly, next day after breakfast we hoisted umbrellas with white covers as a protection against the vertical sun, and crossing the Gran Plaza, found ourselves, after passing a cuadra to the west of it, at the girls' school. A number of the younger pupils were playing in the verandah, which

Accion de Queseras del Medio, 3 de April, 1819.
Batalla de Carabobo, 24 de Junio, 1821.
Accion de la Sabana de la Guardia, 11 de Agosto, 1822.
Asalto de Puerto Cabello en la noche del 7 de Noviembre, 1823.

At Mata de la Miel between the streams Corosito and Guaritico, on the right bank of the Apure, and in the province of that name, about 10 miles to the east of Guasdualito, Paez with a small force attacked Colonel de Francisco Lopez, Governor of Barinas, who had two guns and 1600 men. Of the Spaniards, 400 were slain and an equal number made prisoners, while Paez, lost but 15 killed and had 22 wounded.

At Yagual, also in Apure, a few miles to the south-west of Achagnas, Paez, with some levies hastily collected, again defeated Lopez, who had 1700 horse-men and 400 foot soldiers.

The combat of Guyabal was a victory which only Llaneros, like Paez, could have achieved. He passed the Apure river with 200 horsemen by swimming, and attacked the Spanish leader, Lieut.-Col. Don Salvador Gorrin, who had 1000 cavalry and infantry, and 500 led horses. Paez put the cavalry to flight and carried off the 500 horses, but failed to break the square formed by the infantry.

At Las Mucuritas, a few miles to the W. by N. of Achaguas, Paez with 1100 lancers encountered the Spaniards under La Torre and Calzada, who had 4000 veteran soldiers of all arms and among them 1700 cavalry. Here Paez charged with a part of his men and made a feigned retreat, drawing the enemy's cavalry into an ambush, where they all fell except the European hussars. Paez then set fire to the grass and so obliged the Spanish infantry to retreat, during which movement he repeatedly charged them, and at last drove them into a dense wood. Speaking of this battle, Morillo wrote :— " Fourteen consecutive charges upon my wearied battalions convinced me that those men were not a small gang of cowards, as had been represented to me."

The taking of S. Fernando was preceded by an extraordinary exploit of Paez who, with 50 Lancers, swam to the Spanish gun-boats, boarded and captured them.

After such deeds of valour it is sad, but only characteristic of Republicans, to record that the pictures of these victories have been all defaced by the Liberal Party, while the portrait of Paez himself, their once idolized hero, is utterly destroyed by musket shots.

encircled the inner court. There was a little whispering amongst them, but no noise or embarrassment; and one came forward very politely and asked us to walk into the drawing-room. Here we found the schoolmistress, a lady about forty years of age, who was still good-looking, and who, from her quiet, self-possessed manner, seemed to be well fitted to rule in such an establishment. She said she had fifty pupils, and that the elder girls assisted her in teaching the younger, and that was all the aid she had in managing the school. We were shown pieces of French cambric, from which a number of threads had been drawn out, so that they looked to me like the skeletons of pocket-handkerchiefs. We were then shown how the interstices thus made were filled up with needlework, representing fruits, flowers, and other devices. Rosa, a girl of sixteen, produced a *mouchoir* she was finishing, which was declared to be a miracle of art, and worked at it in our presence. The stitches were so wonderfully fine that our eyes ached in attempting to follow the movements of her needle, but the schoolmistress declared that Rosa never made a false stitch. Hayward seemed very eager to possess this handkerchief, and asked the price, and when it could be got ready. He was told it would be finished in two days, and was valued at fifty dollars. On this, rather to my surprise, he produced the money. I, too, made a few purchases, and then took leave, not without a feeling of regret that so many docile, clever girls should have such scanty means of instruction.

We now walked on to the house of General Paez. I was rather annoyed by Hayward's declining to go in. I entered alone, and found I had plunged into the most talkative family I had ever encountered. In spite of the compliments of my host and hostess, who praised my Spanish, and seemed as if they were wishful to talk on for ever, I managed to effect my retreat, and got back to my house thoroughly tired. On entering, I was rather surprised to find that Hayward was not there, and still more so that he did not return till it was time to ride. When he came in, it struck me that something wrong had happened, for his manner was changed, and, instead of his usual good-humoured smile, he had a depressed and moody look. I told him that there was to be a party that night at Señora Ribera's, and that we really must show ourselves, so as to get an invitation. "Besides," I said, "Antonia Ribera is now quite the reigning beauty. I have not yet seen her, but I am told she has dethroned Erminia; and of course you would not like to leave Valencia without seeing her." Finding I was bent on it, Hayward consented to call. "What is the matter with the fellow?" thought I. "Is he going to have an illness, or has he got into some scrape this afternoon, while he was out by himself? I begin to wish I had not asked him to pay me a visit."

The Señora Ribera was a widow, with three daughters and one son. She had been a great belle, and, though her charms had long since faded, she had still the coquettish ways of a spoiled beauty. Her children were all handsome, but Antonia was said to be the most beautiful woman in Venezuela. The number of suitors she had refused was endless, and a report had gone about that she did not want to marry any one but a foreigner. Some think there is no better cure for a fit of the spleen than a hard gallop, and Hayward seemed to be of that opinion; for I no sooner turned off the high road on to the lake, but he started at a furious pace along a narrow winding path that led across country. In vain I shouted to him to keep a look-out ahead, and to rein in a little. He did not hear me, or would not attend, and the result was just what I expected. At a place where the path twisted a good deal amongst thick bushes, we plumped suddenly on an old fellow riding a stumpy little mule, and, in a moment, Hayward and he came together like two knights in a tournament. Down went the mule, and rolled over and over with the Creole among the bushes, while Hayward's horse made a carambole off the thicket on the other side, and so nearly dismounted Hayward that he lost both his stirrups, and, had he not been a good rider, he would certainly have measured his length on the ground. As it was, he kept his seat, and went on for several hundred yards before he could stop his horse. I pulled up directly, and dismounting, went to lift up the fallen rider and catch his mule. The brute made a vicious kick at me, and I fared little better with his master. He was not much hurt, but so enraged that, if his machete had not tumbled out of his sheath when he fell, he would most likely have given me a taste of it. As it was, he struck at my proffered arm, and sputtered out a string of curses, winding up with one which was quite new to me.

"May you die of the fever," said he; "and may your wife go into a convent!"

By this time Hayward, too, had pulled up, and was coming back to join me. His humour was not much improved by the accident, and I was glad to get back to Valencia. We dressed and went to the Señora Ribera's party, arriving very early. Presently, when all the guests had assembled, the door opened, and in came a young lady,

who, I saw at a glance, from her extraordinary beauty, must
be Antonia. She was very unlike the other Creole ladies I
had seen. Her dress and manner were rather those of an
aristocratic English beauty than of a Creole. Her eyes
were dark blue, her hair a rich brown, her nose Grecian,
her eyebrows arched. Only her lips were fuller than is
usual with English women. Her figure was slender and
graceful, and her step so elastic that she seemed to glide
rather than walk into the room.

"Caballero," she asked me, without the slightest prepara-
tion, "are you married?"

"Upon my word," thought I, "this is too bad." I
looked about for a moment, and saw that all eyes were
directed to me. I could not say I was not married, and I
did not like to own that I was; so, hoping the answer would
be imputed to my imperfect knowledge of Spanish, I replied,
"Algunas veces"—"sometimes."

People tittered, and Antonia smiled, and gave me a look
which seemed to say, "I understand your dilemma."

She then said, "I want to hear about England. I have
always wished to go there."

We entered into a long conversation; and the more I
listened to that singular girl, the more I wondered. She
talked like a bookworm, like a politician, like a diplomatist,
like a savant, but so little like a señorita of eighteen years
of age, that at times I almost forgot I was speaking to a girl.
After a time I remembered that I had brought Hayward on
purpose to introduce him to Antonia. So, making an
excuse, I got up to look for him. To my annoyance, he
was nowhere to be seen, and on asking Madame Ribera
about him, she said he had gone away, not feeling well.

I now began to be really apprehensive about Hayward. His behaviour seemed so odd, that I felt sure there was something wrong. However, I could not have left immediately without exciting remarks, so I sat down and talked to a German lady I knew. She began to tell me about the Riberas. "You see Lucia, the elder sister of Antonia?" she said; "would not you believe her to be the gentlest creature in the world? Well, she is anything but what she seems. I suppose you have heard all about her marriage?"

"Not a word," I said.

"Well, then, I will tell you. Lucia had a cousin about her own age, who was as rich as he was ugly. He fell in love with her, and her mother was determined she should have him. You know girls are not allowed to choose husbands for themselves here. If Lopez had been her uncle instead of her cousin, she would have had to marry him all the same, for the sake of his money. She held out a long time. At last, Madame Ribera, and Lucia's brother, and her male relatives met, and fixed everything; and, in spite of her remonstrances, the marriage took place, and Lucia was carried off by Lopez to his country-house, which he had fitted up with new and elegant furniture. But when he had got her there, he could do nothing with her. She behaved like a maniac. She broke the mirrors, and cut to pieces all the beautiful curtains; and the end of it was, that he was obliged to send for her mother, and she was taken home, and insisted on calling herself Lucia Ribera, and would never acknowledge her husband at all. As for poor Lopez, he was so chagrined that he fell ill and died, and now she has been a year a widow; and report says she is to marry Diego Garcia, who has no money, and a worse temper than she has herself; and it is likely that he will revenge Lopez and punish her as she deserves."

I asked about Antonia, but my German friend declared herself quite puzzled about her, and would only say, " She is an enigma."

As soon as I could get an opportunity, I slipped away and went home. Hayward was not there, and did not come in till I was asleep. When I got up next day, I felt so vexed with him that I determined to leave him to his own devices, and to get rid of him as soon as I could. He talked very little at breakfast, and looked gloomy, but brightened up when a small parcel was brought in to him, containing the handkerchief he had bought at the school. Soon after this he went out, saying he should dine with a friend he had met the other day, who had also invited him to go to his villa, on the borders of the lake. After he had gone out, I could not help saying to my servant Juan that I was afraid there was something the matter with my visitor.

" The matter! yes, sir," said Juan, in a very oracular voice. " It's downright certain there is. If ever I see a man whose place was booked for a passage over Jordan, as my old mother used to call it, it is Mr. Hayward. And then to see him at that house,"—here Juan jerked his head in the direction of Erminia's residence,—" a-going on with that gall——" Juan did not finish his sentence, but stalked off, leaving the rest to my imagination.

The following morning Hayward took leave of me, and went to the house of his Spanish friend, which was about twelve miles off. When he had left, as I felt curious to know what had been going on, I resolved to call on Erminia, and see how affairs stood in that quarter. I was surprised

to find the shutters half closed.  I entered the hall, nevertheless, which in most Venezuelan houses leads to the quad-
rangle round which the rooms are built, and knocked at the
inner door.  It was opened by one of the younger girls, who
had evidently been crying.  "What is the matter?"  I
asked.  "I hope no one is ill."

"Papa is ill," she said; "but you may come in.  Mamma
or Erminia will speak to you."

So saying, she showed me into the drawing-room, and
went to tell them, and I had to wait so long, that I began
to think I had been indiscreet in calling.  At last Erminia
came, with the same little sister who had let me in.

"Papa is very ill," said Erminia; "we have been up all
night with him."

She looked so pale and ill as she said this, that I could
not help thinking she was more in need of being nursed herself than able to attend to others.  After expressing my
regret, and inquiring about the illness of Señor L., I said,
"My English friend, Mr. Hayward, has left me.  I suppose
you did not see him before he started?"

Erminia's pale face flushed, and she said with a sort of
reluctance, "We saw him last evening.  He called; that is,
he was passing by the window, and he stopped to bid me—
mamma, I mean—good-bye."

Just then, the Señora L. herself entered the room, and
Erminia went to take her place by the bedside of the invalid,
so I had no further opportunity of speaking to her that day.

The illness of Señor L. continued without improvement
all the time I remained at Valencia.  I went daily over to
inquire for him, and always saw Erminia, but never alone,
except for half a minute on one occasion.  I then said, "I

want to talk to you about my English friend." Her face flushed, as it had done before when I mentioned his name, and she said, hurriedly, "We shall never be able to speak about that. I am never alone; I am siempre acompañada."

Meantime, I could not help being struck with the love and devotion with which Señor L. was nursed by his family. His daughters, who, when I first came, had every day been seated, radiant with smiles and beautifully dressed, at the windows, now never left the sick-room. I had the pleasure of seeing, in this instance, that the Creole ladies, who to a superficial observer might appear bent only on coquetry, are in reality not to be surpassed in that affection which binds families together. I had before admired Erminia for her beauty: I now esteemed and respected her for her devotion to her father.

One evening, a few days before the date I had fixed upon for leaving Valencia, and about a fortnight after Hayward had left, I was sitting alone, smoking, when some one on horseback came clattering up to my door, and stopped. Presently Juan entered with a letter. With some difficulty I made out that Hayward was very ill, and that Don Pedro Raynal, at whose house he was stopping, earnestly begged me to come over at once and see him. I immediately ordered my horse, and set out on the twelve miles' ride to Don Pedro's house. My surprise was great when, on reaching the villa (which we did about midnight), I discovered by the light which was brought to show me up the steps, that my companion was the very same old Creole who had been so rudely dismounted by Hayward, and who turned out to be one of Don Pedro's servants.

"I hope the Señor Inglis is better," said I, as I sprang up the steps.

Don Pedro shook his head. "You have arrived too late: he is dead."

"Good Heavens!" I exclaimed; "is it possible? What was his illness?"

"He died, Señor, of yellow fever."

After writing to Hayward's friends to tell them of the melancholy termination of his visit to Valencia, I went to sleep; but passed an unquiet night, disturbed by horrid dreams, and was right glad when morning broke and allowed of my return to the city. Two days afterwards I left Valencia, having seen the beautiful Erminia only once more, and then but for a few minutes.

I have since heard, with but little surprise, that her aunt's wish has been gratified, and that she has entered a convent.

# CHAPTER X.



ONE of my first objects on arriving at Valencia was to
expedite the long-desired interview with General Falcon,
the President of the Republic. In my simplicity, I imagined
that my wishes in this respect would now be easily gratified,
and I was not a little surprised when the announcement of
my intention was received everywhere with shrugs. On inquiry, I was told that the president seldom came even to
Valencia; and that if I was bent on seeing him, I should
have to go to Coro or Maracaibo. The distance of these
places was great, but their inaccessibility was greater. "Besides," said my informant, opening his eyes, wider and wider,
as he thought of the difficulties, "Coro is so confoundedly
unhealthy, and you will be sure to die of fever, or to be
eaten by wild beasts in the forest, before you get there.
There are no roads, and no places to put up at, and there is
hardly a misery existing that you will not have to encounter.
Here, just look at the map. You must go back to Puerto
Cabello. That is one of the worst places in the world for
yellow fever, and they have got it there just now. Then,
from Puerto Cabello to the Yaracui and Aroa rivers, you will

o

have to cross a burning waste, in which there is not a single shrub ten feet high to keep off the sun. After that, you will get into the jungles of Coro, through which it is hardly possible to push your way—a regular hot-bed of fever, and swarming with tigers, as they call the jaguars and panthers here. As for the road to Maracaibo, it is a thousand times worse; but I shall say nothing about it, for I am sure you will never get so far."

I could not help smiling at my friend's vehemence, but I did not feel at all deterred, until he further assured me that on arriving at Coro I should very likely find that the president had gone to some other remote region, whither it would be impossible for me to follow him. I then began to feel somewhat as an envoy would, who, on arriving in London, accredited to the Court of St. James, should be told that the queen never came to town, and that he must go to the Orkney Islands, to be presented, with the chance of a further expedition to Cork or Jersey. Not, indeed that any journey by rail or steamboat can compare with one in a country where no such facilities exist, and where, generally speaking, there is—

"Neither horse meat, nor man's meat, nor place to lie down."

After pondering over the matter a good deal, I came to that well-known conclusion—the usual refuge of weak minds—that I would be guided by circumstances. To a man who has serious business on hand, the chase of a Jack o'Lanthorn is not a pleasant pastime, even though the said Jack should be a president and a "grand mariscal." However, I had undertaken the pursuit; and, at last, after being thrown out several times, destiny ordained that I should obtain the interview; but it must be confessed that I owed this, not to the fact that I had come so many miles for the express purpose of seeing the great man, nor to the repeated messages I had sent to him by couriers, but to the breaking out of disturbances in the central and eastern provinces of the republic. As soon as the distant meshes of the political web began to vibrate, the master spinner made his appearance from the recesses of Coro, and the reports of his erratic movements, now to Maracaibo, now to San Felipe, now to Barquisimeto, ceased.

It was a bright hot forenoon in the first week of September when, as I was lazily swinging in my hammock in the Calle de Constitucion at Valencia, the unusual sound of martial music reached my ear. Starting up, I hurried to the Gran Plaza, and was in time to see the Venezuelan army enter. Shades of Brion and Bolivar! what an army it was! I have seen troops of all nations, civilised and uncivilised, from China to Peru, but never any like those. Some of the officers, indeed, were tall and well-made; but the men were the strangest figures—lean old scarecrows and starveling boys not five feet high, the greater number half naked, with huge strips of raw beef twisted round their hats or hanging from their belts. Their skins seemed to have been baked black with exposure to the sun, and their arms and accoutrements were of the most wretched description. Yet they were not contemptible—far from it—but rather weird, repulsive—a sight to make one shudder. My first thought on seeing them was, " What could want, miasma, exposure, or fatigue do to harm these animated skeletons? Could anything make them blacker, grimmer, more fleshless, more miserable? But in this very wretchedness consists their strength; for European soldiers could not exist where these men would thrive."

It was near 1 P.M. before the last of these skeleton bands filed into the great square. I counted them as well as I could, and made out that there were about three thousand men, with eight standards, each standard marking a battalion. They lined the square, and then dispersed to their quarters. They vanished like an army of spectres, and it must be owned, with as little noise. I went about the city a good deal that evening, but I saw but very few of the goblin host that filled the Gran Plaza at noon, and disturbance there was none. This fact made an impression on my mind, and next morning, as I was pulling on my jack-boots preparatory to a long ride to meet General Falcon, I said to my servant, "Quiet fellows those, Juan! Last night I saw only one man drunk out of the three thousand!" "Oh yes, sir, quiet enough, specially when they are going to shoot at you from behind a tree," replied Juan, who had evidently no very exalted opinion of the goblins. "Oh, then they do shoot people sometimes!" I rejoined, in a tone intended to excite Juan's rather irritable mood to the uttermost. "Shoot, sir? I b'lieve you!" he exclaimed, with a snort. "Why, when this gang marched into Carácas, they were very near shooting a lady—Madame R.—because her little boy had a red riband in his cap. You know, red's the colour of the aristocratical party, the same as these chaps call the Godos and Epilepticos, the 'Goths' and 'Epileptics.' Well, sir, there were above a hundred muskets pointed at the balcony where Madame R. was. 'Down with the oligarchs!' 'Down with the red!' they kept shouting; but they weren't a-going to frighten her, I promise you. 'Stead of that, she clapped her hand on her son's cap to keep it on, and called out to them, ' Viva the red !  You *canaille*, he shall wear it!' And then in another moment, not the boy only, but herself too, and every one in that balcony, would have been dyed red in their own blood; but General Guzman Blanco spurred his horse in front, and said that they should shoot him first before they should harm a woman and a child."

By this time I had got on my boots, and had lighted my cigar; so I descended to the street to mount ; for the governor of the province had sent me a message that he should start at 6 A.M., with all the notables of Valencia, to meet the president, and hoped I would ride with him.  I had sent to borrow a horse, and I found a remarkable animal awaiting me.  He was young, full of fire, and very handsome—all but his colour, which was almost that of slate, with white eyes. Altogether he was a good specimen of the Venezuelan horse, a capital charger in miniature, and not more than fourteen hands and a half high.  Punctuality is not one of the Venezuelan virtues, as I found on this occasion.  Although I had been warned that the governor would start exactly at six, I had to wait at least half an hour ; and, as my horse was extremely fresh and fidgety, it was rather fatiguing.  At last we started in a cavalcade of some twenty or thirty horsemen, and, seeing a Spanish friend among them with whom I was rather intimate, I fell into discourse with him about the Venezuelan troops I had seen the day before, and their character.  My friend said they were much better soldiers than they looked. He had no great opinion of their humanity, and not only confirmed Juan's story of Madame R. and her child, but told me several anecdotes not at all suggestive of Venezuelan love of fair play.  Amongst other things, he said that when the party now in power made their triumphal entry into Carácas, one of their officers insulted an officer of the oligarchists. A duel was fought on the spot, in sight of an excited crowd of soldiers and others; and when the democrat was run through the body, the bystanders discharged a whole volley at the conqueror, who fell pierced with twenty bullets. I then asked him his opinion of the president. "Falcon," said he, "deserves a bright page in history for his moderation. Of all the men who have governed Venezuela, Falcon is by far the most humane. Bolivar, as you know, was guilty of many sanguinary acts. On the 14th, 15th, and 16th of February, 1814, he had almost as many persons shot as Robespierre sent to the guillotine. Some of them were aged men of fourscore years, who could not walk, so had to be carried to the place of execution in chairs. The other great revolutionary leaders have been sanguinary, too, and even those associated with Falcon, as Sotillo, are no exception to the rule; but Falcon himself is a shining example of clemency and courage combined. Nor can it be denied that in his case clemency has proved the best policy. I will give you an example. In 1861 he fought a drawn battle with Paez near Carácas. Prisoners were taken on both sides. Falcon treated his well, and, after a few days, sent an officer into Carácas with a flag of truce, and invited an exchange. Paez, it is said, sent for the prisoners he had made, and ordered them to be shot—a command which was immediately carried into execution; then turning to the officer who had come from Falcon, he bade him depart and report what he had seen to his general. Shortly after that officer had returned to his own camp, General Falcon rode up to the place where his prisoners were, and calling out one of them, a Mr. Sutherland, put a paper into his hands; it was the account of the execution at Carácas. Sutherland read the report, handed it back to Falcon, and said, 'Well, general, of course I know our fate is settled. Allow me, however, to thank you for the very kind way in which we have been treated ever since we have been in your hands.' General Falcon bowed, and replied, 'In an hour you will receive notice of my decision.' With these words the general rode away, and Mr. Sutherland and his fellow-prisoners prepared for instant death. In rather less than an hour one of Falcon's aides-de-camp rode up, and brought a sealed paper, which he delivered into Mr. Sutherland's hands, after causing the other prisoners to be brought out. They were brave men; but it is not to be doubted that the pulse of some of them beat fast in that awful moment of suspense, remembering, as they must have done, that even the small boon of a soldier's death was not always granted in some of the barbarous executions of the preceding wars. What was their astonishment, then, when Sutherland read aloud these words: ' General Falcon is unable to retaliate for one barbarity by the perpetration of another. The prisoners taken by him in the late action are free on their parole not to bear arms against him in the present war. And, further, as many of them have great distances to travel to reach their homes, they will each be provided with a sum of money sufficient for the journey!'

"You may be sure that there was a shout of 'Viva Falcon!' on this announcement. But what is more, Sutherland—who had been a steady opponent of Falcon till then—was so touched by his magnanimity, that he hastened to his native place, Maracaibo, and raised the whole province in favour of his benefactor. This mission had an important effect in deciding the issue of the struggle, and from that day to this Maracaibo has continued faithful to Falcon under the guidance of Sutherland, who was elected president of the province."

By the time this anecdote and some others were told, we had got well on our way to Tocuyo, which is about twelve miles distant from Valencia. We were fast approaching the western range of mountains which stretches from Valencia towards Apure, and as we advanced the beauty of the scenery increased. At the same time very threatening clouds were gathering in front of us, and, not wishing to get a soaking, I gave my horse the spur, and soon left every one of my companions behind, and reached the posada of Tocuyo at full gallop. It was well I did so, for a few minutes after I arrived the rain descended in a thunder-plump, which would have drenched me to the skin in an instant. In the midst of this deluge my Valencian friends arrived, and a few minutes afterwards a large body of horsemen made their appearance from the opposite direction, issuing from a gorge in the mountains. Here-upon some fifty tatterdemalion soldiers, who were ensconced in the sheds near the posada, were hastily called out, and presented arms, as a powerfully built man, with a great slouching sombrero, rode up at the head of the horsemen we had seen coming from the mountains.

"So this is Falcon," I said to myself, as the caballero with the slouched hat alighted. He is a man of the Con-rade type, not more than five feet nine inches in height; but his broad shoulders, great swelling chest, and powerful limbs show that he would be a formidable antagonist to encounter. His face is not strictly handsome, perhaps, but more than good-looking. Black hair and moustache, a clear olive complexion, and regular features, do not of themselves imply anything specially attractive; but the expression of Falcon's fine dark eyes is singularly pleasing. Without aiming at a pun, I might say that they are the eyes of a dove rather than of a falcon. Their too great softness is, however, corrected by the firmness and decision of his mouth; and, to sum up, one may say that Falcon's physiognomy announces him to be manly, courageous, and most humane.

While the president was exchanging recognitions with the crowd around him, my friend Don Fernando whispered to me: "There's the man who may truly say, 'Le gouvernement c'est moi,' for he it is who keeps the present party in power, or rather preserves Venezuela from downright anarchy. You know, congress has decreed to him the title of 'Grand Mariscal' of the republic, just as Bolivar was styled the 'Liberator,' and Paez the 'Illustrious Citizen.' Well! Bolivar perished in exile, and almost in want of the necessaries of life. Paez has long been a fugitive. It remains to be seen what will be the fate of the Grand Mariscal."

After the president had greeted his friends, and had been told who I was, he stepped up to me very affably, and inquired if I spoke Spanish. Some of those officious people who are always to be found hovering about a great man, like Falcon, anticipated my answer for me, and exclaimed that I spoke a little; "But," added they, "you, general, can speak to him in French." "No," said Falcon, "I have been too long in the mountains; I cannot speak

French now." Rather amused at this disclaimer, for the Venezuelans had been boasting to me of their president's knowledge of the language of diplomacy, I said that I hoped to make myself intelligible in Spanish. We then conversed for some time, when, on some one mentioning the disturbances which the president had come from Coro to quell, and calling them a revolution, Falcon turned to him and said, in a very loud and decided tone, "There will be no revolution! The interests at stake are too great to admit of change. Were these troubles to continue now, the coffee and cotton crops would be lost. I have every reason to hope, on the contrary, that the English commis-sioner will carry good news to his country."

Just at this moment important despatches were brought in, and the president retired with some of the chief officers to another room to discuss them. I remained, and the apartment where I was grew more and more crowded, as fresh people arrived from the estates in the neighbourhood. Many came in uniforms, not unbecoming, though rather bizarre. I was introduced to a number of persons, and amongst them to a Mr. A., who asked me what part of England I came from. I said, "From London;" where-upon he exclaimed, "Then I dare say you know my family, for they, too, reside in that town." I thought he was joking; but, seeing he looked quite grave, I drew him out a little, and found he had no idea that London was larger than Carácas. As I felt quite sure that he would think me a Munchausen if I told him that the English capital con-tained three times as many persons as all Venezuela, I maintained a discreet silence on that head. I could, how-ever, hardly keep my countenance when he wrote down his name on paper, and added a memorandum that his family lived in London, and I was to find them out and send him the particulars. Presently one of the company informed me that A.'s father was a serjeant, and rose to be a major in Venezuela, where this son was born.

Meantime, a general of cavalry had been preparing lunch, of which I was glad to partake; and when it was over, and we had betaken ourselves to cigars, an officer came and requested me to go to the president. I found Falcon quite alone, swinging, in his hammock; but on seeing me he sprang up, and made me sit on a bed, while he sat in a chair. I said I had been anxious to see him, in order to learn from his own mouth his sentiments regarding the loan. He replied that, from the communications he had received from General Guzman Blanco, he had no doubt that all would be satisfactorily settled. I dwelt on the importance of a scrupulous adherence to the conditions, and of the government's maintaining its character for good faith. He assented. I then said that I had visited the richest districts in Venezuela, and was quite convinced of the enormous productiveness of the soil; but there were two things wanting, *brazos y dinero*—"labour and capital." "It appears to me," I continued, "that the Venezuelan government have the means of becoming rich, and of paying off all the debt of the country." "Ah!" said he, "how so, pray?" "By selling," I replied, "a great tract of country to some European company who would send out large bodies of emigrants." He asked me if that proposition came from the English government or from private individuals; and on my telling him, from the latter, he declared that he was most favourable to such an enterprise.

"There is," he said, "a tract of country between Maracaibo and Carácas, two hundred leagues long and fifty broad, admirably adapted for cultivation, which might be sold to emigrants." After this we spoke of indifferent subjects, and principally of the chase. He told me he had just killed two large panthers and a puma in the forests of Coro. The puma took refuge in an immense tree, the foliage of which was so thick as almost to conceal it, so that he had had great difficulty in shooting it. Finding that I was fond of sport, he expressed his regret that I had not come to Coro, which, indeed, was entirely his own fault, as he had not invited me. His lunch was now brought in, and he asked me to join him at the table; but I said I had already disposed of my appetite, and I took leave, pleased with his manners, but not too deeply convinced of his sincerity.

On coming out, I was shown the diamond star he wears (which is worth, perhaps, two hundred guineas), and his Order of Liberator. "So much," thought I, "for equality, republican simplicity, and all that sort of thing."

# CHAPTER XI.



BEFORE leaving Valencia, that pearl of Venezuelan cities, I resolved to visit the field of Carabobo. The name is little familiar to English ears, yet here Bolivar fought the battle which decided the liberties of the South American republics, and here British valour achieved a victory which deserves to be recorded in bronze and marble.

The battle-field is situated about eighteen miles south of Valencia. As I foresaw it would take some time to examine the ground, besides four or five hours at least for going and returning, and as a tropical sun in August is not agreeable, I determined to drive rather than ride. "What easier!" exclaims my European sightseer. "Order a carriage, and the thing is done." Carriages, however, being non-existent in Valencia, I was obliged to make search for a roofed vehicle of any description. At last my choice was a nondescript, strongly suggestive of the disasters which shortly took place. Into this I mounted with two or three friends about 6 o'clock on the morning of the 29th of August, 186—. We all lit our cigars, gave the word to old Domingo, the driver, and started with a shock that broke one of the traces, and enabled us to get well to the end of our first cigars before even leaving the door.

To say that the streets of Valencia are not adapted for wheels, is to speak in the mild form which the Greeks thought advisable in discoursing of anything preternaturally bad. On this principle, one might say that these streets are paved, just as the Furies were called Eumenides. I had made up my mind to be "jolted to a jelly," but another form of martyrdom was reserved for us. At the first turning there was a chasm, into which we were all but precipitated. At last we cleared it with a portentous jerk, but the triumph cost us so many fractures as to entail a delay which lasted through another cigar. We then got on pretty well through a street and a square, but only to find ourselves in a narrow lane, shelving laterally at an angle of thirty degrees, and full of holes and heaps of broken flagstones. Here we smashed the pole, and the driver went off for a fresh one, and did not return till we had consumed a third cigar.

The sun was already hot before we were off the stones. The road lay in the centre of a valley, which extended north and south as far as eye could reach, and was bounded to east and west by richly wooded ranges of mountains some twenty miles apart, and from one thousand to five thousand feet high. This valley cuts at right angles the far narrower one in which Valencia is built. At its northern extremity is the Lake of Tacarigua, and thence to the field of Carabobo, a distance of twenty-eight miles, there is a succession of plantations, many of them uncultivated since the late war it is true, and now unprofitable to the owners, but not the less luxuriant and pleasing to the eye. Were it not for snakes, insects, a vertical sun, fever, and a too rank crop of liberty, this valley would be Paradise. So we thought, and, falling into a benignant humour, we exchanged civil words with all we met. These were, for the most part, ragged fellows driving mules or asses, or mounted on miserable jades of horses, yet the usual salutation by which they were addressed was, " Good morning, general ;" " Good morning, doctor."

It was past 10 o'clock A.M. before we got to a posada, which is the sole habitation near the Pass of Carabobo. The landlord was only a colonel, but in respectability of appearance he quite thrust several of the generals we had met into the shade. We asked what we could have for breakfast. Like innkeepers everywhere, he informed us we could have whatever we liked; but on our proceeding to name various desirable dishes, it turned out that none of them were forthcoming, and, in the end, we subsided into a meek acquiescence in eggs, which were, in truth, the only thing procurable. For this ovation, and two bottles of wretched wine of the country, the worthy colonel charged us only twenty-one shillings; so that we did not pay much more than a shilling an egg.

Having feasted after this fashion, we sallied forth to reconnoitre the locality in which the battle was fought. It was now past eleven, and the fierce sun made us appreciate what the combatants must have suffered from the heat on the memorable 24th of June, 1821. The English, at least, must have been sorely tried; but as for the natives, we had just then a proof of their power of endurance, for a party of travellers went by, among whom were several girls, who had but a light mantilla drawn over their heads.

And here, after the fashion of the immortal Cervantes, it might be allowable to request the reader to suspend his interest in the battle of Carabobo, and turn aside to a lengthy episode in which could be related an adventure or love passage that befell one or other of our party then, or on some other occasion, or which it might be adroitly pretended that one of the said travellers, *à propos* or otherwise, recounted to us. But, to say truth, the sun was making havoc of my patience, and, so far from seeking matter for an episode, I besought the cicerone of the party to tell us all he knew, and to be brief about it, as I wanted to get under shelter again as fast as possible. The old general, however, had his own way of telling the story, and was not to be thwarted.

"You will never understand the battle," said he, "nor appreciate it, unless you know something of the previous position of affairs. You see we had all been a good deal dissatisfied with Bolivar, who, on the 25th of November, 1820—the year before the battle,—had concluded a truce for six months with the Spanish Captain-General Morillo. This took place at Santa Anna, a village in the province of Trujillo, to the west of Carabobo. It is true we got rid of Morillo by the armistice, for he went off to Spain as soon as it was signed; but he left La Torre, as good a general as himself, at the head of affairs, to say nothing of the famous Morales, who commanded the plundering hordes first raised by Yañes and Bores. And if Morales had not been a traitor, and La Torre had kept his forces together, and prevented Bolivar from joining Paez, who was posted with three thousand men at Achaguas, in Apure, to the south of this, the issue of the struggle might have been different. But Bolivar was right. He no doubt knew that Morales was disaffected because he had not been appointed to succeed Morillo ; and the armistice gave the patriots time to mature their plans and to seize some important places, such as Maracaibo, under cover of the truce."

"All which," I observed, "redounds, of course, very much to the honour of the said patriots, and is a proof of their love of truth and respect for treaties."

" I cannot but think," continued the general, disregarding my interruption, "that, with eleven thousand choice troops such as the Spanish general had—veterans trained in combats with the French, and in many a stubborn fight in this country—the victory might have been wrested from Bolivar, in spite of the thousand British bayonets that supported him. But La Torre, who lay at San Carlos, about one hundred miles to the south of this, was induced by Morales to send some of his best regiments to defend Carácas against Bermudez, one of our ablest officers, who marched on the capital from the east. Bermudez, after many successes, was utterly routed at last under the very walls of Carácas. But, in the mean time, Bolivar had joined Paez, and was advancing against La Torre with equal, if not superior forces. His army, when united, was formed in three divisions. The first, commanded by General Paez, was composed of the Cazadores Britanicos, or ' British light infantry,' which was the remnant of the British Legion, or Elsam's Brigade, and now numbered not more than eight hundred men ; one hundred of the Irish Legion attached to the English corps ; the native regiment, called the Bravos of Apure, eight hundred strong; and one thousand four hundred native cavalry; in all, three thousand one hundred men.

"The second division, commanded by General Cedeño, consisted of the regiments called Tiradores, Boyacá, and Vargas, and of the squadron Sagrado, commanded by Arismendi; in all, about one thousand eight hundred men.

"The third division was commanded by Colonel Ambrosio Plaza, and consisted of the Rifles, a regiment officered by Englishmen, with Colonel Sandes at their head, and the three regiments Granaderos, Vencedor, and Anzuátegui, with one regiment of cavalry, under Colonel Rondon. The numerical strength of this division was, in round numbers, two thousand five hundred men.

"The soldiers of this force were the best in the country. As for our battalion, a great general, it is said, pronounced that Englishmen fight best when well fed; but Carabobo proved that British courage does not depend on food alone. In fact, we English were desperate men, and much in the same mind as that of our forefathers at Agincourt. We were without pay, wretchedly clothed, and with no rations but half-starved bull-beef, which we ate without salt, that being a luxury unknown in Apure. Life itself had become hateful to us, and the men had been driven by distress, not long before, into open mutiny. The zeal of the officers alone extinguished the revolt, but many of us were wounded in quelling it. Order was at last re-established, but after scenes which I do not care to recall. Add to this, our commanding officer, Brigadier Blosset, was killed in a duel with Power of the Irish Legion, and this latter corps, all but the hundred men who were attached to us, mutinied, and, after sacking Rio-Hacha, had been shipped off to Jamaica.

"Well, to go back a little before coming to the battle. I must tell you that it was the 10th of May when our brigade, under Paez, removed from Achaguas, a strong position on the frontier, between the provinces of Apure and Carabobo. We had been stationed there to watch Morales, who lay at Calabozo, about a hundred miles to the north of us. As soon as he retreated on San Carlos we advanced, and passed through the city of Guanares to San Carlos, from which the enemy retired. There we were joined by Bolivar, with Cedeño's division, and halted for four days to prepare for the battle which was now imminent. At this time an order was issued that we English should act independently of the regiment Apure with which we had hitherto been brigaded. This turned out to be a most fortunate occurrence.

" We had now been marching for more than a month, and had suffered terrible privations. We had had to cross the river Apurito, and numerous streams swarming with alligators and, with that still more dangerous pest, the Caribe fish, which, though no bigger than a perch, has teeth which will penetrate a coat of steel, and which, at the scent of blood, comes in such myriads, that the largest animals, and even the alligator itself, are eaten up by them in a moment. Some of our men had thus perished in the water, and others had died on the road from the bites of snakes and venomous reptiles. A far greater number fell victims to want, fatigue, and disease. In short, our sufferings had been such, that there was not a man of us that was not resolved to die, fighting, rather than retrace his steps.

" The opportunity was at hand. On the 21st of June we

marched from San Carlos, due east about a dozen miles, to the village of Tinaco. Our cavalry in advance, under Colonel Silva, had a sharp brush with the enemy, and brought in some prisoners. The same evening the third division, under Plaza, joined us, and brought up our strength to something over seven thousand. Next day, the 22nd, we pushed on due north, through the village of Tinnaquillo, and halted on the road to Carabobo, the enemy's outposts falling back before us, but not without sharp skirmishes.

"We had now the River Chirgua to cross, and then the defile of Buenavista. This is a formidable position, and if it had been occupied by the enemy we could hardly have forced it. Luckily they had resolved on the Pass of Carabobo as the spot where they would give battle, so our advance on the 23rd was unopposed. That day, about noon, our vedettes came in sight of the Spanish army, and Bolivar halted us and formed us as if for the attack. Paez commanded the right, Cedeño the left, and Plaza had the centre. Bolivar then rode from left to right, and addressed each corps as he passed. His words were received by the others with silence, but when he had done speaking to the English, we gave him three hurrahs that were heard a mile off.

"It was only 1 P.M., but Bolivar determined to postpone the attack till next day, either to give us a rest, or because he thought it would be lucky to fight on San Juan's Day. We halted, therefore, and passed the night where we were. And such a night it was! The rain fell in torrents, and those of us who had been at Waterloo reminded one another that it was just the same there, and took it for a good omen.

" The weather in South America is always in extremes, and the sky was cloudless on the 24th, when we stood to arms. Our officers were grouped together, talking over the chances of the day, when an order came from Bolivar for the right division, in which we English were, to advance. It was now that the Creole regiment that was with us, called the Bravos of Apure, claimed to lead the attack. As a matter of right it belonged to us, we being the older corps; but considering the pretension on the part of natives of the country very natural, we conceded the point, and on they went. Our regiment followed, and then came the cavalry, under Paez, led by a squadron called Los Colorados, composed of two hundred supernumerary officers. The morning dawned bright and clear as we moved along the heights opposite the Spaniards. All was calm and still, as if Nature would contrast her peacefulness with the horrid uproar with which man was about to break in.

" We were moving to the west, to get round the enemy's right flank if possible. We could see his guns and some of his infantry; but much of his force was hid by the trees and the broken ground, and a strong body of his men were posted in a ravine, where they were altogether out of sight. But it is time to point out to you his position. This road, by which we came from Valencia, is the high road to San Carlos. The ravine which you see there behind us, coming down to it from the south-east, is called the Manzana, or 'Apple' ravine. Behind that were the head-quarters of the Spanish army. Their forces were in position in front of the ravine, and on the right of the San Carlos road, their guns being on their left flank—on that hill which you see completely commands the road. Had we advanced along the road, our column would have been swept by their guns, and exposed to an attack in flank, which must have proved fatal. On the other hand, the ground on the extreme right of the Spaniards you see there," said the old general, pointing to a series of steep hills and deep ravines, "was quite impracticable for regular troops and cavalry. Bolivar, therefore, after reconnoitring the enemy for about a quarter of an hour, sent us orders to attack by the ravine, which, as you see, lies between the hill on which were the Spanish guns and their infantry. This ravine we found so deep, that, on descending into it, we lost sight of the regiment of Apure. Meantime, the enemy's guns had opened fire, and men began to fall in both the battalions of our brigade.

"The crest of the ravine was lined by the enemy. The ground on which they stood slopes gently towards the mouth of the ravine, which is so steep, that I, for one, was glad to catch hold of the tail of a horse ridden by an officer in front of me. Directly the Apure regiment had got out of the ravine and were beginning to deploy, the enemy's cavalry threatened to charge it, but, either through treachery or cowardice, retreated before our cavalry, who now passed us on our right and charged, but were in their turn driven back by the fire of the Spanish line. Meantime, the Apure Bravos had formed line and advanced to within pistol-shot of the Spaniards, when they received a murderous volley from more than three thousand muskets, besides the fire of the Spanish artillery. Overwhelmed with this storm of shot, the regiment wavered, then broke and fled back in headlong disorder upon us. It was a critical moment, but we managed to keep our ground till the fugitives had got through our ranks back into the ravine, and then

our grenadier company, gallantly led by Captain Minchin,
formed up and poured in their fire upon the Spaniards, who
were only a few paces from them. Checked by this volley,
the enemy fell back a little, while our men, pressing eagerly
on, formed and delivered their fire company after company.

"Receding before our fire and the long line of British
bayonets, the Spaniards fell back to the position from which
they had rushed in pursuit of the Apure Bravos. But from
thence they kept up a tremendous fire upon us, which we
returned as rapidly as we could. As they outnumbered us
in the ratio of four to one, and were strongly posted and
supported by guns, we waited for reinforcements before
storming their position. Not a man, however, came to help
us, and after an hour passed in this manner our ammuni-
tion failed. It then really seemed to be all over with us.
We tried, as best we could, to make signals of our distress ;
the men kept springing their ramrods, and Colonel Thomas
Ferrier, our commanding officer, apprised General Paez of
our situation, and called on him to get up a supply of car-
tridges. It came at last; but by this time many of our
officers and men had fallen, and among them Colonel Ferrier. You may imagine we were not long in breaking open
the ammunition-boxes; the men numbered off anew, and
after delivering a couple of volleys we prepared to charge.
At this moment our cavalry, passing as before by our right
flank, charged, with General Paez at their head. They
went on very gallantly, but soon came galloping back and
passed again to our rear, without having done any execution
on the enemy, while they had themselves suffered considerably.

"Why Bolivar at this time, and indeed during the period

since our first advance, sent us no support, I have never
been able to guess.  Whatever the motive, it is certain that
the second and third divisions of the army quietly looked
on while we were being slaughtered, and made no attempt
to help us.  The curses of our men were loud and deep, but
seeing that they must not expect any help, they made up
their minds to carry the enemy's position, or perish.  Out
of nine hundred men we had not above six hundred left.
Captain Scott, who succeeded Colonel Ferrier, had fallen,
and had bequeathed the command to Captain Minchin; and
the colours of the regiment had seven times changed hands,
and had been literally cut to ribands, and dyed with the
blood of the gallant fellows who carried them.  But, in spite
of all this, the word was passed to charge with the bayonet,
and on we went, keeping our line as steadily as on a parade
day, and with a loud hurrah we were upon them.  I must
do the Spaniards the justice to say they met us gallantly,
and the struggle was for a brief time fierce, and the event
doubtful.  But the bayonet in the hands of British soldiers, more especially such a forlorn hope as we were, is
irresistible.  The Spaniards, five to one as they were,
began to give ground, and at last broke and fled.

"Then it was, and not till then, that two companies of
the Tiradores came up to our help, and our cavalry, hitherto
of little use, fiercely pursued the retreating enemy.  What
followed I tell you on hearsay from others, for I was now
stretched on the field with two balls through my body.  I
know, however, that the famous battalion of royalists called
'Valence,' under their gallant colonel Don Tomas Garcia,
covered the enemy's retreat, and was never broken.  Again
and again this noble regiment turned sullenly on its pur-

suers, and successfully repulsed the attacks of the cavalry and infantry of the third division of our army, which now for the first time left their secure position and pursued the Spaniards.

" It was at this period of the battle that General Cedeño, stung by a rebuke from Bolivar, quitted the third division, which he was commanding, and at the head of a small body of followers, charged the regiment 'Valence,' and found, with all his comrades, the honourable death they sought. So fell ' the bravest of the brave of Columbia.' Plaza also, who commanded the second division, was killed, and also Mallao, another famous hero of the patriots. As for our regiment, it had been too severely handled to join in the pursuit with much vigour. Two men out of every three were killed or wounded. Besides Colonel Ferrier, Lieutenant-Colonel Davy, Captain Scott, Lieutenants Church, Houston, Newel, Stanley, and several others, were killed; and Captains Minchin and Smith, Lieutenants Hubble, Matthew, Hand, Talbot, and others, were wounded. The remains of the corps passed before the Liberator with trailed arms at double-quick, and received with a cheer, but without halting, his words, ' Salvadores de mi patria ! '—Saviours of my country.

" On getting across the bridge you see there, the enemy made an effort to retrieve the day, and opened fire with the guns still left to them. Our men then charged, took one of the guns, and got across the bridge, when they had to form square to repel some squadrons of cavalry that attacked them. Our well-directed fire soon broke them, and the rout now became general. The battalion 'Valence ' alone maintained the order of its ranks all the way to Valencia, baffling for eighteen miles the unceasing attacks of our cavalry. Under the walls of Valencia itself it was, for the last time, charged by the rifles and the grenadiers of Bolivar's Guard, mounted on horseback by order of the Liberator. In this final conflict the gallant Spaniards continued unbroken, and were no further molested, but reaching at 10 P.M. the foot of the mountains, they made good their retreat to Puerto Cabello to the number of nine hundred men.

" All the rest of the Spanish army was completely dissolved, and Carácas, the capital, La Guaira, and the other towns still in the hands of the royalists, at once surrendered. In short, the independence of Columbia was achieved by the battle of Carabobo; and that the victory was entirely owing to the English is proved by the fact that they lost six hundred men out of nine hundred, while all the rest of Bolivar's army, amounting to more than six thousand men, lost but two hundred ! "

The old general here concluded his harangue. We then ascended the hill on which the Spanish guns were planted, examined the deep ravine through which the English had passed to the attack, and the slope on which the Spaniards had been drawn up, and returned to Valencia impressed with the belief that the English soldier had never better maintained his reputation than at Carabobo.

# CHAPTER XII.



I RESOLVED, before quitting Valencia, to inspect more closely that broad expanse of beautiful vegetation which surrounds the lake. Two gentlemen, resident in the city of Valencia, one a Spaniard, the other a German, agreed to accompany me on an expedition to the plantations. We fortunately secured a better vehicle than that in which we had gone to Carabobo, and on the 8th of September, at 7 A.M., we started. We drove first due north, over the bridge to the hill called the Morro, and then turned off to the right in the direction of the lake, abandoning the main road, which goes to Maracai and Victoria. For three miles the track was tolerably good, though we saw that rain would turn it into deep mud, as there were neither stones nor gravel to give it consistency, nor ditch nor drain for the water to escape. Traffic, in fact, made the road, and nature keeps it up, after a fashion, by filling the holes with rubbish from the jungle on both sides. Very ugly was this same low jungle, with no flower to beautify it, except a common dog-rose. There was good grass, however, enough for innumerable kine to nibble, but I saw no cattle. After the third mile, we entered a broad belt of luxuriant cultivation. The scenery charmed us; but, *en revanche*, the way grew narrower and the ruts deeper till the cigars were all but jolted out of our mouths. Nathless we so endured, though conversation flagged, as we had to speak with great caution for fear of biting off the ends of our tongues in the fearful bumpings that ensued. After five miles or so of this agony, we arrived at Las Tinájas, "the large-mouthed Jars," a hacienda so-called, belonging to the Señores Mesa. Here we alighted, drank coffee, and saw sugar and rum made on a grand scale.

The first thing that struck me in this tour of inspection was that a vertical sun, the fumes of rum, and the millions of flies, which improve each shining hour by continually perching on the noses of those human beings who come forth to work, are not conducive to persevering labour. There were a good number of men in the factory, but their attitude was for the most part that of repose, and they seemed to have sought out the shadiest nooks possible, at the furthest attainable distance from the cocina and alembique— the boilers and distillery. Even the steam-engine, made at Glasgow, was doing nothing, with its 16-horse power, to re-imburse its master for the 1200 dollars he had laid out on it. The shed in which it stood must have been 300 feet long, and I counted about a hundred enormous vats in it for rum. The tenant told me he paid 450 dollars a month as rent for this cane farm. He had a nice little cottage, in which our breakfast was being prepared. On asking him how he had escaped during the war, he shook his head, and replied that the Federals had killed some of his labourers, had stolen all

his cattle, and had three times forced him to fly into
Valencia. So much for the moderation of patriots!

At 9 A.M. I mounted a horse belonging to the planter, and
rode, with my two companions, to the lake, which we reached
at 10 o'clock, though the distance is only five miles. On
either side the road were coffee estates or cane plantations,
and, beyond them, hills beautifully wooded. This continued
to within a quarter of a mile of the lake, when we entered a
belt of prodigiously tall reeds and grass, excellent cover for
wild boar and tigers, but I did not hear that there were any
such animals there. We got round to the shore opposite to
Valencia, and saw the city gleaming white in the distance.
In front of us was the Culebra, or Snake Island, and beyond
it other islets. The water of the lake is fed by fourteen
small streams, but it is brackish. It contains four kind of
fish—the guarina, which is voracious, the vagra, sardina,
and bava. Calculating by what we know has taken place, as
regards the diminution of the water, since Humboldt's
visit,* it may be expected that the lake will be dried up in
100 years. An immensely fertile soil will be left at the end
of this desiccatory process, and, supposing that the streams,
which at present feed the lake, suffice for irrigation, the productiveness of the Valley of Araguas will be increased. The
fevers, also, now so rife on the margin of the lake, would
probably, in the case mentioned, disappear. On the other
hand, the streams may diminish as the air becomes more
dry, when the prodigious evaporation, which is now going on
from the lake, ceases, and then, notwithanding a black soil
of 90 feet in depth, cultivation would fall off. As for the

* Humboldt says the Lake is ten leagues or 28,800 toises long, and 2·3
leagues or 6500 toises broad.

fevers, they might be prevented by cutting down the stifling jungle of reeds which now borders the water. On the whole, one may regret that the Venezuelans make no attempt to maintain their beautiful lake by bringing back to it the stream of the Pao, which was once its largest feeder, and the course of which was diverted from it to the south at the end of the 17th century.* If only as being the principal ornament of one of the loveliest scenes in the world, the Lake of Tacarigua ought to be preserved. So we thought, as we looked across its breadth to Valencia and summed up the attractions of the view; a glittering expanse of silver water, studded with fairy islets, rich masses of foliage of every hue, a city in the distance, that seemed built of white marble, and hills that gradually swelled into blue mountains.

I know not how long we might have feasted our eyes with the scenery, but the sun had grown so fierce as to make itself felt even under the spreading branches of the rather diminutive trees that grow near the lake. We turned back, therefore, and galloped all the way to Las Tinajas, arriving at 10.30 A.M. We breakfasted, and one of the superintendents, addressing me in tolerable English, asked me if I would hear him read Richard the Third, which he did in a way very creditable to a man who had never had but one or two lessons at wide intervals. We returned to Valencia at 4 P.M., and I agreed with the coachman to hire his vehicle as far as Victoria on my return journey to Carácas, and to start on the 13th.

When the morning of departure arrived, I got up and dressed at 4 o'clock, having agreed with Antonio, the Creole coachman, to start at 5. But it pleased my lord Antonio, in

* Humboldt, vol. iv., p. 149.

the exercise of his republican rights, to be an hour behind
time.  He offered no apology—not he; but, getting down
from the box, seated himself on a large stone, and began to
smoke.  Hereupon Juan, who was not in the sweetest temper
at having been kept waiting, requested him to assist in
bringing down my luggage.  My lord Antonio did not so
much as vouchsafe an articulate reply to this entreaty, but
simply shook his head, and continued to smoke.  Now, had
we not been in a city, but in some lonely spot, my belief is
that Juan would have shaken my lord out of his habiliments
as a reward for this aggravating conduct.  As it was, Juan
had to bring down the things himself, and when he had done
so, my lord Antonio, although he had seen all the luggage
five days before, now remarked that it was too heavy for his
coach, and he could not take it.  At this, Juan fell into such
a transport of fury as no pen, but that of the immortal
Cervantes, could describe.  An interminable wrangle ensued,
carried on in Spanish with such surprising volubility and
*abandon*, that, finding I could not get in a word edgeways, I
went off to present a bouquet to a lady, and did not return
for half an hour, at the end of which period I came back,
expecting to find nothing left of the disputants but the tails
of their cigars.  To my surprise, the hubbub had ceased; and
there was Antonio on the box, ready to start, and Juan and
an ill-favoured individual piling my luggage into a cart.  In
fact, the high contracting parties, Juan and Antonio, had
agreed that I should lead the way with a young German
friend and Juan in the coach, and that my luggage should
follow as best it could in the cart.  I was thus made to pay
the expenses of the late wordy war, and should risk the loss
of my things into the bargain.  So much time had been

lost, however, that I accepted the situation, and on we went.

At 8.30 we reached Las Guias, a neat village four and a half miles from Valencia, and about as far from the lake, and in an hour more we were at Guicara, and at 10 A.M, at San Joaquin, distant respectively eleven and seventeen miles from Valencia, and both of them villages on the northern coast of the lake. Before noon, still travelling in the same direction, we reached the coffee and cotton plantation of the Señores Gascue and Careño. Here we alighted to breakfast. The situation of the house is most picturesque. It abuts on a hill, 200 feet high, densely clothed with shrubs. Beyond this was a belt of wood, and then a line of glorious mountains. Panthers, they said, were numerous in these mountains, and they pointed out a spot where a very large one was known to have his den. He had done a great deal of mischief, but no one was bold enough to attack him in his steep retreat. An aqueduct had been built to the side of the nearest mountain, and along this a fine stream of water was leaping in mid-air, foaming and glittering. It fell close to the mill where the coffee was being husked, and they said it was usual for travellers to take a bathe in it. However, not wishing to get a chill, and, perhaps, fever, I declined the experiment.

Before we went to breakfast another guest arrived, a Don Realte, who, it appeared, was the owner of a neighbouring plantation. He told us that the committee for the enlistment of soldiers was sitting at no great distance, and that a detachment of 160 men had been sent to him to obtain recruits among his labourers. As soon as he heard that the detachment was approaching, he, like a true patriot, sent off every man on his estate, except the lame, the halt, and the blind, to hide in the mountains. The officer in command of the detachment was so enraged at this that he enlisted all these "miserables," but at length, on Realte's threatening to go to Valencia to complain, he released his victims and went away. In the discussion that ensued I heard enough to show that the military service was detested, and that the enlisting parties were often resisted by force. In the combats that ensued loss of life was frequent.

After breakfast, I looked at the books and went over the works. It appeared that the men who laboured on the estate made four, five, and six reals a day, according to their activity. The women get two or three reals. The men were small, but well proportioned; and some of the women were decidedly pretty and even graceful in their figures. I remarked an order that in case of rain out-door work was to be stopped, as exposure to wet brought on fever. The husking-mill was worked by water. It stood in a paved yard, one hundred and fifty feet square, where the coffee berry was being dried.

At 3 P.M. we attempted to start, but, the roads being heavy, the pole snapped, which detained us an hour. At 6 P.M. we arrived at the village of Mariala, twenty-six miles from Valencia. There was a pretty cascade on the left of the village which seemed to have a fall of eighty feet. After this the road passed through very fine potreros, or "grazing-grounds," where we saw a good many horses. We were close to the lake, and the road in some places was covered with water. Two severe actions were fought in this locality in the old wars of Bolivar. At 7 P.M. we reached Maracai, about thirty miles from Valencia, and found an excellent posada, where, to avoid the importunate mosquitos, I turned into a hammock, and, covered with a mosquito net, which I had luckily brought with me, slept profoundly.

We rose on the 14th at 5 A.M., and, having paid ten dollars for coffee and our night's lodging, we started. About two miles from Maracai we passed the foot of Cabrera, on the summit of a lofty hill, which dominates the lake. For the sake of the view it is worth ascending this hill, in spite of the snakes, which are unpleasantly numerous. At 10 A.M. we reached the hacienda of Palmár, a fine coffee plantation belonging to a German, about sixteen miles east of Maracai. The road passed through beautiful scenery and rich cultivation. We were now beyond the eastern extremity of the lake. The small river Aragua, from which the whole valley is called, falls into the lake on this side. On arriving at Palmár a novel difficulty presented itself, in the shape of an aqueduct carried across the road, at such a height as just to catch the top of a carriage. To make things more pleasant the ground below the aqueduct was very muddy, and, indeed, had it not been so, the coach could not possibly have passed. As we were hot, hungry, and in haste, we jumped out into the mud, and leaning with all our weight on the doors of the coach brought it down on the springs, so as to admit of its passing, though a g—r—ating noise showed that it was literally a real scrape we had got into. Juan, who had to stoop considerably to pass under the duct, indulged in various chuckling reflections as to what would have been our fate if we had arrived at night, and I have no doubt would have joyfully risked his own brains for the pleasure of seeing the carriage decapitated.

The proprietor of the estate and his wife, finding I could

speak German, welcomed us most warmly. After a cup of
coffee we walked over the works, and found everything in
the finest order possible. Besides the mill for husking
coffee, there was a cane-mill worked by water. A remarkably handsome girl was serving this mill with canes, and
the planter drew my attention to her with the exclamation,
" Bonita muchácha." " Ein hübsches mädchen ! " I replied,
" but pray tell me are all the labourers here women, for I
don't see half a dozen men about the place ? " " You are
right," said the planter ; " I have as few men as possible,
because, you see, the women work nearly as well, and then
they cannot be taken for soldiers. It is the recruiting that
ruins the plantations."

We did not breakfast till past noon, and I had a delicious
bathe where the water from the aqueduct came tumbling
down five or six feet into a reservoir, deep enough for a
swim. After breakfast mine host played on the piano, and
mine hostess, a very tall and comely young matron, gave me
an account of an agreeable visit they had had some weeks
before. They had been awakened before dawn one day by
an unaccountable noise in the verandah, attended by a
tremendous commotion amongst the live stock of the establishment. At first they thought a panther had come down
from the hills, but what puzzled them was a curious hissing
sound which arose occasionally, but which appeared to be
much too loud to be made by a snake. They waited with
much anxiety until it was light, and then went down-stairs,
monsieur le mari, gun in hand, to reconnoitre. To their
horror they discovered an enormous boa constrictor, curled
round one of the pillars of the verandah, and apparently
determined to hold his own against all comers. In such a

state of things the women labourers were of not much use, but all the men they could muster assembled, and a regular combat took place. On being wounded at the first discharge of the gun the serpent uncoiled himself and charged his assailants, who fled like the wind. They were in hopes that he would make off after his victory, but he returned to the verandah, and it was only after firing repeatedly and after a furious battle with machetes and clubs that the monster was killed. He measured over eighteen feet.

Among other things mine host told me that he had been music mad, and that, while his father was living on the estate, he ran away and joined a company of strolling musicians, who were *en route* for Maracaibo. They issued bills at Valencia for a concert, but, as very few tickets were sold, one of their number, a Pole, proposed that they should give it gratis, and in the open air at the Gran Plaza. This they did, and thousands of people assembled. It was a complete success in all respects, save as to money. They did not receive one real, and after a few more similar performances with similar results, the runaway returned to his father, half starved, and with his musical ardour considerably abated.

At 3·30 P.M. we left the hospitable mansion of our German host and his fair wife, and a little after four o'clock passed a long row of huts, three miles to the east of Palmár, which are called a town, and are dignified with the name of San Mateo. From this point the road became infamously bad; in fact, a mere succession of holes and deep ruts, in passing which we gradually dissipated all the good humour we had been accumulating at Palmár. In vain nature presented us with wood-crowned hills and a perpetual series of the richest plantations in the valley below, the road was really too bad for us to enjoy the scenery. A mile from San Mateo we passed a house on a lofty hill with a cane estate surrounding it. In it Bolivar was born, and from it he went forth to lead the rebellion, in which thousands died, to leave their country poorer, more discontented, and with infinitely less chance of a tranquil future than under the government of Spain. Yet Bolivar was called a patriot! Patriot—how the word is abused; how often it is bestowed on men whom selfish ambition, a love of notoriety, or an unruly spirit, urges to take up arms against a government! Bolivar murdered thousands of prisoners in cold blood, entered Carácas in a triumphal car drawn by beautiful women, and made a general of a notorious coward, whose sister he carried about with him as a mistress. Such is the modern idea of a patriot! Bolivar was a man of blood, and the house in which he lived met with a fate worthy of its owner. It was held by Recaurte against the Spaniards, and when at last they had forced their way into it, he blew it and them, and himself up, *à la* Clerkenwell. The present building is new, and it is to be hoped that the existing race of patriots will let it alone, and blow themselves up where they can do no harm.

The long succession of fine plantations ended at last with a lovely hacienda, which stands at the entrance of Victoria, with the house as usual built on an eminence. I had heard much of the valley of Araguas and of its luxuriant cultivation, but the reality surpassed anticipation. We drove at once to the posada in Victoria, and alighted at 5 P.M. The first man I met was a brother of General Guzman Blanco. I believe he had a very narrow escape of being shot by the Government of Rojas. Times were changed now, and he had come down to choose an estate in the far-famed valley. Let us hope his residence will meet with a better destiny than Bolivar's—*pero quien sabé!* Our dinner consisted of stewed potatoes, among which some diminutive fragment of a fowl lay in ambush. This was washed down with bad beer and worse wine. My German companion walked out to call on a Dane, who had a pretty daughter. The father had been a posadero and his wife was the cocinera. They had soon saved up money enough to open a *magasin de nouveautés*, which, though less remunerative, was considered a step up in the land of equality.

I awoke, or rather, arose, at 5 on the morning of the 15th, having been literally devoured by fleas, stifled with heat, and suffocated with innumerable stenches. Had it not been for my hammock, which placed me above the most stupendous efforts of the vermin that covered the patriotic floor, and left me to fight it out with those who had already effected a lodgment in my clothes, I believe that nothing of me would have been left after that sanguinary encounter. Escaping from the posada as soon as possible, I walked about till it was time to breakfast with the Dane, of whom I had hired mules to carry me to Carácas. The meat was excellent, and I observed that the daughter of the house, who had so skilfully prepared the *cotelettes de mouton*, had reserved the sheep's eyes for a young gentleman who sate at table with us, and who repaid *les yeux doux* with interest. He informed me that he had just returned from the province of Apúre, and that Sotillo, who reigns there after the fashion of Paez, had been enquiring for his share of the loan, and would probably raise disturbances unless a considerable portion were set aside for him. At 3 P.M. my luggage, which had been continually in the rear ever since the *fracas* with Antonio, arrived, and I engaged a boy and two asses to convey it. My German companion had gone back to Valencia, and I settled to start with Juan at dawn next day for Carácas. I dined with the Dane, and rode over the town with him. It contains several thousand inhabitants, and in the hands of the Yankees, or the English, would by this time have probably contained a quarter of a million. The country around it is the richest in the world, but the people are all, more or less, Antonios.

At 4 A.M. on the 16th, thanks to the *pulgas*, I was ready for the saddle. The mules, however, did not come till six o'clock, so that I had abundant time to reflect on the extortionate charges of my posadero, who made me pay twenty-one dollars for the stewed potatoes on the night of the 14th, and the filthy place in which I had twice endeavoured to sleep. The ·Dane had charged me twenty-eight dollars for the mules and the asses, and when I told him of the bill at the posada, his mind was so full of his own account, he kept repeating—twenty-eight dollars—*aber das ist zu stark— das ist abscheulich !* From the expression of his face, however, I judged that so far from sympathising with me he was regretting, on hearing of the preposterous bill at the posada and that I had reluctantly paid it, that he had not charged more himself. In short, I was reminded of the story of some one, who had been robbed at an hotel, and complained to the waiter, saying that he had lost forty sovereigns. On this the waiter's face, instead of evincing regret, dilated with a grin of wild delight, and the wretch, rubbing his hands, exclaimed, " Forty sovereigns ! my ——, what a haul ! "

Leaving Victoria at 6·30, we rode slowly along for two

hours. The valley gradually contracted, the mountains grew higher, and the vegetation became less luxuriant. At 8·30 we passed Consejo, " council-house," a large village, which lay a little to the right. At 9 we got to Las Coquillas, an estate so called, Juan informed me, from a plant which he pointed out resembling the aloe. Two miles on we came to the river Tuy, a clear, very rapid stream, about twenty yards in breadth and two feet deep. A handsome Creole girl forded it just in front of us, displaying with great cruelty *deux jambes parfaitement faites.* There was a mill on the far side, where several men were drinking an early glass under some magnificent trees. I inquired of them the way, and they pointed to a very narrow, rugged, and steep path which ascended the side of a lofty mountain in front of us. Here, then, we bade adieu to the famous valley of Araguas, and began to climb back to Carácas. We had come about ten miles from Victoria, and we had still between fifteen and twenty to go to Los Teques, where we were to halt for the night. Unfortunately, at this moment Juan's knee became so swollen and painful that he declared he could ride no longer. However, after a rest of half an hour,—during which the sturdy little *gamin* with the asses, a boy of not more than twelve years, trudged past us,—I persuaded my giant to make another effort. Up and up we went for more than four thousand feet, until we got to the top of the mountain, the views at every turn being really worthy the pencil of a Claude, especially the one which looked back on the Coquillas and Victoria. But the view which pleased Juan most was that of the small posada of Limon, where we alighted and got his knee rubbed and fomented. I had some eggs and chocolate, for which

I paid twelve reals. At 1·30 p.m. the asses arrived, and at 2 p.m. we went on. Our path lay along the summit of the mountains, the ridge being from thirty to a hundred yards broad at top, while on either side we gazed down four thousand or five thousand feet into valleys, beyond which rose other mountains as tall or taller than those we had surmounted. After riding about a league, the sun, which had been shining brightly, suddenly veiled itself in clouds. A mist, thin at first, but rapidly becoming denser, began to drift over the heights. At the same time we descended some hundred feet and entered a thick forest. I had just time to wrap myself up in my waterproof when down came the rain with that vigour with which it usually descends in the tropics, and the wind swept in fierce gusts along our path. Having endured this for some time, we looked about for shelter, and, seeing a low hut on the side of the road, we made up to it and knocked. The door was opened by a short, but very square-built, woman of middle age and forbidding appearance, who objected strongly to our entering. However, the storm looked even uglier than she did, so we would not take a denial, but went in, and seated ourselves on a rude bench. I asked her how she could live alone in such a wild forest. She said she had had a friend, who had been killed by a snake, but that she was not afraid to stop, though by herself. She added that she should very likely be bitten by a snake too, for serpents of all kinds were most numerous, particularly cascabels (rattlesnakes). There were also tigres (panthers), she said, but she did not fear them so much. It did not occur to me at the time, but I think it very likely that she was a leper, and consequently safe from human savages, and necessarily an outcast.

Before long the storm passed over, and we sallied forth again. The road now began to descend rapidly, and the forest ended, at least on the ridge we were crossing, though the sides of the mountains were crowded with dense jungle. Here and there a coffee plantation showed itself, and I was astonished at the seeming inaccessibility of the places in which this cultivation was carried on. The winding paths which, doubtless, led to them from the valleys were entirely hidden by trees from our sight. We reached Teques before 7 P.M., and the boy with the luggage came in an hour afterwards. We found a posada in the little town, which looked clean, but contained even more fleas than that at Victoria. After writhing in misery for some time, I shouted for the posadero, and told him I was being devoured alive. He went away for a moment, and returned with a vast bottle of gin, which he put down before me, and saying, "*Aqui el remedio*," retired. But not "poppy nor mandragora," nor even gin, could relieve my sufferings, and, spite of my long ride, I hardly closed my eyes all night.

Next morning I went into a sort of coffee-room to get breakfast, and began reading a paper. Presently a man said to me in English, "Guess you'll not get much out of that." I looked up, and said nothing, on which the same individual remarked, interrogatively, " Arrived by last packet ?" I said " No," and was thinking of retreating, when a very gentlemanly man began to talk to me in French, and made himself so agreeable that I entered into a long conversation with him. Moreover, he had some excellent claret, which he pressed upon me, so that I enjoyed my breakfast much. Among other things, he told me that his sister had married an Englishman, an officer in the Hussars. This officer had received two balls in the battle of Toulouse, one in the shoulder and the other in the knee, and was for a long time detained in the town by his wounds. The doctor who attended him was also the doctor who attended the family of my informant, and hence an acquaintance arose. The Frenchman's sister was beautiful, and the Hussar received a third wound, which was beyond the power of doctors to cure. Whenever his departure to England was mentioned he always said, " I shall come back for Zoe." At last the doctor pronounced him able to travel, and he took leave. His last words were, " I shall come back for Zoe." Days and months went on, and months grew into years, and the light of hope faded in the French maiden's beautiful hazel eyes. Many suitors had come for her hand and had gone away disappointed, and the *foi d'Anglais* seemed to be a broken link to all but her to whom it was plighted. At last one of the rejected suitors returned, and Zoe's family pressed her to bestow on him a gracious answer. She yielded at length so far as to promise to give him her answer from her own lips. It was a bright day in June when he came for it. The windows were all open, and a sweet smell of flowers floated into the room. Zoe was seated at a table, with a book before her, but her eyes saw not the pages — she was thinking of one far, far away. The rejected suitor entered, and pleaded well and passionately; but Zoe made no reply — in truth, she heard him not, for her thoughts were far away. Suddenly an electric shock seemed to pass through her frame. She started up, her eyes flashing, and the bright colour rushing to her temples. The Frenchman recoiled in alarm, thinking that madness had seized her brain. A moment afterwards a hasty step was heard coming up the garden path. The door opened, and an excited voice exclaimed, "I have come for Zoe;" but Zoe heard it not—she had fainted in the arms of her long-looked for Hussar.

At 1·30 P.M. on the 17th of September we started in the coach from Los Teques for Carácas. The distance was only eighteen miles, and we did it in a little more than two hours. The road is, in fact, very good, and, were it ever repaired, would be, I need not say, better. It was made in 1850 by a Frenchman, one M. Le Grand. It is a rapid descent the whole way, with some very ugly precipices and sharp turns, but not in the least degree dangerous. The scenery, of course, is tame in comparison of that between Victoria and Teques.

Before leaving Carácas, I gave a dinner to the acting Vice-President of the Republic and to those gentlemen who had shown me attention. Owing to the number of refusals, we had at last to sit down the ominous number of thirteen. There is the same superstition in Venezuela as to that number that there is among us, and consequently there was not a little joking about it. Next morning, very early, Mr. —— came to my rooms, and said, "Have you heard the news?" "What news?" I asked. "General ——, who sate next you at dinner last night, is dead." "Good Heavens!" I replied, really very much shocked; "how singular. The General was the very *man* we were quizzing about the number thirteen." An hour afterwards, all Carácas was talking about the melancholy, sudden death, and I believe not an individual in the whole city would at any price have made one of a party of thirteen that day.

However, just as we had acquired the most solemn belief in the *presagio*, I was scandalised by seeing the General who had been declared defunct walk into my apartment. After some desultory conversation, during which I was endeavouring to control my sense of the wrong he had committed by falsifying a story which had been accepted so generally, he suddenly exclaimed, " Do you know some one has been spreading an absurd story of my death ? " " Indeed," I said, making a vain effort to look *tout effaré*, " and pray how could such an absurd rumour have arisen ? " " 'Egad," he replied, " that's just what puzzles me, except it was the nonsense we were talking last night at dinner, or maybe because General ——, who lives next door, took it into his head to go off suddenly." " Oh, it must have been your neighbour dying," I said, " that did it. No one would have been such a fool as to believe the superstition." " I don't know about that," rejoined the General, taking up his hat ; " people are such fools. But I only wish I could find out the man who first spread the report—by ——, I'd make him swallow it."

I left Carácas on the 3rd of October. On the night of the 2nd I went out to wish some friends good-bye, and in one of my visits had the ill-luck to be bitten in the calf of the leg by a large dog. The bite was extremely painful, but I did not pay much attention to it, and did not even look at it until I arrived at La Guaira. Then, after a hot and dusty drive in the coach from 6 to 9·40 A.M., I took a cold bath with half a bottle of rum in the water, a recipe which I recommend to travellers. Finding my leg smart abominably, I looked and found it much bruised and slightly wounded where the dog had bitten me. Now, in South

America, it is by no means safe to bathe with an open wound in cold water. So, upon the whole, I thought it would be better to send for a doctor. Accordingly, as soon as I had dressed, I called for Juan, and, as no answer was returned, went in search of him. I found him in his room lying on the floor, attacked with fever, and looking as woe-begone as possible. He said he had heard me call, but really felt too ill to get up. I said it did not matter, that I wanted to send some one for a doctor, but I would find some other messenger. "A doctor," said Juan, still with the same dismal countenance; "who wants a doctor?" "I do," I replied. "I have been bitten by a dog, and from the way it rushed out and ran down the street, I have some suspicion it may have been mad. At all events, I should like to show the wound to a doctor, and at the same time he can prescribe for you." "Bitten by a mad dog!" ejaculated Juan, opening wide his half-closed eyes, and half raising himself from the ground, while his countenance lighted up with evident satisfaction. "I'll go myself—no time to be lost—have it cut out and cork-dried." "No, no, Juan," I replied, not particularly pleased at this alacrity; "no need for your going, with fever on you, while the sun is so fierce. And as for the cauterizing, or cork-drying, as you call it, I fancy it won't be at all necessary." With these words I left him, and despatched another servant for the doctor. My announcement, however, had effected a magical change in Juan. In a very short time he made his appearance, and I was quite astounded at his extraordinary recovery. His haggard look was gone, and in its place he wore his usual jaunty smile. In fact, the possibility of my having hydrophobia had acted as a complete tonic. Not that he wished me harm—far from it—but it was part of his idio-syncrasy to find a pleasurable excitement in any coming disaster.

It was lucky for me that the dog that bit me was not mad, for I certainly should not have been saved by the promptitude of the doctor. In half an hour, the servant I had sent returned, and said the doctor was asleep, and his domestic said he could not be awakened on any account. "Did you tell the man I had been bitten by a mad dog?" I asked. "Yes, señor," replied the servant, "I told him, but he said that made no difference. The doctor could not be disturbed if all the people in the town had been bitten by mad dogs." In short, I had to wait five hours, at the end of which time the medico made his appearance. He was a German, of a phlegmatic temperament, and without much ado proceeded to burn a hole in the calf of my leg with something he poured upon it. I inquired if, supposing the dog to have been mad, I might, after that unpleasant operation, consider myself safe. He fell to reckoning the hours that had elapsed since I was bitten, and then, pulling out his watch and looking very oracular, informed me that had I sent to him four hours before I should have been safe, but, as it was, he could only hope the dog was not mad. "But, doctor," I said, "I did send to you five hours ago, and your servant said you were asleep and could not be disturbed." "No; did he?" replied the medico; "how unlucky, and yet one can hardly be angry with the fellow. Do you know I really believe he would let half my patients die, rather than let me over-fatigue myself." With these words, and a hasty bow, the doctor vanished, and I was left to the sympathies of Juan, who was really very attentive, though he could not forbear indulging ever and anon in doleful prognostics, and recounted to me more than once the history of his late master's illness, and how he suffered on board a ship. " You see, sir," said Juan, " he never thought he would die, no more than you do, and that made him the more impatient. It's always the best to make up your mind, you know, sir." " Yes, Juan," said I, " and that is just what I have done. I am sure the dog was not mad, so say no more about it."

However, in spite of the confident way I spoke, I must own to having been very uneasy. My leg became very painful, and the wound grew more and more inflamed. My sufferings were aggravated by the intense heat, and I was unable to take exercise. One day, indeed, I drove out a little way from the town, and paid a visit to some ladies. They asked me why I limped, and I told them the reason. " Oh ! " said they, " we have a dog that bites too; and the other day he almost killed a boy. He bit him in several places, and the people could hardly prevent him from tearing him to pieces. Would you like to see him ? He is as big as a bear nearly, and so savage." Hereupon they sent for " Leon," as the brute was called, and he came, led by a man, who had hold of his chain. He was, in fact, the largest mastiff I have ever seen, and the fair Creoles laughed immoderately as they described how he had shaken the boy.

Such was my last reminiscence of Venezuela. On the 9th of October I embarked in the small steamer that used to ply between La Guaira and St. Thomas. Before my departure I had the satisfaction of knowing that the bills, which had been drawn with my concurrence by the Venezuelan Government to clear the export duties of all claims, had been paid; that the American claim for the Aves Island, and French claims, amounting to one million two hundred thousand francs had been settled; and that the Venezuelans had been once more placed in a position, in which, by good management, they might free themselves from all difficulties.

# CHAPTER XIII.



NOTWITHSTANDING the labours of Humboldt, of Boussingault, of Codazzi, and of some more recent travellers, it is very difficult to form a just estimate of the resources of Venezuela. The ruinous civil wars, which have been carried on for so many years, have kept down the population, and destroyed the agriculture and trade of the country; while epidemics have done their part in devastating the plains of Apure, though still rich in cattle. No census has been taken of late, and the commercial statistics of recent years do not appear to be deserving of implicit confidence. What follows is based on Colonel Codazzi's statements, corrected as far as possible, for the present time, by data obtained partly from the public offices, and partly from private individuals.

Venezuela is the most northern region of South America. It is entirely a tropical country, lying between 1° 15′ and 12° 20′ N. lat., 60° 51′ 45″ and 75° 53′ 45″ W. long., but its climates range from cold too intense for human life to be supported, down to the greatest heat known on the earth's surface. On its extreme west the gigantic ridge of the

Andes running north and south forms its limit, and from this ridge three sierras, or mountain chains, extend with gradually diminishing altitude to the east, until they are lost in the interminable plains of Apure and Guayana, the latter covered with a primeval forest. The highest of these sierras is that which begins in Merida, with peaks fifteen thousand seven hundred and ninety eight feet above the sea. It rapidly decreases in altitude as it passes through the province of Barinas, and is lost in skirting Apure. It is one hundred and sixty five Spanish leagues long and six broad. The sierras to the north of it are separated from the Andes by the Great Lake of Maracaibo, the area of which is six thousand three hundred square miles. The more southern sierra of these two runs parallel to the coast, and is therefore called Costanera. Its highest peaks are the Pico de Nirguata and the Silla, which latter is eight thousand six hundred feet high. The whole sierra is estimated to be sixty leagues long and six broad. The most northern sierra, beginning in Coro, is submerged by the sea till it reaches the island of Tortuga. It is then again submerged and reappears in the island of Margarita. From the Andes, and from the sierras just mentioned, innumerable streams flow down into the plains of Apure and Guayana, and unite into the mighty river Orinoco, which bisects Guayana, and as it passes Ciudad Bolivar pours, even when at its lowest, a flood of two hundred and forty thousand cubic feet of water per second towards the ocean, or as much as the Ganges brings down when highest.[*]

Codazzi divides Venezuela into three different systems or regions. The first is the Alpine region, which joins the

* Codazzi, p. 623.

mountains of Nueva Granada, that is, the Andes, and lies between six thousand feet and fifteen thousand nine hundred feet above the level of the sea. Here are the wastes called páramos or Cold Deserts, where an icy and furious blast chills the blood. During the civil wars whole regiments have perished in attempting to cross these wastes. Yet at the foot of the mountains are immense woods, in which the cacao tree, the theobroma, grows wild. In this region, too, are the sabánas, or plains of Barinas, surrounded by an amphitheatre of hills, which rise in successive stages. At the summit of each stage are table-lands that might be cultivated. There is no population, however, save in the centre. There coffee, potatoes, wheat, barley, and most of the cereals and legumes of the temperate zone are grown. This region contains one thousand seven hundred and fifty-five Spanish square leagues.

The second region begins at the height of one thousand eight hundred and ninety feet above the sea, and is that of the cordilleras, or mountain chains which run parallel to the coast. Between them lie the rich valleys of Valencia, Araguas, and Tui. Here are grown coffee, cacao, maize, cotton, indigo, sugar cane, yuca, and the plantain. The soil is a deep black mould of marvellous fertility. The area of this rich land is one thousand four hundred and fifty four Spanish square leagues.

The third region is that of Parima or Guayana. In shape it resembles an immense convex dish slightly elevated and corrugated by lines of hills, which are sometimes regular, sometimes broken by gigantic rocks, covered with grass, or bare, and in the shape of pyramids, towers, and ruined ramparts. In this region there are five thousand one hundred and four square leagues of virgin forest. There are, besides the vast sabánas of Apure, pastures, of which Don Ramon Paez says :—" They are characterised by a luxuriant growth of various grasses, which, like those of the Portuguesa, preserve a uniform verdure throughout the year. These grasses, some of which are soft and pliable as silk, are most important in the economy of cattle-breeding. The prodigious increase of animals in these plains is mainly owing to the superiority of the pastures over those of the upper regions of the Llanos, from whence the farmer is compelled to migrate with his stock every summer. There are three varieties of grass which, in richness of flavour and nutrition, can hardly be surpassed by any other fodder plants of the temperate zones. In the early part of the rainy season the granadilla, a grass reaching to about four feet in height, with tender succulent blades and panicles of seed, not unlike some varieties of broom-corn, starts with the earliest showers of spring. It grows with great rapidity, and is greedily sought by all ruminants; but being an annual soon disappears. In the alluvial bottom-lands subject to the periodical inundation, two other grasses, no less esteemed for their nutriment, have an uninterrupted growth and luxuriance, which the hottest season cannot blast ; these are the carretera, named from the beautiful prairie-goose that feeds on it ; and the lambedora, so termed on account of its softness."

In the middle of these sabánas, which form part of an immense plain that stretches for a thousand miles to the foot of the Bolivian Andes, rises a central plateau called the Mesa of Guanipe, the height of which above the sea varies from two hundred and ninety to four hundred and sixty-four yards.

Around it are many secondary plateaux, and from all these issue tiny rills of water, which the traveller, when he first observes them shewing themselves from beneath the palm-trees, thinks will soon be absorbed in the soil. Far from being lost, however, they grow and grow till they become streams, and then, uniting, form rivers. In fact, the whole land is full of springs, and the map indicates the course of one thousand and sixty rivers, all navigable, of which seven are of the 1st class, thirty of the 2nd, twenty-two of the 3rd, and nine hundred and sixty-three of the 4th. There are besides many lakes, of which that of Maracaibo is the largest, its circumference, including bays, being two hundred and fourteen Spanish leagues.

The total area of Venezuela is thirty-five thousand nine hundred and fifty-one Spanish square leagues, or four hundred and twenty-nine thousand and thirty-five square miles, or more than that of France, Spain, and Portugal taken together. Though only one-seventh of the extent of the United States, and one-seventh of that of Brazil, it is larger than N. Granada, Ecuador, Bolivia, Chili, or Paraguay. Codazzi divides Venezuela into three zones; the agricultural zone, pasture-land, and forest. The first of these contains eight thousand seven hundred and thirty-seven square leagues, of which five hundred only had been cleared in 1840. There were in 1840 only six hundred thousand and fifty inhabitants in this zone, which could support seven millions. Of pasture land there are nine thousand square leagues, with but thirty-nine thousand inhabitants. There are eighteen thousand two hundred and fourteen square leagues in the forest zone, of which but nine were cleared in 1840, while twelve thousand were covered with dense virgin forest, and three thousand are classed, by Codazzi, as hills on which sheep might graze, seven hundred and ninety seven as sabánas fit for cattle, and the rest as steep mountain or lake. This zone, which has perhaps about sixty thousand inhabitants, could support sixteen millions.

In Codazzi's map Venezuela is divided into thirteen provinces, which, beginning from the south-east, and reckoning in a westerly direction, may be enumerated as follows :—1. Guayana ; 2. Cumaná ; 3. Barcelona ; 4. Margarita ; 5. Carácas; 6. Carabobo; 7. Apure; 8. Barinas; 9. Barquisimeto; 10. Coro; 11. Trujillo; 12. Merida; 13. Maracaibo. In the more modern map of 1865, will be found the new distribution into twenty-one provinces, which, reckoning in the same order from south-east to west are as follows:—

|  | Inhabitants. |
|---|---|
| 1. Guayana with . | 60,000 |
| 2. Maturin . | 45,000* |
| 3. Cumaná . | 75,000* |
| 4. Nueva Esparta . | 24,000 |
| 5. Barcelona . | 90,000 |
| 6. Guárico . | 18,000 |
| 7. Bolivar . | 120,000 |
| 8. Araguas . . | 140,000 |
| 9. Distrito Federal | 80,000 |
| 10. Apure . . | 25,000 |
| 11. Zamora . | 80,000 |
| 12. Portuguesa | 85,000* |
| 13. Cojedes . | 60,000 |
| 14. Carabobo . | 170,000* |
| 15. Yaracui . . . | 80,000 |
| 16. Nueva Cegovia . . | 23,000 |
| 17. Coro . . | 80,000 |
| 18. Los Andes . . | 80,000 |
| 19. Táchira . . | 65,000 |
| 20. Mérida | 90,000 |
| 21. Zulia | 75,000 |
|  | Total  1,565,000 |

* These provinces have united for representative purposes.

Upon the whole, Guayana must be regarded as the most important province of Venezuela. It is by far the largest, and is permeated by the magnificent flood of the Orinoco, by which and by its tributary streams the whole continent of South America might almost be crossed from east to west; while on the south it is joined by the Casaquiare to the Amazon, and so renders all Brazil accessible for ships from the coast of Venezuela. The commerce which will one day be developed on this great river will, without a doubt, be of immense importance. Of what it is at present an idea may be formed, from the fact that an American Company, who have had the privilege of carrying on the steam navigation there for the last eighteen years, have offered half a million of dollars for the renewal of their charter. Cotton grows wild in Guayana, especially in the canton of Rio Negro, where there is a species which resists the rains that fall during almost the whole year in this province. It is called *rejuco* (furnished with tendrils), and clings to trees for support. The woods of Guayana are of infinite variety, and can be turned to every useful purpose. For the names of some of them see Appendix B. Cattle and skins might be brought down the Orinoco to supply all the markets in Europe. It is an ancient tradition that gold is to be found in abundance in Guayana, and it was here that from 1535, the Spaniards, and our Raleigh after them, sought for the Golden City. So Milton writes—*

> " Yet unspoil'd
> Guayana, whose great city Geryon's sons
> Call El Dorado."

Time has proved that the wondrous legends of the Caribes

* Paradise Lost, B. XI. v. 406.

as to this city are false, but it is not to be supposed that they were utterly without foundation—that the precious metal is never to be met with in this vast province. On the contrary, the best living authorities declare,* that even in the vicinity of Angostura gold exists, and is scattered more lavishly over the remoter districts. Indeed, there is reason to think the gold fields of Guayana may yet attract thousands to Venezuela.

In 1576 the Jesuits, Ignacio Llauri and Julian Vergara, founded the town of Santo Tomas, opposite the island of Fajardo, but the Dutch destroyed it in 1579. Don Antonio Berrio, who came from Nueva Granada, refounded Santo Tomas in 1591, where Old Guayana now is, and the province thenceforward became a dependency of N. Granada, at least as far as ecclesiastical matters. In 1595 the first expedition, which went from this side, set forth in quest of El Dorado. In 1618 Walter Raleigh took Santo Tomas, killing Palomeque, the governor, and setting fire to the town. Next year it was rebuilt by Fernando Berrio in the same place. In 1764, the city now called Angostura was commenced by Mendoza, the governor, fifty-two leagues further up the river, and was at first called Santo Tomas de la Nueva Guayana, a name which was too lengthy to survive, and gave place to that of Angostura, "The Straits." In fact, the Orinoco, whose general breadth in this part is from four thousand two hundred to four thousand six hundred yards, narrows near the ancient forts of S. Gabriel and S. Rafael to eight hundred and eighty-five yards. In the middle of the stream rises the famous rock called Piedra del Medio, which has never been submerged, but which serves as a meter to the people of

* See Appendix C.

Angostura to gauge the rise of the river. This, when highest, appears to be fifty-six feet above the summer level. On the 20th of November, 1818, Bolivar issued his declaration or the independence of Venezuela from Angostura, which in his honour was named Ciudad Bolivar. It is built in the shape of an amphitheatre, on the slope of a hill, in part destitute or vegetation. Many of the houses are of stone, showing there is little danger from earthquakes. The streets run parallel to the course of the river. Humboldt attributes the unhealthiness of the place to the marshes on the south-east.

The capital of Guayana is Ciudad Bolivar, founded by Mendoza in 1764, on the right bank of the Orinoco. It has ten thousand inhabitants, and Upata,* about one hundred miles nearer the sea, has six thousand. San Fernando, near the confluence of the Atabapo and the Guairare, is also a good-sized town. In Ciudad Bolivar is made the far famed tonic called Angostura Bitters, for which prizes have been awarded at the English Exhibitions.

In addition to its other claims on the attention of Englishmen, it must be remembered that Guayana borders on English territory, being conterminous with British Guayana on the south-east, and only a few miles from Trinidad on the north-east. The question of emigration from England to Venezuelan Guayana is one that deserves more attention than it has received. It is true that Ciudad Bolivar has an evil reputation at present for yellow fever, and that generally the climate of Guayana is said to be unfavourable to Europeans, but that does not appear to have been always the case. Raleigh, in his " Discoverie of the Large, Rich, and Bewti-

* Here are important gold fields.

full Empire of Guayana," writes, p. 112, "Moreover the countrey is so healthfull, as one hundred persons and more, which lay (without shift, most sluggishly, and were every day almost melted with heat in rowing and marching, and suddenly wet againe with great showers, and did eate of all sorts of corrupt fruits, and made meales of fresh fish without seasoning, of tortugas, of lagartos, and of al sorts, good and bad, without either order or messure, and besides lodged in the open ayre every night) *we lost not any one*, nor had one ill disposed to my knowledge, nor found anie callentura, or other of those pestilent diseases which dwell in all hote regions, and so nere the equinoctiall line." And this testimony to the healthfulness of Guayana is remarkably confirmed by Sir Robert Schomburgk, who says in a note on the above passage, "During the eight years of our rambles through the thick forests, over the hills and the extensive savannahs, though our night's lodging was often merely the shelter of an umbrageous tree, though often drenched by rains and exposed to the heat of the tropical sun, our fare that of the Indians,—yet our health, after we had passed the first fevers in the commencement of the expedition, was seldom interrupted by disease. And this remark applies likewise to the Europeans who accompanied us. Indeed, if we except the melancholy death of Mr. Reiss, by the upsetting of a boat in descending a cataract, we did not lose a single individual of our European companions by disease brought on by the climate or our hardships. It is otherwise, however, in the coast regions, where injurious miasmata render the sojourn frequently dangerous to Europeans."

In fact, at the distance of about fifteen or twenty miles from the banks of the Orinoco, the ground rises from two hundred to five hundred feet, and at this elevation the climate is comparatively healthy. In case of emigration care should be taken to select high land for the first settlements, and there is no reason to apprehend much sickness in such spots.

The province of Maturin formed part of Cumaná in the time of Codazzi, 1840. Its principal towns are Maturin, the capital, with seven thousand inhabitants; Aragua, close to the frontier of Cumaná, on the northern limit of Maturin, and Barrancas on the southern. The town of Maturin is celebrated in the history of the Republic for the many attacks it has sustained. It is situated in a fine sabána, or grassy plain, on the right shore of the river Guarapiche, which is navigable to a place called Point Colorado, within eight leagues of the town. Maturin is a not unimportant mart for cattle and agricultural produce.

Aragua, on the southern slope of the mountains of Caripe, is a town as large as Maturin. In its vicinity is the celebrated Cave of Guácharo or Caripe, in which tobacco of peculiar excellence is grown, which Humboldt visited and described. He makes its length two thousand eight hundred feet, but Codazzi gives more detailed measurements, dividing the cave into three parts, of which the first is nine hundred and seventy-five yards long and from ten to twelve wide, the second two hundred and twenty-five yards long and from one to three wide, and the third one hundred and thirty-five yards long and fourteen wide. The first division, which is from seventy to eighty feet high, is inhabited by an innumerable multitude of birds called guácharos, and from them the Indians in Humboldt's time made one hundred and sixty bottles of fat oil yearly. The roof and sides of this division are covered with petrifactions and stalactites, which may be seen in the act of formation. A stream, from fifteen to twenty feet broad, but shallow, runs through this part of the cave. In the second division, which is so low that one must stoop to pass through it, there are neither birds nor petrifactions. The third, which is the most beautiful of all, on account of the petrifactions, is full of the curious animal called the lapa, which is exceedingly good to eat. The mines at Aragua contain an inexhaustible supply of pure salt.

At Guayúta and Punceres in this province are mines of sulphur, of salt, and petroleum. Maturin carries on a trade with Trinidad in cattle, horses, and mules.

The Province of Cumaná, which lies to the north of Maturin, is an important one on many accounts, but especially for its magnificent harbours. Humboldt says of the Gulf of Cariaco, on which the capital, Cumaná, is situated, that it is "a large and sheltered harbour, able to contain all the fleets of Europe put together, having in its bay the creek Obispes, which is one of the handsomest harbours in America." The port of Mochima, further to the west, is also one of the finest harbours in the world, and beyond it is Manare, also excellent. The capital, Cumaná, is the most ancient of all the towns on the mainland, but its population is only five thousand. Humboldt says that it has for ages been the focus of the most tremendous earthquakes, and eighteen months before his arrival it was entirely overthrown by one of those fearful visitations. The coast of Cumaná was first discovered by Columbus in his third voyage in 1498. In 1520 Gonzalo Ocampo built, half a league from the *embouchement* of the river Cumaná, now called Manzanáres, the town of Toledo. Next year Jácome Castallan completed a fortress begun by Las Casas, and called the place New Cordoba, the Capital of New Andalusia, as the province was then styled. In 1530 this fortress was thrown down by an earthquake, during which the sea rose twenty feet above its level. In 1766 Cumaná was destroyed by another earthquake, and shocks recurred for fourteen months. In 1794 there was again an earthquake, as also in 1797, 1802, 1805, and 1839.

Carúpano, another town of this province, has ten thousand inhabitants. It is situated near the sea, and would become a populous mart but for the unhealthiness of the lowlands near it. Cariaco, founded in 1600, and first called San Felipe, is surrounded by lands of marvellous fertility. It is situated within a few miles of the inner extremity of the gulf of the same name. Cumanacoa, five and a half Spanish leagues to the south-east of Cumaná, is placed in a fertile plain, between two rivers. To the south of it rise the peaks of the Bergantie mountains, some of which are eight thousand feet high. The scenery is exquisitely beautiful, but the most remarkable feature in it is the flames, which show themselves at the height of seven hundred feet from the hill of Cuchivano, and which arise from an inflammable gas, but are thought by the common people to be the soul of the tyrant Lopez d'Aguirre. The climate of the province is, upon the whole, favourable to health, except near the lands liable to be submerged. The average temperature is 81° of Fahrenheit.

The commerce of Cumaná consists in coffee, cocoa, cotton, sugar, and tobacco. It also exports cattle and horses, salt and petroleum. The cuspa, or cinchona, here grows to twenty feet high; it is more bitter than Peruvian bark, and less irritant. It blossoms at the end of November.

Nueva Esparta, formerly called Margarita, consists of the island of that name and the isles in the vicinity. Asuncion, the capital, has four thousand inhabitants, and is situated in a green valley, watered by a stream of the same name, about a league from the sea and one hundred and twenty-nine yards above its level. The climate is hot, but singularly healthy. The port of Pampatar is the principal harbour in the island, and is quite safe. Indeed storms are so uncommon in the sea near Margarita that Humboldt says it might be navigated in an open boat. Margarita was discovered by Columbus in 1498, and next year Cristobal Gueara obtained there the first pearls that were brought from America to Europe. The pearl fishery was carried on with great success during the sixteenth century, but has now fallen to decay. Instead of pearls, fish are now taken in great abundance and form the chief commerce of the island, together with turtles, and tortoise-shell, which are exported to Cumaná and Trinidad. Nets, two hundred yards long, are drawn twice a day, and usually bring up from ten to twelve hundred-weights of fish, and sometimes so many that it is requisite to cut the meshes and let some escape.

Barcelona is separated on the south from Guayana by the river Orinoco, on the west from Guarico by the rivers Unare and Suata, and on the east from Maturin and Cumaná by the river Los Pazos, the Mesas of Morichal, Guanipa, Pelua and Urica, and by the lofty range of the Bergantin mountains. On the north is the sea. The anchoring ground is very inferior to that along the coast of Cumaná.

Barcelona, the capital, is a town of twelve thousand inhabitants. It is situated a league from the sea, and from it verdant pasture lands extend all the way to the Orinoco, where much cattle is reared. Barcelona was built in 1671 by the Governor Sancho Fernandez de Angulo. It was the scene of many sanguinary combats during the war of Independence, and on the 6th of April, 1817, Bolivar abandoned here Colonel Chamberlain and one thousand men, who most of them perished, after Colonel Chamberlain had destroyed himself and his wife with his own hand.*

Aragua, fourteen Spanish leagues due south of Barcelona, is a town of about eight thousand inhabitants  There are also the small towns of Píritu, Onato, S. Mateo, S. Diego, Pao and Soledad, which last faces Ciudad Bolivar, being placed on the northern shore of the Orinoco. All the above towns have from two thousand to four thousand inhabitants. The foreign commerce of Barcelona consists in the same articles as that of Cumaná, but is less extensive.

The province of Guárico has been formed by detaching from the ancient province of Carácas the three vast districts of Orituco, Chaguaramas, and Calabozo. The capital, Calabozo, is a town of ten thousand inhabitants. It was founded by the Guipuzcoan Company in the beginning of the eighteenth century, close to the river Guárico, whence the province has its name, and stands so low that it is sometimes quite surrounded by the floods of the said river. The Guárico falls into the Apurito, and that again falls into the Orinoco near Caicara. Calabozo is surrounded by immense pastures where vast herds of cattle are bred. It is an ex-

* Ducoudray Holstein, p. 245.

tremely well-built city, with streets at right angles. The houses rank with the best at Carácas, and there are many fine churches. The rose here grows to twenty feet high, and two trees will support a hammock.

Orchuco, the capital of the district so called, is a town of six thousand inhabitants, situated in a fertile plain at the foot of the range of hills which separates the valleys of the Tui from the *llanuras* or "pastures." The river Orituco falls into the Guárico.

Chaguaramas is a town of about five thousand inhabitants, who are for the most part engaged in breeding cattle. It suffers from want of water. It is situated about eleven Spanish leagues to the south and by east of Orituco. The commerce of this province is less important than that of most of the other provinces.

The province of Bolivar has likewise been formed from that of Carácas by detaching from it the districts of Petare, Guarenas, Caucagua, Rio-Chico, Santa Lucia, and Ocumare. Petare, the capital, is a town of six thousand inhabitants, ten miles to the east of the city of Carácas. It is beautifully situated on the banks of the river Guaire, and overlooking the valley of that name.

Eighteen miles due east of Petare is the small but pleasantly situated town of Guarenas, and about the same distance to the south of the latter is S. Lucia in a fertile valley, watered by the Guaire. All around are fine plantations and dense woods. Twenty miles to the south-southwest of S. Lucia is Ocumare with a population of nine thousand. It is at a little distance from the Tui, in a rich country covered with woods and plantations. Forty miles to the east by north is Caucagua on a stream of the same name, which falls into the River Tui, and as the river is navigable to this point Caucagua is excellently placed for commerce. Lastly, twenty-eight miles east by north of Caucagua is Rio Chico, with twelve thousand inhabitants, on the spot where the Tui formerly flowed into the sea. It is near a lake called Tacarigua which abounds in fish, and on this account and owing to the rich lands by which it is surrounded, is enabled to carry on a brisk commerce; but it is rather feverish and unhealthy. The whole province exports considerable quantities of coffee, chocolate, sugar-cane, indigo, and tobacco.

The next province, Araguas, one of the most populous and richest in all Venezuela, has been constituted recently, of districts taken from the ancient province of Carácas. These are Victoria, Turmero, Maracai, Cura, and San Sebastian. Victoria, the capital, is situated almost exactly in the centre of the province. It is a town of nine thousand inhabitants, surrounded on all sides by calcareous hills covered with trees. The eye is delighted by the sight of the most luxuriant plantations and the richest cultivation extending in every direction. A stream called Calanche passes through the town and flows into the river Aragua, which descends into the Lake of Valencia. To the south and south-east rise the lofty mountains of La Palma, Guaracina, Tiara, and Guiripa, and beyond them are the vast plains which extend past Calabozo. Examination of the neighbouring hills shows that the Lake of Valencia, or Tacarigua, in bye-gone ages covered the present site of Victoria. Two high roads lead from Victoria; one passes by the north of the lake to San Carlos and Barinas, the other on the south of the lake leads to the plains of Apure. It is here that colonists should come. They would find the richest soil in the world, the most beautiful scenery imaginable, and a delicious and healthy climate, the whole of the province being more than one thousand six hundred and ninety feet above the level of the sea.

Five miles west of Victoria is Turmero, where is the former residence of the Governor-General of the Valleys of Aragua. It is now converted into a church. There are eight thousand inhabitants in Turmero, which is rather an agricultural than a trading town, being at a little distance from the high road. Three streams, the Guaire, Paya, and Turmero, unite near it.

The town of Maracai lies twelve miles west of Turmero, and is about the same size, having a population of nearly eight thousand. It is three miles to the north of the Lake of Valencia, and from the neighbouring height of Calvario there is a magnificent view over the lake. All around are plantations and meadows, in which numbers of horses are pastured. Cura, eighteen miles south-west of Victoria, and San Sebastian twenty miles south of Victoria, are both situated on the river Pao, which falls into the Guárico. This stream, however, near Cura, is called the Tucutunemo, and presents the strange phenomenon of a disappearance under ground for several leagues. The singular hills called the Morros of S. Juan, near Cura, are a marvel to the geologist. They are full of caves, of which one is of large dimensions. Cura has eight thousand inhabitants, S. Sebastian about two thousand. The latter is one of the oldest Spanish towns in the country, and owes its origin to the belief that gold-mines existed in the vicinity. Curious caves are to be seen near it, and at Ostig, one of the districts dependent on it, bones of the mastodon have been found. The chief export of San Sebastian is indigo, which is also grown at Maracai. Cotton and tobacco are grown at Maracai and Cura, cocoa at Turmero, and coffee and sugar-cane at all the chief places in Araguas.

The Federal District is formed of the districts of Carácas and La Guaira, part of the ancient province of Carácas. Carácas, the capital, has been fully described in the third chapter of this book. The population is fifty thousand. La Guaira also has been described. It has nine thousand inhabitants. The products of the districts dependent on these two cities are coffee, cocoa, and sugar-cane.

The province of Apure is inhabited by a race of men who make the best soldiers in South America. These Llaneros, "plainsmen" are matchless horsemen, passing the greatest part of their lives in the saddle, and accustomed to lasso from horseback the wild cattle. To use the words of Don Ramon Paez :*—"Cast upon a wild and apparently interminable plain, the domain of savage beasts and poisonous reptiles, their lot is to pass all their life in a perpetual struggle, not only with the primitive possessors of the land, but with the elements themselves, often as fierce as they are grand." These Llaneros are a mixed race, from Spaniards, Indians, and Negroes, and according to M. de Larayesse, possess a more healthy and vigorous constitution and more vital energy than either Europeans or Africans. Hence, in the War of Independence, and in the civil wars that have since occurred, the Llaneros have always played a most conspicuous part, and have produced the most celebrated soldiers, such as Paez, Boves and Morales, and more lately Sotillo.

* Wild Scenes in South America, p. 41.

The present province of Apure, though much curtailed, is about three hundred and thirty miles long, and one hundred and five miles broad. The rivers Meta and Orinoco separate it from Guayana on the south and east, and the river Apure flows between it on the north and the provinces of Zamora and Gaárico. On the west it is bounded by New Granada. The climate is hot, but in general healthy. From December to February the sky is cloudless. Rains begin in April, and fall with great violence in June, July, and August. In these months Eastern Apure is changed into a vast lake, and except for the hardy and experienced natives the whole province becomes impassable. Numberless cattle are then destroyed by the jaguars, the alligators, and the yet more troublesome caribe fish, or are drowned in the waters. Notwithstanding this the herds abound to such an extent as to surpass the power of description. Some idea of their number may be formed, however, from the following circumstance. It has been found impossible for any cattle-owner to brand more than ten thousand animals in a year. But there are at least ten proprietors who have more than that number born in their herds annually. Consequently they are allowed to purchase the privilege of claiming all the unmarked animals near their pastures. Now, if we consider how great must be the herd which supplies more than ten thousand fresh animals every year, and that certificates are issued to ten proprietors of their having such a herd, while many other claimants to the certificate exist, and several thousand proprietors who possess herds of various classes below that first rank, it will be evident that the cattle must be reckoned by hundreds of thousands, if not by millions.

The capital of Apure is San Fernando, a town of six thousand inhabitants, situated near the spot where the river Portuguesa falls into the Apure. This latter river is here two hundred and thirty-six toises broad, when at its lowest ebb, but its usual breadth is one thousand yards. Considerable traffic is carried on by the river, which receives boats bringing goods from Barinas and Carácas for Ciudad Bolivar. But neither S. Fernando, nor any other town of Apure, adds to the traffic. Of course, if freight were less high a trade might be carried on in cattle and hides, for a two year old animal sells for one shilling and sixpence, and a full grown bull for half a crown.

The town of Achaguas, thirty-six miles to the south-south-west of S. Fernando, has a population of about four thousand. It was founded as a mission by the Friar Alonso in 1774, and was originally the capital of Apure, when it was formed from Barinas into a separate province in 1824. It is situated near the confluence of the Apurita with the Matiyure. Mantecal, on the river Caicaro, fifty miles to the west of Achaguas and Guasdualito, in the extreme west of the province, are the only other towns of Apure worth notice. Each has about three thousand inhabitants. Among the noteworthy things in Apure are the Saman trees, a species of mimosa, which afford good timber, and are of such a gigantic size as to overshadow several acres.

The province of Zamora has been formed out of the ancient one of Barinas, Obispo, Pedraza, and Nutrias. The new province has Merida, Los Andes, Portuguesa, and Cojedes to the north, Guarico to the. east, Apure to the south, and Táchira to the west.

Barinas, the capital, is a town of six thousand inhabitants.

It is situated in the northern part of the province near a hill, where the river Domingo has its source. It was built in 1576 by Juan Andres Varela, and was first called Altamira de Cáceres. Codazzi declares that no province possesses equal advantages, since its inhabitants may be agriculturists, cattle breeders, and merchants at once. Tobacco of a superior kind is produced here.

Obispo, eleven miles to the east by south of Barinas, is a town fully as large. The river Domingo, which passes near it, is navigable, and communicates with the Apure and Orinoco. Caroni, two leagues off on the Domingo, is the port of Obispo.

Pedraza, eighteen miles to the south-west of Barinas, is a town of three thousand inhabitants. It was founded in 1601 by Gonzalo Piño Ladueño, who called it by the name of the town in Estremadura in which he was born. In 1614 it was destroyed by the Indians, and rebuilt on its present site by Diego de Lima. It stands in a lovely sabána on the banks of the river Canagua. To the west of it is the great forest of Ticoporo, which covers eighty square leagues, and in which the cacao tree grows wild. The Canagua is navigable not far from Pedraza, so that goods can be carried down from it to Ciudad Bolivar.

About sixty miles to the south-east of Obispo is Nutrias on the Apure river, a town with considerable commerce and about six thousand five hundred inhabitants. It is the general port of the province of Barinas, and the following articles are interchanged at it. To Ciudad Bolivar Barinas sends coffee, cocoa, hides, indigo, timber, rice, cotton, maize, sugar, papalon, potatoes, chick-peas, tares, shoe-leather, drugs, Indian barley, brandy, horns, mules, mares, cattle, receiving in exchange dry goods, soap, delf, rum, wine, gin, cheese, oil, vinegar and salt. To Carácas and Puerto Cabello, Barinas sends indigo, hides, cocoa, asses, pigs and cattle, and receives groceries in exchange. From Barquisimeto Barinas receives leather, morocco leather, shoes, hammocks, linen, sacks, drugs, onions, garlic, preserves, tiles, belts, chick-peas, sugar, papelon; and gives in return maize, beans, rice, cheese, fish, money and cattle. From Tocuyo Barinas receives flour, cotton, blankets, sweetmeats, salt, morocco leather, garlic and onions; and returns hides and money. From Boconó, in Trujillo, Barinas receives flour, Indian barley, tares, chick-peas, sugar, white cabbages, potatoes and drugs; returning piece-goods and money. Mucuchico sends to Barinas drugs, potatoes, tares, and flour; and gets in exchange cattle, cocoa, and fish. The traffic with Merida consists in the things just named, and in robes made of furs, skins, blankets, and hammocks, which Barinas sends also to Apure, getting back cattle from Guasdualito and Achaguas.

The new province of Portugueza has been formed from the ancient Merida by detaching the districts of Guanare, Ospino, Araure, and Guanarito.

Guanare, the capital of Portugueza, is situated at about four miles to the north of the Guanarito river, and contains seven thousand inhabitants. It was founded by Juan Fernandez de Leon in 1593, or according to Oviedo in 1609. The soil about it is most fertile, and the woods rich in valuable timber. Its chief wealth, however, consists in cattle.

Ospino, situated thirty-four miles to the north by east of Guanare, and midway to Araure, contains about three thousand inhabitants. There are excellent pasturages near the town, which is especially famous for its herds of swine, with which it carries on a brisk trade to Carabobo and Carácas.

Thirty-four miles again to the north by east of Ospino is Araure, a town of six thousand inhabitants. It is three leagues from the canal Durigua, which is navigable, and leads to the river Sarare, which conducts to the Cojedes, and this latter to the Portugueza. This again falls into the Apure, and the Apure into the Orinoco. Near it is the pine forest of Turen. The cocoa, coffee, sugar-cane, tobacco, and indigo here are excellent. In 1813 a celebrated battle was fought here which liberated all Barinas. It is also the birth-place of Paez. Lastly, Guanarito, on the river of the same name, is a town of four thousand five hundred inhabitants, in the south-east part of the province. In few places is fish so abundant. Cattle also are reared in great numbers.

The principal trade of the province is in cocoa, indigo, coffee, cotton.

The modern province of Cojedes has been formed by detaching from Carabobo the districts of San Carlos and Pao.

The capital, San Carlos, is a town of nine thousand inhabitants, and is situated in a fine plain near the river Madrina, which falls into the Portugueza. The hills to the north of the town extend far into the province of Carabobo, and along them is the famous pass called the galera, which divides the plains of Valencia from those to the south of San Carlos. The town is well built, and the edifices are a sign of the wealth of the inhabitants, who carry on a considerable trade in cattle. San Carlos also exports quantities of oranges, which fruit grows there in great abundance. The climate is hot, and fevers are prevalent.

Seven miles to the east of San Carlos is Tinaco, with six thousand inhabitants, and twelve miles to the east-north-east of Tinaco is Pao, with about the same population. The trade of these places is chiefly in coffee and sugar.

The most populous of all the provinces of Venezuela is Carabobo, which also possesses the richest soil, the most beautiful scenery, and, upon the whole, the most delightful climate. It has been so much curtailed by the separation of the districts which form the new province of Cojedes, that it is now no more than forty-five miles square, yet it contains more than double as many inhabitants as most of the other provinces. Its coast can boast of some of the finest harbours in the world, the principal of which is Puerto Cabello, the chief port of Venezuela. Cata, Ocumare, and Turiamo, are also excellent harbours.

Valencia, the capital of the province, has been already described in Chapter VIII. It has a population of about twenty-five thousand, was founded by Alonso Dias Moreno in 1555, and is consequently twelve years older than Carácas. Seven miles from it is the beautiful lake described in Chapter XII.

Twenty-five miles in a direct line from Valencia is Puerto Cabello, which by the road is at least forty. It contains nine thousand inhabitants, and would be far more populous but for the fevers which prevail there and arise from the rank vegetation, stagnant waters and the mangrove forest. The roots of this tree exposed to the sun send forth deadly exhalations. The principal part of the coffee and cocoa trade of Venezuela is carried on at this port.

Eighteen miles to the east of Puerto Cabello is the town of Ocumare with two thousand inhabitants.

The modern province of Yaracui has been formed out of the provinces of Carabobo and Barquisimeto, by detaching from the former the districts of Nirqua and Montalban, and from the latter those of San Felipe and Yaritagua.

San Felipe, the capital, situated almost exactly in the centre of the province, has eight thousand inhabitants. The Guipuzcoan Company finding the village of Cocoroto commodiously situated for trade with the interior, built their stores there, and the town of San Felipe grew up under their support. Six miles to the east flows the river Yaracui, which gives its name to the province, and carries down a considerable amount of merchandize in small vessels to the sea. Fifteen miles to the north runs the river Aroa, by which the copper from the mines of Aroa, a village six leagues to the north-west of San Felipe, is brought down to the sea. The copper of Aroa is superior to that of Coquimbo and of Europe, but the district in which it is found is extremely unhealthy, as indeed is that which intervenes between San Felipe and Puerto Cabello. Aroa also is infamous for the massacre of Englishmen there, who were employed at the mines, and were barbarously murdered by the native miners some years ago. A railroad from Puerto Cabello to San Felipe has been commenced, and would prove of immense advantage to the country, but this useful work is at present suspended.

Yaritagua, about twenty-six miles to the south of San Felipe, and Montalban, at the same distance to the south-east, have a population respectively of about three and two thousand. Yaritagua is hot but healthy, and is well placed for trade between San Felipe and Barquisimeto. The mountains which separate it from Nirgua are very steep and difficult of passage.

Montalban stands in a plain at the foot of hills and with immense woods covering them and stretching away to the sea. The land in the vicinity is of excellent quality.

Nirgua, fifteen miles south of Montalban, was first founded in 1555, and several times deserted and reoccupied. In 1625 D. Juan de Meneses y Padilla, exterminated the hostile tribe of Jirabaras and refounded the town with the name of Our Lady of the Victory of the Field of Talavera, a title which was too long to continue in vogue. Nirgua is three thousand feet above the level of the sea, and the mountains near it are more than six thousand. Its climate is cool and pleasant, but it is very difficult of access.

The trade of this province is in copper, indigo, coffee, cocoa, and sugar.

The province of Nueva Cegovia represents that which was formerly called Barquisimeto, with the exception of the districts of San Felipe and Yaritagua, which, as mentioned above, have been assigned to Yaracui.

Nueva Cegovia is separated from Coro on the north by a line of mountains uninhabited and little explored, and by lands liable to be submerged by the river Tocuyo. This river, whose course is nearly four hundred miles long, divides Nueva Cegovia into two equal parts, and after flowing nearly due north for about one hundred and twenty miles through the entire province, turns to the east and forms the boundary between Nueva Cegovia and Coro. It then flows through Coro for seventy miles, being navigable the whole way, and falls into the sea. On the east the mountains of Duaca, three thousand eight hundred feet high, and the river Barquisimeto, separate Nueva Cegovia from Yaracui, and on the south and west the ranges of Trujillo and Carache, with the peaks of Jabon, Cavimbu, and Rosas rising to the height of from twelve to thirteen thousand feet, divide it from the provinces of Los Andes and Zulia. The climate of the province varies according to the elevation from extreme cold to great heat.

The capital, Barquisimeto, situated near the eastern frontier, in a plain, where the roads to Coro and to Carabobo and Barinas meet, has a population of ten thousand inhabitants. It was founded in 1552 by D. Juan de Villegas, and was called Nueva Cegovia after the country of his birth. Here the famous Lope de Aguirre, called the Tyrant, after having destroyed his own daughter, was put to death by Don Diego Garcia de Parédes. In 1812 the city was almost destroyed by the same earthquake which overthrew Carácas, and a whole division of the so-called patriot troops under Colonel Diego Jalon, perished in the ruins. The scenery which surrounds the town is beautiful, especially towards the south, where the river, from which the town has its present name, flows through a fertile valley, full of valuable plantations. Rich pastures afford every opportunity for breeding cattle, the hills produce excellent corn, and the valleys the finest cocoa. Cotton, indigo, and cereals also flourish.

Twenty-eight miles south-south-west of Barquisimeto is Quibor, with about two thousand inhabitants, situated in a dry and arid plain. Good mules and asses are bred here. Tocuyo, ten miles due south of Quibor, has seven thousand inhabitants. It was founded in 1545 by Juan de Carvajal, and was first called N. Señora de la Concepcion. It is built in a beautiful valley watered by the river of the same name. On the east and west, ranges of hills shut out the view of the Andes, notwithstanding their vast height. On their skirts in the directions named are the small towns of Sanare, Guárico, and Barbacoas, with fertile lands and a delightful climate. The corn of Tocuyo is equal to the best in the world. There is a brisk trade also in wool and salt. Tocuyo boasts of a college and good schools.

Sixty-three miles almost due west of Barquisimeto is Carora, a town of six thousand inhabitants. It was founded in 1572 by Diego de Montes. The soil is dry, and the only neighbouring stream is the Morere, the waters of which is at times insufficient. Carora owes its population to its excellent climate. In the hills of Guacamuco, which are at no great distance, odoriferous balsams and aromatic gums abound. The cochineal insect is found here.

Coro, a province of the second class in point of size, owes its present importance to its being the birth-place of the President, General Falcon, and to the prominent part its levies took in the late war. Its greatest length from east to west is two hundred and twenty miles, and its breadth from north to south two hundred and fifty miles, reckoning from the extremity of the Peninsula of Paraguana, Cape Roman, where the sabánas of Tatarabare join the province of Nueva Cegovia. The principal port in the long line of coast is La Vela, at two leagues from the capital, where there is good anchorage. Macalla, also to the west of Cape Roman, is an excellent harbour, as is Los Taques and Agana.

The climate is in general dry and hot. Near the rivers Tocuyo and Aroa it is more humid and excessively unhealthy.

Nevertheless, Coro possesses a considerable tract of territory, which is probably better adapted for colonization by Europeans than almost any part of Venezuela. This is the mountain range of San Luis, which traverses the centre of the province, and rises to the height of five thousand feet above the sea. Here the land is fertile, and the air cool and pleasant.

The capital, Coro, has a population of seven thousand inhabitants. It was founded on the 26th of July, 1527, by Juan de Nugaes, who disembarked on the coast with sixty men. Next year Ambrosio de Alfinjer and Bartolome Sailler, both Germans, brought a reinforcement of four hundred Spaniards. In 1578 D. Juan Pimentel transferred the government of the country from Coro to Carácas. In 1818 Coro was erected into a province. The town is situated in a barren plain, one hundred and twenty feet above the sea, and distant from it about two miles.

Twenty-eight miles south of Coro, the capital, is the town of San Luis, situated in the healthy and fertile mountain range of the same name. Here are plantations of coffee and sugar-cane.

The towns of Cumarebo, of Pueblo-Nuevo, in the peninsula of Paraguaná, and of San Miguel del Tocuyo, at the mouth of the river of that name on the eastern shore of the province, as also Casigua in the south-west, are deserving of mention.

The trade of Coro is chiefly in cotton, coffee, and cocoa. But in Paraguaná there is a rich salt mine at Guaranao, from which many vessels are loaded yearly with that useful article. The province also carries on a brisk trade with the Dutch islands, Curazao and Oruba exporting to them hides, maize, hammocks, horns, mules, asses, goats, sheep, salt, wool, cheese, timber, and cocoa.

The appellation of Los Andes has been given to the province formerly called from its chief town Trujillo. It is a small province, twenty Spanish leagues broad from east to west, and twenty-six long from north to south, divided from Nueva Cegovia on the north and east, from Zulia on the west, and from Merida and Zamora on the south by lofty mountains, of which the peaks Volcan, Caldera, Niquitao, Rosario, Jabon, Rosas, Cabimbú, Tuñame, Zelàs, Linares, Atajo, Tonoco, and many others, rise from ten thousand five hundred to seventeen thousand feet in height. Most of these are covered with eternal snow, and in their neighbourhood are wastes called Páramos, in which a furious wind prevails, so cold as to destroy animal life. There are, however, deep valleys full of luxuriant vegetation and suitable for agriculture and cattle-breeding. The climate is in general cold, or cool and refreshing. The hills looking towards the Lake of Maracaibo are, however, feverish and unhealthy.

Trujillo, the capital, is a town of seven thousand inhabitants. A town of the same name was first founded by Diego Garcia Parédes in 1552 near Matatua, but the locality was several times changed until it came to be fixed where it now is, a little to the south by east of the centre of the province. In 1668, the pirate Francisco Gramont burned the town, which was long before it recovered. It is placed between two hills on a steep slope towards the river Jacinto. The air is pure and cool, but the water produces the goitre. The town stands at an elevation of three thousand four hundred feet above the sea. On the 15th of June, 1813,

Bolivar issued from this town the decree of " war to the death," and on the 26th of November, 1820, he here signed the Convention of Santa Ana, a village four leagues off, by which the cruel reprisals of the seven years' war ceased.

Next to the capital, the principal town is Escuque, with six thousand inhabitants, and twenty-three miles to the west by north of Trujillo. It lies in a fair plain on the slope of the hills towards the Lake of Maracaibo. The river Escuque, formed by the confluence of the Colorado and Blanco, flows at the foot of the town. To the north-east, on the road to the small town of Betijoque, is a mine of petroleum. The oil made from it gives a bright light, not easily extinguished. Near the mine are many copious springs of cold and excellent water. The rich lands near Escuque, are excellently suited for cocoa, coffee, cereals and sugar-cane, of which large crops are grown.

Bocono, sixteen miles to the south-east of Trujillo, is a town somewhat smaller than Escuque. It is situated in a rich valley one thousand five hundred and seventy-two Spanish yards above the sea's level. It is surrounded by lofty mountains, in which are the wintry wastes called the Páramos of Volcan, Caldera, Niquitao, Rosario, Cabimbu, Tonoco, Atajo, Linares, Teta, and Tuñame ; all of them from six thousand to seven thousand feet above Bocono itself, and consequently from twelve thousand to thirteen thousand feet above the level of the sea. To the south-east flows the river Bocono and to the north-east the Burate, which receive innumerable torrents, and at last unite near the town.

Carache is a small town twenty-five miles to the north-east of Trujillo, at the foot of the mountain range of

Aguaobispo, which separates the province of Los Andes from that of N. Cegovia. The climate is delicious and healthy. A river of the same name washes the town. The village of Santa Ana, famous for the armistice between Bolivar and Morillo, is in one of the districts dependent on Carache, and half way between it and Trujillo. It was ordered that a pyramid should be erected on the spot where the two Generals met; but, with the characteristic levity of Republicans, the order was never carried into execution.

The commerce of this province is principally with Maracaibo, or, as it is now called, Zulia, from which it receives groceries, liquors, and salt; sending in exchange cocoa, coffee, preserves, and sugar. To the towns of Guanara and Barinas Trujillo sends coffee, sugar, papelon, flour, and various extracts, and receives back cattle and rice. From Carora and Tocuyo Los Andes receives belts, shoes, and soap, and returns cocoa, coffee, hides, mules and cattle.

Táchira is a province, formed by detaching from Mérida its south-western districts, viz. Bailadores, Grita, San Cristóbal, and San Antonio.

This province is forty-six Spanish leagues long from east to west, and nineteen broad from north to south. It has Mérida to the north, Zamora to the east, and the foreign territory of N. Granada,* or, as it is now called, Columbia, to the west and south. From Pamplono, in the Columbian territory, a branch of the Andes traverses Táchira and Merida in a north-easterly direction, and continually increases in elevation. Beginning with the Páramo of Tama

---

* It is now three years since New Granada assumed the name of Columbia, which properly belonged to the united territory of Ecuador, New Granada and Venezuela.

it, near the river Frio, leaves a chasm, through which flows the larger stream of the Torbes. Passing to the south of S. Cristóbal it forms the wintry heights of Zumbador, Agrias, Batallon, and Portachuelo, which rise from three thousand to three thousand eight hundred and forty Spanish yards above the sea; thence, throwing out several spurs, it passes to the Sierra-Nevada of Merida, whose peaks are covered with perpetual snow. This is the highest land in Venezuela, being five thousand four hundred and sixty to five thousand four hundred and seventy-nine Spanish yards above the level of the sea; and from it seventy-five rivers descend towards the Orinoco. The climate of this province, as might be expected from its elevation, is cold. The air is in general cool, bracing, and healthy. The rains begin in March and last till November, falling in torrents during July and August.

The capital of the province is San Cristóbal situated on a hill, at the foot of which flows the river Torbes. It has six thousand inhabitants, and is advantageously placed for commerce with Maracaibo and Pamplona, as well as with the Llanos. Its exports are sugar, indigo, coffee, cocoa, and cotton.

San Antonio, eighteen miles west of San Cristóbal, is a much smaller town, situated at the foot of a hill which dominates a small plain through which flows the Tachira. This river gives its name to the province, and then, falling into the Zulia, loses its own. The Zulia disembogues into the Lake of Maracaibo. The climate here is warm.

Thirty-five miles to the north-east of San Cristóbal is Grita, a town somewhat smaller than San Cristóbal. It stands near the river of the same name, which is navigable

for fourteen leagues, and falls, like the Táchira, into the
Zulia. By this river Grita is well able to carry on a trade
with Maracaibo, and by the river Uribante which flows in
the opposite direction, and falls into the Apure, it is equally
well situated for commerce with Apure and the eastern
provinces.

Bailadores, fifteen miles to the north-east of Grita, is a
smaller town situated on elevated ground, which dominates
the valley washed by the river Mocotuyes, and covered
with plantations and cultivation. Excellent tobacco is
grown here, as well as cocoa, sugar-cane, plantains, corn,
barley, and potatoes.

Táchira sends sugar, indigo, coffee and cocoa to Maracaibo, and receives in exchange groceries, liquors, and salt.
To Apure it sends flour, brandy, salt, garlic, onions, and
cereals; and receives cattle, which it exchanges in the
valleys of Cuenta in Columbia for groceries and salt.

Mérida is a province of about the same size as Táchira,
which, till lately, formed a part of it, and is of the same
character.

The capital, Mérida, situate in the south-east part of the
province, has a population of nine thousand inhabitants.
It was founded in 1558 by Juan Rodriguez Suárez, and was
first called Santiago de los Caballeros. Rodriguez was a
native of Merida in Estramadura. The town stands in a fine
table land one thousand nine hundred and seventy-one Spanish
yards above the sea's level, which is washed on all sides
but the north by the rivers Mucujun, Alvaregas, and Chama.
The scenery is beautiful, the magnificent snowy peaks of
the Sierra-Nevada being full in view. On all sides are lofty
mountains, in which are delightful valleys well suited for the

habitation of man. There are hot mineral springs in a hill near, and medicinal plants, gums, and resins abound. Mérida, suffered much from the earthquake, which destroyed Cuenca in 1644, and was reduced to ruins by that which overthrew Carácas in 1812. It was soon rebuilt, however, and is now the seat of a bishop, and possesses a college, many schools, and a nunnery.

The small town of Mucuchies, about twenty miles to the north-east of Mérida, is remarkable as being the highest inhabited locality in Venezuela. It is two thousand eight hundred and twenty three Spanish yards above the level of the sea.

Egido, seven miles to the west of Mérida, is a small town about three miles from the river Chama. Fifteen miles to west of it is the village of Lagunilla, remarkable for a lake, in which is a mine of *urao*, like that which is found at Trona in Africa. It has been declared by M. Boussingault to be sesqui-carbonate of soda.

The trade of Mérida resembles that of Táchira.

Zulia, till lately called Maracaibo, is the largest province in Venezuela, next to Guayana, and has a superficies, including the lake, of two thousand seven hundred and eighty Spanish square leagues. It has Columbia to the west, Mérida to the south, the sea to the north, and Coro, New Cegovia, and Los Andes to the east.

On the north-west the peninsula of Guajira projects far beyond the line of the eastern coast of Zulia. Cape Chichibaco in the peninsula forms the point of demarcation between Columbia and Venezuela. If a line be carried from the said Cape across the Sierra Aciete, and the mountains of Oca, to the heads of the rivers Soldado and Hacha, it will mark out the country of the independent Indian

tribe of Guajiros. These and some other tribes use poisoned
arrows, with which and by their valour they have all along
been able to repulse the Spaniards.

The most remarkable feature in the province is the lake.
Its navigation is impeded by a bar at its mouth, which
cannot be safely crossed by vessels drawing more than nine
feet of water, and which at all times requires a good pilot to
clear it. The water of the lake is sweet. It takes its name
from a cacique of the Indians in 1529. Its shores are covered
with vegetation, and are hot and unhealthy. An American
Company has lately had the monopoly of the navigation, and
it is said large profits have been made by them.

Maracaibo, the capital of Zulia, has a population of
twenty-five thousand. The place was first visited by Europeans in 1499, when Ojeda and Vespucci entered the gulf,
and gave it the name of Venice. Alfinjer, in 1529, built a
few houses on the spot the city now occupies, and in 1571,
Alonso Pacheco founded a town there, which he called N.
Zamora. The soil is sandy and the climate hot and dry.
The place is subject to most terrific thunderstorms, and
nowhere in the world is the noise of the thunder so loud or
the lightning so destructive. Deluges of rain fall and often
do great injury to buildings. The principal part of the
town is built on the shore of a creek two miles wide; the
rest on an eminence to the north which looks over the lake
to the town of Altagracia on the opposite shore. There are
a college and a naval school at Maracaibo; and Depons
speaks highly of the natural talents of the natives and their
love of music. Excellent timber is found on the shores of
the lake, and the best vessels which navigate the neighbouring seas are built at Maracaibo.

Altagracia, opposite to Maracaibo, is a town of about two thousand inhabitants. Cocoa, cotton, and sugar-cane are grown in the lands near it. The lake here is but two leagues broad.

Perija, sixty miles to the south-west of Maracaibo, is a town of two thousand inhabitants. It is built on a slight eminence in the midst of a beautiful plain. There is but little cultivation near it, the people being for the most part cattle-breeders.

On the south coast of the lake the only town is Gibraltar. Here the cocoa-tree grows wild in the woods. The vegetation here is most luxuriant, and numerous streams descend from the hills to the lake. The climate is unhealthy.

The commerce of Zulia is carried on chiefly by the lake. The exports are indigo, cocoa, coffee, sugar, honey, straw hats, besides cotton and wax.

According to Codazzi, the population of Venezuela was, in 1800, composed as follows :—

| | |
|---|---:|
| Whites . | 200,000 |
| Mixed races, including civilised Indians | 406,000 |
| Slaves . | 62,000 |
| Catechised Indians . | 37,000 |
| Independent Indians | 83,000 |
| Total | 788,000 |

In 1839 the following were the classes of the population according to the same authority :—

| | |
|---|---:|
| Whites . | 260,000 |
| Mixed Races . | 414,151 |
| Slaves . | 49,782 |
| Civilized Indians . | 155,000 |
| Catechised Indians . | 14,000 |
| Independent Indians | 52,415 |
| Total | 945,348 |

In 1844 the census gave the total of one million two hundred and eighteen thousand souls, and in 1865 the population had risen to one million five hundred and sixty-five thousand, but no details of the census are known in this country. The item " Slaves " will have to be added to that of the " Mixed races," and supposing the rate of progression in all the classes to have continued as from 1800 to 1839, the Whites may be reckoned at a fourth of the entire population. The Indians* are not of very much weight in political questions, and considering that the whites have ever shown themselves the leaders in every great movement, and that they are much more than half as numerous as the Mixed races, there is little danger of any contest for supremacy. Negroes are not found in any number, except at the seaports, and in districts like the Valley of Araguas, where there were extensive sugar-cane plantations cultivated by slave labour.

The form of Government is modelled on that of the United States of North America. The Executive is represented by the President, who appoints the ministers, and is himself elected by the majority of votes in the different States, for a period of four years, beginning from the 20th of February.

The President appoints the ministers, who are strictly his organs, and vacate office with him.

The Legislature consists of a House of Senators and one of Deputies, which meet in Congress on fixed occasions, or when either House declares it to be necessary. The Senators are chosen, two from each State, with two supplementaries to fill vacancies, and must be Venezuelans by

---

* For curious proofs of the S. Americans and Egyptians being one race, consult " American Antiquities," by J. T. C. Heaviside. Trübner, 1868.

birth and thirty years of age. The Chamber of Deputies is formed by each State choosing one Deputy for every twenty-five thousand inhabitants, and a second Deputy for any number in excess beyond twelve thousand.

The High Federal Court examines causes against the Ministers of State, Diplomatic officers, and the high functionaries of the different States, declares where laws clash which is to prevail, and discharges other important duties. It consists of five members, who are chosen by the majority of the States.

The States, which form the Union, reciprocally acknowledge the rights of one another to self-government, declare themselves equal as political units, and retain in their plenitude all sovereign rights not expressly delegated by the Constitution. In one particular the English Government might, perhaps, borrow an idea from the Constitution of Venezuela. The Venezuelan Ministers have the right to speak in either Chamber of the Legislature, and are obliged to attend when called upon to give information.

The scheme of the Venezuelan Republic, further particulars of which will be found in Appendix C, looks well on paper, but unfortunately does not work well. The States are governed in the same way as the Union, and form an *imperium in imperio.* They attend but little to the orders of the general government, and have appropriated its revenue to their own purposes. Under a very determined and popular President they might be reduced to obedience, but at present they are quite beyond control.

These remarks lead to the consideration of what the revenue of the general government is, a subject on which the Constitution is by no means explicit. The principal source of national revenue in Venezuela is the Custom-houses. By Section 14 of Article 13 of the Constitution, each State binds itself " not to establish Custom-houses for the collection of dues, so that the National Custom-houses may be the only ones."

The principal Custom-houses are eight, according to Codazzi. Trade was then only commencing :—

Duties levied in 1839 according to Codazzi.

| | |
|---|---|
| La Guaira . . . . . | $774,930 |
| Puerto Cabello . . . | 197,344 |
| Ciudad Bolivar . . . | 171,201 |
| Maracaibo . . . . . | 115,179 |
| Cumaná . . . . . | 25,140 |
| Barcelona . . . . . | 42,314 |
| Coro . . . . . | 44,907 |
| Margarita (not given) . . . | |
| | ——$1,371,015 |

Subaltern Custom-houses are :—

| | |
|---|---|
| Pampatar . . . . | 127 |
| Carupano . . . . | 11,557 |
| Maturin . . . . | 19,158 |
| Higuerote . . . . . | 2,063 |
| Guiria . . . . | 5,635 |
| Adicora . . . | 900 |
| Juan Griego . . | 1,009 |
| • Cumarebo . . . . . | 628 |
| Rio Caribe . . . | 4,158 |
| Barrancas, &c. . . | |
| | —— 45,235 |
| Total | $1,416,250 |

What the amount of export and import duties now collected at these places is, is not exactly known. But the following paper, in which some of the stations are omitted, gives an approximate estimate. It will be seen that there is no mention of Maracaibo, where the receipts are probably as large as those at Bolivar.

| CUSTOM-HOUSE. | 1865—66. Dollars. | Cents. | 1866—67. Dollars. | Cents. |
|---|---|---|---|---|
| La Guaira . | 2,719,829 | 53 | 2,037,389 | 79 |
| Puerto Cabello . . . | 1,560,234 | 00 | 1,233,447 | 13 |
| Ciudad Bolivar . | 422,615 | 90 | 406,024 | 51 |
| La Vela . . . . | 158,243 | 23 | 152,263 | 57 |
| Maturin . . . | 91,470 | 13 | 79,197 | 12 |
| Pampatar . . . | 6,626 | 80 | 6,464 | 87 |
| Juan Griego . | 5,654 | 94 | 4,379 | 60 |
| Guiria . . | 78,917 | 98 | 53,849 | 30 |
| Carupano . | 93,040 | 23 | 149,257 | 22 |
| Barcelona . . . . | 36,168 | 74 | 50,551 | 63 |
| Cumaná . . | 26,741 | 30 | 28,716 | 17 |
| Táchira . . . | 34,545 | 75 | 63,828 | 62 |
| Total | 5,234,088 | 53 | 4,265,369 | 53 |

The Minister of Finance in his Report to Congress, dated Carácas, 1865, states at p. 20, that "there are no accounts, no statistics, whereby the Government can know what its revenue is." At p. 19, he says, "the Eastern Aduanas, or Custom-houses, other than Ciudad Bolivar, are all heavily mortgaged, and pay nothing to the National Treasury. The same remark applies to the Custom-houses of the West, and it is not even known how their revenues are applied, except those of Coro !" The duties collected at Maracaibo, a most important station, inferior only to La Guaira and Puerto Cabello have, ever since General Falcon came into power, been usurped by Mr. Sutherland, the President of Zulia. The State of Cumaná applies the duties to its own purposes. Táchira never so much as sent a reply to the communications of the General Government on the subject of the Custom-houses. Puerto Cabello and La Guaira being under the immediate superintendence of the General Government the collectors at those places have at least furnished accounts. With this exception, the only State that has shown itself loyal to the Constitution, and honourably faithful to its promises, is Ciudad Bolivar. The other States, in the same spirit of rebellion and license in which they first threw off their allegiance to Spain,* and then continually raised the standard of insurrection against every succeeding government, have remained contumacious and insensible to their pledges. This is the true spirit of democracy, and we may be quite sure that, if successful, it would maintain its character here as there. In the meantime, what has been the result of the long democratic struggle in Columbia, and of the fratricidal war of twenty-five years' duration? The answer, as regards Venezuela, shall be given by a late President: "Horrible situation! Not only the army was in want of the necessaries of life. Civil officials had no pay. The widows and orphans who had been pensioned were dying of hunger. The wives and children of the soldiers on service could obtain no means of support. We called on the Custom-house at La Guaira for money, and the answer was — There is none! We asked assistance from the mercantile community, and received for reply—Credit is destroyed! We applied to our citizens, and found that not a dollar could be raised without the most rigorous measures. What recollections! What agony! What horror!" The miseries here spoken of were relieved by the Loan of

* It is not pretended that the Government of Spain was a good one. It was despotic, bigoted, ignorant; but at least the country was at peace under its rule. Since the rebellion there has been continual war, terrible and incessant carnage, augmentation of Debt and loss of National Credit. Ever since the successful rebellion of North America it has been assumed that the overthrow of a Government implies improvement. But what is the advantage of overthrowing even a bad government if it is to be replaced by a worse? Even as regards the United States, it is an open question whether they would not have been as happy and prosperous if they had continued loyal. It is rather too much to assume the contrary, as a matter of course, with the example of Canada before us.

1862, but the situation soon recurred. In the same strain, the Minister of Finance for 1865 declares that "Venezuela *agonises* for the means of support." "The public revenue," he says, "will be, instead of an advantage, a calamity, if it continue to be the aim of all who thirst to grow rich at the expense of their country."

But, in spite of the almost impenetrable obscurity which envelopes every question connected with Venezuelan finance, it is absolutely necessary to make an attempt to arrive at an approximate estimate of what the general revenue of the Republic ought to be. The Venezuelan Government must not expect that, if it has really assigned to it ample revenues, which it is too negligent or pusillanimous to collect, the British bondholders will remain passive and display similar indifference and irresolution. In making the inquiry into the state of the Custom-houses, it must be premised that the import duties amount to a far larger sum than those on the exports. The latter dues have, indeed, always been regarded unfavourably by the public in Venezuela. Agriculture suffers too much as it is from the want of roads and other means of communication, and from the usury of money-lenders, who supply money at from twenty to thirty per cent. to the cultivators. A hundred per cent. duty on exports; such as has been raised on imports, could not be tolerated for a moment; and it is very doubtful if, under present circumstances, twenty per cent. would be borne with equanimity. By Article 103 of the New Constitution of 1865, it has been decreed that the export duties cannot be increased, and that, when once the mortgages upon them have been paid off, the export trade of the country is to be for ever free. The first consideration, then, is what should be the amount of the import duties received by the Venezuelan Government? Now in order to determine this, assistance may be borrowed from the official statements of the total amounts of imports into the country, and of the rates at which duties have been levied upon them. The rates then are as follows :—

| | | |
|---|---|---|
| The Tariff of 1830 fixed 27 per cent. on articles of general consumption ; on non-specified articles 32 per cent.; and on luxuries, 37 per cent.—average | | 34·00 |
| ,, | 1834 added 10 per cent. on the above rate on specified ; and 5 per cent. on ad valorem | |
| ,, | 1836 added 10 per cent. on the above rate, giving a base of | 38·09 |
| ,, | 1838 added a subsidiary 3 per cent. on the above . | 39·11 |
| ,, | 1847 | 39·52 |
| ,, | 1848 | 40·93 |
| ,, | 1853 ½ per cent. for churches | 41·10 |
| ,, | 1854 4 per cent. subsidiary | 42·29 |
| ,, | 1857 | 58·28 |
| ,, | May 25, 1857, subsidiary 10 per cent. on the above | |
| ,, | By the Convention of Valencia, Nov. 29, 1858 . | 56·26 |
| ,, | Nov. 14, 1861, Dictator Paez added 50 per cent. on the above | 63·94 |
| ,, | Aug. 12, 1862, 75 per cent. on the above . | 74·58 |
| ,, | Sept. 12, 1863 | 85·26 |

Since then the rate has been further increased, and as much as one hundred per cent has been paid. Thus, a barrel of flour of two hundred pounds, the cost price of which is eight dollars, has paid eight dollars duty.

The next thing to be ascertained is the actual yearly amount of imports. Now, according to the report of the Minister of Finance, the actual amount of imports for the first sixteen years of the Republic was two hundred millions, of which no less than one hundred and twenty-nine and a half millions were smuggled. Seventy and a half millions, therefore, passed through the Custom-houses yearly, or about four millions four hundred thousand pounds' worth a year. In corroboration of this statement may be quoted that of Brandt, who calculates that the government lost in the first seventeen years of the Republic forty-eight millions by defalcation; that is, nearly three millions a year, or fifty per cent. on an annual amount of six millions of imports kept back from the knowledge of government. The yearly estimate of frauds on the Customs-houses is given as follows :—

| | |
|---|---|
| Contrabando aventurado, that is, smuggling unknown to officials } | $2,000,000 |
| ,, connived at by officials | 3,000,000 |
| False marks concealing the value of goods<br>Frauds by the boatmen<br>Bribes to officials } | 1,000,000 |
| Total | $6,000,000 |

It must be observed that the frauds practised in the export department are comparatively insignificant.

In the twenty-two years from 1830 to 1852 there were, according to Iribarren, frauds on the customs to the extent of fifty-three and a half millions of dollars. These allegations of fraud are supported by very convincing evidence. Thus the Custom-house reports make the annual amount of imports for the first seventeen years to have been $3,791,667, or at the rate of three dollars and seventy-nine cents per head for the whole population; whereas even the slaves cost for their clothes alone five dollars per head, and all their clothing was imported, and, according to a calculation in *El Liberal*, each Venezuelan really consumes twelve dollars of imports yearly. In the same way Brandt shows that the customs' reports were so incorrect that they made the price of sugar vary from thirteen reals to thirty-eight dollars per quintal, or hundredweight; and he asserts that, in the period he brings under review, all mention of no less than ten thousand vessels freighted with imports was suppressed. Again, according to the statistics of the Custom-houses no more than twenty-five thousand barrels of flour are imported into Venezuela in a year, but the province of Carácas alone expends that amount of imported flour in two hundred and fifty days.

The Statistics of Trade published by foreign powers satisfactorily confute those of the Venezuelan Custom-house officials. Thus, French documents show that in the two years, 1840, 1841, France sent to Venezuela silk-thread to the value of twenty-one thousand and ninety dollars; whereas, according to the statement of the Venezuelan authorities, only one thousand, two hundred, and eighty-eight dollars' worth of silk-thread was imported in three years into Venezuela from all countries put together.

According to the published Reports of the United States, that country in 1858 had a trade with Venezuela amounting to six million one hundred and seventy-one thousand six hundred and ninety-eight dollars, while Venezuelan accounts show only an amount of three million six hundred and seventy-six thousand three hundred and eighty-one dollars. Similar discrepancies might be advanced at great length, but enough has probably been said to make it apparent that the frauds on the Venezuelan Custom-houses are enormous, and amount to at least two-thirds of the whole sum received by government. But the losses by fraud have been calculated by the Minister of Finance at six millions of dollars.*  We may, therefore, fairly estimate the imports which actually pass through the Custom-houses at nine millions, and reckoning the duty at fifty per cent.,—which can be paid, considering that it is only one half of what was levied some years back,—the import duties may be reckoned at four and a half millions of dollars, which would be collected were the collection entrusted to Englishmen.

The next point to be considered is the amount of the Export duties.  The basis of calculation will be the minimum estimate furnished by Messrs. Boulton & Co. of the export duties of La Guaira and Puerto Cabello for the year 1864, each item being taken at the lowest.  The estimate is as follows :—

| Article. | Duty. |
|---|---|
| Coffee, 300,000 quintals, at 12 reals per quintal | $450,000 |
| Cocoa, 40,000 fanegas, at 33 reals per fanega | 166,666 |
| Cotton, 50,000 quintals, at 16 reals per quintal | 100,000 |
| Hides, 50,000, at 6 reals per hide | 37,500 |
| Sundries . | 25,000 |
| Total | $779,166 |

Subsequent experience proved that this minimum estimate was considerably below the actual receipts, which never fall below eight hundred and fifty thousand dollars. But the receipts at Maracaibo, Ciudad Bolivar, and at all the other Custom-houses, cannot be taken at a less sum than those at the two principal stations.

* It is unfortunate that the value of the dollar in English money is not stated in these calculations.  It is understood that it has been fixed of late at 5 francs, or 4s. 2d. ; but previously the dollar was a money of account, and was reckoned about $6¼ to the pound sterling.

An approximate estimate of the national revenue of Venezuela, therefore, may be taken as follows :—

| | |
|---|---:|
| Import Duties . . . . . . \$4,500,000 |
| Export Duties . . | 1,700,000 |
| Salinas or Salt Mines . . . . | 400,000 |
| Papel Sellado, Stamp Duty . . . . | 400,000 |
| 10 per cent. on the Revenues of the States, say | 1,000,000 |
| Sundries . . . . . . . . | 300,000 |
| Total | **\$8,300,000** |

This is the least that the Government ought to realize; but the item for the salt mines has been struck out by the constitution of 1865. The remaining sum, however, five millions nine hundred thousand dollars, would more than pay the expenses of the state, which, inclusive of three millions of dollars for the interest of the public debt, and of no less a sum than one hundred and sixty thousand dollars paid to General Falcon, amounted in 1865 to only five millions eight hundred and twenty-seven thousand four hundred and thirty dollars.

The debt of Venezuela, according to the official report presented to Congress in February, 1867, is as follows :—

| | | |
|---|---:|---|
| Home | . \$10,995,149 | (54) cts. |
| Foreign . . . . . | 46,851,511 | (63) |

DETAILS OF THE FOREIGN DEBT.

| | | |
|---|---:|---|
| Active, Old Debt . . . . . | 18,280,112 | (50) |
| Passive ,, . | 8,985,275 | (00) |
| Interest of the Active | 1,827,865 | (01) |
| ,, Passive . | 449,414 | (87) |
| Bonds of 6 per Cent. | 1,366,365 | (00) |
| Interest on the Bonds . | 204,954 | (75) |
| Loan of 1862 . . | 5,966,350 | (00) |
| Interest on ditto . | 721,324 | (50) |
| Loan of 1864 . | *9,049,950 | (00) |
| Total | **\$46,851,511** | (63) |

* £1,392,300, at \$6½ to the pound sterling. The last item apparently includes both capital and overdue interest.

The statement of the Foreign Debt of Venezuela, according to Messrs. Baring & Co., is as follows :—

The present Debt of Venezuela (exclusive of arrears of interest) is as follows :—

| | |
|---|---|
| £2,812,325 . . | 3 per Cent. Bonds. |
| 1,382,350 . | 1½ per Cent. Bonds. |
| 210,210 . . | 6 per Cent. Bonds, issued for arrears of Interest. |
| 917,900 | 6 per Cent. Bonds. Loan of 1862. |

| | | |
|---|---|---|
| The amount of the Loan was | . . | £1,000,000 |
| Redeemed by Sinking Fund | . | 82,100 |
| | | £917,900 |

The above debts are represented by Messrs. Baring, Brothers, & Co., and were guaranteed by the assignment of 55 per Cent. of Import Duties in La Guaira and Puerto Cabello.

According to the General Credit Company, the debt on the Loan of 1864 is as follows :—

VENEZUELA 1864 LOAN, AS STATED BY THE GENERAL CREDIT COMPANY.

| | |
|---|---|
| Stock issued in 1864 . . . . . | £1,500,000 |
| Cancelled . . . . | 213,200 |
| | £1,286,800 |

DIVIDENDS IN ARREAR.

| | |
|---|---|
| Balance of dividend due 1st April, 1867, at 12s. 6d. per cent. . . . . . | £8,042 |
| Dividend due 1st October, 1867. . . . | 38,604 |
| „ „ 1st April, 1867 . . | 38,604 |
| | £85,250 |

30th April, 1868.

In the absence of reliable statistics it is impossible to give more than a conjectural estimate of the total value of the trade of Venezuela, but it can hardly be reckoned at less than twenty-three millions of dollars. In 1839 Codazzi reckoned it at only nine millions six hundred and four thousand seven hundred and thirty-four dollars; but it has been shown that so long back as 1858 the United States alone had a trade of more than six millions of dollars with Venezuela, and the trade of Venezuela with France, Holland, and Germany is very considerable, probably not less than double that with the United States. Iribarren, indeed, reckons the imports alone at twenty-five millions of dollars, so that to assume twenty-three millions as the total of exports and imports will no doubt be considerably within the mark. According to the map published at New York in 1865, the total value of the trade of Venezuela was twenty-five millions of dollars; the amount of the duties levied at the Customs-houses nine millions; and the total revenue of the Republic ten millions of dollars.

The following is a summary of the resources of Venezuela as regards mineral and vegetable wealth. There are gold-fields in Guayana, known to be very extensive, and probably among the largest in the world. Gold is found in several parts of the old province of Carácas, and especially at Guaicaipuro. There is a silver mine in the mountain of St. Paúl, between Aroa and Nirgua. The Quebrada mines of red copper, in the Aroa district, yield an ore superior to that of Sweden, of Coquimbo in Chili, and of Australia. There are copper mines also in Coro, Carabobo, Barquisimeto, and Merida, and at Tucuticnemo, in Carácas, and on the ridge of the Pao. Iron is found in several districts, and is abundant in Parima, in Guayana. There is a lead mine in Tocuyo, and tin mines exist in several places. Coal is found in Coro and elsewhere. Bitumen is plentiful in Maracaibo, where it is used instead of tar for ships. Trujillo and Cumaná have rich mines of petroleum, and the latter province has a most valuable salt mine at Aragua, abundance of earth suitable for porcelain at Azaveches, and a sulphur mine. Garnets are found in the Silla mountain, near La Guaira, and along the sierra of the coast there are inexhaustible supplies of marble, slate, rock crystal, granite, gypsum and lime.

Among trees, those deserving of especial mention are, first, the palms, which grow at any altitude from the level of the sea to three thousand three hundred feet above it. They yield fruit, a vegetable like the cabbage, oil, cordage, thread, hats, roofs for the cottages of the Indians, rafters, wine, ship-timber, wax, mats, bread, soup, sieves and baskets, and many other things useful for man, according to their kinds, which number at least a hundred. The tuna, or cactus, is valuable not so much for its pleasant fruit and its repulsive spicula, which render it the best of all hedges, as for being the abode of the cochineal insect, which is found also on the pear-tree in Coro, Maracaibo, and Barcelona. The candela tree, called also arbol de la manteca, and by the Indians cuajo, supplies tallow for candles, an excellent oil for lamps, and a beverage, which is made from its toasted fruit. More curious still, and the most wonderful of all trees, is the palo de Lecha, or milk tree, which supplies a milk like that of cows, but thicker; analysed, this product is found to consist of water, animal milk, and wax as pure as that of bees. Mixed with cotton, this milk is used for candles. To the parched traveller the bejuco de agua supplies the place of wells and fountains, for from each yard of it a pint bottle of water can be obtained. Not less useful in its own peculiar locality is the frailejon, which grows at the height of thirteen thousand five hundred feet above the sea, in the region of the icy wastes called Páramos. Even in these wildernesses of death, the frailejon keeps the human body warm. It yields a turpentine superior to Venice turpentine.

Of medicinal plants the first in rank is the quina, or Peruvian bark, which abounds in the forests of Guayana. The cuspa, or bark of Angostura, is still more bitter, and possesses the same valuable qualities. The guaco has many useful properties which have not yet been fully appreciated. It is declared by the Indians to be a specific against the poison of snakes and of hydrophobia, and there is probably some foundation for this assertion. Similar value is assigned to the raiz de mato, which is also said to be a remedy against cholera. The zarzaparilla, which is of three kinds, red, white, and black; the tamarind; the copaiba, or arbol de aceite; the piñon, or pine nut; the cana fistula, or purgative cassia, need only to be mentioned to have their uses recognised. The carapa also yields a medicinal oil, which is likewise adapted for burning in lamps, as does the ceiba, or five-leaved silk-cotton tree; and the carana yields a resin good for curing wounds. From this last tree a syrup is prepared which is said to be good in cases of phthisis, while the fruit of the guaruche, or unona arometica, is a febrifuge.

Of trees useful for timber the vera, or palo sano, the zigophyllum arboreum, deserves to be placed first as producing the strongest wood known, which is well adapted for the keels of ships; it grows to the height of ninety feet. The mague cocui, or maguesis, yields a spirit stronger and more palatable than rum. The pita, or cocuina aloe, supplies material for cordage and sacks. The algarubo, or carob tree, counts high for usefulness as furnishing varnish from its roots and good wood for machinery from its trunk. Cork is made of the alcornoque, and its roots are employed for medicinal purposes. The wood of the divi-divi is good for wheels, and its bark for tanning. The bucare and the guamo protect coffee plantations from the too fierce heat of the sun. The totuma supplies gourds for drinking. The wood of the granadilla is useful for many purposes, and is as hard as iron. Dyes are obtained from the caruto, the paraguatan, the murcielago, and the sangre de drago. The leaves of the lechose are used as soap to bleach lace, muslin, and chintz. The black cedar, or cedrela odorata, grows to one hundred feet in height and fifteen feet in circumference; the cahobo, or swietenia mahogani, to sixty feet in height and twelve in circumference. The caracoli and the guarapa are useful for ship timber, the carnesto-lendus, bombax gossypium, for canvas. The white cedar and the gasifali supply good wood for furniture, and the latter yields a dye. Resin is got from the tacamahaca, and canoes which hold ten persons are made of its bark. The matapato supplies caoutchouc, and its bark makes bags, and the seringa, or concho, gives India rubber, while aromatic caoutchouc is obtained from the guariman. The wood of the sassafras is incorruptible. Oil is obtained from the aguacate, and the Indians make clothes of the marinna. From the camarruba, cupana, and purpuro, the Indians make a kind of soup, and from the guava tree a delicious preserve. The limoncillo, nazareno, and piz, afford good wood for veneering, and the urape elastic bark. Furniture is made of the pardillo, and wheels and machines of the trompillo. A durable, round, hollow wood is got from the tara, and planks from the apamete. A colouring for sauces is supplied by the onoto, and incense by the tree that bears the same name. The miopero, or medlar tree, with its delicious fruit, is common in the forest, where the otoba, or nutmeg tree, is also found. Finally, the wood of the araguanei is hard and proof against wet, and that of the chacarrondai imitates the delicate shades of the tortoise-shell. The leaves of the peoque and the beparia are fragrant, and those of the latter attract bees. From the niopo the Indians make an intoxicating snuff.

From the foregoing brief notice it will be seen how great are the resources of Venezuela in mines and forests; but more important still are those she possesses in her plantations of coffee, cocoa, cotton, sugar-cane, tobacco, and indigo. Coffee was first cultivated in Venezuela in 1784, and the yearly crop may be now reckoned at four hundred and fifty thousand hundredweights, of which twenty per cent., or ninety thousand hundredweights, is lost for want of hands to get in the harvest. The value, therefore, which Venezuela ought to receive for her coffee crop, reckoning the price at two pounds sixteen shillings the hundredweight, and supposing the full harvest to be got in and sold, is one million two hundred and sixty thousand pounds. Coffee plantations flourish at any altitude from seven hundred to seven thousand five hundred feet above the sea. The plant bears in between two and three years, and continues in bearing on an average forty-five years. About thirteen hundred trees are planted in an acre, and each will give at the least one pound and a half of coffee, but instances have been known of a single tree yielding sixteen pounds. The cost of production is about twenty-one shillings per hundredweight.

The cacao, or cocoa tree, theobroma cacao, is indigenous in Venezuela, and no doubt for ages its fruit formed part of the food of the Indians. The taste for it passed into Spain soon after 1522, and was carried by Spanish friars into France in 1661, where A. de Richelieu was the first to patronize the new beverage. Codazzi gives the altitude at which in Venezuela the tree ceases to flourish at six hundred and fifty-two yards above the level of the sea, and later writers fix it at one thousand eight hundred feet above the same level. According to Humboldt, cocoa occupies the same place in point of utility to man in South America as rice does in Africa. Like the coffee plantations, those of cacao are shaded by the bucare, or plantain. The cacao tree begins to bear at from six to eight years after the germination of the seed, and lasts from thirty to fifty years, the latter period only near the sea. Codazzi reckons the total produce of the country in 1840 at one hundred and seventy-six thousand fanegas, of one hundred and ten pounds each. The value at twenty-one dollars the fanega was three million six hundred and ninety-six thousand dollars. The total produce now is not known in this country, but is probably, at least, one-half more.

The cotton of Venezuela is not inferior to the best kinds known in the European markets. The following report, from a native writer thoroughly conversant with the subject, contains an exhaustive account of the mode and expense of cultivation and of the kinds of the plant which have been introduced into Venezuela.

*From the " Venezuelan Agricultor,"* by José Antonio Diaz.*

COTTON : *Gossypium unoglandulosum. Natural order : Mallowworts (Malraceæ), Monadelphia, Polyandria.* A branched, herbaceous plant, lives four years, and may be considered as a semi-shrub. It is of various species : the indigenous, which is called " Pajarito," seed-vessel, white and small, but yielding an abundance of cotton and tough fibre ; and the species raised from foreign seeds, whose seed-vessels are white or straw-coloured, and of larger size. In the torrid zone and in dry situations, which suit it best, it grows to the height of two or three yards. Its leaves are alternate and palmate, divided into five segments, like those of the vine, though somewhat smaller. Its flowers are of a beautiful light yellow colour. Corolla, of five showy petals, heart-shaped, expanding towards the exterior, flat at the broadest part, and united at the base. Calix double, the external one larger than the internal, is divided to its base into three broad leaflets ; the internal calix is undivided. Stamens numerous, united into one column, springing from the corolla, and of which the free anthers form the capital. Seed-vessel single and globular, pointed at the top. Style single, arising from the seed-vessel, inclosed in the same column, and of the same height as the stamens. Stigma deeply cleft, so as to appear like three or four stigmas growing together. Nectaries varying from three to four as the stigmas. The fruit is an oval, almost round, capsule, opening when ripe by three, sometimes four, valves, and divided internally into as many cells, each containing from three to seven seeds, egg-shaped, black or grey, according to the species, and wrapped in a covering of fine down, brilliantly white, which unfolds and falls off at maturity.

According to Codazzi, as late as the year 1782 the largest of the Creole plantations did not contain more than a hundred plants ; and it was at that period that trials of cotton gave better results than those of indigo. Subsequently cotton was cultivated in Aragua, Valencia, Barinas, Cumaná, the province of Carácas, Barcelona, and Maracaibo. In 1794 the exports were ten thousand

---

* I am indebted to Mr. Consul Hemming for this Report.

quintals, and they rose to twenty-five thousand in the year 1803, since which the cultivation of cotton in Venezuela, owing to a decline in price, fell off till the year 1838, when, consequent upon a heavy demand and rise in value, it was urged forward ardently ; new plantations were opened, and the following year, 1839, twenty-seven thousand quintals were exported. But the ardour was of short duration. Partly from the plague of the caterpillar, partly from loss of crops, occasioned by the northern rains, some of the growers lost heart, and others turned their attention to coffee.

Cotton grows under all temperatures, and neither requires a very fertile nor a very moist soil. On the contrary, at the period of its inflorescence and fructification it is injured by rain, and it thrives best in dry positions, sheltered from the north winds. Nevertheless, according to the same Codazzi, in the vast territory of the Rio Negro, where it rains during nine months out of the twelve, and the remaining three are not without showers, at an elevation of three hundred yards, and a mean temperature of $26°$, cotton is growing all the year round, and plants in flower are seen, besides plants bearing seed.

*Culture.*—From what we have said above, it appears that, with the exception of the Rio Negro district, those localities in which northern rains prevail, or which are exposed to the winds from that quarter, are not favourable to the growth of cotton.

Whatever may be the class of cotton, it is sown, with the dibble, in the months of May and June. Three seeds are deposited in each hole, and the holes are a yard apart, in rows a yard and a half one from another. The plants come up from the ground in fifteen days, and bear seeds in seven months. When the seed-vessel opens, it must be gathered within a few days, because the seeds do not remain in the pod longer than six to eight days, after which they escape and fall to the ground, and are lost, or are carried away by the wind, on the out-spread flocks of cotton. In the cooler zone, the plant requires more than seven months to ripen its seed, and, at an elevation of fifteen hundred yards, as much as nine months. Two clearings are sufficient ; the first when the plant is a foot above the ground, and the second when it begins to put forth knops ; but, as it is necessary to make old ground profitable by growing minor crops till the cotton harvest arrives, the clearing, whether done with the hoe or the hook, must be made dependent on the requirements of these crops, bearing in mind that in all cases the cotton should be clear at harvest-time. If the tips of the shoots be nipped off, not only of the main stem, but also of the branches, the plant will become more bushy, and will flower at a greater number of points ; though this operation is more applicable to the foreign descriptions, with large seed-vessels, than to the Creole or Pajarito, of which the ramifications and inflorescence are naturally profuse.

*Harvesting by Cleaning.*—The harvest takes place in the summer, during the months of December, January, and February, according to the period of inflorescence. The capsules are gathered one by one, the labourers (men or women) being provided with baskets to deposit them in. Formerly one real was paid for the filling a basket of the capacity of 6 almuds (21 almuds = 100 litres), moderately compressed ; and the most nimble fingers could scarcely collect three baskets-full. To clean the cotton—that is, to separate it from the seeds—two rollers of hard wood or iron were formerly employed. These were connected by cog-wheels fixed on their axles, and worked one against the other. A crank was attached to one of these rollers, and connected by a cord to a foot-board ; so that the same person who fed the rollers gave motion to the machine with his foot. The cotton passed through and left the seeds behind. But this contrivance did not answer well ; and many crushed seeds found their way through, to the deterioration of the cotton. Afterwards carding cylinders were introduced to lay hold of the filaments and leave the seed perfectly clean ; but these also have their disadvantage : for, although they give out a cleaner cotton, yet they tear it to pieces, and almost pulverize it ; so that, were there not a cloth hood placed over the machine, it would be scattered to a distance in the air. At first, before cotton became a staple article of commerce, it was separated from the seed by hand labour ; and, if time and expense could be disregarded, this plan would still be the best, because, while the cotton would be perfectly cleaned, its fibre would be preserved unbroken, and, as may be logically concluded, would work up into threads and cloths of increased strength. Nevertheless, the material is so delicate and pliable, that, prepared in the carding-cylinders, it is still sufficiently strong when re-united and manufactured.

*Packing the Cotton in Bales.*—When the cotton has been gathered and cleared of the seed, it has yet to be pressed into bales before it can be sent to market. This is the operation we are about to describe. A strong square box is constructed one yard broad and long, and a yard and three quarters deep. The sides of this box are removeable, and above it is fixed a screw-press. The box being put in its place and the sides taken away, four thongs of hide, or stout ropes, are laid across the bottom at equal distances in opposite directions, and over these is stretched a piece of stout canvas a yard and a quarter broad and three yards long. The sides of the box are now put in position and a quintal of cleaned cotton (*net* weight) having been weighed out into bags, the box is filled with it as full as it will hold. The cover of the box, which is square and adjusted to fit the interior of the box, is then put on and forced down with the press little by little as far as possible. When it will yield no further, it is left for a couple of hours; and then, as the whole of the quintal weighed out has not yet been taken in, the press is unscrewed and the box filled up, and pressure again applied until the whole of the quintal of cotton is compressed into three quarters of a yard, in which state it is left for twenty-four hours under the press, so that it may lose most of its elasticity, and yield to packing in a bale. The next day the press is unscrewed, and in the mouth of the box is placed a piece of canvas similar to the piece below, but laid in a different direction, so as to form a cross with it. These pieces of canvas, being divided into three parts, the middle part coincides with the area of the box, and the ends remain over. The cover is next placed upon the top canvas, which is forced down by the press closely upon the cotton in the box. Then the press is made fast, the sides of the box removed, the pieces of canvas sewed together just in the position they are in, and the press being raised as quickly as possible, the cords are tied tight, or the leathern bands are sewed together with thinner strips of the same hide with all possible despatch. It is evident that if these tie-bands are of hide, as is best, the hide must be supple so that holes for sewing may be pierced through it with a sharp stiletto. The bale being now finished, it is removed to make room for another.

From the Society of " Friends of the Country."

On the various species of Cotton :—

1. *Wild Cotton* (which the French call " cotumna," and the English of Jamaica "withy wood") has long and weak branches easily broken. This bad sort was originally introduced into the plantation of that species of cotton known as yarum, or añal cotton, with which it is frequently found, and it has maintained its hold through the size it attains and the great number of capsules it produces, though its cotton falls off, and what remains in the pod is stained by rain or dew. It reaches to a height of nine feet and spreads seventeen or eighteen feet. It flowers once a year, but although it promises largely, it does not give half an ounce of cotton per plant, while the yarum, which does not exceed six feet in height or in spread, yields, under similar circumstances, as much as seven ounces. Wild cotton, though so called, is only found in the plantations. Its flock is not more coarse than that of the yarum, but it approaches to an ash-colour.

2. *Small-flock Cotton.*—Produces little.

3. *Green-crowned Cotton.*—So called from the tip being covered with a down of that colour, which in time becomes a dark gray. It was peculiar to Martinique, where it is called "fine cotton," and is highly esteemed on account of its good quality and colour ; in which, however, it does not equal the Indian cotton, nor the white cotton of Siam. The flocks of cotton fall off, and if it rains at harvest-time, the half-ripe capsules stain the cotton. But if no rain falls till the cotton is quite matured, it retains its whiteness, and is esteemed by the trade. The harvest begins early in November, and lasts seven or eight months. It only gives two and a half ounces per plant. It does not grow higher than three feet, or spread more than four or five.

4 and 5. *Red and Green Sorrel.*—The plant called "Sorrel" by the English is the " Bibisco Sadariffa" of Linnæus, of which there are two varieties—one having the flower-stem and calix green,

the other red. The same peculiarities obtain in the two species of "Sorrel" cotton, whence probably their name. The planters consider them as one species only; but in this they are mistaken, to the detriment of their interest.

The green sorrel has the stem, calix and leaf-veins green, while in the others these parts have a reddish hue. Its cotton falls as soon as ripe—that of the red sorrel does not fall. It gives four ounces of cotton, while the yield of the red is seven and a half ounces.

The red sorrel is preferable not only to the green, but also to the yarum or añal cotton, whose produce is less abundant, while it has the disadvantage of not bringing it forward at fixed periods of the year, as the red sorrel does, but little by little, so that it is necessary to go over the plantation every week, or part of the crop is lost. The flock of the yarum easily separates itself from the pod, either by its own weight or from the influence of rain or wind; and when on the ground it becomes foul and rotten, whence arises the necessity of gathering it from the plant every week. The red sorrel remains on the plant, and is not injured either by wind or rain, except in the case of a hurricane that brings down tree and all. Moreover, the red sorrel gives a white and superior cotton, and does not take up so much space as the yarum, as, at the most, it does not exceed five feet in height and four and a half in diameter.

6. *Algodon Barbiagudo* (cotton with a pointed beard) grows seven feet high and eight wide. Bears once a year, giving scarcely three ounces of cotton. It is frequently planted with the yarum.

7. *Algodon de Gancho Barbado* (cotton with a bearded hook) is often cultivated with other sorts, especially with the yarum. The plant grows to the same size as the yarum; and its cotton is not inferior in quality. It only bears once a year, and the crop is consequently liable to fail, but when this does not happen, the yield is five ounces a tree.

8. *Añal Cotton.*—The coarse sort is mostly cultivated, and is called also Jamaica or San Domingo cotton. We have already observed that its yield is slow, and lasts almost all the year. It rises to a height of six feet, and spreads as much. It usually gives seven ounces per tree. The finer sort is met with in Puerto Rico,

and is the earliest of all that Rohr was acquainted with. Its cotton is of very good quality.

9. *Large-flock Cotton*, formerly was much cultivated, but has latterly sunk in estimation, because it only bears once a year, is stained by rain, and, when attacked by caterpillars, yields nothing. Through negligence of the planter, it is often found mixed with the yarum. It grows six feet high and eight feet wide, and scarcely gives four ounces of cotton per tree. Rohr met, in San Tomas, with a plant of this species, which had spread as much as sixteen feet, and in March, 1710, had already given a pound and three quarters of cotton, promising another copious yield during the remainder of the year. Its flocks of cotton did not fall off, nor were they stained by the rains, and in fineness they approached those of the green-crowned variety.

10. *Guayana Cotton.*—Highly esteemed in Europe on account of the whiteness, length, and strength of its fibre. Known in commerce as Cayenne, Berbice, Demerara, or Essequibo cotton. Gives two crops in the year, but the rains do not allow them both to be turned to account, for they make the green or half-ripe capsules fall from the tree. The ordinary yield is three-quarters of a pound. Under another sky, and more carefully cultivated, it has given as much as a pound and three-quarters.

11. *Brazilian Cotton* is the most esteemed in Europe, but Rohr had not time to notice it attentively.

12. *Indian Cotton.*—" I met with this," says Rohr, " on the mainland between Santa Martha and Cartagena, cultivated by an Indian, whom I used to visit frequently for the sake of the rich store of useful knowledge which he communicated to me. I have never seen trees that bear like his, which was probably due to the fertility of the soil, naturally flat and dry, and to the abundant irrigation obtained by means of numerous ditches and flood-gates. This cotton gives two crops a year. The flocks are very white, and remain a long time on the tree, and are not stained by the pods when wetted with rain. They are more readily cleaned of the seed than those of any of the species I have hitherto described. The lower leaves are always convex, and the branches divergent."

13. Four species bear the name of Siamese, of which three,

called by the French "smooth-crowned" (No. 16) and "downy" (No. 25), yield a cotton of a reddish chestnut colour, somewhat like that of Nanquin. The smooth cotton-tree of Siam grows higher than any other ; in two years it attains a height of twelve feet and a diameter of eight feet. It bears once a year, from February till April, and on this account its cultivation cannot be recommended. Its capsules usually fall as soon as ripe ; but, whether they fall or remain on the tree, they do not open fully, so that it is necessary to break the valves to extract the cotton, which adheres to them firmly, and is separated with difficulty. The yield looks abundant to the eye, but the cotton is so thin in fibre that when weighed the product scarcely comes up to three ounces a tree.

14. *San Tomas Cotton.*—Yields once a year, from February to May, or even till June. Height, eleven feet ; breadth, twenty feet. Product, about six ounces. The cotton is more delicate and white than that of the yarum or añal, and its staple much longer ; but it adheres so strongly to the seed that it cannot be detached from it without carrying off some particles of the epidermis, which have to be separated before spinning, because otherwise the thread breaks every time they present themselves—a peculiarity that has not been observed in other species.

15. *Los Cayos Cotton.*—Similar to the preceding in growth, time of harvest, and quality of cotton, but does not adhere so firmly to the seed, and only gives two and a half ounces per tree.

16. *Grey-crowned Cotton of Siam.*—Paler than No. 13. The ripe capsules burst without falling off, which facilitates the gathering ; but if this is delayed, the cotton falls to the ground, becomes foul, and loses its elasticity and value. It yields twice a year, in February and May, but the two together do not give more than three ounces ; and, as the tree takes up a space of six feet diameter, its cultivation cannot be recommended, unless, indeed, the singular colour of the cotton should render it valuable.

17. *Small-flocked Cotton of Cartagena.*—According to Rohr, this is grown in the province of Carthagena (Columbia), but he adds that it is brought to market in the rough state, not cleared of the seed. Cultivated by Rohr in Santa Cruz, it gave once a year, from February to the end of April, a yield of two and three-quarter

ounces per tree of the finest and whitest cotton. It seems that the capsules fall off as soon as ripe, and this renders it unfit for cultivation.

18. *Large-flocked Cotton of Carthagena.* — This tree is the largest of all hitherto described. It yields once a year. The flocks are as long as eight inches, and remain on the tree without staining. The produce is abundant, but Rohr had not time to ascertain its precise quantity.

19. *White Cotton of Siam.*—Very white, and does not stain on the tree, but its capsules sometimes drop before they reach maturity. Produce, six ounces. In growth, size, leaves, flowers, and capsules, it exactly resembles No. 16. Yields twice a year, in January and June.

20. "I call," says Rohr, "by the name of Curazao Cotton, that which grows naturally on the rocks which overlook the port of Willemstadt in the island of that name. It was there that I first saw it." This cotton is extremely fine, its seeds are half the usual size, its capsules are likewise small, and consequently contain little cotton, though closely packed, which gives it a very bad look at harvest-time, though when it is cleaned it has quite a different appearance, being very white and fine. It is employed in the island in weaving stockings, which are of remarkable fineness and durability, but it is not exported from the island. These trees, planted at distances of four feet in rows five feet apart, yield annually one ounce and two drachms of cotton ; but the harvest lasts much less time than if they were planted, as is usual, at double the distance. In this case, each tree would give more than seven ounces, and the harvest would last from February till June.

21. *Crowned Cotton of San Domingo.*—Bears twice a year, from November to January, and from April to May, and, when the season is favourable, until June. In quality it approaches to Indian cotton, but it is cleaned with difficulty. Its branches are very divergent. It grows seven feet high and ten broad. The ripe capsules fall off, which detracts from its value, notwithstanding the abundance of its yield.

22. *Trailing Cotton.*—Indigenous to Guinea. The stem is covered and the branches bend, so that the lower ones drag on

the ground. Its flocks of cotton closely resemble in shape those of the Indian cotton, but those of the red-leaved cotton (No. 27) resemble them still more; such at least is the opinion of the European manufacturers. It gives one harvest only, from November till March.

23. *Smooth-stained Cotton.*—This name has reference to the appearance of the seeds, which exhibit towards the base a large smooth stain. Its cotton is fine and white.

24. *Coarse Cotton.*—Called in Trinidad Hairy Cotton. Grows seven feet high and four broad, and gives only one harvest, from February to May. Remains on the tree a long time after it is matured, and is very easily cleaned, but does not yield more than two and a half ounces per tree.

25. *Red Downy Cotton of Siam.*—The cotton which it produces is of an Isabel colour, very strong and elastic.

26. *Muslin Cotton.*—In all its four varieties it is so difficult to clean that the operation has to be performed with the fingers, at the cost of sixteen hours' labour for every pound. The red variety and the Raminez Cotton (so called from the islands of that name off Cayenne) requires still more time. It only gives one crop a year, small in quantity, and not of good quality.

27. *Red-leaved Cotton.*—The tender bark of the shoots, and the leaf-veins, are flesh-coloured; a great many of the leaves and the outsides of the calices and of the capsules assume the same colour, when the cotton reaches maturity. Those which do not, become stained with red. It only yields one crop a year, from February to March, producing one ounce and three drachms per tree. Its cotton is as white and fine as the Indian cotton, but it cannot be cleaned by machine, and one pound demands at least thirteen hours of hand labour. Height, seven feet; diameter, eight feet.

28. *Monjas Cotton.*—That of Tranquebar has the leaves lobed, the lobes being lanceolate and pointed, and the side lobes jagged. That of Cambaya has the leaves divided into three elliptic and parabolic lobes, those at the side being cut into, sometimes so deeply as to make it appear that the leaf has five lobes. Both varieties present one capsule only on the principal nerve of the leaf, and even this is apt to be wanting in that of Cambaya. The

flowers are very beautiful, of a fine yellow, with a large spot of blood-colour towards the base. The Tranquebar variety grows three feet high by two broad, and the Cambayan four feet each way. The capsules of the former are the smallest known, those of the latter being rather larger ; but both produce very little cotton, exceedingly difficult to clean. That of Tranquebar requires thirty hours of hand labour per pound, and that of Cambaya a little less·

29. *Porto Rico Cotton.*—Very similar to that of Guayana in size, growth, and configuration of all its organs, but is much more difficult to clean. No idea can be formed of its intrinsic value, because the European manufacturers receive it mixed with many other sorts ; for in Porto Rico every species, except the best, is cultivated indifferently.

It is probable that the experiments of Rohr, repeated in other parts, would give results somewhat different as regards the duration and yield of the crops, and consequently as regards the aptness of certain species for the cultivation. But the fundamental idea of distinguishing the species, and electing those best suited to each locality, rejecting the rest, is applicable to all cotton-growing countries, and requires neither outlay of money nor scientific knowledge.

Rohr is also of opinion that it would be possible to mingle the species, and thus obtain varieties that would be preferable to any of those at present known. There is a species (that of Curazao, for example,) which gives a very fine cotton, but whose capsules are too small. What must be done, then ? Let the anthers be taken away before they open, and the pistils impregnated with pollen from the Carthagenan plant whose cotton flocks are large. Let the seed thus obtained be sowed, and see whether the capsules of the resulting plant will be of a larger size. It may perchance happen that this hybrid variety, imitating its parent plant, will give only one crop, because the hardness of its bark will not allow the flower-buds to pierce it more than once a year. Let us marry it, then, to the red sorrel, or to the white Siam cotton, and see if we can obtain an equal yield in less time, or in two single crops during the year.

By impregnating in this manner the flowers of the Indian cotton with the pollen of the Brazilian cotton, not only have I succeeded in correcting the divergency of the branches of the former, but in rendering them more convergent than in the latter species ; and it even happened that the growth of the variety was more rapid than that of both. These trials may be infinitely varied, and bring about results that will leave far behind the experiments of those who are not naturalists. Who would have foretold that, from that miserable wild berry, so hard and disagreeable, would have sprung all those rich and delicate apples now known under different names ? Shall we, then, deem it impossible to obtain, by following the same steps, a cotton superior to all those now cultivated, perhaps even a cotton without seeds, which would save the growers a deal of labour and expense ? A fruit full of pips was brought by Captain Schmat to contain none at all, and to show no traces of a capsule. The Corinth grape contains no seeds ; and who has ever seen any in the banana (Musa paradisiaca), or in the cambure or guineo (Musa sapientum) ? Such a variety of cotton once obtained, it would be easy to multiply it by means of cuttings ; for the tender branches cut off and put into the earth soon take root. But the best way of improving the species is to become acquainted with them and cultivate them well.

There is grown in the United States a species of cotton, straw-coloured, brilliant, and fine to the touch, the seed of which seems to have been brought from Sicily.

---

### Cultivation of Cotton in Venezuela.

Three sorts of cotton are at present cultivated at Venezuela, called Creole, Marañon, and New Orleans Cotton.

The first is longer and finer in staple than the others ; the second, which probably derives its name from the river so called, as the third does from the place of its origin (New Orleans) is short and rough in fibre.

The plant of the two first classes rises to a height of three yards, or even rather more in low and fertile districts, such as the margin of lakes and rivers. Lands of this sort, or those which, although not bordering on a lake or river, are yet low, damp, light and level, or at least fulfil the two latter conditions, and are in no way composed of dead sand or clay, are those which are best suited to the growth of every species of cotton.

The culture of the cotton is conducted in the following manner :—

After the ground has been cleaned and prepared so that the rain-water or the waters of irrigation may flow off as soon as the two or three first showers after the spring have fallen, lines, the breadth of a hoe (azada), are marked upon it by means of a line and hoe at distances of three yards from centre to centre in the best, or two and a half to two yards in inferior soils. In the middle of these lines holes, two or three inches deep, are made with an iron or wooden dibble (chicura). These holes are three-quarters to a yard apart, according as the soil is more or less fertile, and in them the seed, selected and prepared in the usual way, is deposited to the number of six to eight grains in each hole ; these are then covered lightly over with earth, and, as soon as they come up, those holes out of which two plants at least do not appear are re-sown. When the plants are four or five inches high, they are thinned out by hand, two or three of the most robust, according to the strength of the soil, being left. The plants are trimmed every thirty or forty days, beginning as soon as they reach the height of eighteen or twenty inches. This operation (called by the labourers "capada") is performed by taking away with the fingers the tender sprouts from all the branches, and plucking up the suckers that spring up at the foot of the plant. It is suspended before the inflorescence is announced by means of the pistil, which generally comes enveloped in leaflets, commonly called "mariposa" (butterfly). The ground must be constantly weeded with the hoe until the branches of the cotton-plants, crossing in all directions, form a shade that prohibits any under-growth.

The harvest usually begins in January and ends in March, but if the soil is sufficiently moist it lasts, in most cases, until the first rains.

The plants may be left for another year, cutting them down with a sharp pruning-hook to half their height after the crop is gathered and before the rains come on. A plantation thus prepared is called "troncon" (pollard), and, if kept well weeded, it will sometimes produce as large a crop as the first year (in which it is called "plantilla "). The pollard plants are never trimmed.

In such descriptions of land as are above indicated, a plot of one hundred yards square will produce in a good year, under the system of cultivation just described, one hundred to one hundred and twenty "arrobas brutas," or, on an average, one hundred and twelve and a half, which, at the rate of twelve arrobas to a net quintal, give nine quintals. The total of the costs and charges on a single quintal amounts to nine dollars eighty cents, as shown by the annexed estimate.

The New Orleans seed, which was brought from that port a few years back, is green and hairy, and the plant rises to a height of from a yard and a quarter to a yard and a half (five to six cuarbas). Its culture is as follows :—

In April or May, after a couple of good showers have fallen, the ground having been cleaned and prepared as mentioned above, maize is sown, in rows a yard and a quarter to a yard and a half apart, according to the fertility of the soil. This maize will be ripe in August, and it is then doubled up so that it may dry thoroughly, and lines are immediately marked out between the rows of maize and cotton sown at distances of three-quarters of a yard to a yard. The operations of re-sowing and thinning-out are performed as before described, and the cotton-plants are trimmed once only—when they are a half to three-quarters of a yard high. The plantation must be kept well cleaned until flowering com-mences. The harvest takes place at the same time as with the other sorts, except that, if the soil is sufficiently good, it is usual with the plant in question to come into bearing again spon-taneously and yield some cotton, which is called "reposicion" (after-crop). This plant is never left in pollard, because it would bear little, and would hinder the re-sowing of the maize at its proper time, without mentioning that the crops would injure each other with their shade.

This sort of cotton is short and stout in fibre like the Marañon, and enjoys the same advantage, even in a higher degree, of requir-ing less cotton in the rough to make up a quintal of clean cotton than the black-seeded Creole, since only ten and a half to eleven arrobas of the two former sorts are needed to form a quintal, if the cotton has been gathered from the plant and kept very clean, while twelve to thirteen arrobas of the Creole in the same condition are required.

In all these sorts, the cotton is separated from the seeds in carding-machines (máquinas de sierra), imported from the United States since the year 1818, up to which time the only machines known were the iron cylinders, by which only twenty-five to thirty-five pounds a day could be cleaned, and this frequently turned out of very bad quality, because many of the seeds were crushed and passed through the rollers to the deterioration of the cotton.

The following is an estimate of the cost and expenses of a quintal of cotton in the best lands of the province of Aragua, the ground being supposed to be covered with brushwood, and not with a virgin forest. The "tarea de socalo," *i.e.*, the task or job (tarea) of clearing wood with a bill, is usually a space of thirty brazadas long by six wide, equal to seven hundred and twenty square yards. Consequently, a plot of ten thousand square yards contains approximately :—

| | | | | |
|---|---|---|---|---:|
| 14 "tareas de socalo," | . | . | at 3 reals each | $5·25 |
| 14 tareas felling with an axe | . | ,, | | 5·25 |
| 2 ,, cutting up the wood | . . | ,, | | 75 |
| 2 ,, collecting it into heaps | . . | ,, | | 75 |
| 1 ,, burning it | . . . . | ,, | | 38 |
| 1 ,, re-collecting and re-burning | | ,, | | 38 |

    A plot of 100 yards square contains 40 rows at an average distance of 2½ yards one from another.

| | |
|---|---:|
| 2 tareas laying out the rows and sowing, at 3 reals each | 75 |

    Weeding 6 times, at 8 rows per tarea :—

| | |
|---|---:|
| 30 tareas at 3 reals each . . . . . . . | 11·25 |

    Trimming 4 times at 2 tareas to the plot :—

| | |
|---|---:|
| 8 tareas at 2 reals each . . . . . . | 2·00 |
| | $26·76 |

    The 26 dollars 76 centavos shown by the preceding estimate being divided among 9 quintals, which is the average yield of a plot 100 yards square, give for each quintal . . . . . . . $2·97

The cost of gathering 12 arrobas of cotton for each quintal, at 2 reals each . . . . . . . 3·00
Freight on 1 quintal from the valleys of Aragua to Puerto Cabello . . . . . . . . 1·50
Rent of the land at the rate of 3 dollars per plot, gives for each quintal . . . . . . . . 0·33
Cleaning of each quintal (total cost) . 2·00

Total cost of 1 quintal of cotton $9·80

It must be observed that this estimate does not include freight or carriage of cotton from farms, that do not possess machines for cleaning the cotton, to establishments where such machines are to be found.

Neither is any notice taken of the additional expense that would attend the clearing of a virgin forest, beyond that of clearing such wood of lesser growth, as we have supposed.

It must also be borne in mind that the clearing, whether of copse or of forest, is an expense for the first time only, and which will not have to be incurred again while the land remains under cultivation.

The sugar-cane cultivated in Venezuela is of three kinds, introduced from India, Tahiti, and Java. The cane flourishes at any altitude above the level of the sea up to three thousand three hundred feet, and bears in from eleven to fourteen months. Each cane yields a tenth of its own weight in sugar. An acre will contain nine thousand canes, planted at four feet distance. The Tahiti cane yields one-third more sugar than the Indian, but requires to be resown every ten years. That of Java is the best for rum. Near Valencia plantations have yielded twenty-five consecutive harvests without requiring renewal.

Indigo grows at from three hundred to three thousand feet above the sea, is full grown in from two and a half to three and a half years, lasts a year and a half, and yields two harvests a year. One pound of dye is got from every seventy-two plants.

Tobacco thrives at any altitude from the sea's level to six thousand feet above it, and yields two crops a year, and half a pound of dry tobacco for every five plants. The best sorts of tobacco are those of Rio Negro, Cumanacoa, and Barinas. The latter kind is used by Germans for the pipe.

After what has been said of the resources of Venezuela, of its various products, of the fertility of the soil, of the extent of its territory, the richness of its gold fields, and the moderate amount of its debt in comparison with what ought to be that of the national revenue, it will not be difficult to imagine what must be the answer as to the question, Can Venezuela pay the interest of its debt? With common prudence, Venezuela can pay that interest and all the necessary expenses of the state, and still have a small surplus. It will not be possible for her, indeed, to assign to General Falcon one hundred and sixty thousand dollars out of a single year's income, and thus to bestow on him a salary equal to that of eight cabinet ministers in England; but she can afford to pay her president and ministers well, and yet keep faith with her foreign creditors. The best proof of this assertion is that, besides the payment of the expenses of government on a liberal scale, the Republic has since 1864 discharged nearly all its foreign liabilities in the shape of claims, and has also enriched enormously many of its executive officers, as, for example, the Grand Mariscal. All that is required is a resolute head of the government, and the name of Venezuela will soon be removed from the list of insolvents.

Relations of Venezuela with Foreign Powers—Assistance rendered to Venezuela by England in men and money—History of Venezuelan Debt—Causes of the Decay of English Influence—The Question of the Loans—Plans for solving the Difficulty—The Foreign Office View—The Appeal to Force—The Compensation Plan—The Best Plan.

SPAIN and England are the only European powers with which Venezuela has had very intimate relations. The nature of those relations will appear presently. The consideration of them may be waived for a moment in order to notice very briefly such intercourse as has taken place between Venezuela and other states, whether European or American. The proximity of the Dutch island of Curazao to the coast of Coro has led not only to a flourishing trade, but also to interminable smuggling transactions, to claims and counter-claims between the Dutch and their Creole neighbours. Curazao has continually been the rendezvous of conspirators and intriguers against the government of Carácas, and also of those who, from the righteousness of their cause, deserve a better name. Thus, on the 16th of March, 1848, Don Ramon Paez, son of the renowned soldier and patriot, General Paez, sailed from Curazao to join in a movement in Coro against Monagas.

With New Granada and Ecuador, Venezuela was once united into a great country, which, under the name of Columbia, handed down the memory of its first discoverer, Colon, or Columbus. Within the last five years attempts have been made to renew the union of these three republics, and Signor Antonio Guzman was appointed Venezuelan commissioner to effect that object. The negotiation failed, however, owing, it is said, to the opposition of General Falcon.

Brazil has always been on friendly terms with Venezuela, and a Brazilian minister resides constantly at Carácas. The line of frontier between the two states has been amicably settled.

From the United States of North America Venezuela has on several occasions received sympathy and assistance. After the great earthquake of 1812, North America despatched several vessels laden with provisions for the relief of the sufferers at Carácas. Paez and many other illustrious refugees from Venezuela have found a second and a safer home in New York. On the 25th of November, 1858, Paez, after ten years' sojourn at New York, during which time he "enjoyed every political and social privilege under a free and enlightened government," embarked on board a steamer placed at his disposal by the government of the United States, and sailed for Cumaná. His expedition was unsuccessful, and he returned to North America, where he still lives, at the age of between 80 and 90 years. A minister from the Government of Washington resides at Carácas, and a considerable trade is carried on between that city and New York. Nor did North America fail to take an active part in the war of independence. So long back as the 3rd of November, 1812, the President of Quito, Don Toribio Montes, executed Macaulay, a North American officer, who had successfully defended Popayan against the

Spanish forces, and, after Macaulay's death, others of his compatriots took part in the war.

France and Germany both carry on a not inconsiderable trade with Venezuela, and some Frenchmen and a far greater number of Germans are resident in Venezuelan territories, but, with the exception of the crude designs of the first Napoleon, no intention of political interference has been manifested by either of the said European powers with reference to the government of Carácas.

The long and cruel war which was waged between Columbia and the mother-country, Spain, seems to have left the seeds of hatred and aversion to Spain deep-sown in the breast of every Venezuelan. It is sad that there should be such feelings between the two countries, and that parent and child should have parted on such terms; but the wrongs on both sides were such that centuries must elapse before the memory of them fades entirely away. Meanwhile, the history of the dealings of Spain with her South American colonies, especially with Columbia, deserves to be studied by all nations, and should prove a beacon to mark out errors in colonial government for all time. The grievances which the South Americans alleged as the ground of their revolt were, first, their exclusion from office; secondly, the pride of the Spaniards; thirdly, the Inquisition; fourthly, restrictions on education; fifthly, commercial restrictions. On the first, second, and fourth of these, England will do well to ponder in her dealings with India. The Inquisition alone, it must be owned, formed a reasonable ground of separation from Spain, and the whole list of wrongs justified, perhaps, war, if war be ever justifiable; but such was the prostration of Columbia under

Spanish rule, that it is doubtful whether she would ever have rebelled but for the successful example of the United States of North America. As it was, the rebellion began feebly, and the struggle was long protracted, owing to many causes, such as the dispersion of the population, the division of castes, difficulty of communication, the ignorance of the people, their long habits of obedience, the want of experienced Creole officers, the general ignorance of war, and the influence of Spanish officials. All these things retarded the independence of the Columbians, and the longer they fought the more embittered the strife became;—hence the rancour it has left.

After dwelling on the great struggle between Spain and her colonies, the mind is naturally led to inquire and estimate the result of the victory. An impartial examination will find it hard to determine whether the end attained was an evil or a good. On the one hand, it must be freely admitted that the government of Spain over her South American colonies was odiously selfish, despotic, and unjust; but the worst possible government is perhaps better than chronic civil war and a restless appetite for change, which grows with every fresh revolution. Slavery and the inquisition are monstrous evils, but rebellion and scepticism are as bad, if not worse. If any one is disposed to dispute this statement, let him hear the testimony of Ducoudray Holstein, who, himself a French republican and chief of the staff to the president liberator, was not likely to be too favourable to despotism. After speaking of the material prosperity of Columbia while under Spain, he says: " All this wealth, comfort, and agreeable society have now disappeared. The greater part of the distinguished families

in Venezuela and New Granada have left the country, and
the few that remain are ruined." " Were the inhabitants
in a worse condition under the dominion of Spain, bad as it
was, than they are now, under the bayonets of the dictator
liberator ? "   As to the war itself, and the manner in which
it was conducted, it will be sufficient to state that, according
to the estimate of Restrepo, the republican secretary of
state, 400,000 persons perished in it, and, at the same time,
to quote the words of an Englishman, who was himself
engaged in it : " There is no power," says Colonel Hip-
pesley, " to be acquired in the starvation and perils of the
tedious voyage, whatever there may be in the after war ;
and even in the conflict the author can scarcely imagine the
Briton engaged, who would not shrink in disgust and
horror, rather than rise in the pride of triumph, at the
merciless massacre of unarmed prisoners, and the infernal
sporting with human sufferings.   The utter want of a commissariat, and the intolerable heat of the climate, involve
a complication of miseries which no European constitution
can withstand ; and the author has to lament the death of
the great majority of his companions, who perished like
infected lepers, without sustenance and without aid from
the unfeeling wretches* in whose behalf they fell."   Those
who think that the overthrow of a bad government implies
the inauguration of a better will do well to ponder over
these remarks, and the more they reflect upon them and
study the history of the events to which they refer, the less
will be their sympathy with the revolutionary principles
which are spreading so rapidly in Europe.

* If this be meant as imputing inhumanity to the Venezuelans generally,
the author feels bound to deny the charge.

Whatever the results of the war of independence, whether they have been beneficial to Venezuela or the reverse, that country certainly owes some gratitude to England for the part she took in it. The policy of the English Government was, perhaps, to a certain extent, selfish in aiding the Creoles against Spain, but the majority of Englishmen went to serve Columbia very much from sympathy with a people struggling for freedom; and if this be questioned, a sufficient proof of the truth of the observation will be found in the fact that no Englishman could be induced to enlist on the side of despotism.

England assisted Columbia with both soldiers and treasure in the war with Spain. So early as the year 1813, the troops of Socorro were brought into admirable discipline by a British officer, Gregor MacGregor. These men did good service under Don Antonio Nariño, of Santafé, who was the prime mover of the revolt. MacGregor afterwards rose to be a general, and in 1816 commanded a small army which marched from Maracai to Barcelona and took that important town, after winning a great battle against the Spanish General Lopez, and repeatedly defeating the royalists in lesser engagements. After taking Barcelona, MacGregor united his column with the troops of Piar, and defeated the sanguinary Morales with great slaughter. Another English officer who very early distinguished himself in the war was Captain, afterwards Colonel Virgo, who is first mentioned by Restrepo as doing eminent service at the battle of Palace, near Popayan, on the 30th of December, 1813. From that time forth Englishmen were constantly engaged on the side of the patriots, and to notice all their exploits would be equivalent to writing a history of the War of Independence. It will be sufficient, then, to say that in the two decisive battles by which the power of Spain was overthrown, and especially in the latter, which was the crowning victory, the honours of the day belonged to the British soldiers. Thus, on the 7th of August, 1819, the battalion of rifles under Lieut.-Col. Arthur Sandes, and that called Albion, commanded by Lieut.-Col. Rook, bore the brunt of the battle at the Bridge of Boyacá, near the city of Tunja. "The results of this victory," says the historian Baralt, "were immense, for the Spanish army was destroyed, and New Granada was set free." More decisive still was the battle of Carabobo, a full account of which has been given in a preceding chapter, and in which the British Legion alone carried the Spanish position, losing two men out of every three killed or wounded. On that occasion the valour of the English extorted from Bolivar the address, "Saviours of my country!"

The pecuniary assistance rendered by England to Venezuela has been of such a nature that a full account of it cannot be given without narrating the whole history of the Venezuelan debt. The debt of Venezuela, then, is of two kinds, domestic and foreign. The domestic debt is that portion of the domestic debt of Columbia which fell to the share of Venezuela when it separated from New Granada and Ecuador, the two republics which, with Venezuela, made up the grand Republic of Columbia. The domestic debt of Columbia had its origin in sums raised by the Spanish Government by mortgaging the treasuries in New Granada and Venezuela. For these sums the Spanish Government paid, in some cases, three per cent., in others four, and in others five per cent. Other sums raised by the

Spanish Government were styled funds of amortizacion, as it was supposed that they were intended to form a sinking fund to pay off the bonds of that government. Besides these, there was the debt of the Panama States, for which Columbia became liable, since on that condition those states threw off their allegiance to Spain. So also with the debt of Guayaquil, which Columbia, on similar grounds, took on itself. To these liabilities were added debts incurred by the Republic of Columbia after it had declared its independence in 1810. The young republic had a scanty revenue, insufficient for its wants even in times of peace, and this, notwithstanding the exigencies of war, it, with the usual imprudence of republics, still further reduced by abolishing many imposts which were unpopular with the citizens. Hence, up to 1822, the epoch when foreign loans were negociated, a considerable amount of debt had been incurred on account of stores supplied to the commissariat and of pay due to the army, and this debt was not paid off with the proceeds of the foreign loans. Up to May, 1824, then, the debt of Columbia stood as follows :—

| | |
|---|---:|
| For sums raised by the Spanish Government at various amounts of interest | $900,000 |
| Interest thereon | 468,138 |
| For ditto raised by ditto for amortization | 1,250,000 |
| Interest thereon | 937,500 |
| Debt of the States in the Isthmus of Panama | 252,000 |
| Interest thereon | 48,000 |
| Debt of Guayaquil | 800,000 |
| Liquidated domestic Debt | 1,200,000 |
| Unliquidated, with Interest | 3,800,000 |
| Pay due to civil officers up to 1st January, 1822 | 1,500,000 |
| A third of the same retained by law | 1,650,000 |
| Loans received in cash | 1,000,000 |
| Pay due to military | 3,500,000 |
| Foreign Loan of March, 1822 | 10,000,000 |
| ,, May, 1824 | 20,000,000 |
| Total | $46,505,638 |

The foreign debt of Columbia began in 1816, when some English houses and other foreigners supplied Bolivar with the means of making his expedition to Angostura. After the battle of Boyacá, Bolivar determined to send an envoy to London to settle the claims then existing against his government. Accordingly, in 1820, he despatched Francisco Antonio Zea to England, and that officer issued a number of debentures in payment of the foreign claims to the amount of £547,783. In March,* 1822, Zea contracted a loan of £2,000,000 with Messrs. Herring, Graham, and Powles, at £80 for the £100, by which the former debt of £547,783 was paid off. On the 15th of May, 1824, a further loan of $20,000,000, or £4,750,000, was taken from Messrs. B. A. Goldsmith & Co.

On the 25th of December, 1834, Señor Santos Michelena, Plenipotentiary on the part of Venezuela, and Señor Luis de Pombo, on that of N. Granada, without the concurrence of the Plenipotentiary of Ecuador, agreed that the foreign Columbian Debt for the two loans, should be divided amongst the three Republics, Venezuela making itself liable for $\frac{28\frac{1}{2}}{100}$ and N. Granada for $\frac{50}{100}$, while the remainder, or $\frac{21\frac{1}{2}}{100}$, fell to the responsibility of Ecuador. Hence the foreign debt of Venezuela became $11,698,049·93 cents, or £1,888,395 15s. This Convention was ratified by Venezuela on the 26th of July, 1837; by N. Granada on the 25th of August; and by Ecuador on the 26th of November, 1837. The domestic debt of Columbia was divided at the same time, and $7,217,915·12 cents, fell to the share of Venezuela. The total of the Venezuelan share of both foreign and domestic debt thus amounted to $19,215,965·05 cents, or 76,875,860f. and 20 centimes.

* Codazzi, p. 289, gives May 13, 1822, as the date of this Loan.

The dividends on the foreign debt were paid faithfully during the Presidentship of General Paez, and up to the year 1848, when the General went into exile, and they were stopped. On the 23rd of February, 1859, a meeting of bondholders was held in London, when it was agreed to accept the proposal of Señor Rodriguez, the Venezuelan Minister, to pay 3 per cent. on active, and 1½ per cent. on deferred Venezuelan bonds. Only two coupons were paid upon the reserved bonds, and in 1862, the sum of £214,000 of arrear dividends had accrued.

In January, 1862, Señor Hilarion Nadal, the agent of General Paez, arrived in London to raise a fresh loan of one million. At a general meeting of bondholders held on the 20th of June, 1862, it was agreed to accept the proposal of Señor Nadal, in order to obtain the special hypothecation of 55 per cent. of the import duties, and by freeing the customs from usurious claims to enable the Venezuelan Government to recommence paying the dividends. At this time the foreign debt of Venezuela amounted to £4,412,000, carrying an annual interest of £118,000. The following is the account given by Señor Pedro* José Rojas, the Secretary-General, and successor of General Paez, of the manner in which the funds realised by this loan were expended :—

£1,000,000 at 63 per cent. = £630,000 = at $6·48 the pound sterling . . . . . . . . . . $4,082,620·54

| *Expenses and Commissions.* | £ | s. | d. |
|---|---|---|---|
| Baring, Brothers, and Company . . . | 12,102 | 0 | 0 |
| Brokerage . . . . . . . . | 1,939 | 2 | 6 |
| Mr. Mocatta's Travelling Expenses . . . | 1,747 | 9 | 6 |
| Estimate of expenses for which Messrs. Baring will account . . . . . . . | 3,012 | 15 | 0 |
| | | £18,801 | 7  0 |

* Vindicacion, Carácas, 1863, p. 114. The statements of Mr. Mocatta and of Messrs. Baring will be found in the Appendix.

|  | £ | s. | d. |
|---|---|---|---|
| Brought forward . . | 18,801 | 7 | 0 |
| Petty expenses . . . . . . . | 89 | 2 | 10 |
| Freight and insurance of £100,000 . . . . | 2,587 | 14 | 0 |
| Seymour and other agents for assistance rendered | 21,800 | 0 | 0 |
| Commission to Señor Nadal . . . . | 16,000 | 0 | 0 |
| His expenses . . . . . . | 3,000 | 0 | 0 |
|  | £62,278 | 3 | 10 |

The same in dollars at $6·50 the pound sterling, $469,808·21 cts.

Freight from St. Thomas    1,652

$471,460·21

*Dividends in arrear and advance on the old and new English debt.*

|  | £ | s. | d. |
|---|---|---|---|
| 20 per cent. on £9,600 arrears of interest from 1840 to 1847 on old Bonds at 6 per cent. converted into 3 per cents., on condition of paying the said 3 per cent. . . . . . | 1,920 | 0 | 0 |

|  | £ | s. | d. |  | £ | s. | d. |
|---|---|---|---|---|---|---|---|
| 6 months' interest due July 1, 1862, on £2,810,850 active Bonds at 2 per cent. . . . . | 28,108 | 10 | 0 |  |  |  |  |
| On £1,385,450 deferred at 1 per ct. | 6,927 | 5 | 0 |  |  |  |  |
| Commission 1 per cent. . . | 350 | 7 | 0 |  | 35,386 | 2 | 0 |
| 6 months' interest due July 1, 1862, on £210,210 6 per cent. Bonds, issued for dividend in arrear from July, 1860, to Jan. 1862, on the 3 and 1½ Bonds . . . . | 6,306 | 6 | 0 |  |  |  |  |
| Commission 1 per cent. . . | 63 | 1 | 3 |  | 6,369 | 7 | 3 |

|  | £ | s. | d. |
|---|---|---|---|
| 6 months' interest of Jan. 1863, on £2,810,850 Bonds of 3 per cent. to 2 . . . . . | 28,108 | 10 | 0 |
| On £1,385,250 Bonds of 1½ per cent. at 1 . . | 6,927 | 5 | 0 |
| On £210,210 6 per cent. Bonds . . . . | 6,306 | 6 | 0 |
| Commission at 1 per cent. . . . . . | 413 | 8 | 4 |
| 6 months' interest due Nov. 1862, on 1 million sterling at 6 per cent. . . . . . | 30,000 | 0 | 0 |
| Ditto, due May, 1863, on ditto at ditto . . | 30,000 | 0 | 0 |
|  | £145,430 | 18 | 7 |

at $6·50     $945,291·04

|  | £ | s. | d. |
|---|---|---|---|
| Baring, Brothers, & Co., for sums due to them | £14,719 | 1 | 3 |

at $6·50     $95,673·90

Brought forward   .   .   .   .                    $1,512,425·15

*Bank of Venezuela.* *

|                                                  | Dollars. | Cts. |
|--------------------------------------------------|---------:|------|
| On account of account current        .   .   .   | 740,250·34 | |
| For Notes in circulation    .           .   .    | 1,644,021·16 | |
| Shares .   .   .   .   .   .           .   .      | 2,714,500 | |
| Equivalent for Public Debt 3 per cent.   .       | 10,858,000 | |

$13,942,871·50

Paid on account in cash   .   .   .   .   .   .   .   .   $234,895·63

*Diplomatic Claims.*

| | |
|---|---:|
| United States   .   .   .   .   .   .   . | 100,000 |
| Ditto,   Aves Island          .   .   . | 13,000 |
| British Legation  .   .   .   .      .   . | 97,278·43 |
| Consul-General of Denmark   .      .   . | 63,106·60 |
| ,,   ,,   Netherlands   .   .   .   . | 15,139·66 |

$288,578·69

Orders on the Custom-House at La Guaira .   .   .   .   . 133,591·62
Various public creditors paid by E. Mocatta, by bills on London   456,522·50
War expenses remitted to the provinces, and common expenses
  of the Treasury paid by the Custom-house at La Guaira   .   . 219,224·55
Paid in the same departments by the Treasury .   .   .   . 407,382·40
Balance in the hands of Baring, Brothers, £20,000   .   . 130,000·00

† $4,082,620·54

General Páez having hypothecated 55 per cent. of the import duties at La Guaira and Puerto Cabello, for payment of the dividends of this loan, a decree was issued on the 1st of November, 1862, duly signed by the General and the Secretary of State. This was lodged at the Custom-house, published in the official gazette, and by bando or beat of drum.

* "We allotted," writes Señor Rojas, "a large sum for the amortization of the ordinary Shares of the Bank of Venezuela. These Shares consisted of Public Debt. The capital purchased amounted to eleven millions; for the balance bills (vales) were given with security on certain Custom-houses of the Republic. This was certainly not one of the least important advantages of the Loan." (Vindicacion, p. 112.) "A respectable committee of merchants and the Directors of the Bank of Carácas, allotted the money assigned to pay the sums due" (valores) to the Bank of Venezuela. (Vind., p. 113.)

† It will be seen that there are several mistakes in the addition of figures in this statement, and that the total is $700,000 out. The statement is, however, an exact transcript of the Spanish.

"A few months afterwards General Falcon and General Blanco assumed the Presidency and Vice-Presidency of the Republic, and the aforesaid decree was respected and acted upon for two years. On one occasion the sum of $75,000 was appropriated by the authorities as a loan, on the plea of necessity, but that sum was restored by General Blanco in London. In October, 1863, General Blanco received and accepted from Messrs. Baring the complete and final account of the loan of 1862, together with a balance of about £21,000." Suddenly, on the 3rd of December, 1864, the Government of Venezuela issued a decree suspending the payment of the 55 per cent. to the British bondholders, and actually forced the agents of the bondholders to return $18,443 that had been paid to them.*

In the meantime, however, General Falcon and General Blanco had secured the proceeds of the loan of 1864, and had relieved the Government from the army claims and other pressing demands, as has been shown in a preceding chapter. It, therefore, appears in the clearest way, that England not only aided the Venezuelans with gallant soldiers in winning their independence, but supplied them in all the most critical emergencies with treasure to defray their expenses. Surely, under the circumstances, the influence of this country in Venezuela ought to be great. How is it, then, that the exact contrary is the case, and that the representations of our Ministers at Carácas with respect to the loans, have had no weight whatever? A distinct and decisive answer to this question cannot be given, except before a Committee of the House of Commons. It involves the whole subject of the organisation of the Foreign

* Statement by the Committee of Venezuelan Bondholders, London, 1866.

Office; an organisation which could barely be tolerated in
1782, but which is so unsuited for the present time that
nothing but the intense ignorance and consequent indifference of the general public regarding it, allows of its being
maintained for a moment.

But, though all that is known cannot be told, unless
under due authorisation, one great cause of the decay of
British influence in foreign countries, and especially with
reference to the recovery of debts owed by the Governments
of those countries to British subjects, can be pointed out.
This is, that the English Government gratuitously parades
its determination not to enforce the claims of its subjects.*
Now, whatever the intentions of a claimant may be, it is
surely very unwise to proclaim beforehand that resort will
not be had to ulterior measures. It is like putting up a
board to warn trespassers that they will *not* be prosecuted.
Such a course may be declared quite unreasonable, without
going at all into the question whether war for the recovery
of a debt is justifiable by international law, or is to be
regarded only as a matter of discretion. But the fact is, it
is a course adopted by Government in order to stand well
with Parliament and the general public, who, from selfish
motives, are opposed to such expenditure as a war necessitates for the recovery of the property of a comparatively
small number of persons. " Why should we be taxed that
they may be indemnified ? " is the thought that pervades

---

* This extreme candour amounts to almost touting for injuries, and reminds
one of Jack in the Tale of the Tub, who "would stand in the turning of a
street, and calling to those who passed by, would cry to one, ' Worthy, sir,
do me the honour of a good slap in the chaps.' " It is, perhaps, unnecessary
to add that the remarks here made are intended to apply to the traditional
policy of the Foreign Office, not to that of the Ministers now in power.

the public mind, and finds its echo in Parliament. The same thought gave rise to all the fables that were told about the difficulties of the Abyssinian campaign,—the unhealthiness of the climate, and the impracticability of reaching Magdala. This *lâcheté* has been properly punished in the case of Abyssinia, by the enormous and unnecessary expense of sending an army to accomplish what might well have been performed by a single brigade. But the selfish taxpayer exaggerated the difficulties of the expedition in order to prevent it altogether, and, of course, no government would incur the responsibility of sending only 3,000 men to do what every one was declaring could not be achieved by five times that number.*

It is not to be supposed, however, that Government would admit the dread of unpopularity, or of Parliamentary censure, to be the reasons for its meek acquiescence in the wrongs of the Venezuelan bondholders, and the contemptuous disregard of its remonstrances in their favour. A very different ground for this patient endurance was put forward on a previous and similar occasion by Lord Palmerston in his memorable circular of January, 1848. It is there alleged, that Government abstained from action in order to discourage the investment of English capital abroad instead of at home. Twenty years have passed away

---

* The idea of sending an Ambassador with three thousand men originated with the author of this book. See Athenæum, No. 2057, March 30, 1867, p. 419. "It has been clearly ascertained that the road from Massowah into Tigré is quite practicable. Would it not be better to send an ambassador with an escort to treat with Theodorus ? Twelve hundred horse, two thousand infantry, a brigade of guns and a couple of mortars would suffice for the escort." This was not a mere guess, but was based on a careful comparison of what Sale had done in a country as difficult as that between Annesley Bay and Magdala, and against incomparably better soldiers than the Abyssinians.

since this plausible excuse was made, and the increasing
investments in foreign loans during each year have rendered
it less and less specious, but even now it would probably
be again employed. It is requisite, therefore, to examine
the whole question of the right and expediency of enforcing
the performance of justice to the citizens of this country in
reference to the debts owing to them by foreign nations,
with the view of showing that, neither on the ground alleged
by Lord Palmerston, nor on any other, can action be any
longer delayed.

It will be as well, then, to begin with quoting Lord Palmerston's circular *in extenso*, in order to dispose of the
pretext for inaction which he thought it politic to put forward. This document* is as follows :—


FOREIGN OFFICE, *January*, 1848.

Her Majesty's Government have frequently had occasion
to instruct Her Majesty's representatives in various foreign
States to make earnest and friendly, but not authoritative
representations in support of the unsatisfied claims of
British subjects, who are holders of public bonds and
money securities of those States.

As some misconception appears to exist in some of those
States with regard to the just right of Her Majesty's Government to interfere authoritatively, if it should think fit to do
so, in support of those claims, I have to inform you, as the
representative of Her Majesty in one of the States against
which British subjects have such claims, that it is for
the British Government entirely a question of discretion,
and by no means a question of international right, whether

* The *Times*, April 21, 1849.

they should, or should not, make this matter the subject of diplomatic negociation. If the question is to be considered simply in its bearing upon international right, there can be no doubt whatever of the perfect right which the Government of every country possesses to take up, as a matter of diplomatic negociation, any well-founded complaint which any of its subjects may prefer against the government of another country, or any wrong which from such foreign government those subjects may have sustained; and if the government of one country is entitled to demand redress for any one individual among its subjects who may have a just, but unsatisfied, pecuniary claim upon the government of another country, the right so to require redress cannot be diminished merely because the extent of the wrong is increased, and, because, instead of there being one individual claiming a comparatively small sum, there are a great number of individuals to whom a very large amount is due.

It is, therefore, simply a question of discretion with the British Government whether this matter should or should not be taken up by diplomatic negociation, and the decision of that question of discretion turns entirely upon British and domestic considerations.

It has hitherto been thought by the successive governments of Great Britain undesirable that British subjects should invest their capital in loans to foreign governments instead of employing it in profitable undertakings at home; and, with a view to discourage hazardous loans to foreign governments, who may be either unable or unwilling to pay the stipulated interest thereupon, the British Government, has hitherto thought it the best policy to abstain from taking up as international questions the complaints made by British subjects against foreign governments which have failed to make good their engagements in regard to such pecuniary transactions.

For the British Government has considered that the losses of imprudent men, who have placed mistaken confidence in the good faith of foreign governments, would prove a salutary warning to others, and would prevent any other foreign loans from being raised in Great Britain, except by governments of known good faith and of ascertained solvency. But, nevertheless, it might happen that the loss occasioned to British subjects by the non-payment of interest upon loans made by them to foreign governments might become so great that it would be too high a price for the nation to pay for such a warning as to the future, and, in such a state of things, it might become the duty of the British Government to make these matters the subject of diplomatic negociation.

In any conversation which you may hereafter hold with the —— Ministers upon this subject, you will not fail to communicate to them the views which Her Majesty's Government entertain thereupon, as set forth in this despatch.

Signed,          PALMERSTON.

With reference to this important circular, the first thing to be considered is the principle, which is said to have been the animating one of successive British governments as regards loans to foreign states—viz., discouragement of them, in order that English capital might be invested at home. But money, like every other export, will always seek the best market, and to discourage it from doing so is simply opposition to the principles of free trade. Supposing the foreign state to fulfil its engagements and to pay a higher interest than home investments would, it is obviously beneficial to England that foreign loans should be negociated in the London market. But should the foreign state not fulfil its engagements, England loses the whole capital lent, unless payment be enforced. If payment be enforced, the capital returns to England, and fraudulent borrowers are deterred from coming to the English market. In a word, there are two ways of discouraging hazardous loans—the one is to punish the English lender by neglecting his rights, in which case British capital is lost; the other is to enforce payment and punish the foreign fraudulent borrower, in which case English capital is recovered, and that, too, without loss to the state, for the borrower would have, of course, to pay the expenses of coercion. But, in truth, if successive British Governments really did imagine that they could put down foreign loans by ignoring the rights of English bond-holders, when, even at the time of Lord Palmerston's circular, the capital lent to foreign governments had grown up· to £150,000,000, all that can be said is, *O, sancta simplicitas!* At all events, the notion must be dead now, when the capital owed to Englishmen by foreign states amounts to something like half the national debt, a sum much too vast to be made the subject of mistaken theories.

In point of fact, the language of Lord Palmerston's circular, like that of all diplomatic documents, is intentionally guarded, and represents only the square root of what his lordship really felt to be right. This is shown by what he said in the House of Commons, in a debate which was the real *fons et origo* of the circular above cited. The debate took place in June, 1847, when Lord Bentinck brought forward a motion—" That an address be presented to Her Majesty, humbly praying that Her Majesty may be graciously pleased to take such steps as may be deemed advisable to secure for the British holders of unpaid foreign* bonds redress from the respective governments." Lord Palmerston then said : " Although I entreat the house, upon grounds of public policy, not to impose at present upon Her Majesty's Government the obligation which the proposed address would throw upon them, yet I would take this opportunity of warning foreign governments, who are debtors to British subjects, that the time may come when this house will no longer sit patient under the wrongs and injustice inflicted upon the subjects of this country. I would warn them that the time may come when the British nation will not see with tranquillity the sum of £150,000,000 due to British subjects, and the interest, not paid ; and I would warn them that, if they do not make proper efforts adequately to fulfil their engagements, the government of this country, whatever men may be in office, may be 'compelled, by the force of public opinion and by the votes of Parliament, to depart from that which has hitherto been the established practice of England, and *to insist* upon the payment of debts due to British subjects. That we have the means of *enforcing* the rights of British subjects I am not prepared to dispute. It is not because we are afraid of those states, or all of them put together, that we have refrained from taking the steps to which my noble friend (Lord George Bentinck) would urge us. England, I trust, will always have the means of obtaining justice for its subjects from any country upon the face of the earth. But this is a question of expediency, and not a

* The immediate occasion of the motion was the non-payment of Spanish bonds.

question of power; therefore, let no foreign country that has done wrong to British subjects deceive itself by a false impression, either that the British nation or the British Parliament will for ever remain patient acquiescents in the wrong, or that, if called upon to enforce the rights of the people of England, the Government of England will not have ample means at its command to obtain justice for them."

Here Lord Palmerston distinctly warns defaulting foreign states that a time may come when payment will be enforced from them.   This warning was uttered more than 20 years ago: is it to remain a *brutum fulmen?* or can there ever be a case in which the menace it contains could be more justly executed than that of Venezuela, where, be it remembered, no less a sum than $7,000,000 is at stake?   But before exhibiting in one view the strength of that case, it may be desirable to support Lord Palmerston's declaration by quotations from the best authorities on international law.

In Phillimore's "Commentaries upon International Law" (ed. 1855, v. 2, c. iii., p. 8), it is said : " The right of interference on the part of a state, for the purpose of enforcing the performance of justice to its citizens from a foreign state, *stands upon an unquestionable foundation,* when the foreign state has become itself the debtor of these citizens."

Vattel (v. 2, c. xiv., p. 216) writes : " Les emprunts faits pour le service de l'État, les dettes créées dans l'administration des affaires publiques, sont des contrats de droit étroit, obligatoire s pour l'État et la nation entière. Rien ne peut la dispenser d'acquitter ces dettes-là. Dès qu'elles ont été contractées par une puissance légitime, le droit du créancier est inébranlable.   Que l'argent emprunté ait tourné au profit de l'État, ou qu'il ait été dissipé en folles dépenses, ce n'est pas l'affaire de celui qui l'a prêté. Il a confié son bien à la nation ; elle doit le lui rendre. Tant pis pour elle, si elle a remis le soin de ses affaires en mauvaises mains."

The same writer, further on (c. 18, s. 343), says : "It is only for an evidently just cause, *and for a clear* * *and undeni-*

* Mr. Gerstenberg in his excellent Report of 1865, and Messrs. Baring in their Memorial to Earl Russell under date the 25th of March in the same year, have so completely disposed of all attempts to evade the obligation of the Debt of 1862, by the device of a reference to the High Court of Venezuela and other pretences, that it is unnecessary to add anything on the subject here. With regard to one point, however, which seems to have some weight with the Venezuelans themselves, though it can have none with those who really understand the question, it may be as well to cite the authority of Wheaton (International Law, ed. 1863, p. 41). "As to public debts—whether due to or from the revolutionized State—a mere change in the form of government, or in the person of the ruler, does not affect their obligation. The essential form of the State, that which constitutes it an independent community, remains the same ; its accidental form only is changed. The debts being contracted in the name of the State, by its authorized agents, for its public use, the nation continues liable for them, notwithstanding the change in its internal constitution. The new government succeeds to the fiscal rights, and is bound to fulfil the fiscal obligations of the former government." As to the general question it is right to add the opinions of the Members for the City of London, which are thus expressed :—

New Court, 10th July, 1865.

My Lord,—The Chairman of the Committee of Venezuelan Bondholders has invited me to write to your Lordship respecting the Venezuelan Loan, contracted in 1862, and to state my opinion of the conduct of the Venezuelan Government.

I cannot help complying with the request of that gentleman, and I beg to say that I consider it a case in which the Bondholders may expect every assistance from your Lordship, in obtaining the fulfilment of the contract entered into by the Government of Venezuela with the British Bondholders.

Recommending their claims, therefore, to your Lordship's assistance, and apologising for troubling your Lordship,

I have the honour to be, my Lord,

Your Lordship's very obedient Servant,

(Signed)    Lionel de Rothschild.

The Right Honourable
    The Earl Russell, K.G.

*able debt*, that the law of nations allows us to make reprisals."

———

LONDON, *7th July*, 1865.

MY LORD,—The Chairman of the Committee of Venezuelan Bondholders has shown me a copy of a letter of the 25th of last March, addressed to your Lordship by Messrs. Baring Brothers & Co., setting forth the faithless conduct of the Venezuelan Government towards the British Bondholders; and he has further submitted to me some resolutions of the Committee, dated the 30th of June last, appealing to your Lordship for help in their endeavour to recover the 55 per cent. of Import duties, especially hypothecated to them, and now unjustly confiscated.

Having been requested to give my support to this appeal, and having carefully examined the subject, I have no hesitation in saying that the case of the Venezuelan Bondholders is a very hard one, fully deserving the active and energetic interference of Her Majesty's Government, and I therefore beg respectfully to solicit your Lordship to grant to them the protection and assistance they seek at your Lordship's hands.

By such action, not only the rights and just claims of British Bondholders will be protected, but a signal service will be conferred upon the people of Venezuela, whose interests will be considerably benefited by the observance of public engagements on the part of their Government.

I have the honour to subscribe myself,

Your Lordship's most obedient, humble Servant,

(Signed)     G. J. GÖSCHEN.

To the Right Honourable
    The Earl Russell, K.G.,
Her Majesty's Principal Secretary of State for Foreign Affairs, &c., &c., &c.

———

71, OLD BROAD STREET, *12th July*, 1865.

MY LORD,—Having been prevented by my public engagements from accompanying the deputation which waited on your Lordship, on Monday last, with reference to certain complaints of the Venezuelan Bondholders, in respect of the acts of that Government as set forth in Messrs. Baring Brothers & Co.'s letter of the 25th March, 1865, I now address your Lordship for the purpose of recommending the claims of my constituents to the early consideration of Her Majesty's Government, with a view to such communications being made to the Government of Venezuela as will ensure justice being done in the matter.

I am,

Your Lordship's obedient Servant,

(Signed)     R. W. CRAWFORD.

To the Right Honourable
    The Earl Russell, K.G., &c.

Travers Twiss, " On the Rights and Duties of Nations in time of War " (ed. 1863, p. 20), states : " If a nation has refused to pay a debt to, or has inflicted an injury upon, the subjects of another nation, and the former has refused to make satisfaction or to give redress, the latter may proceed to do justice to its subjects by making reprisals upon the former."

Wheaton (ed. 1863, p. 508, Notes) quotes the words of President Jackson, in his message to Congress of December, 1834, as follows : " It is a well-settled principle of the international code that, when one nation owes another a liquidated debt, which it refuses or neglects to pay, the aggrieved party may seize on property belonging to the other, its citizens, or subjects, sufficient to pay the debt, without giving just cause for war. I recommend that a law be passed, authorising reprisals upon French property, in case provision shall not be made for the payment of the debt at the approaching session of the French chambers." Wheaton then refers to the convention of the 31st of October, 1861, between England, Spain, and France, to obtain redress, by combined operations, from Mexico. Earl Russell, in his instructions to Sir C. Wyke, after saying that it has not been usual to interfere to enforce the claims of bondholders, and that the case of the Mexican bondholders has not been an exception to the rule, goes on to declare that the government will now interfere on the ground of the arrangements made with the Government at Vera Cruz, by which customs' receipts were in certain proportions to be assigned to the holders of the bonds. And, though the agreement never assumed the form of a treaty, it is insisted that their (the Mexican bondholders) claims have assumed the character of international obligations.

This statement of Lord Russell forms a very suitable *point-de-départ* in summarizing the case of the Venezuelan bondholders; for, if the agreement to assign a proportion of the Customs' receipts to the Mexican bondholders, gave to their claims the character of an international obligation, what must be the strength of the claim advanced by the Venezuelan bondholders, whose agents, British subjects, under the authority of a solemn agreement with the Venezuelan Government, themselves collected the duties, and paid to the British Minister and British Consuls a large annuity for their assistance in the collection? Briefly, the whole case of the Venezuelan bondholders stands thus :— Two millions and a half have recently been lent to the Venezuelan Government by British subjects, on the faith of contracts entered into between them and the authorised representatives of that government, in which specified portions of the proceeds of the Venezuelan Custom-houses have been hypothecated for the payment of the debtor. The collection of the Customs has been made over under a distinct agreement to the agents* of the bondholders, those agents being British subjects. The British Minister has been present at the negociation of the loan, and that negociation has been protracted, broken off, and finally concluded in accordance with his demands. The British Government have authorised its representative to aid in the negociation of the loans, and has obtained the settlement of the claims of its subjects, amounting to considerable sums, by the loans. The British Minister and Consuls have been permitted by the British Government to draw yearly salaries, amounting to nearly £2,000, for aiding

---

* In the case of the Loan of 1864.

in collecting the Customs hypothecated for payment of the loans. All the papers connected with the loans have been registered and deposited in the British Mission; and, in the case of the loan of 1862, the British Minister was appointed the colleague of the bondholders, and agent in settling the claims which should be paid out of the proceeds of the loan.

On the one hand, then, there are in favour of the bond-holders all the above-mentioned undeniable facts; on the other, there is the decree of the Venezuelan Government of the 3rd of December, 1864, suddenly, wrongfully, and violently suspending the 55 per cent. duties hypothecated to the British bondholders, and actually forcing their agents to return $18,443, that had been already paid to them. And this, too, notwithstanding that, on the 9th of November, 1864, not a month before the issuing of the decree, General Blanco had spontaneously addressed a letter to Messrs. Baring, " solemnly promising the faithful observance of the contract of 1862, and offering to refund any sums that might have been hitherto abstracted."* There is next, the arbitrary suspension of payment for the loan of 1864, and the wresting of the solemnly-pledged Export Duties from the hands of the British agents, in spite of their protest and the protest of the British Minister.

Now, there is no attempt to lay down the doctrine that, in all cases of loans to foreign States, the English bondholders are to have the additional security of an immediate appeal to war. But let the British public well reflect how vast a sum is owed to England by foreign Powers; how terrible a calamity it would be if anything like general repudiation of

* Debt of Venezuela, p. 8.

that debt were to set in; how easily creditors, and especially foreign creditors, incline to evade their liabilities, when they are apprised by example that there is no restraint upon their inclinations but that of moral principle; and then let them decide whether they will submit to injuries and indignities, which Venezuela would not venture to inflict on the subjects of France or of the United States. The case of Venezuelan repudiation is altogether an exceptionally strong one, and requires exceptionally strong measures; and it is a case so flagrant, that should it be passed over, it would be utterly inconsistent to have recourse to coercion on any future occasion. At the same time, there are many steps to be taken short of war. There is the breaking off of diplomatic relations, there are reprisals, embargo, and blockade—measures which throw the responsibility of declaring war on the wrongdoer, where it ought to rest.

Having said thus much of the coercive steps which might be taken, and rightly taken as regards international law, it remains to appeal, in the interests of peace, and for their own best interests, to the justice and good feeling of the Venezuelan nation. It is undeniable that Venezuela has derived nothing but advantage from her intercourse with England. It has been shown how British troops took a prominent part in winning the independence of Venezuela; and how, in all the most critical emergencies, England was ever ready to supply funds, by the aid of which Venezuela recovered from exhaustion. And if such has been the past, the future may be expected to be like it, if Venezuela, the recipient of so many favours, will but reciprocate friendship and maintain her engagements.

Now, strong evidence has been brought forward to show

that Venezuela is well able, if she will but exert herself, to pay the interest of her debt. But admitting, for the sake of argument, that her funds are temporarily insufficient, there are ways by which the revenue might be supplemented. There are vast tracts of valuable waste lands at the disposal of the general Government. It is well known that the neighbouring States of Ecuador and N. Granada have assigned to their foreign creditors portions of their territories in compensation for diminished interest on their debts. The example might possibly be followed by Venezuela. Again the steam navigation of the Orinoco and of the great Lake of Maracaibo are valuable monopolies, which have been in the hands of Americans, but which might well be offered to those who have real claims on the State. In a word, there are means, if there be only the will, by which the Venezuelan Government might regain its credit.* All these, no doubt, must be matter of inquiry and negociation, and at present there is no representative of the bond-holders, through whom such negociations would have to be carried on.

These remarks naturally lead to the consideration of the proposition which has been made by the Venezuelan Government, that the bondholders should send out a Commissioner to Carácas. Such a step would evidently be a very great concession to that Government, which is in no sense entitled to demand it. It would be a concession involving considerable expense to those who have already suffered loss unjustly; and the least that could be expected

---

* The Plan for settling matters suggested by Mr. Engelke, which has been mentioned in chap. 6, might, perhaps, under the change of circumstances, be now worthy of consideration.

in return would be, that the Venezuelans should undertake to do their best to satisfy the Commissioner, and should render him every assistance, not only at the capital, but in any part of their territories he might find it necessary to visit. Under such circumstances, and with the support of the British Minister for Foreign Affairs, there is little room to suppose that the long pending claims of the bondholders could not be finally settled. Twenty years ago the Venezuelans had the reputation of being a mild, equitable, and law-fearing people: surely, they cannot regard the present state of things as indicative of progress! To continue the course they have lately adopted is to seal for ever the fate of the national credit. Let us hope that, while the door is still open to them, they will retrace their steps, and return to wiser counsels, in which case it is quite certain that a bright and prosperous career is before them.

# APPENDIX.

⸺•⸺

## (A)

*Prospectus of Messrs. Matheson's Loan.—Venezuela Six per Cent. Bonds for £1,000,000 sterling, in Bonds of £100, £200, and £500 each.— June, 1863.*

The Government of Venezuela having invested Signor Giacomo Servadio with full powers, as its fiscal agent, to carry out certain financial and banking arrangements for the benefit of the republic, and with a view to these objects, to issue securities to the extent of £1,000,000 sterling, Messrs. Matheson & Co., acting on behalf of the Government, have been instructed to offer to the public Bonds to that amount on the following terms :—

The Bonds are to bear interest at the rate of six per cent. per annum, payable half-yearly, at the counting-house of Messrs. Matheson & Co., on the 1st day of February and the 1st day of August, and are to be issued at 60 per cent.

The principal and interest will be secured on the revenue derived from export duties, established by a Law of the 24th February, 1863, upon the produce of the country shipped from the ports of La Guaira, Porto Cabello, and Ciudad Bolivar, which are calculated to produce from £130,000 to £140,000 per annum, and now yield at that rate, of which £100,000 per annum will be specially appropriated to the discharge of the Bonds.

The above sum of £100,000 will be applied, firstly, to the payment of the annual interest, and the residue to form an annual sinking fund, of which £20,000 will be employed in the redemption of Bonds of that nominal value by drawing in the usual manner at par, commencing on 1st February, 1865, and the balance of £20,000, increasing annually by the amount no longer required for interest on the cancelled Bonds, in the purchase of Bonds in the open market at the price of the day when at or below par ; if above par, by drawings, as before provided.

The consent of Earl Russell, Her Majesty's Secretary of State for Foreign Affairs, has been obtained for the collection of the above duties by Her Majesty's consuls at the several ports where they are levied.

The instalments are to be payable as follows :—

| | | | |
|---|---|---|---|
| £ 5 per £100 Bond on | | | application. |
| 10 | „ | „ | allotment. |
| 20 | „ | „ | 20th August. |
| 15 | „ | „ | 15th September. |
| 10 | „ | „ | 1st October. |
| £60 | | | |

Interest on the full amount of the Bond will commence from the 1st August next.

No part of the proceeds of the Loan will be paid over until the ratification of the arrangements shall have been received from the Government of Venezuela.

A moiety of the proceeds of the Bonds will be applied to the requirements of the Government, which the recent course of events has firmly established, and a second moiety will be devoted to the following object :—

At present there is almost an entire absence of banking accommodation in Venezuela. Possessed of every advantage of climate and soil, within sixteen days' sail of England, the existing monetary facilities are quite inadequate to the commerce of the country, and to the increasing production and rapidly extending exports of its coffee, cocoa, cotton, hides, &c.

The Venezuela Government has therefore determined to establish at the capital, Carácas, a National Bank, with the object of developing the great internal wealth of the country, and promoting its foreign trade, thereby creating new sources of revenue. The advantages of this institution will be obvious to all either politically or financially interested in the prosperity of Venezuela, and as the rates of interest range from 10 to 15 per cent. per annum, the profits may be expected to be considerable.

£300,000 of the proceeds of the Bonds will be invested in 3 per Cent. Consols, to form the basis of an issue of notes by this Bank.

As a guarantee for the proper management of the Bank, the manager at Carácas will be appointed by the agents for the bondholders, on whose behalf they will also be entitled to an equal share with the Government in the nomination of a board of three directors, and Messrs. Smith, Payne, and Smiths, will act as the agents to the Bank in this country.

As an additional security to the holders of the Bonds, it has been agreed that the capital of the Bank shall be charged with their redemption, and that the annual profits shall also be liable for the payment of the half-yearly interest.

Applications for the Bonds are to be made to Messrs. Matheson & Co., 3, Lombard-street; and forms of application may be obtained of Messrs. Mullens, Marshall, & Co., 3, Lombard-street.

FORM OF APPLICATION.

*Venezuelan Six per Cent. Bonds.*

London, E.C., June, 1863.

Messrs. Matheson & Co., 3, Lombard-street, London.

GENTLEMEN,—

I request that you will allot to me £         in the above Loan, on which I enclose the required deposit of 5 per cent., or £         ; and I agree to accept that amount of stock, or any less sum that may be allotted to me, and to pay the further instalments thereon, according to the terms of your circular.

I am, Gentlemen,

Your obedient servant,

Name in full

Address

Quality

PRICES OF THE VENEZUELA 1862 LOAN FROM THE
"ECONOMIST."

| | | | | | | | | |
|---|---|---|---|---|---|---|---|---|
| 31 Aug. | 1863 | ... | $58\frac{1}{2}$ | | 2 June | ,, | ... | $56\frac{1}{2}$ ex. div. |
| 30 Sept. | ,, | ... | $61\frac{3}{4}$ | | 1 July | ,, | ... | $56\frac{7}{8}$ |
| 31 Oct. | ,, | ... | $61\frac{5}{8}$ c. div. | | 29 ,, | ,, | ... | 58 |
| 1 Dec. | ,, | ... | 56 x. div. | | 30 Aug. | ,, | ... | $56\frac{3}{4}$ |
| 31 Dec. | ,, | ... | $55\frac{1}{4}$ | | 1 Oct. | ,, | ... | $55\frac{3}{8}$ |
| 1 Feb. | 1864 | ... | 55 | | 31 ,, | ,, | ... | 55 c. div. |
| 1 March | ,, | ... | $59\frac{1}{4}$ | | 31 Nov. | ,, | ... | 51 ex. div. |
| 1 April | ,, | ... | 61 | | 29 Dec. | ,, | ... | $52\frac{1}{8}$ |
| 30 ,, | ,, | ... | $58\frac{1}{4}$ c. div. | | | | | |

PRICES OF THE VENEZUELA 1864 LOAN FROM THE
"ECONOMIST."

| | | | | | | Price | | Disc. |
|---|---|---|---|---|---|---|---|---|
| SCRIP | £15 paid | 9 May, 1864 | ... | | | 10 | ... = | 5 |
| ,, | 15 ,, | 1 June ,, | ... | | | $10\frac{3}{4}$ | ... = | $4\frac{1}{4}$ |
| ,, | 30 ,, | 16 ,, ,, | ... | | | $24\frac{1}{4}$ | ... = | $5\frac{3}{4}$ |
| ,, | 45 ,, | 4 Aug. ,, | ... | | | 36 | ... = | 9 |
| ,, | 15 ,, | 30 ,, ,, | ... | | | 35 | ... = | 10 |

FULLY PAID UP, £60.

| Date | | | Price | | Date | | | Price | |
|---|---|---|---|---|---|---|---|---|---|
| 1 Oct. | 1864 | | $44\frac{1}{4}$ | | 30 April | 1866 | | 32 | |
| 31 ,, | ,, | ... | 42 | | 31 May | ,, | | $30\frac{2}{3}$ | |
| 1 Dec. | ,, | ... | 41 | | 2 July | ,, | ... | 31 | |
| 28 ,, | ,, | ... | $44\frac{3}{8}$ | | 1 Aug. | ,, | ... | 27 | |
| 1 Feb. | 1865 | ... | $42\frac{1}{4}$ | | 1 Sept. | ,, | ... | $27\frac{3}{4}$ | |
| 1 March | ,, | ... | 40 | | 2 Oct. | ,, | ... | $22\frac{1}{2}$ ex. div. | |
| 2 April | ,, | ... | 38 ex. div. | | 2 Nov. | ,, | ... | $30\frac{1}{4}$ | |
| 2 May | ,, | ... | 40 | | 3 Dec. | ,, | ... | $27\frac{1}{4}$ | |
| 1 June | ,, | ... | $40\frac{1}{4}$ | | 1 Jan. | 1867 | ... | $27\frac{3}{4}$ | |
| 2 July | ,, | ... | 41 | | 1 Feb. | ,, | ... | $30\frac{1}{2}$ | |
| 29 ,, | ,, | ... | 41 | | 1 March | ,, | ... | $31\frac{5}{8}$ | |
| 1 Sept. | ,, | ... | $42\frac{1}{2}$ | | 2 April | ,, | ... | $30\frac{3}{4}$ ex. div. | |
| 2 Oct. | ,, | ... | $39\frac{1}{8}$ ex. div. | | 2 May | ,, | ... | $17\frac{5}{8}$ | |
| 2 Nov. | ,, | ... | $37\frac{3}{4}$ | | 3 June | ,, | .. | 23 | |
| 30 ,, | ,, | ... | $37\frac{1}{8}$ | | 29 July | ,, | ... | 20 | |
| 20 Dec. | ,, | ... | $37\frac{1}{4}$ | | 9 Aug. | ,, | ... | 18 | |
| 30 ,, | ,, | ... | 37 | | 3 Sept. | ,, | ... | 19 | |
| 1 Feb. | 1866 | ... | $35\frac{3}{4}$ | | 4 Oct. | ,, | ... | $20\frac{1}{4}$ | |
| 1 March | ,, | ... | $38\frac{1}{2}$ | | 31 ,, | ,, | ... | $21\frac{1}{4}$ | |
| 4 April | ,, | ... | $33\frac{1}{4}$ ex. div. | | 3 Dec. | ,, | ... | $18\frac{1}{8}$ | |

*Extract from " Apology for Sinking Funds." By Wm. Lucas Sargant. London, 1868 : Williams & Norgate.*

" In 1862 M. Block [*] gave the following as the rates at which European nations could borrow :—10 per cent., Turkey ; 6 to 7 per cent., Italy, Portugal, Austria, and Spain ; 5 per cent., Russia ; over 4 and under 5 per cent., France, Sweden, and Prussia ; 4 per cent., Holland ; something over $3\frac{3}{4}$ per cent., Belgium and Denmark ; $3\frac{1}{4}$ per cent., Great Britain only.   Considerable changes have since taken place : Russia cannot borrow at 5 per cent., much less can Italy borrow under 7 per cent."

*Letter from the General Credit Company to Lord Stanley, stating the history of the Loan of 1864.*

6, VICTORIA STREET, WESTMINSTER ABBEY,<br>
*25th June,* 1867.

MY LORD,

Your Lordship was good enough to grant an interview on the 31st ultimo to the Committee appointed at a public meeting of the Bondholders of the Venezuelan Loan of 1864, at which interview your Lordship requested that the facts of the case might be re-stated in writing, with a view of being laid before the law officers of the Crown.

We now proceed to comply with your Lordship's request, and would

[*] " Puissance Comparée, Gotha," 1862. 166.

merely wish, at the outset, to call your Lordship's attention to the general outline of the circumstances (so far as they had then occurred) which we submitted to your Lordship by our letters of the 13th August and 11th December last, and to state that since the interview between your Lordship and the Committee, information has been received that the Venezuelan Government have decreed a further reduction of the duties hypothecated to the Bondholders, beginning from the 1st October next.

The document referring to this decree shall be set out in its proper order.

The history of the Loan is as follows :—

In the year 1863 the President of Venezuela, Marshal Falcon (who is still the President) duly empowered General A. Guzman Blanco, Vice-President of the Republic, and Minister of Finance and of Foreign Affairs, to raise a Loan of not exceeding £2,000,000 on the security of the Import and Export Duties of the Republic.

In October, 1863, General Blanco entered into a contract with the General Credit and Finance Company of London (Limited) for the negotiation by that company for the Government of Venezuela of a Loan of £1,500,000.

The terms of this contract are set out at considerable length in the definitive Bonds of the Loan, one of which for £100 (hereinafter referred to as document B), we have the honour of transmitting to your Lordship with this statement, and shall be obliged by its return when it is not further required.

The contract was duly approved and ratified by the Constituent Assembly of Venezuela in the month of January, 1864.

The Loan was offered to the public in the month of April, 1864, and subscriptions were invited in the terms of the prospectus, a copy of which is left herewith (marked A).

This prospectus was duly authorized and approved by the Venezuelan Minister, General Blanco. The copy of it signed by him is now in the possession of the General Credit Company.

In due course the definitive Bonds of the Loan were delivered to the subscribers, each Bond being signed in London by General Blanco in his capacity of Vice-President, and Minister of Finance and of Foreign Affairs, and Fiscal Commissary of the Republic of Venezuela.

These Bonds recite the main facts including, as we have said, the contract with the General Credit Company. They also gave the particulars of the special security hypothecated to the Bondholders, and on the faith of which the Loan was subscribed.

One of the Bonds, marked B., accompanies this statement.

The special security hypothecated to the Bondholders was the whole of the *Export Duties* at the ports of the Republic, which were guaranteed to be uncharged and of sufficient amount to pay the annual sum required, viz., £120,000 for interest, and the sinking fund of the Loan.

Before paying over the proceeds of the Loan to the Venezuelan Government, the General Credit Company in June, 1864, sent a special commissioner to Venezuela, Mr. Edward Backhouse Eastwick (formerly of the British Legation, Teheran), in order to see that the Export Duties so specifically mortgaged were free from incumbrances, and with full power to put resident agents in receipt of them from week to week, as stipulated by the contract.

These functions Mr. Eastwick duly executed to the satisfaction of everybody, including the Venezuelan Government. He was assured and was satisfied that the Export Duties were free from all charges, and he appointed Messrs. H. L. Boulton & Co., of La Guaira, and Messrs. Boulton & Co., of Puerto Cabello (who are British subjects) the agents for the receipt of the duties and their transmission to England.

The accompanying printed pamphlet (marked C*), entitled "Extracts from Correspondence," and official documents, contain full information of the transactions which took place between Mr. Eastwick and the Venezuelan authorities, and Messrs. Boulton & Co., and we beg your Lordship's particular attention to them, as from them it will be seen that in the most solemn and deliberate manner the Export Duties were declared to be free from incumbrances, and that Mr. Eastwick and Messrs. Boulton & Co. were put into possession of them.

The duties were duly received by Messrs. Boulton & Co. without interruption from the 23rd July, 1864, up to the 2nd July, 1866, when, without any warning, and on the pretence of the necessities of the State they were detained by the Government under the authority of a resolution, a copy of which (marked D) is left herewith, together with copies of letters to the General Credit Company from Messrs. Boulton & Co.† dated 9th July, 1866, and from General Blanco dated 1st and 5th August, 1866 (marked E, F, and G).

It was on our being informed of this proceeding that we wrote to your

---

* This having been published in a separate pamphlet is not subjoined here.

† This letter being marked private is not given.

Lordship our letter of the 13th August, 1866, stating the facts, and sending copies of several documents.

On the 24th September, 1866, the Government resolved that the suspension of the payment of the duties should cease from the 1st November following (see copy of Resolution herewith, marked H), but Messrs. Boulton & Co. wrote on the 9th November stating that the Resolution had not been acted upon, and that they believed the Government contemplated reducing the duties by one half, and charging part of the other half with a new loan (see copy of this letter herewith marked I).

It was at this stage of the proceedings that we addressed to your Lordship our letter of the 11th December last.

The decree which followed is dated the 30th November, and under it the Export Duties were reduced to two-thirds of the old rates, and by a Resolution of the same date 75 per cent. of the new duties were ordered to be applied to the payment of the Loan of 1864, and the remaining 25 per cent. retained by the Government to pay off a domestic Loan (see copy of Resolutions and Decree herewith marked K).

This arrangement reduced by about 50 per cent. the duties which the Bondholders were entitled to receive.

From this time till March, 1867, Messrs. Boulton & Co. received the duties only at the reduced rates (see copy of their letter to us of the 8th December, marked L).

Translations of these documents of the 30th November, were transmitted by Her Majesty's chargé d'affaires at Carácas, and your Lordship was good enough to inform us thereof on the 23rd January last.

Then, on the 15th March, the Government proceeded to the extremity of again entirely stopping the payment of the duties, reduced as they were by the Decree of November.

We enclosed a copy of the translation of the Decree and of the letter from the Government to the General Credit Company referring thereto, dated the 23rd March last (see the copies herewith marked M. and N.), and of extract from letter from Messrs. Boulton & Co., dated the 25th March (marked O), referring to the same transaction, and enclosing a copy of their letter to Mr. Fagan and his reply (marked P).

During the time the General Credit Company were in receipt of the full amount of the duties, they were more than sufficient to meet the annual charge upon them of £120,000 as provided by the contract, and indeed at the end of each of the years 1864 and 1865, there was a surplus balance paid over to the Government after meeting all expenses.

We now beg to call your Lordship's attention to the Resolutions which were passed at a public meeting of the Bondholders held at the London Tavern on the 23rd ultimo; a copy of them (marked Q) is sent herewith, together with a copy of the proceedings at the meeting (marked R).

The next step was the interview with your Lordship on the 31st ultimo, and, as we before intimated, a letter has subsequently, on the 14th instant, been received from Messrs. H. L. Boulton & Co., dated La Guaira, 25th ultimo, notifying the intention of the Venezuelan Government as from the 1st October next to further reduce the duties (see copy of this letter herewith marked S).

The above are the main facts of the case, and the Bondholders beg in all earnestness to appeal through us to your Lordship to afford to them the active interference of Her Majesty's Government to redress the grievous wrongs which have been perpetrated upon them and their property by the Venezuelan Government, in not only arbitrarily and without notice dispossessing them of the duties solemnly pledged to them and placed in their possession, but in reducing the tariff to such an extent as there is every reason to fear will render the duties (when their receipt shall be resumed) totally inadequate to the amount of the annual charge of £120,000 due under the contract.

Hoping soon to receive a favourable reply from your Lordship, we have the honour to be, my Lord,

Your Lordship's most obedient servants,

(Signed)　　　　　　　BAXTER, ROSE, NORTON & Co.,

For the General Credit and Discount<br>Company (Limited) and the Bond-<br>holders of 1864.

---

(D)

[Translated from the Spanish.]

OFFICIAL SECTION.

UNITED STATES OF VENEZUELA.

CHANCELLOR OF THE EXCHEQUER'S OFFICE, SECTIONS 2ND, 3RD,<br>AND 8TH.

CARÁCAS, 2nd July, 1866.

Resolved,—Peace, the most important condition of the country, having been broken, all the revenues set aside for paying the fiscal debt must be devoted to the all-important object of re-establishing and consolidating it ; and, therefore, it has been resolved by the Executive, in conformity with Article 4 of the Budget, so to do.

The Great Marshal Citizen, President of the Union, while exercising legal powers, without which the very existence of the Government would not be possible, has not overlooked the obligations weighing upon the Treasury, proposing to himself to discharge and fulfil them with justice, and without inflicting losses upon legitimate interests, so soon as the circumstances which demand the present determination shall have ceased to exist.

Therefore, the collecting offices shall hold at the disposal of this Exchequer the proceeds of the export duties, which are destined for the public service by the 2nd Article of the Budget Law above mentioned.

For communication and publicity.

For the Marshal President, the Chancellor of the Exchequer,

(Signed)      R. ARVELO.

It is a copy.—The Secretary to the Chancellor of the Exchequer's Office.—(Signed) P. BERMUDEZ.

*Local Newspaper Remarks.*—We print, in continuation, a most important Resolution of the Government, by which that protecting power fulfils the wishes of the country, and the claims of agriculture, and other great interests of the country, which are at present in a distressing state.

We give our cordial support to this Administrative Act, reserving to ourselves to dwell upon it at greater length as the subject deserves it.

---

## UNITED STATES OF VENEZUELA.

CHANCELLOR OF THE EXCHEQUER'S OFFICE, SECTION 2ND, 3RD, AND 8TH.

CARÁCAS, *July 3rd*, 1866.

Resolved,—The Great Marshal Citizen President has firmly resolved to regulate the Exchequer and the credit of the nation in a uniform and firm manner, upon equitable bases for all interests concerned therein, and with such economical and administrative measures as will inspire a solid confidence in the conduct of matters calculated to exercise such a great influence in consolidating the public peace, and in developing the natural resources of the country. And since, to accomplish so laudable

A A

an object, the assistance of intelligent and patriotic, as well as practical and experienced persons, must be invoked to help in the important works which the subject demands, the Great Marshal Citizen President has resolved upon taking the collective opinion of the citizens Senators Jacinto Gutierrez and Pascual Caranova, and Citizens Carlos Engelke and Dr. Modesto Urbaneja, upon all and each of the branches and dependencies of the Exchequer and Public Credit. The President is confident that those citizens will, along with their opinion, also recommend the measures which they may deem convenient to adopt.

To enable them to do so, the citizens afore mentioned shall have the power to ask for, or to personally take from the public State offices and custom-houses, or any other public offices, all the notes and information which they may require.

The Marshal President recommends to them to discharge this duty with the least possible delay compatible with the study and meditation which so delicate a duty necessitates and counsels, because the Government, without losing sight of the multifarious and varied obligations of the Treasury, and the powers vested upon the Government by the Constitution and the laws, acknowledges and feels the urgency of giving attentive and due consideration to the unfortunate state of industry, and specially to agriculture, on account of the grave consequences which, among other causes, spring from the unevenness and great burden of the taxes, and from the inactivity and deplorable depreciation of all public and private securities, which constitute the wealth of the country.

To be communicated to the citizens afore named, to the officers of state, to the customs offices, and other public offices, and published.

For the Marshal President, the Chancellor of the Exchequer,

(Signed)      R. ARVELO.

It is a copy.—The Secretary to the Exchequer's Office,

P. BERMUDEZ.

---

[Copy.]

CARÁCAS, July 4th, 1866.

SIR,

As agents of the General Credit and Finance Company (Limited) of London, for the collection of the export duties at the ports of La Guaira, Puerto Cabello, Ciudad Bolivar, and Maracaibo, specially mortgaged to them for the redemption of a Loan of £1,500,000 sterling, contracted by that company with the Government of Venezuela, we have the honour, according to our instructions, of enclosing a legalised copy of our formal protest, entered this day at the Register Office in this city, against the arbitrary detention of the export duties at La Guaira, ordered by the Government in violation of their engagements with the British creditors, and in the name of the company beg you to protect their interests.

We remain, sir,<br>
Your most obedient humble servants,<br>
(Signed)     H. L. BOULTON & Co.

George Fagan, Esq., H.B.M. Chargé d'Affaires
and Consul-General, &c. &c. &c., Carácas.

---

(E)

[Translation.—Copy.]

James Macdonald, Esq.

PARIS, *August 1st*, 1866.

MY DEAR SIR,

Although I have not yet recovered from the surprise which the correspondence from Venezuela caused me yesterday evening by the announcement that the delivery of the Export duties had been suspended, I think that perhaps in the midst of your own correspondence it may have occurred to you to ask me how such an event can have taken place.

I think it useless to tell you that I repudiate such a proceeding, and that I never even considered it possible that any one could propose the like.

To-day I am writing at great length on the matter, and hope to alter affairs ; but, in the meantime, if you can manage to pacify the Bondholders of 1864, be good enough to do so. The moment I feel myself better I will start for Venezuela, and will endeavour to re-establish so sacred a claim.

It appears that there has been a disturbance in the south of the Republic, and they have taken part of the Export duties to prepare the troops that have been despatched to re-establish order.

I feel certain that the whole thing will end immediately, and on my return I will point out to Marshal Falcon what our duty is, and he will not only order the delivery to your agents of the Export duties, but will decide upon the manner in which the portion already taken is to be redeemed.

Yours very truly,<br>(Signed)     A. GUZMAN BLANCO.

---

*To the Right Honourable Lord Stanley, H.M. Secretary of State for Foreign Affairs.*

6, VICTORIA STREET, WESTMINSTER,<br>*August* 13th, 1866.

MY LORD,

Seeing by the newspapers that a deputation has recently been received by your Lordship of persons interested in the Venezuelan Loan of 1862 (commonly known as "Baring's Loan") we think it right that your Lordship should also be aware of the position in which the Bond-holders of a more recent Loan to the Venezuelan Government are now placed by a recent act of that Government.

We refer to the Loan of 1864 contracted by the existing Government of Venezuela.

This loan was for £1,500,000 sterling, and was principally subscribed on the London market, and by the terms of the contract the whole of the Export duties levyable at the ports of the Republic, La Guaira, Puerto Cabello, Maracaibo, and Ciudad Bolivar, were hypothecated for the payment of the interest and of the sinking fund for redemption of the loan, and were to be handed over weekly as they were received by the Government officers, to the duly authorised agents of the contractors.

Before the proceeds of the subscription were paid over to the Government, the General Credit Company sent out Mr. E. B. Eastwick to Carácas as their representative, to ascertain that all prior charges had been cleared off, and to take formal possession in their name of the Export duties, and arrange for their future receipt.

This gentleman, with the full approval of the Government, when in Venezuela, appointed Messrs. H. L. Boulton & Co., an eminent firm at La Guaira, to act as the future agents of the contractors during the continuance of the Loan.

Up to a recent date, the duties were paid over to these gentlemen with scrupulous regularity, so that not only has the interest on the Loan been punctually paid, but the purchases on account of the sinking fund have been duly made up to the present time in accordance with the contract, and the General Credit and Finance Company of London (Limited), who acted as the agents of the Government, have now in hand sufficient for the payment of the dividend falling due in October next, with a small surplus over.

By the last mail information was received from Messrs. Boulton that, without any previous warning, the Government had ordered the retention of the duties under the authority of a decree which attempts to justify the step by the anticipation of internal war.

The announcement of this proceeding, which is in distinct violation of the contract, has caused the greatest anxiety and alarm among the Bondholders of the Loan of 1864, and your Lordship cannot fail to see that any default by the Venezuelan Government in connection with the Loan of 1864 would be a much more aggravated breach of faith than can have been brought before your Lordship by the claimants under any prior Loan, as in this case the Decree for suspending payment actually emanates from the same Government, composed of the same individuals with whom the Loan of 1864 was contracted, and to whom the money has been paid.

The Bondholders do not, at the present moment, ask for the interference of Her Majesty's Government on their behalf. But they have felt it to be their duty to bring under your Lordship's notice this statement of the facts.

They trust that circumstances may not arise to render any interference necessary, but rather that the Government of Venezuela may be acting under some misconception, and that it will take the earliest opportunity of retracing a step so fatal to its own reputation and to the credit of the country.

The Bondholders are confirmed in this view by a letter addressed to the manager of the General Credit Company by His Excellency Guzman Blanco, the late Vice-President and Minister of Finance of the Republic, with whom the Loan was originally negociated, and who, being now at Paris, writes to deplore the step adopted in his absence, and to assure them that he will use his utmost endeavours to obtain its immediate reversal.

We have the honour to enclose to your Lordship a copy of His Excellency's letter, together with a copy of the letter of Messrs. Boulton, and accompanying documents, including the Decree before referred to.

We think it also proper to forward for your Lordship's information a copy of the Prospectus issued in 1864, upon the terms of which the Loan was subscribed for by the Bondholders.

Praying your Lordship to pardon the length of these details,

We have the honour to remain,

Your Lordship's most obedient humble servants,

(Signed)    BAXTER, ROSE, NORTON & Co.

---

[Copy.]

CONSULATE OF VENEZUELA,
25, MOORGATE STREET,
*January 11th*, 1867.

DEAR SIR,

I have received a letter from General Guzman Blanco, written at St. Mazaire on the day of his embarkation from that port in the French mail steamer for Venezuela, from which I send you the following. After stating how greatly fatigued he was from the exertions of preparing for his departure, he says: "I have not time to write to Mr. Macdonald, but I desire that you should fortify him, as also the Bondholders of 1864, in the assurance that the Government of Marshal Falcon will pay with all punctuality the dividends on the Loan contracted by me in his name.

"According to my last advices, the agents had already begun to receive the part of the Export duties which corresponds with the present harvest. The diminution of duty will never exceed the surplus which, up to this time, the Company had always returned.

"I know the probity of Marshal Falcon, and therefore do not hesitate to repeat these assurances."

I thought it best to send you his message in his own words, and I have done the same to the Bondholders, and shall send the same extract this evening to all the papers for to-morrow.

I am, dear sir,

Yours faithfully,

(Signed)    FRED. H. HEMMING, Consul.

To James Macdonald, Esq., General Manager, &c.,
27, Austin Friars.

---

## (K)

## UNITED STATES OF VENEZUELA.

CHANCELLOR OF THE EXCHEQUER'S OFFICES.—SECTION 3RD AND 8TH.

CARÁCAS, *November 30th*, 1866.

Resolved,—By order of the National Executive the Export duties received shall be distributed in the following manner. Seventy five per cent. is to be applied to fulfil the obligations undertaken by the contract for the Loan, which was signed in London on the 3rd October, 1863, under the understanding that should it prove not to be sufficient for that purpose, the Government shall cover with other funds any deficiency that there may be. The remaining 25 per cent. shall be applied to redeem the Loan for $150,000, contracted on the 24th March last, with various merchants, to whom it was offered to pay them with the residue which there might be left from the Export duties during the year closed in the month of October last, after payment of the sums due during the same year, towards covering the exterior debt of the Federation. This 25 per cent. shall be paid in proportion as it is received, to Messrs. F. Echena-gucia & Co., at the ports of La Guaira, Puerto Cabello, Ciudad Bolivar, and Maracaibo, to which the present resolution is referred to.

To be communicated to whomsoever it may concern, and published.

For the Citizen General first appointed to the office of President.

(Signed)     I. M. ALVAREZ DE LUGO.

[It is a copy].

The Secretary to the Chancellor of the Exchequer.

NICOLAS SILVA.

---

## (L)

[Copy.   Per W. I. Mail].

LA GUAIRA, *December 8th,* 1866.

*The General Credit and Finance Company of London (Limited), London.*

GENTLEMEN,

We beg to confirm our letter of the 24th November, duplicate of which we enclose, and have to acknowledge the receipt of your favour of the 16th ultimo, contents of which claim our best attention.

On the 20th ultimo Government published a Decree announcing the reduction of Export duties to two-thirds of the old rates. Another Decree of the same date states that 75 per cent. of the new duties will be applied to the payment of the Loan of 1864, and the remaining 25 per cent. will be retained by Government to pay off a domestic Loan of $150,000; this arrangement makes it equal to a reduction of just 50 per cent. on what the Bondholders formerly received.

By this mail we send you Carácas newspapers, the *Federalista* and *Porvenir* containing these Decrees, and on this date we have received a communication from Government under date of the 5th instant confirming the same.

Acting upon this communication we applied at the Custom-house for the proceeds of the duties, and we are pleased to inform you that, at the last moment, we received the sum of \$2,141·89 cents, being 75 per cent. of the total Export duties at this Custom-house for the week ending the 8th instant. We shall remit this amount by next mail; it is too late to do so by this.

We remain, Gentlemen, yours obediently,

(Signed)      H. L. Boulton & Co.

Exchange, London, 6·50.

---

(Q)

[Copy].

*Extract from Messrs. H. L. Boulton & Co.'s letter, dated La Guaira, March 25th, 1867, to General Credit and Discount Company.*

We regret to inform you of another suspension of payment of Export duties, of which step Government will advise you direct according to a note passed to us on this subject under date of 15th instant, copy of which we beg to enclose. We at once protested in due form, and beg to hand you enclosed our protests drawn up here and at Puerto Cabello, copies of which we have handed to Mr. Fagan, H.B.M. chargé d'affaires in Carácas.

We learn that Government is anxious that you should send out an agent to judge for himself how utterly impossible it is for it to fulfil its engagements, meanwhile we shall keep you advised of all that takes place in reference to this matter.

We enclose copy of our letter to Mr. Fagan, and of his reply to the same.

We remain, Gentlemen,

Yours obediently,

(Signed)      H. L. Boulton & Co.

---

[Copy].

Carácas, March 16th, 1867.

Sir,

We have the honour to accompany herewith an official copy of the protest we have entered this day at the Register Office, as agents of the General Credit and Discount Company of London (Limited) against

the order given by the Minister of Finance of the United States of
Venezuela suspending the payment of the Export duties mortgaged for
the interest and redemption of the Loan of 1864.

We have the honour to be, Sir,

Your most obedient humble servants,

(Signed) H. L. BOULTON & Co.

GEO. FAGAN, ESQ.,

H.B.M. Chargé d'Affaires and Consul General, &c.,
Carácas.

---

[Copy].

CARÁCAS, *March 19th*, 1867.

GENTLEMEN,

I beg to acknowledge the receipt of your communication of the
16th instant, transmitting a legal copy of the protest you have entered at
the Register Office, as agents of the General Credit and Discount Company
of London (Limited) against the order given by the Minister of Finance
of the United States of Venezuela suspending the payment of the Export
duties mortgaged for the interest and redemption of the Loan of 1864.

I have the honour to be, Gentlemen,

Your most obedient humble servant,

(Signed) GEORGE FAGAN.

---

## (B)

*Catalogue of Articles Exhibited from the South American
Republic of Venezuela, in the International Exhibition
at London, in 1862.*

---

The following have mostly been collected and forwarded by a Committee appointed by the Venezuelan Government, consisting of Señor
Lino J. Revenga, Señor Carlos Hahn, and Señor Carlos J. Marxen, and
having been delayed on the voyage, were too late to be inserted in the
first Catalogue published by H.M.'s Commissioners.

The Exhibitors, when not otherwise stated, are residents in Venezuela.

---

*N.B.—The second numbers refer to the different articles in the same Class.*

|   |   | *Exhibitor.* |
|---|---|---|
| 1 | NATIONAL ARMS OF VENEZUELA, worked in feathers of natural colours | *The Government.* |
| 2 | Bouquet of Flowers, worked in same | *Señor A. Schibbye.* |
| 3 | Roses, of the same | ,, ,, |

*Exhibitor.*

| 4 | | A coffee tree, in wax . . . . . | *Señora Guadalupe Novel.* |
|---|---|---|---|
| 5 | | Fruits of Venezuela, in wax, the names of each are attached thereto . . . . | ,, ,, |
| 5A | | A branch of cotton tree in wax . . | ,, ,, |
| 6 | | Two cases of stuffed birds . | *Mr. F. L. Davis,* 13, *Blandford-street.* |
| 7 | | A case of butterflies . . . | ,, ,, |
| 8 | | A totuma carved with a knife . . | ,, ,, |
| 9 | | A ditto, with Masonic emblems . . | *Señor Edo. Calcano.* |
| 10 | | Three ditto, two plain, one painted . | *Mrs. F. H. Hemming,* 104, *Gloucester-place.* |
| 11 | | A hammock, made in Margarita of cotton grown in that island . . . | *Mr. F. Meyer, Hamburg.* |
| 12 | 1 | A hammock, made by Indians of Rio Negro, ornamented with feathers . | *N. P. B. Ulstrup.* |
| 13 | 2 | A hammock, ditto ditto . . . | ,, ,, |
| 14 | | A pocket handkerchief from Maracaibo, worked in Venezuelan style . . | *The Committee.* |
| 15 | | One ditto, made of one piece of linen . . | ,, |
| 16 | | A shirt worked in Carácas . . . . | *Edo. Culcano.* |
| 17 | 3 | A table, top of Macanilla palm wood, stand of ebony, pinavete, and gateado woods | *The Committee.* |
| 18 | 50 | A box, top of gateado, cut horizontally, the inside of bitter cedar, the outsides of gateado, caimeto, cahobo, and algarrobo, the lower edge of chiria . . | *Señor Avila.* |
| 19 | | A box, of Macanilla palm wood . . | *N. B. P. Ulstrup.* |
| 20 | | A box ,, ,, . . . | ,, |
| 21 | 119 | A picture frame and sample of ditto . . | ,, |
| 22 | | A piece of unbleached cotton cloth from the first manufactory established in Venezuela . . . . . | *Señor Machado.* |
| 23 | 67 | 10lb. of cotton wick, from ditto . . | ,, |
| 24 | | Rope used for ships' cables, made of fibres from Rio Negro . . . . | *The Committee.* |
| 25 | | Rope of the cocuiza plant from Maracaibo . | ,, |
| 26 | | Cloth made from same . . . | *Mr. F. Meyer, Hamburg.* |
| 27 | 98 | Washed coffee, estate of J. J. Rivas . | *The Committee.* |
| | 99 | ,, Ovidio Diaz, Macarao . . | |
| | 100 | ,, Pinango, Tibron . . | |
| | 101 | ,, Edo. Pacheco, La Laguua . | |
| | 103 | ,, Lizarraga, Laguenta . . | |
| | 105 | ,, Quintana, Bucaral . . | |
| | 104 | Egg-shaped coffee . . . | |
| | 102 | Unwashed coffee—cold climate . . | |
| | 126 | Egg-shaped coffee . . . . | *Señor Nadal.* |
| | 130 | Sample coffee from St. Antonio . . | *Mr. F. Meyer, Hamburg.* |
| | | Coffee from Valleys of Aragua . . | |

*Exhibitor.*

|  |  |  |  |  |
|---|---|---|---|---|
| 28 | 94 | Cocoa from Ocumare | | *The Committee.* |
|  | 95 | ,,  ,,  Choroni | | |
|  | 96 | ,,  ,,  Carúpano | | |
|  | 97 | ,,  ,,  Rio Caribe | | |
|  | 110 | ,,  ,,  Tuy | | |
|  | 122 | ,,  ,,  ,, | | |
|  | 144 | ,,  ,,  ,, | | |
|  | 01 | ,,  ,,  Carácas | | *Mr. F. Meyer, Hamburg.* |

| 29 | 131 | Indian beans | *The Committee.* |
|---|---|---|---|
|  | 132 | Black-eyed ,, | |
|  | 133 | Brown ,, | |
|  | 134 | Black spotted ,, (Poncha) | |
|  | 135 | Brown ,, | |
|  | 136 | Common black ,, | |
|  | 137 | Grey ,, | |
|  | 138 | Grey ,, | |
|  | 139 | Small white ,, | |
|  | 140 | Brown spotted ,, | |

| 30 | 141 | Indian Corn | ,, |
|---|---|---|---|
|  | 142 | ,, | ,, |
| 31 | 88 | Dividivi from Maracaibo | ,, |
| 31 | 85 | Cochineal from Carácas | ,, |
| 33 | 75 | Cebadilla | *Go. Sturup.* |
| 34 | 74 | Vanilla | ,, |
| 35 | 18 | Starch extracted from root of Yuca plant | *The Committee.* |
| 36 | 87 | Tonquin beans | ,, |
| 37 | 76 | Simarruba | *Go. Sturup.* |
| 38 | 86 | Sereipa from Guayana | *The Committee.* |
| 39 | 45 | Secua Escandinava de Decandio; antidote against certain poisons, and against rust in steel and iron | ,, |
| 40 | 44 | Curara, Indian remedy for the cure of hæmorrhage, cuts, wounds, and ulcers | *Fco. Conde.* |
| 41 | 46 | Espino—used for same purpose | ,, |
| 42 | | 6 bottles of Indian balsam | *Señor N. A. Gil.* |

It is requested by the Exhibitor that these bottles of balsam may afterwards be presented to the hospitals, that its wonderful efficacy may be tested.

| 43 | | Root of Sarsaparilla | *Go. Sturup.* |
|---|---|---|---|
| 44 | | Extract of Sarsaparilla | ,, |

Prepared from the *green root* by immense pressure, possessing greatly concentrated strength.

| 45 | 117 | Ten bottles of Pectoral oil | *Mo. Espinal.* |
|---|---|---|---|
| 46 | 118 | Sample of Ajoujoli seed (Sesame) from which the above is made | *Mo. Espinal.* |

| | | | Exhibitor. |
|---|---|---|---|
| 47 | 11 | Ten bottles of bitters from Maracaibo . . | *Catalan and Co.* |
| 48 | | Twelve ,, ,, Angostura . . | *Syers, Braach and Co.* |
| 49 | | Twelve ,, ,, ,, . | { *M. S. Warburg, 16, Devonshire-sq. E.C.* |

These bitters are celebrated as a very agreeable tonic, and as most efficacious in removing various disorders.

| | | | |
|---|---|---|---|
| 49A | | White Rum of 30 deg. from Guartire. | |
| 50 | | Three tins of preserved oranges . . . | *The Committee.* |
| 51 | | Bottle of preserved quinces . . . . | ,, |
| 52 | 57 | Boxes preserved Guayaba . . | ,, |
| 53 | 58 | ,, ,, Guanábana . . . . | ,, |
| 54 | | ,, ,, quinces . . . | ,, |
| 55 | | ,, ,, peaches . . . | ,, |
| 56 | | Soap, in imitation of English . | ,, |
| 57 | | ,, ,, Spanish . . | ,, |
| 58 | | Candles of stearine from Auauco . | ,, |
| 59 | | Four samples of wax . . . . | *Dr. Bolet.* |
| 60 | | White wax from Carapita . . . | *Carl Hahn.* |
| 61 | | Yellow ,, ,, . . . . | ,, |
| 62 | | Vegetable wax, with fruit and leaf of the tree from which produced . . . | *The Committee.* |
| 63 | | Sugar from Guatire . . . . . | *The Committee.* |
| 64 | | Chocolate with almonds . . . | *J. Barnola.* |
| 65 | | ,, ,, Vanille . . . . | ,, |
| 66 | | ,, ,, cinnamon . . . | ,, |
| 67 | | ,, ,, cocoa . . . | ,, |
| 68 | | Chocolate . . . . . . | *C. Mayo.* |
| 69 | 7 | Tobacco leaf, from Guanape . . . . | *The Committee* |
| 70 | 8 | ,, ,, Cumanacoa . . . | ,, |

Venezuela produces many varieties of tobacco adapted for cigars, the pipe, or snuff, but there happened not to be any in Carácas when this consignment was made.

| | | | |
|---|---|---|---|
| 71 | 52 | Cigars from Cumanacoa . . . . | ,, |
| 72 | 53 | ,, ,, Carácas . . | ,, |
| 73 | 70 | ,, ,, Carapita . . . | *Carl Hahn.* |
| 74 | 71 | ,, ,, Turmero . . . | ,, |
| 75 | | Four bottles natural snuff . . . | |
| 76 | | Two ,, simple rose snuff . . <br> Four ,, flavoured . . . . <br> Four ,, highly flavoured snuff . | *Fco. Garrido.* |
| 77 | | Two ,, simple rhoda . . . <br> Four ,, flavoured . . . <br> Four ,, highly flavoured . . | |
| 78 | 91 | Tacamahaca . . . | *The Committee.* |

*Exhibitor.*

79  43  Resin of Algarrobo   .   .     .  .  *The Committee.*

80       Ten pounds of wool from Coro  .   .   .  *,,*

81       Goat skins from Coro  .   .   .   .  *Carl Hahn.*

82       Deer skins from Carácas  .   .   .   .  *,,*

83       Two bales of plantain leaf, from which excellent paper is made  .   .   .   .  *Ruete, Röhl, and Co.*

84  66  Bale of cotton from valleys of Aragua  .  *,,     ,,*

85 116  Small bag of cotton  .   .   .   .  .  *,,     ,,*

86       Sample of cotton from Maracaibo, from Sea Island seed  .   .   .  *Stolterfoht, Sons & Co., Liverpool.*

87       Sample of the same  .   .   .  *T. Bazley, Esq. M.P., Manchester.*

88       The same in several states of manufacture .  *,,*

          The above are from 15 bales of cotton from Maracaibo, bought by T. Bazley, Esq., M.P., Manchester, on April 14, at 2*s.* 5*d.* per lb., and kindly supplied by him. Maracaibo can supply immense quantities of this quality, if British capital and enterprise be introduced.

89       Cotton from Barquisimeto .    *Mr. F. Meyer, Hamburg.*

90       Cotton  ,,    ,,  .   .   .  *Mr. F. Meyer, Hamburg.*
91       Cotton  ,,  Puerto Cabello  .  .

92       Five samples of wild cotton from Upata Guayana  .   .   .   .   .   .  *Carl Hahn.*

92A     Four samples of cotton, recently sent from different portions of the Aroa district, where it can be grown in large quantities, severally valued from 1*s.* 6*d.* to 2*s.* per lb. .  .   .   .   .  *The Quebrada Land and Mining Company.*

## OIL PAINTINGS.

*Painted by* MARTIN TOVAR Y TOVAR.

2,861  The Cattle Drovers of Venezuela   .  .  *The Artist.*

2,862  Study of a Drunken Mulatto .     .  *,,*

Woods collected by Dr. VARGAS, formerly President of the Republic, and placed in the University at Carácas.

| No. | NAME. | Specific Weight. | No. | NAME. | Specific Weight. |
|---|---|---|---|---|---|
| 1 | Granadilla, Couroupita odoratissima, *Seem.* | 1,2367 | 26 | Tijerita | 0,8301 |
| 2 | Nazareno, Hymenæa floribunda, *Kth.* | 1,1744 | 27 | Angelino, Audira inermis, *Kth.* | 0,8186 |
| 3 | Dividivi, (152) Cæsalpinia coriacea, *Lin.* | 1,2189 | 28 | Naranjillo, Swartzia 3-phylla? *Willd.* | 0,8586 |
| 4 | Palma real, Oreodoxa regia, *Kth.* | 1,0787 | 29 | Paraguatan, Condaminea tinctoria, *De C.* | 0,8026 |
|  | Cocos butyracea, *Lin.* |  | 30 | Laurel Angelino, Nectandria Laurel, *Meiss.* | 0,5505 |
| 5 | Fiama | 1,3003 | 31 | Pardillo negro | 0,7017 |
| 6 | Araguaney | 1,0985 | 32 | Toco, Cratæva gynandra, *Lin.* | 0,6099 |
| 7 | Guayacan, (158) Tecoma Guayacan, *Seem.* | 1,3068 | 33 | Cartan, cold country (9) | 0,7537 |
| 8 | Gateado, (107, 119, 128, 159) Acacia riparia? *Kth.* | 1,0034 | 34 | Olivo, (99, 174) Capparis intermedia, *Kth.* | 0,6213 |
|  |  |  | 35 | Coba longa | 0,8911 |
| 9 | Cartan, from the hot country; (33) | 0,8171 | 36 | Cedro dulce, Cedrela odorata, *Lin.* | 0,5293 |
| 10 | Urape negro, Bauhinia (Pauletia) multineroia, *De C.* | 0,8577 | 37 | Guarataro, (77) Couratari Guianensis, *Aubl.* | 0,7950 |
| 11 | Guayabo encanado, Psidium? | 1,0946 | 38 | Capuchino | 0,6284 |
| 12 | Urape rosado, Bauhinia (Pauletia) glandulosa, *De C.* | 0,9842 | 39 | Cedro amargo, Simaba cedron | 0,2579 |
| 13 | Hayo, Acacia peregrina? *Willd.* | 1,1107 | 40 | Caimito, (145) Chrysophyllum Caimito, *Lin.* | 1,0869 |
| 14 | Vera, Guaiacum arborcum, *De C.* | 1,2479 | 41 | Grifo | 0,8017 |
| 15 | Guayabo rosado, Psidium pomiferum | 1,0206 | 42 | Lecherito, Brosimum? | 0,9877 |
| 16 | Cañafistola, Cassia brasiliensis, *Lin.* | 0,8575 | 43 | Laurel Mangou | 0,6818 |
| 17 | Guayabo blanco, Psidium pomiferum sp. | 1,0503 | 44 | Estoraque, (154) Styrax tomentosum, *Kth.* | 0,8482 |
| 18 | Nogal, Juglans cinerea | 0,5587 | 45 | Guama, Juga Bonplandiana, *Kth.* | 0,6058 |
| 19 | Majomo | 0,8434 |  | Juga vera, *Willd.* |  |
| 20 | Roble, Tecoma pentaphylla, *Juss.* | 0,8758 | 46 | Laurel Aguacate, Persea gratissima, *Lin.* | 0,5885 |
| 21 | Guayabo pauji, Bumelia buxifolia, *Willd.* | 1,0244 | 47 | Almendro, Geoffroya superba, *Kth.* | 0,8771 |
| 22 | Naranjo dulce, Citrus aurantium, *Lin.* | 0,8015 | 48 | Lecherito pintado | 0,7770 |
| 23 | Huecito | 1,0019 | 49 | Aguanoso | 0,5628 |
| 24 | Zapatero, Hymenæa venosa? *Vahl.* | 0,9311 | 50 | Sereipo, Avicennia nitida, *Lin.* | 0,7668 |
| 25 | Guayabo racino | 1,0715 | 51 | Croton, Croton coriaceum? | 0,4500 |
|  |  |  | 52 | Cedrillo horcon | 0,6557 |
|  |  |  | 53 | Tigron | 1,0151 |
|  |  |  | 54 | Cerezo, Burchosia glauca, *Kth.* | 1,0260 |
|  |  |  | 55 | Atata | 1,0271 |

| No. | NAME. | Specific Weight. | No. | NAME. | Specific Weight. |
|---|---|---|---|---|---|
| 56 | Tabacote . . . . | 0,5227 | 70 | Apamate . . . | 0,6443 |
| 57 | Tasí, Tasi (Tachi) Myroxylon pubescens, *Kth.* | 1,2432 | 71 | Lechoso, Carica papaya . | 0,7864 |
| 58 | Naranjillo, Swartzia tomentosa, *De C.* . . | 1,0207 | 72 | Curtidor . . . . | 0,8719 |
| 59 | Limoncillo, Citrosma laurifolium, *Kth.* . . | 0,9183 | 73 | Pinabete . . . | 0,5885 |
| 60 | Chupon colorado, Gustavia (Pirigara) speciosa, *De C.* . . . | 1,0169 | 74 | Haya criolla, Rhopala polystachya? *Kth.* . | 0,7832 |
| 61 | Guisanda . . . | 0,9719 | 75 | Guamo, Juga insignis, *Kth.* . . . . | 0,8921 |
| 62 | Narauli . . . . | 0,8239 | 76 | Pui * . . . . | 1,0194 |
| 63 | Guayabo sabanero . . | 1,0265 | 77 | Guarataro, (37) Couratori Guianensis, † *Aubl.* . | 0,8777 |
| 64 | Roseta . . . . | 0,8821 | 78 | Llaguero ‡ . . . | |
| 65 | Chupon, Gustavia fastuosa? *Willd.* . . | 0,9461 | 79 | Aguacate cimarron, Persea sp. ? § . . . | 0,5337 |
| 66 | Espuelita, Juga microphylla ? *Kth.* . . | 0,9473 | 80 | Aguagate dulce, Persea gratissima, ‖ *Lin.* . . | 0,5021 |
| 67 | Sasafras, Nectandra cymbarum . . . | 0,7313 | | Cuji ¶ . . . . | 1,0538 |
| 68 | Rosa de Montana, Brownea grandiceps, *Jacq.* . | 0,8477 | 81 | Balsamillo, Elaphrium Jacquinianum, *Kth.* * * | 0,8533 |
| 69 | Canilla de venado . . | 0,7646 | 82 | Amarillo, Xanthoxylum Cumanense, *Kth.* . | 0,8591 |
| | | | 83 | | |

* Very hard, adapted for large beams, joists, &c.

† Hard, produces large planks and joists from 30 to 35 feet long.

‡ Like the cedar in colour and weight; for tables, planks, &c., of large grain.

§ Weight and colour of cedar, but fine grain.

‖ For tables, planks, &c.

¶ For strong pillars, axles for carts, being very strong and hard.

* * Very hard, for veneering for boards, tables, and furniture; the same colour as mahogany.

*Exhibited by* RUETE, ROHL, & Co., *La Guaira.*

84 Alcornoquio (132), Bowditchia Virgilioides, *Kth.*
85 Apamate.
86 Asajarito.
87 Caoba (Mahogany) (126, 139), Swietenia Mahogani, *Lin.*
88 Caritivar, Prosopis sp.
89 Cotoperis, Myrtus Erythroxyloides, *Kth.*
90 Cuchoro (124), Oreocallis grandiflora, *R. Br.*
91 Cuji (80, 136), Juga cinerea, *Kth.*
92 Curarire (143), Lasciostoma Curari, *Kth.*
93 Ebano, Brya Ebenus, *De C.*
94 Flor Amarilla (155).
95 Guaimaro (157).
96 Guayavo (156), Psidium pyriferum, *Lin.*
97 Hatata.
98 Lata.
99 Olivo (34, 174), Capparis intermedia, *Kth.*

100 Pardillo (177).
101 Vera (14, 123), Coccoloba Caracasana, *Meiss.*
102 Virote.
103 Canalete (146).
104 Cedro (150), Cedrela odorata, *Lin.*
105 Roble (20), Tecoma pentaphylla, *Juss.*
106 Zapatero (24), Hymenæa venosa ? *Vahl.*
107 Gateado (8, 119, 159), Acacia riparia ? *Kth.*
108 Mamon de venado, Melicocca sp.?
109 Paraguatan (29), Condaminea tinctoria, *De C.*
110 Trompillo, Lætia guazumæfolia, *Kth.*
111 Gateado amarillo, Acacia sp.
112 Canafistola de Semana Santa, Cassia Brasiliensis, *Lin.*
113 Canafistola Marimari, Cassia Bouplandiana, *De C.*
114 Mosa, Mosa (Palodo moza) Machœrium, sp.

*Exhibited by* Fo. CONDE, *Carácas.*

115 Araguanei (6).
116 Algarrobo, Hymenæa Courbaril, *Lin.*
117 Algarrobo, Prosopis pallida, *Kth.*
118 Chinca.
119 Gateado (8, 107, 128, 159), Acacia riparia ? *Kth.*
120 Chica, Lundia Chica, *De C.*
121 Tussara.
122 Betuu.

123 Vera, (14, 101) Coccoloba Caracasana ?
124 Cucharo, (90) Oreocallis grandiflora, *R. Br.*
125 (Not named).
126 Caoba, (87, 139) Swietenia Mahogani, *Lin.*
127 Macanilla, Hippomane Maucinella, *Lin.*
128 Gateado, (8, 107, 119, 159) Acacia riparia, *Kth.*

*Exhibited by* TARTARET & Co., *Carácas.*

129 Block of Red Gateado.

*Recently arrived from Maracaibo.*

130 Amargo, Simaruba glauca?
131 Accituno, Calophyllum longi-
folium, *Kth.*
132 Alcornoquio (84), Bowditchia
Virgilioides, *Kth.*
133 Balaustre.
134 Brazil, Coulteria tinctoria, *Kth.*
Poinciana insignis.
135 Balsamo, Myrospermum tolui-
ferum, *Lin.*
136 Cuji (91), Juga cinerea, *Kth.*
137 Clemon.
138 Ceiba, Eriodendron anfractuosum,
*De C.*
139 Caoba (87—126) Swietenia Mahogani, *Lin.*
140 Canjaro.
141 Caritiva (88), Prosopis sp.
142 Canada.
143 Curarire (92), Lasiostoma Curari,
*Kth.*
144 Caobilla.
145 Caimeto (40), Chrysophyllum
Caimito, *Lin.*
146 Canalete (103).
147 Carangano.
148 Cardon.
149 Carreto.
150 Cedro (104), Cedrela odorata,
*Lin.*
151 Daguero.
152 Dividivi (3), Cæsalpinia coriaria,
*Lin.*
153 Ebano (93), Brya Ebenus, *De C.*
154 Estoraque (44), Styrax tomento-
sum, *Kth.*
155 Flor-amarillo (94).
156 Guayabo (96), Psidium pyriferum, *Lin.*
157 Guaimaro (95)
158 Guayacaus (7), Tecoma Guayacan,
*Seem.*

159 Gateado (8, 107, 119), Acacia
riparia? *Kth.*
160 Lata (98).
161 Llalla.
162 Mocquillo, Moquilea Guianensis,
*Aubl.*
163 Marfil, Phytelephas macrocarpa,
*Kth.*
In Brazilian Guiana the name of
*Marfin* is also given to the
Cordia tetraphylla.
164 Membrillo, comun (166), Gustavia superba, *Lin.*
165 Moral, Mora excelsa.
166 Membrillo (164), Gustavia angus-
tifolia, *Benth.*
167 Maria, Triplaris Caracasana,
*Cham.*
168 Macarutu.
169 Mccoque.
170 Mamon, Melicocca bijuga, *Lin.*
171 Mangle-blanco, Odontandra acu-
minata, *Kth.*
172 Mangle-colorado, Avicenna tomen-
tosa, *Lin.*
173 Olla de mono, Lecythis Ollaria,
*Lin.*
174 Olivo (34, 99), Capparis intermedia, *Kth.*
175 Panjil.
176 Penda.
177 Pardillo (100).
178 Quiebra-hacha, Cæsalpinia sp.?
179 Roble (20), Tecoma pentaphylla,
*Juss.*
180 Vera (14, 101, 123), Coccoloba
Caracasana?
181 Zapatero (24), Hymenæa venosa?
*Vahl.*
182 Hoja-ancha, Nectandra poly-
phylla? *Juss.*

## MINERALS, &c.

Exhibitor.

93 {
　13 Copper ores from Teques . . . . *Marcano & Co.*
　121 ,, ,, . . . . . ,,
　72 ,, ,, . . . . . *Dr. Betancourt.*

94　　Copper assayed by Johnson and Matthey } *F. H. Hemming, 104, Gloucester-place.*

95　41 Iron ore . . . . . . . . *C. Hahn.*

96　149 Silver and lead ore from Carupano . . *J. P. Romero.*

97　62 Silver ore, mine of "Gran Pobre," Carupano *Dr. Rodriguez.*

98　17 Gold from Caratal, Guayana . . . . *C. Hahn.*

99　　Gold quartz, from Guayana . . . } *Mr. F. Meyer, Hamburg.*

This quartz was assayed at the "Ecole des Mines," Paris, and produced nearly 100 oz. to the ton.

100　　Gold quartz, from Caratal, Canton of Upata, Province of Guayana . . } *C. Hahn.*

These specimens are selected promiscuously from 22 bags, containing 1650 lb., now in the Venezuelan Court, which were lately collected by Mr. C. Hahn.

Attention has only recently been drawn to these gold-fields in Guayana, which from their vast extent and great richness of ore, it is thought, fully confirm the reports made by the aborigines to the Spaniards, at the time they originally became possessed of this country, when it was generally designated as "El Dorado."

101　61 Green marble from Carácas . . . *L. J. Revenga.*

102　69 Red marble . . . . . .

103　64 Rock crystal . . . .

104　63 Petrified vera wood . . . . . .

105　　Specimens of copper ore, with their assays, from the celebrated mines in the Aroa district, now about to be worked by an English Company . . . . } *The Quebrada Land and Mining Company.*

---

*The following articles are mostly from the province of Maracaibo :—*

106　A pocket-handkerchief, handsomely worked.
107　A worked pillow-case.
108　Eight pairs of alpargatas, or sandals.
109　Cups and jugs of totuma, painted and gilt.
110　Four models of cocoa in wax, in different states.
111　Three tins of preserves.
112　One tin of chocolate.
113　One tin of dried camburitos.
114　Five bottles of spirits, varied.
115　One bottle of vinegar from aloes.

116  A bunch of grapes and two lemons, grown in bottles.
117  Three cocoa-nuts, of very great size.
118  A stuffed bird.
119  A bow and arrows of the Indians ; the arrows poisoned.
120  A hat made from rabbit-skins, and a skin from which they are made.
121  Articles made in bone by prisoners.
122  A bough, with oranges made in wool.
123  Samples of coffee.
124  Sample of cocoa.
125  Samples of cotton.
126  A SAMPLE OF COAL from the island of Joas, of which large quantities are said to exist.
127  Two large cakes and 100 candles of very fine STEARINE, manufactured and exhibited by SENOR MARTIN TOVAR GALINDO, in CARÁCAS, and the first ever sent from South America to England.
128  "THE DECLARATION OF INDEPENDENCE," and THE ARMS OF VENE-ZUELA, worked in hair, upon satin.—*Exhibited by Mr. Wesselhoeft, Puerto Cabello.*

---

*Medals and Honourable Mentions awarded by the International Juries to the Exhibitors in the Court of Venezuela.*

| Page in Award. | No. in Catalogue. | Name of Exhibitor. | Award. | Objects rewarded, and reasons for the award. |
|---|---|---|---|---|
| 52 | | Exhibition Committee, Carácas | A Medal | Collection of agricultural produce. |
| 71 | 27 & 28 | Exhibition Committee, Carácas | A Medal | Coffee and cocoa—excellence of quality. |
| 96 | 47 | J. M. Catalan and Co., Maracaibo | Honourable Mention | Bitter liqueur—goodness of quality. |
| ,, | 48 | Dr. Siegert, Ciudad Bolivar | Honourable Mention. | Aromatic bitters—goodness of quality. |
| 132 | 8 | F. L. Davis, 13, Blandford-st., W. | A Medal | For the excellent workmanship of the totuma, or cup, carved out of the shell of a fruit. |
| ,, | 91 | Ferd. Meyer, Hamburg | A Medal | For cotton, medium staple value, 1s. 1d. per lb. |
| ,, | 84 | Ruete, Rohl, and Co., La Guaira | A Medal | For cotton, value 1s. per lb. |
| ,, | 86 | Stolterfoht, Sons, and Co., Liverpool | A Medal | For exceedingly fine cotton, with long staple, value 2s. 5d. per lb. |

## Appendix (C).

*Sketch of the Gold Mine of the Yuruari in Venezuelan Guiana.*

The extension of the auriferous territory is very great ; the whole surface of Guayana may indeed be considered as auriferous, if we except a few patches of land here and there. I can give as proof of it, that the worked part of the Yuruari * is considered a central point, while the English Mining Company is established on the banks of the Yuruari, at about two hundred and twenty-five miles east of Tupuquen,† upon the Yuruari. I can present samples from old mines, and from gold washings in the Upper Orinoco, in the river Graviare, and other streams, as also samples brought from Caicara,‡ which is situated about three hundred miles west of Ciudad Bolivar, and from the washings in the district of the Paragua,§ at about one hundred and eighty miles from Tupuquen, on the Yuruari, as the most conclusive proof of the general auriferous character of the country. Lastly, I can speak of the presence of gold in French Guayana, south of the Yuruari, and on the other side of the great range of the mountains Parima and Anaparima. We cannot doubt, then, that the gold-bearing grounds extend from the banks of the Orinoco on the north, to the aforesaid mountains of Parima and Anaparima on the south, and from the table land of Rio Negro on the west, to the Atlantic Ocean and English colony of Demerara on the east.

The evidence of gold, rather slight on the banks of the Orinoco, begins to be more conspicuous about sixty miles to the south of that river, and about one hundred miles farther the appearance is richer,

---

* The copyist seems to have made some blunder here. There are two rivers, one called Yuruari, and one called Yuruan or Juruan, which fall into the Cuyuni, the former flowing from N. to S. and joining the Cuyuni on its left bank, and the other flowing in an opposite direction, and joining the Cuyuni on the right bank. According to this there must be a third river of similar name, not given in Codazzi's map.

† Tupuquen is about 70 miles S.E. of Upata.

‡ Caicara is on the right bank of the Orinoco at its confluence with the Apure.

§ The Paragua falls into the Caroni 70 miles S.S.W. of Upata.

and at about one hundred and fifty miles, in the country through which the Yuruari runs, we are in the full development of the formation, though, perhaps, not yet in the richest places, which, methinks, must lie nearer the large mountain range mentioned above.

Mining remains as yet limited to the river Yuruari and neighbouring ground on the south side of the river, in the midst of a splendid forest.

There has been very little progress, indeed; which may be attributed to the want of knowledge of the miners, who have been, to the present day, but unintelligent workmen, unable to make any progress in discovery.

The working of the mines has remained where it is, for it was on that spot that Dr. L. Plassard made the first discovery of gold in April, 1849.

In different trips I have made through the country, above all in 1858, I have run over a tract of land of about forty thousand square miles; a surface extending from the Orinoco on the north to beyond the river Sapauro, or Avertuca, on the south, and from the river Caroni on the west, to the river Cuyuni on the east. Upon this great surface gold is to be found; first, as gold dust, in all the rivers and torrents mixed with the sand and mud, and even with the earth in the open fields or savanas, in many places where there grows nothing but scanty grass and a very few stunted trees.

Secondly.—It is found in small grains and nuggets (pieces) of all sizes, from ounces to many pounds' weight, in the gold-bearing clay under ground of the whole country, which occurs at very different depths, from one yard to twenty-five yards. This clay, which offers a thickness of two to eight inches, is commonly yellow, with veins sometimes brown, sometimes green or white. In other mines, as in the bed of the Yuruari, the clay is whitish, with yellow or dark veins. In all cases the auriferous clay contains a great many small pebbles and broken pieces of stones of all descriptions, pyrites, oxydated iron, garnet, zircon, and small grains of platina.

Thirdly.—Gold is found in grains and pieces of various sizes in earth of a fine red poppy colour, imparted to it by peroxydated iron. That earth, soft and unctuous to the touch, and of a thickness between thirty and forty inches, contains generally a great many loose gold-bearing quartz stones in its bed, fine gold being mixed throughout with the earth, and grains and pieces of gold being found at the bottom of the bed mixed with a great many broken pieces of rock, as in the clay. As this red earth lies on the surface, it is easy to be found. The miners call it tierra de flor ("surface earth") for this very reason.

Fourthly.—Gold is to be found in the quartz rock. The quartz is very abundant everywhere—in pieces and loose stones of different sizes, in blocks, in beds or strata, and in well-formed veins between the metamorphic rocks. All these descriptions or varieties of shape of quartz are met with, both on the surface of the ground and at every depth. The loose stones and blocks are sometimes well impregnated with gold in veins and crystals. The strata and veins of quartz are very often richly traversed by abundant and numerous veins of gold, as may be seen in some of the samples I have brought, not the richest either.

The miners do not use any machinery at all. The only tools they use are the American pick, or pickaxe, the shovel, the mining bar, to work the ground ; mining implements to blow up the rocks ; hammers of different sizes and weights, to break the quartz stones into small pieces ; a mortar, to pound those pieces of quartz, which they pulverize with a flat stone and a round one, after burning them to soften them ; sieves, to pass the powdered stone till it is fine enough to be amalgamated ; and, lastly, a batea (sort of wooden bowl) to wash the auriferous quartz dust with mercury ; after which they sift the amalgamated gold with a piece of thick linen, and burn the mass till most of the mercury evaporates and leaves a hard yellow cake of gold containing still a small quantity of quicksilver.

This batea is the only instrument used to wash the clay.

All these operations are very coarsely performed, and a rather large quantity of gold and quicksilver is lost in the process.

I have said before that mining is still limited to a few spots in the vicinity of the Yuruari. The first place inhabited by the miners was the old mission of Tupuquen, a village at about one mile from the river on its left bank. In 1856 to 1857 they began some works on the right bank, at about three miles south of the Yuruari. They built there a few huts, which were the origin of the present village called Nueva Providencia, or Caratal, as the miners prefer to call it, from the leaf of a palm called carata, which served to cover the huts. It must be observed here that they give the same name of Caratal to the whole forest, which extends along the banks of the river Yuruari, with a length of forty-five miles from the west to the east, and a breadth of twenty to twenty-four miles from north to south. The river Yuruari runs from the west to the east in that part of the country.

Nueva Providencia, now-a-days a pretty village, being considered as the centre of the very few places discovered and worked up to this day, we may say that the places most distant from the village, a place called Cicli, is only four to five miles from Nueva Providencia. The other places called Peru, Panama, Callado, &c., are all near the village.

There is, indeed, very little progress in the discoveries, though at the end of last year the miners (I mean the persons working the mines) numbered between six hundred and seven hundred. Since May last their number must have increased. At that time, when I left Caratal, or Nueva Providencia, the whole population of those mountains amounted to about five thousand inhabitants, and was increasing rapidly.

We have seen that the red earth is found lying on the surface ; the miners have but to dig it and carry it to the water-side to wash it. For this they choose generally the rainy season, when they have not to go very far to find water to wash the dirt off. I have said, too, that the gold-bearing clay was to be found at very different depths. In the spots called Chili and Peru the clay is met at one or two yards from the surface ; in others at eight, at twelve, at sixteen, and more yards deep. In the red earth there are, as already mentioned, loose gold-bearing quartz stones, and in the shafts dug to reach the clay, the last layer upon the gold-bearing clay is always composed of loose rocks of different sorts, and above all of quartz, generally impregnated with gold, and worth working. As to the quartz rock itself, it is so very common that I may well say that where you do not see it, you may still look for it under ground, and you are sure to come to it at any depth. Thus, the miners met by chance very rich quartz on the hill called Tigre, and in Callado ; at twenty-five yards depth in the first case, and at twelve to twenty in the second. I must state, too, that up to this day the miners have never had the idea that gold could be found at a much greater depth, and have besides no means to undertake such works. The way they work is ruinous, and yet, notwithstanding the great difficulties they meet, and the want of means and implements. they get a good return.

In general, when you speak of mines to any one, you will be asked directly— " Well, well, but tell me how much gold is got per hundred-weight of earth or stones, and how many men are employed to extract it, in order that I may know the average produce of your mines ?"

We must try to solve the problem in another way, because, in the first place, there is no regularity, as every one knows, in the richness of gold-diggings ; and because, in the second place, our miners of the Caratal work without the least regularity, work when they please—to-day a little, to-morrow much, and the day after to-morrow not at all.

One day they will continue working four hours, another day two hours, another day the whole day, and, where they find a large piece of gold, they will remain a fortnight without doing anything—enjoying themselves. On the other hand, they never weigh anything like dirt, clay or rock ; they do not take time into account, because for them time is not money. Being so, we must content ourselves, if we have no time or money to undertake to work mines for our own account—we must be contented, I say, with looking on, and see how things go, and do our best to calculate the aforesaid average product, so much looked for by those who are inclined to take shares in a gold-mining company.

I will, then, state first that our miners of the Caratal do not go on working their claims when the red earth and the clay do not produce more than four shillings per hundredweight, and, be it observed here, that they miss entirely the black gold, which exists everywhere, and requires to be extracted by a second washing, after exposing the earth or clay in the open air. I must state, too, their coarse way of pulverising the stone with which the gold is amalgamated is the cause of a loss that may be valued at from five to ten per cent. Again, the miners, when breaking the quartz rock to pick out the pieces containing gold, throw away such a quantity of gold-bearing stones that a great number of women and children make a very good day's work out of what they can pick up, and it would be a very good business for a company to collect those rejected stones of quartz and work them. The miners in Caratal may have sometimes thought that washing earth for gold-dust would be a good business, but they never tried it.

These facts adduced here detract from the general product of the mines, and make the average product very uncertain.

The miners work claims about seven yards on each side ; they pay three shillings and fourpence per month duty. According to the points they must reach, and to the difficulties of the ground, they join two or three together. We have said already that, in some places, they find the gold-bearing clay at one yard to two yards below the surface, and in other places they must sink a shaft of twenty and even twenty-five yards. Between these two extremes there is a great variety as to the depth of the clay. The digging of a square or round hole of a yard or two yards in depth and one and a half yards in breadth will take about two days. The digging of a shaft twenty to twenty-five yards deep will take so much more time in comparison ; and, again, sometimes the diggings of a yard to two yards may be richer than those of twenty to twenty-five yards. What a difference in the average product then !

Generally, when the two or three men working a claim do not get at least an ounce of gold per day, they consider it a bad business. I have said that they leave the digging when the earth or clay gives only four shillings per hundredweight. I have seen claims giving two to three ounces per day ; I have seen others giving eight to ten ounces, and a few giving twenty to thirty and more per day ; and, again, a piece of gold of a few pounds' weight is found now and then. How difficult it is, in such conditions, to give an average product !

The working of the quartz, in stones on the surface, in the bed of the red earth, lying on the auriferous clay, in blocks, strata, or veins, would give a regular product if worked by a company. As the quartz is generally rich, the miners are sure to get well repaid for a day's labour. Sometimes a loose stone of thirty to sixty pounds will give ounces, even pounds of gold ; sometimes the gold veins will give such wondrous results that I scarcely dare to write them down. I have seen pieces of quartz extracted from a vein, as in the Tigre, contain more gold than stone. One piece of twelve pounds gave seven pounds and some ounces.

In the auriferous quartz, which is so very abundant, that I may call it inexhaustible—and we know nothing as yet of the lower or deeper strata of that rock, as no shaft has been sunk deeper than twenty-five yards—in the gold-bearing quartz rock, I say, the lowest average product cannot be valued at less than eight to ten pounds per ton weight. Some quartz veins will give forty to sixty pounds sterling. Some other quartz veins will give, as I have seen, hundreds of pounds sterling per ton.

The quantity of melted gold exported from the mines to Ciudad Bolivar, during the months of December, 1866, January, February, March, and April, 1867, was about four thousand ounces of gold per month ; and I may well say that all the gold extracted was not exported. During the time spoken of, the number of the miners, I mean people at the diggings, was between six hundred and seven hundred.

I left the diggings, where I had arrived in January, at the beginning of June. In May the population was already on the increase, so that I can say nothing of this last month.

As I have, during three months and a half, studied with care the mountains of Caratal (forty-five thousand square miles), I beg leave to say that I have stated nothing but what I have seen, and that I have come to such a certainty of the richness of the mines, that I fear they will be under-rated in this short sketch, which I had not even time to make up correctly.

All the country between the Orinoco, Superino, Cuyuni, and Caroni, which I have registered, is composed of low table lands, hills, and small mountains. Low plains and marshes are very scarce in those parts of Guayana. The very forests of Caratal are a sort of table lands, small plains, high valleys, and mountains, everywhere covered with beautiful trees. The heat varies in the different plains ; it is, near the Orinoco, between 74° and 92° Fahrenheit ; in the interior of the missions of Upata between 70° and 86° ; further in the mining district between 72° and 88°. Upata itself is a very healthy place, as well as the other ancient missions raised by the Spanish friars. Santa Maria, Yuasipati, Tecumrevero, and Miano, may be cited as uncommonly healthy places. Why may we not say the same of the mountains of Caratal and others ? Surely, living in a thick forest, sleeping generally in the open air, often for want of houses, working in the diggings, people that are new to such hard work, taking sometimes bad food, making use of strong drinks and liquors, gambling and dancing sometimes the whole night—these are, methinks, sufficient causes to explain the few diseases that have reigned in the mining districts. Besides these, every-day people, unaccustomed to such travels, come to the works, and are sometimes without means to take any repose. They are tried by the journey—by the heat of the sun ; they ought to keep quiet some days ; but they have no means, they must go to work ; they then go to the diggings, sleep in the mountains, and now and then encounter a shower of rain when their body is over-excited by the work. How is it possible for them not to fall sick ? It would be rather a wonder should it not be so.

I have lived over twenty years as a physician in Venezuelan Guayana, and may well say, that if you except the borders of the large rivers, you will find the country pretty healthy. I think that measures being taken to avoid the causes above alluded to, you can keep even strangers in a pretty good state of health in our country.

Two roads lead from Ciudad Bolivar, the chief town of the State of

Guayana, to the mines.  The first one, and the shortest, goes from Ciudad Bolivar by land in a south-east direction to the mining districts.  The distance is about two hundred miles.  Cars with loads may be driven to the mines, but with many difficulties.  People use mules and donkeys for this purpose, but a good road can easily be made, as there are no mountains, nor other great difficulties.  When I left Ciudad Bolivar, the merchants of that town had raised a sum of money to make the survey of the works wanted ; the commission named for this object was on its way to begin the inspection of the roads.

The second road to the mines goes down the Orinoco to a small port named " Puerto de Tablas," ninety miles from Ciudad Bolivar.  From the port, the road goes through the small town of Upata to the Yuruari.  The distance from the river to the mines is about one hundred and fifty miles.  This last road, as may be seen, is somewhat longer than the first.  A pretty good road might be made, too, that way, but I think it presents greater difficulties than the first one.

It has been said very justly, I think, that the Republic of Venezuela is often disturbed by periodical political movements ; that there is no security, no guarantee for people that would like to undertake something in that country ; that there is no protection from the Government, no reliance to be put in promises made by it ; and so on.

Though I agree in all other things, I beg leave to point out the situation of the State of Guayana, on the left bank of the river Orinoco.  This situation is the very cause why Ciudad Bolivar has passed through the period of five years' disturbances and revolutions in Venezuela without any conflicts, without sufferings common to revolutionary times.  The river Orinoco is the stronghold of Guayana, and will always preserve her from any attack on the part of the other States.  It is well worth while to pay attention to this particular disposition of Guayana.  It is to be remarked, too, that the State of Guayana, larger in surface than France, has but the scanty population of twenty-five thousand * inhabitants.

How easy it will be to transform the country.  When immigrations on a larger scale take place, the present population will be soon absorbed, and disappear in the general increase of population.

Security may then be depended upon in Guayana, at least to a much greater extent than in the other States.  But, if we consider the want of protection, may we not here refer to the vicinity of English Guayana, the

* Sixty thousand according to other authorities.

mines of which province are blasting up quartz on the Cuyuni, at but two hundred and twenty-five miles east of Caratal, in a country where roads could easily be made to bring men and goods from America up to the right banks of the river Caroni. I only mention this to prove that protection, if refused by the authorities of the State of Guayana, could be found somewhere else.

---

## Appendix (C.)

### *Constitution of the United States of Venezuela. Translated from the Official Edition, printed at Carácas, May 10th, 1864.*

The Constituent Assembly, invoking the Supreme Author and Legistor of the Universe, and under the authority of the people of Venezuela, decrees :—

### DIVISION I.—THE NATION.

#### FIRST SECTION.—TERRITORIES.

Art. 1. The Provinces of Apure, Aragua, Barcelona, Barinas, Barquisimeto, Carabobo, Carácas, Cojédes, Coro, Cumaná, Guarico, Guayana, Maracaibo, Maturin, Mérida, Margarita, Portuguesa, Táchira, Trujillo, and Yaracui : declare themselves Independent States, and unite to form a free and sovereign nation, under the name of the United States of Venezuela.

Art. 2. The boundaries of each State will be those which the Law of the 28th April, 1856, announced to the Provinces, when it fixed the last territorial division.

Art. 3. The boundaries of the United States, which compose the Federation of Venezuela, are the same as those which, in the year 1810, corresponded to the ancient Captaincy-General of Venezuela.

Art. 4. The political individualities mentioned in Article 1 reserve to themselves the power of uniting, two or more of them, so as to form one State ; retaining always liberty to resume their original quality of individual States. In either case, they will communicate their intention to the National Executive, to Congress, and to the other States of the Union.

Art. 5. The States, which may have availed themselves of the power accorded in the preceding Article, will retain their votes for the Presidentship of the United States, for the nomination of Senators, and for the empowerment of voters for the High Federal Court.

SECOND SECTION.—CITIZENSHIP.

Art. 6. Citizens of Venezuela are :—

1st. All persons born in the territory of Venezuela, whatever the nationality of their parents may be.

2nd. Children of a Venezuelan mother or father, born in alien territory, if they come to domicile themselves in the country, and express a wish to become citizens.

3rd. Strangers who may have obtained letters of naturalization ; and

4th. Persons born in any of the Spanish-American Republics, or in the Spanish Antilles ; always providing that they have fixed their residence in the territory of the Union and desire citizenship.

Art. 7. Those Venezuelans who fix their domicile and acquire nationality in a foreign State do not lose their Venezuelan citizenship.

Art. 8. All Venezuelans, who are males of twenty-one years of age, are eligible to office, with the exceptions contained in this charter of the Constitution.

Art. 9. All Venezuelans are bound to serve the nation, as the laws decree, at the sacrifice of their goods and life, if required, for its defence.

Art. 10. Venezuelans, in whatever territory they may be, are bound by the same duties and retain the same rights as those Venezuelans who are living in Venezuela.

Art. 11. The Law will determine the rights belonging to strangers.

DIVISION II.—BASES OF THE UNION.

Art. 12. The States, which form the Union, reciprocally acknowledge their rights to self-government, each of the others declare themselves equal as political units, and retain in their plenitude all sovereign rights, not expressly delegated by this Constitution.

Art. 13. The said States bind themselves to self-defence against all violence injurious to their independence and the integrity of the Union ; and further bind themselves to establish fundamental regulations for their guidance and internal government, and remain under engagement:—

1st. To adopt an organisation in conformity with the principles of popular, elective, federal representation, alternate and responsible government.

2nd. Not to alienate any part of their territory to a foreign Power, nor to seek its protection.

3rd. To give up to the nation such lands as may be required for the federal district.

4th. Not to close by imposts or otherwise the navigation of the rivers or other navigable waters, which have not required the aid of canals made by man's labour.

5th. Not to tax before they are exposed for sale products which have been subjected to national imposts.

6th. Not to tax goods or merchandise, which are in transit from one State to another.

7th. Not to impose duties on the national officers, except in their quality of members of the State, or as far as their duties may not be incompatible with the public service of the nation.

8th. To defer and submit themselves to the decision of Congress, to the National Executive, and to the High Federal Court in all disputes which may arise between two or more States, when an amicable arrangement cannot be arrived at ; but in no case can a State declare or make war against another State.  If, for any reason, they may fail to designate the arbiter to whose authority they will submit, they remain bound by the very nature of things to submit to the decision of Congress.

9th. To observe strict neutrality in the disputes which may arise in other States.

10th. Not to join themselves or alienate themselves to any other nation, nor by separation to impair the nationality and territory of Venezuela.

11th. To obey and carry out the Constitution and the laws of the Union, and the decrees and orders, which the National Executive and the Tribunals and Judges of the Union may issue in the exercise of the powers belonging to them.

12th. In their several constitutions to subscribe to the extradition of criminals as a political principle.

13th. To keep at a distance from the frontier those individuals who, from political motives, take refuge in a State, provided that a State interested in their seclusion demands it.

14th. Not to establish Custom-houses for the collection of imposts, so that the national Custom-houses may be the only ones.

15th. Not to permit in the States of the Union enrolments or levies, which have or might have for their object to attack the liberty or independence, or to disturb the public order of other States, or of any other nation.

16th. To leave to each State the free management of its own natural products : consequently, those States which possess salt-works may manage them in complete independence of the general government.

17th. To reserve from the national rents for the benefit of those States which do not possess mines, which are being worked, the sum of $20,000, which must be fixed in the annual estimate of public expenses, and must be paid to those States three months beforehand.

18th. To supply the contingent force which may fall to their share in the composition of the public national army in time of peace or of war.

19th. Not to prohibit the consumption of the products of other States, nor to burthen them with differential charges.

20th. To leave to the government of the Union the free administration of the territories of the Amazons and of Goajira, until they may choose to be acknowledged as States.

21st. To respect the possessions in towns, parks, and forts belonging to the nation.

22nd. To maintain for all one and the same substantive civil and criminal legislation.

23rd. To establish in the popular elections the direct and secret suffrage.

### DIVISION III.—RIGHTS GUARANTEED TO VENEZUELANS.

Art. 14. The nation guarantees to Venezuelans :—

1st. The inviolability of life, capital punishment being abolished, whatever law may establish it.

2nd. Property, with all its rights; this will be subject only to the contributions decreed by the legislative authority, to the decision of judges, and to requisitions for public works, after indemnification or adverse decision.

3rd. The inviolability and secresy of correspondence and other papers.

4th. Inviolability of the domestic hearth, which cannot be entered except to prevent crime, in conformity with the law's decree.

5th. Liberty of the person, and consequently, 1st, forced military enlistment is abolished ; 2nd, slavery is for ever abolished ; 3rd, slaves that arrive in Venezuelan territory become free ; 4th, all are at liberty to do or execute everything that does not prejudice another.

6th. Liberty of thought, expressed by word of mouth or through the medium of the press, without any restriction whatever.

7th. Liberty of transit without passports, and to change domicile, observing the forms established in the States, and to absent oneself from and return to the Republic taking away one's goods.

8th. Liberty of industry, and, consequently, the ownership of things discovered or produced. The law will assign to owners a temporary privilege, or a mode of indemnification in case the inventor should agree to make public his invention.

9th. Liberty to assemble or meet together without arms, publicly or privately, the authorities not having any right of inspection.

10th. Liberty of petition, and the right of obtaining a decision. This liberty would apply to the petitioning of any functionary, authority, or corporation. If the petition be made by a number of persons, the first five will be answerable for the authenticity of the signatures, and all will be responsible for the truth of the facts.

11th. Liberty of suffrage at the popular elections, without any restriction except that of being under eighteen years old.

12th. Free right of being educated, which will be protected in its full extension. The power of the State remains under obligation to establish gratis a course of primary education and of the arts and employments.

13th. Religious liberty; but the Catholic, Apostolic and Roman religion alone may perform public service out of the sacred edifices.

14th. Security of the individual, and therefore, 1st, no Venezuelan can be taken or arrested by force for debts which do not originate in fraud or crime; 2nd, no one is obliged to receive soldiers into his house to be lodged there or quartered upon him; 3rd, no one is to be judged before special tribunals or commissions, but only by his natural judges, or in virtue of the laws delivered before the crime or action to be judged; 4th, no one is to be made prisoner or to be arrested without previous distinct information of his having committed a crime deserving corporal punishment, or written order of the functionary who decrees the arrest, with notification of the motive of the arrest, unless he be taken in the act; 5th, nor is he to be prohibited from holding intercourse with others on any account or pretext; 6th, nor is he to be obliged to take oath, nor to undergo examination in criminal causes against himself or his relations within the fourth degree of consanguinity or the second of affinity, or against his or her spouse; 7th, nor to be kept in prison when the grounds of his imprisonment cease to exist; 8th, nor is he to be condemned to suffer any penalty in a criminal matter until his cause has been legally heard; 9th, nor is he to be condemned to corporal punishment for more than ten years ; 10th, nor is he to be deprived of his liberty for political reasons after order has been re-established.

15th. Equality, in virtue of which, 1st, all must be judged by one and the same laws, and must be subjected to the same duties, services, and contributions ; 2nd, titles of nobility, honours, or hereditary distinctions are not to be granted, nor employments or offices whose pay or emoluments last beyond the time of service ; 3rd, no official address is to be adopted towards persons in office or corporations except that of citizen and *usted*, " you."

Art. 15. What has been just set forth does not restrain the liberty of States to grant to their inhabitants other guarantees.

Art. 16. The laws in the several States will fix punishments for those who violate those guarantees, and will fix the judicial process for making them effective.

Art. 17. Those who issue, sign, or execute, or cause to be executed decrees, orders, or resolutions, which violate or infringe any of the guarantees accorded to Venezuelans, are culpable, and must be punished as the law may direct. Every citizen is entitled to accuse them.

DIVISION IV.—OF THE NATIONAL LEGISLATURE.

FIRST SECTION.

Art. 18. The National Legislature is composed of two Chambers—one of the Senators, the other of the Deputies.

Art. 19. The States shall determine the mode of appointing the Senators and the Deputies.

SECOND SECTION.—OF THE CHAMBER OF DEPUTIES.

Art. 20. In order to form the Chamber of Deputies, each State will choose one Deputy for every 25,000 inhabitants, and a second Deputy for a number in excess beyond 12,000. They will also elect an equal number of supplementaries.

Art. 21. Deputies will keep their functions two years, and then will all be re-elected.

Art. 22. The following are the duties of the Chamber of Deputies :—

1st. To examine the annual account which the President of the United States of Venezuela will lay before them.

2nd. To pass votes of censure on the Ministers of State, and, by the fact of such votes, the appointments of those to whom they refer will be rendered vacant.

3rd. To hear accusations against the officer charged with the national executive for treason to his country, or for common offences; and against the ministers and other national officers for infraction of the laws and for malversation, in conformity with Art. 82 of the Constitution. This power is preventive, and does not detract from the powers which other authorities hold to judge and punish.

Art. 23. When an accusation is brought forward by a Deputy, or by any corporation or individual, the following rules will be observed:—

1st. A committee of three Deputies will be nominated by a secret vote.

2nd. The committee will deliver judgment within three days, and declare whether there are grounds for trial or not.

3rd. The Chamber will consider the report, and will decide by the vote of the absolute majority of members present, the Deputy who accuses abstaining from voting.

Art. 24. Declaration of there being grounds for trial will, *ipso facto,* suspend the accused, and incapacitate him from the discharge of any public office during the trial.

### THIRD SECTION.—THE CHAMBER OF SENATORS.

Art. 25. To form this Chamber each State will elect two principal Senators, and two supplementaries to fill vacancies.

Art. 26. To become Senator it is requisite : to be a Venezuelan by birth, and to be thirty years of age.

Art. 27. Senators will remain in office four years, and will be re-elected every two years. When, through any circumstance, they are all re-elected, the election shall be for two years.

Art. 28. The duty of the Senate is to support and determine the judgments initiated by the Chamber of Deputies.

Art. 29. If a trial be not finished during the Session, the Senate will prolong its Session, solely with the object of terminating the trial. In this case the Senators will not receive allowances.

### FOURTH SECTION.—GENERAL REGULATIONS FOR THE CHAMBERS.

Art. 30. The Legislature will assemble every year in the capital of the United States, on the 20th of February, or as soon as possible afterwards, without waiting to be summoned ; and the Session will last seventy days, with the power of prolongation to ninety.

Art. 31. The Chambers will open their Session with at least two-thirds of their members ; and failing this number, those present will form themselves into a preparatory Committee and determine means for obtaining the presence of the absentees.

Art. 32. The Session, when opened, can be carried on with two-thirds of those by whom it was opened, provided that the number does not descend below half the whole number of nominated members.

Art. 33. Though the Chambers discharge their functions separately, they will meet in Congress, on occasions fixed by the Constitution and the Law, or when one of the two Chambers declares it to be necessary. If the Chamber to which the requisition is made assents to it, it shall fix the day and hour for the meeting.

Art. 34. The Sessions shall be public, and secret when the Chamber agrees to hold a secret Session.

Art. 35. The Chambers have the right :

1st. To make rules to be observed during the Sessions and debates.

2nd. To bring those who infringe rules to order.

3rd. To cause the observance of courteous behaviour in the House during Session.

4th. To punish or correct spectators who infringe the rules of order.

5th. To remove obstacles which may oppose the free exercise of their functions.

6th. To cause to be executed their resolutions for depriving officials of their appointments.

7th. To admit members and hear resignations.

Art. 36. Either of the Chambers has no power to suspend its Session, or change its place of meeting, without the consent of the other ; in case of disagreement they are to meet, and what the majority decide must be carried out.

Art. 37. The exercise of any public function is incompatible with that of a Senator or Deputy during the Session ; the law will declare the indemnifications which they will receive for their services, and these cannot be increased during the period for which they may be constitutionally fixed.

Art. 38. From the 20th of January every year, until thirty days after the close of the Session, the Senators and Deputies shall enjoy immunity;

and this shall consist in the suspension of all procedure against them from whatever cause it may originate, or whatever be its nature. When any Senator or Deputy commits an act meriting corporal punishment, the judicial inquiry shall be carried on to the termination of the summary, and remain in that state until the period of immunity is over.

Art. 39. Congress shall be presided over by the President of the Senate, and the President of the Chamber of Deputies shall be the Vice-President.

Art. 40. Members of the Chambers are not responsible for the opinions or speeches they there deliver.

Art. 41. Senators and Deputies cannot accept appointments or offices from the National Executive for one year after the period for which they were nominated has expired. The appointments of Ministers of State, and of diplomatic officers and military commands in time of war, are excepted from this vote ; but the acceptance of such employments vacates that previously held in the Chamber.

Art. 42. Nor can Senators or Deputies make contracts with the general Government, nor conduct the causes of others who have claims on the Government.

### FIFTH SECTION.—DUTIES OF THE LEGISLATURE.

Art. 43. The National Legislature has to discharge the following duties :

1st. To settle disputes which may arise between the States.

2nd. To establish and organise the Federal District in an uninhabited part of the country, not to exceed ten square miles, in which the capital city of the Union is to be built. This district shall be neutral, and shall not deal with any other elections but such as the law shall determine for its locality. Provisionally this district shall be that designated by the Constitutional Assembly, or that which the National Legislature shall fix.

3rd. To organise all that relates to the Custom-houses, whose receipts shall form the treasure of the Union, until others are substituted.

4th. To decide all that relates to the equipment and security of the ports, and of the maritime coasts.

5th. To create and organise the offices of the national post, and fix the sums to be charged for the carriage of letters.

6th. To make the national codes in accordance with paragraph 22 of Article B.

7th. To fix the value, mould, law, weight, and milling of the national money, and decide as to the admission and circulation of foreign money.

8th. To declare the shield of arms and flag of the nation, which shall be the same for all the States.

9th. To appoint and remove the national officers, and settle their pay.

10th. To determine everything that has reference to the national debt.

11th. To contract loans on the security of the national credit.

12th. To dictate the measures necessary for taking the census of the population and other national statistics.

13th. To fix annually the armed force by sea and land, and to make the military regulations.

14th. To make the regulations for the formation and replacement of the forces noted in the preceding paragraph.

15th. To declare war and call on the National Executive to negociate for peace.

16th. To approve or reject diplomatic treaties or conventions. Without this necessary preliminary the said treaties or conventions cannot be ratified or modified.

17th. To approve or reject contracts which the President of the Union may make for public national works, the said approval being essential for their being carried out.

18th. To make the yearly estimate of the public expenses.

19th. To promote all that conduces to the prosperity of the country, and to its progress in the knowledge of the arts and sciences.

20th. To fix the national weights and measures, and render them uniform.

21st. To grant amnesties.

22nd. To fix with the denomination of their territories the special government under which uninhabited regions, or those inhabited only by uncivilized tribes, are to be temporarily ruled ; such territories shall be under the immediate control of the Executive of the Union.

23rd. To fix the judicial processes and declare the penalties which the Senate has to impose in causes initiated in the Chamber of Deputies.

24th. To augment the constituencies for the election of Deputies.

25th. To admit foreigners to the public service, or exclude them from it.

26th. To transmit the law of elections to the President of the Union.

27th. To make laws for the retirement and retiring allowances of soldiers.

28th. To declare the law as to the responsibility of all the national officers.

29th. To determine the mode of assigning military rank and promotion.

Art. 44. Besides the points enumerated above, the National Legislature will make all laws of a general nature that may be required.

### SIXTH SECTION.—OF THE PASSING OF LAWS.

Art. 45. The laws and ordinances of the National Legislature may be initiated by the members of either Chamber, or in any manner enacted by their regulations.

Art. 46. As soon as a Bill has been presented, a discussion shall take place as to whether it shall be brought in ; if permitted to be brought in, there shall be three debates on it with the interval of at least one day between each ; the rules for debates being observed.

Art. 47. Bills approved in the Chamber in which they are initiated shall be sent up to the other to go through the stages in the preceding paragraph, and if not rejected shall be returned to the Chamber whence they originated, with the alterations which they may have undergone.

Art. 48. If the Chamber which initiates a Bill is unwilling to accept the alterations, it can insist on its remaining unmodified and send up its reasons in writing to the other Chamber. The Chambers can also assemble in Congress and go into a Committee of the two Houses to consider on the mode of coming to an agreement, but if this agreement cannot be arrived at, the Bill must be abandoned as soon as the Chamber of initiation comes to that decision.

Art. 49. When the Bills of either Chamber are passed, the days on which they have been discussed must be mentioned.

Art. 50. A law to regulate another law must be drawn out in full, and the former law becomes entirely repealed.

Art. 51. The following formula is to be observed in laws :—" The Congress of the United States of Venezuela decrees."

Art. 52. Bills rejected by one Legislature cannot be brought forward again until a new one comes in.

Art. 53. Bills which are under discussion in one of the Chambers at the end of the Sessions, must be debated again three times in the following Sessions.

Art. 54. Laws are to be repealed with the same formalities with which they are passed.

Art. 55. When the Ministers of State have maintained in a Chamber that a measure is unconstitutional, and it is nevertheless passed as a law, the Executive of the Union may submit it to the nation represented in the Legislatures of the States.

Art. 56. In the case contemplated in the preceding Article, each State shall represent a vote, expressed by the majority of the members present in the Houses of Legislature, and shall send the result to the High Federal Court, in this form : " I confirm," or " I object."

Art. 57. If the majority of the States agree with the Executive, the Court shall order the law to be suspended and shall report to Congress, transmitting an account of all that has taken place.

Art. 58. Laws shall not be in force until published with the established ceremonies.

Art. 59. The power granted to sanction a law cannot be delegated.

Art. 60. No legislative enactment shall have a retrospective force, except in the matter of a judicial process, or in a case where punishment not capital is imposed.

### DIVISION V.—OF THE NATIONAL EXECUTIVE.

#### FIRST SECTION.—OF THE CHIEF OF THE GENERAL ADMINISTRATION.

Art. 61. Everything relative to the general administration of the nation, not entrusted by this Constitution to other authority, shall be the duty of a magistrate, who shall be called President of the United States of Venezuela.

Art. 62. To be President it is necessary to be a Venezuelan by birth, and to be thirty years of age.

Art. 63. The President shall be elected by the citizens of all the States, by direct and secret vote according to the rule for State voting, namely, by the relative majority of each State's electors.

Art. 64. On the eighth day of the Session of Congress the Chambers shall meet to hold a scrutiny. If by that time all the registers have not been received, measures shall be taken to obtain them, the scrutiny being deferred in case of necessity for forty days. After that term the scrutiny may be taken with the registers that have been received, provided that they be not less than two-thirds of the whole number.

Art. 65. In the case of the election being made according to the preceding Article, whoever obtains the absolute majority of votes will be declared President. If no one has it, Congress will select the two who have the greatest number of votes. The votes will then be taken by States, each State having one vote, and unless two-thirds of the States agree, the election will not hold good. The vote of each State is that of the absolute majority of its Representatives and Senators ; and in case of an equality of votes the decision shall be by lot.

Art. 66. During the scrutiny none of the members assembled can leave the Session, without the consent of Congress.

Art. 67. Two designated Presidents will be annually chosen by the Chambers jointly to fill up the occasional absences of the President, or an absolute vacancy.

Art. 68. The President will remain in office four years, reckoning from the 20th of February, on which day he will quit his duties and will summon the person who is to replace him, even though the period of four years has not completely expired.

Art. 69. When there occurs an absolute vacancy in the Presidentship during the two first years of a period, Congress shall decree a new election for the appointment of another President who shall continue in office for the time wanting to make a complete period of four years.

Art. 70. The President, or his substitute in the case contemplated in the preceding Article, cannot be elected for the period immediately following his term of office.

Art. 71. The law will fix the pay which the President and his substitutes are to receive ; and the amount cannot be augmented nor diminished during the period for which the law fixes it.

### SECOND SECTION.—OF THE DUTIES OF THE PRESIDENT OF THE UNITED STATES OF VENEZUELA.

Art. 72. The President of the Union has the following duties to perform :

1st. To preserve the nation from every external attack.

2nd. To order the laws and decrees of the National Legislature to be executed, and to see to their execution.

3rd. To take care of and watch over the collection of the national rents.

4th. To manage the waste lands according to law.

5th. To convoke the National Legislature at its periodical assemblies, and on extraordinary occasions, when the gravity of any event demands it.

6th. To appoint persons to fill diplomatic offices, Consul-Generalships, and Consulships ; being bound to see that Venezuelans by birth are appointed to the first and second class of offices.

7th. To direct the negociations and ratify all kinds of treaties with other nations after submitting them to the National Legislature.

8th. To ratify the contracts which are of national importance in conformity with the law, and submit them to the Legislature.

9th. To nominate and remove the Ministers of State.

10th. To appoint the officers of finance, whose nomination is not assigned to other functionaries. For these offices the nominees must be Venezuelans by birth.

11th. To remove and suspend officials, who are appointed by himself alone, and to order them to be tried should there be ground for it.

12th. To grant letters of naturalization conformably to law.

13th. To issue commissions to the ships of the nation.

14th. To declare war in the name of the Republic, when Congress has decreed it.

15th. In case of foreign war he has power : 1st, to apply to the States for the assistance required for the national defence ; 2nd, to call by anticipation for contributions, or to negociate loans decreed by Congress, if the ordinary rents are insufficient ; 3rd, to arrest or expel individuals who belong to the nation with which the country may be at war, and who may be an impediment to the defence of the country ; 4th, to suspend the guarantees which may be incompatible with the defence of the independence of the country, except that of life ; 5th, to designate the place to which the National Executive may have to remove temporarily, when there are grave reasons for it ; 6th, to bring to trial for treason such Venezuelans who may in any way be opposed to the national defence ; 7th, to issue letters of marque and reprisals, and to lay down the rules to be followed in cases of capture.

16th. To make use of the public forces, and of the powers contained in Numbers 1, 2, and 5 of the preceding functions, with the view of re-establishing constitutional order in case of armed insurrection against the political institutions which the nation has assumed.

17th. To dispose of the public force in order to put an end to the armed collision between two or more States, and require of them to lay aside their arms and submit their controversies to the decision of the national authorities, according to Paragraph 8 of Article 13.

18th. To direct the war or command the army in person in the cases contemplated in this Article. He may also quit the capital, when the public interests require it.

19th. To grant general or particular amnesties.

20th. To defend the territory marked out for the Federal District, when there are well-founded fears of invasion by hostile forces.

21st. To discharge the other functions assigned to him by the national laws.

Art. 73. When the National Executive may have made use of all or several of the powers accorded to it in the preceding Article, it will report hereon to the Congress within the eight first days of its next assembling.

THIRD SECTION.—OF THE MINISTERS OF STATE.

Art. 74. The President of the United States of Venezuela will have those Ministers of State which the law decrees. The law will determine their functions and duties, and will organise the Secretariats.

Art. 75. In order to be Minister of State it is requisite to be twenty-five years of age, to be a Venezuelan by birth, or to have been naturalised five years.

Art. 76. The Ministers are naturally and strictly the organs of the President of the Union : they will subscribe all his acts ; and without this formulary his orders will not be performed or executed by the authorities, officially, or by private persons.

Art. 77. All the acts of the Ministers must be regulated by this Constitution and by the laws : they do not escape responsibility by the order of the President, even though they receive it in writing.

Art. 78. The decision of all matters, which are not included in the routine of the Secretariats, shall be arrived at by the Ministers in Council, and their responsibility is collective.

Art. 79. In the first five Sessions of each year the Ministers shall report to the Chambers what they may have done or intend to do in their respective departments. They will also furnish memoranda of information or verbal statements, when called upon, reserving only what may be unsuitable to publish in diplomatic negociations or in war.

Art. 80. Within the same term they will lay before the National Legislature the estimate of the public expenses, and the account current of the preceding year.

Art. 81. Ministers have the right to speak in the Chambers, and are obliged to attend when called on to give information.

Art. 82. Ministers are responsible :

1st. For treason.

2nd. For violating the Constitution or the Laws.

3rd. For malversation of the public funds.

4th. For expending sums beyond estimates.

5th. For bribery or corruption in the discharge of their functions, or in appointments to public offices.

### FOURTH SECTION.

Art. 83. The National Executive is exercised by the President of the Union, or his *locum tenens*, in union with the Ministers of State, who are his organs.

Art. 84. The functions of the National Executive cannot be exercised beyond the Federal District, except in the case contemplated in section 5 of the 15th Paragraph of Article 72. When the President takes command of the army, or absents himself from the Federal District, availing himself of the 18th Power in the same Article 72, he will be replaced as ordained in Articles 72 and 102 of this Constitution.

### DIVISION VI.—OF THE HIGH FEDERAL COURT.

#### FIRST SECTION.—OF ITS FORMATION.

Art. 85. The High Federal Court shall be composed of five Members, with power of voting, who must have the following qualifications :

1st. The being a Venezuelan by birth or naturalized ten years.

2nd. The having completed thirty years of age.

Art. 86. For the appointment of these Members the Legislature of each State shall present to Congress a list equalling in numbers the places to be filled, and the Congress shall declare him elected who shall have most votes in the united lists of the sections that follow.

1st. Cumána, Margarita, Maturin, and Barcelona.

2nd. Guayana, Apure, Barinas and Portuguesa.

3rd. Carácas, Aragua, Guárico, and Carabobo.

4th. Cojédes, Yaracuy, Barquisimeto, and Coro.

5th. Maracaibo, Trujillo, Mérida, and Táchira.

Where the votes are equal Congress shall decide.

Art. 87. The law shall determine the different functions of the members, and of the other officers of the High Federal Court.

Art. 88. The Members, and their respective substitutes, who shall be appointed in the same way as the principals, shall continue in office four years. The principals, or the substitutes in office, cannot accept any employment from the Executive during the above period, even though they should resign their Membership of the Court.

### SECOND SECTION.—DUTIES OF THE HIGH FEDERAL COURT.

Art. 89. The High Court is competent to deal with the following matters :

1st. To take cognizance of civil or criminal causes which relate to diplomatic officers, in the cases permitted by the public right of nations.

2nd. To take cognizance of causes in which the President orders the trial of his Ministers, and in case of the suspension of a Minister being decreed, a report will be made by the Court to the President.

3rd. To examine causes against the Ministers of State, when they are accused in the cases contemplated by this Constitution. Should it be necessary to suspend the accused from his functions, the Court will call on the President to suspend him, and the President will comply.

4th. To take cognizance of causes in which diplomatic agents accredited to other nations are put on trial for misconduct.

5th. To examine causes in which the high functionaries of the different States are put on trial for criminal acts or other misconduct, provided that the laws of those estates sanction that form of procedure.

6th. To inquire into the action of the civil tribunals when required by the nation and sanctioned by law.

7th. To settle disputes between the officers of the different States in matters of judicature or competency.

8th. To take cognizance of all matters which the States wish to submit to their consideration.

9th. To declare what is the law in force when the national laws clash, or those of the nation with those of the States, or the laws of the same State with one another.

10th. To take cognizance of disputes which arise from contracts or negociations ratified by the President of the Union.

11th. To try cases of capture.

12th. To exercise the other functions assigned to it by law.

DIVISION VII.—REGULATIONS NECESSARY TO COMPLETE THE SUBJECTS TO BE DEALT WITH.

Art. 90. Everything not expressly assigned by this Constitution to the general administration of the nation, falls within the competency of the States.

Art. 91. The tribunals of justice in the States are independent: causes commenced in them in conformity with their special procedure, and on subjects of their exclusive competency, shall be settled in the States themselves, without being subjected to investigation by any external authority.

Art. 92. Every act of Congress or of the National Executive, which may violate the rights guaranteed to those States by this Constitution, or infringe their independence, shall be declared null by the High Court, always provided that the majority of the Legislatures should require it.

Art. 93. The public force of the nation is divided into naval and military; and shall be composed of the militia of citizens, which the States organize in conformity with their laws.

Art. 94. The force maintained by the Union shall be formed of individual volunteers with a contingent from each State in proportion to its resources, the citizens of the State being called upon to serve, and being bound to obey according to the laws.

Art. 95. In case of war the contingent may be augmented from the citizen militia up to the number of men required to meet the demand of the National Government.

Art. 96. The National Government has the power to change the leaders of the public force which the States furnish in the cases, and with the formalities that the military law of the nation may appoint, and the States will then be required to furnish substitutes.

Art. 97. The military and civil authority shall never be exercised by one and the same person or corporation.

Art. 98. The nation possesses the right of ecclesiastical patronage, and will exercise it as the law shall direct.

Art. 99. The Government of the Union shall not possess in the States resident officers with jurisdiction and authority, other than the officers of the States themselves. From this rule are excepted the officers of finance, and of the forces which garrison national fortresses, or which protect parks created by the law, stations for soldiers and inhabited posts, and these will have jurisdiction only in what belongs to their respective duties, or within the precincts of the fortresses and quarters where they command ; and they are not thereby exempt from being under the general laws of the State where they reside. All the material of war which at present exists belongs to the National Government.

Art. 100. The National Government cannot locate in a State a force or military chief with a command, though belonging to that State or otherwise, without the permission of the Government of the State in which the force is to be placed.

Art. 101. Neither the National Executive, nor the Executives of the States, can make an armed intervention in the domestic disputes of a State : they are only allowed to tender their good offices to bring about a peaceable solution of the disputes.

Art. 102. When the Presidentship is vacant, or temporarily vacated, and cannot be filled up by a Designated President, one of the Ministers of State will fill it, elected in public session by all his colleagues. In this case the person so elected will be summoned, and will report his election to the States.

Art. 103. The National Congress cannot augment the imposts which are levied on the exports, nor increase the mortgages upon them ; and when once the existing mortgages upon them are removed by payment, compensation, or substitution, the exportation of the national products will be for ever free.

Art. 104. All usurped authority is without effect ; its acts are null. Every decision arrived at by the direct or indirect demand of the armed force, or by the assembling of the people in a subversive attitude, is *ipso facto* null and inconsequent.

Art. 105. No corporation or official is permitted to discharge any function whatever, which is not conferred on him by the Constitution or the laws.

Art. 106. Any citizen may accuse the national officers before the Chamber of Deputies, before his respective superiors, or before the authorities indicated by the law.

Art. 107. Officers appointed by the free voice of the President of the Union finish with him their term of office in each constitutional period ; but will continue in office until relieved.

Art. 108. No disbursement is to be made from the National Treasury, for which a sum has not been expressly applied by Congress in the annual estimate, and those who infringe this rule will be civilly responsible to the National Treasury for the sums they have so disbursed. In all distributions of the public treasure, the ordinary expenses will be attended to before the extraordinary.

Art. 109. The departments for collecting the national contributions and those for payments will be always kept separate ; the former have not the power to make any other payments but what are due to the officials employed in them as salary.

Art. 110. When for any reason the estimate corresponding to a fiscal period has not been voted, that of the period immediately preceding shall be continued in force.

Art. 111. In the periods of the national elections, and those of the States, the public force shall be disarmed; and the respective laws of the States shall determine the mode of disarmament.

Art. 112. In commercial and friendly international treaties the clause shall be inserted, "all differences between the contracting parties shall be decided without appeal to war by the arbitration of some power or powers."

Art. 113. No individual can discharge more than one office under the nomination of the Congress or the National Executive. The acceptance of any other appointment is equivalent to the resignation of the first. Removable officers cease in their appointments to be capable of receiving the post of Senator or Deputy, when dependent on the National Executive.

Art. 114. The law shall create and define the other national tribunals which may be necessary.

Art. 115. The national officers cannot accept presents, trusts, honours, or recompenses from foreign nations, without the permission of the National Legislature.

Art. 116. The armed force cannot deliberate ; its duty is to be passive and obedient. No armed corps can make requisitions, nor ask for subsidies of any kind except from the civil authorities, and in the mode and form defined by law.

Art. 117. The nation and the States will promote immigration and colonization by foreigners under the rule of their respective laws.

Art. 118. One law shall regulate the manner in which the national officers shall be bound to make oath or declaration as to the discharge of their duties on entering upon their appointments.

Art. 119. The National Executive shall negociate with the Governments of America for treaties of alliance or confederation.

Art. 120. The rights of nations fall under the department of the National Legislature : its rules shall be the standard, especially in cases of civil war. Consequently civil war may be terminated by treaties between the belligerents, who must respect the humane practices of Christian and civilized nations.

Art. 121. The Laws and Regulations of the government of the States shall remain in force, until the new Legislatures which are about to be appointed can bring them into harmony with the present Constitution ; and this must be done within the space of four months.

Art. 122. This Constitution may be remodelled entirely or partially by the National Legislature, if the majority of the Legislatures of the States require it ; but the modification shall not take place except with regard to points which the States desire to have changed.

Art. 123. The present Constitution will come into force from the day of its official publication in each State ; and from that day the date of the Federation, the 20th of February, 1859, shall be stated in all the public acts and official documents, as also that of the present law.

Given and sealed in the Hall of the Sessions of the Constituent Assembly in Carácas on the 28th of March, 1864, the first of the Law and sixth of the Federation.

> President of the Assembly, Eugenio A. Rivera, Deputy for Barinas.
>
> Vice-President, Manuel N. Vetancourt, Deputy for Cumaná, and seventy other Deputies.

## Appendix (D).

## *Mr. Mocatta's Statement of the Disposal of the Money raised by the Loan of 1862.*

Brighton, *October 13th*, 1865.

Messieurs Baring, Brothers, & Co., London.

Gentlemen,

The letter addressed to you, of the 29th September last, by Señor A. L. Guzman, lays a distinct charge that your agents failed in their duties with respect to the Loan of 1862.

Owing to the lamented demise of F. D. Orme, Esq., C.B., Her Majesty's Chargé d'Affaires, I am left alone to reply thereto ; this, however, is not a difficult task, as I am able by documents to disprove the false charges brought against us.

At page 2—Allusion is made to a previous hypothecation, and refers to a letter of Dr. H. Nadal ; this is answered by the fact of the creditors who represented the $4,240,000 having accepted the terms offered them at public meetings on the 1st and 8th May, 1862. As this took place prior to the Loan, it is necessary to state the particulars :—It was agreed that a common fund of 27 per cent. of the duties of Imports should be substituted for the 38 per cent., which had been paid to that date ; the directors of the bank notified the acceptance of this new agreement to the Government. This new arrangement proves that the hypothecation of the 38 per cent. ceased, and no formal cancelment was needful. Owing to the stopping of the bank, Mr. Carl Hahn, director thereof, made a written proposal to the Government for a new arrangement, based on the 27 per cent. security. In the *Independiente* of the 26th June, 1862, the bank directors published a notice declaring that the shareholders accepted a proposal made by the Government to purchase the capital of the bank at 50 per cent., payable in five years ; this was sanctioned and approved at a general meeting held on the 3rd July, 1862, at the bank premises, and presided over by his Excellency the Secretary-General ; the vote passed with only one dissentient (Dr. D. B. Urbaneja) ; the whole was published in the Carácas papers ; this was binding to all interested, whether citizens or foreigners. And this brings me to the case laid before the High Federal Court ; as it was put, it certainly did not require the learned judges to say that a prior mortgage took precedence of a second claim, for a schoolboy would be deemed a dunce did he not know this. Had the case with all its bearings been referred to the High Federal Court, the sentence must have been different, and it is evident the present Government thought very little of it, as by a stroke of the pen they reduced it to 15 per cent., not only for the parties interested, but for all the internal creditors.

At page 3—Señor Guzman states that your agents directly interfered, by partial arrangements which they made with some of the creditors ; this is untrue, as they simply fulfilled the instructions of his Excellency the Secretary of State, which were to take up the shares held by Messrs. Pardo & Co., and others, on a consideration being made to the Government for the advance of payment ; in this your agents could make no demur, as the funds of the Loan were ample for all just claims, as shown in my letter of the 10th April, 1863, in document No. 1.

At page 4—Much stress is laid on the French and Spanish claims, which were in the hands of their respective representatives, and must have been * unadjusted, or they would have come forward, together with the other diplomatic claims. Again, had the parties holding the shares and notes of the bank presented them to the Commission, they would have received the instalments in November, 1862 ; thus your agents had no cognizance or intervention therein, and cannot be justly accused of neglect of duty. I know, however, that several payments were made in money to the order of Monsieur Millinet, the French Chargé d'Affaires.

At page 6—It is asserted that the internal creditors were not paid nor even consulted ; this is untrue, as another agreement was entered into at a public meeting, and from this emanated the decree of the 15th November for the settlement of the bank claims.

At page 8—It is said, by not calling a general meeting of the internal creditors, the agents prevented the settlement of their claims ; this, to say the least of it, is ludicrous, and I should like to know what Señor or General Guzman would have said to the agent of the 1864 Loan, had he presumed to call a meeting of the creditors of the Export Duties.

It is stated that the law of Venezuela requires that a Loan should be

* Sic in orig.

registered ; if this is so, why was the agent of the 1864 Loan not made to register, and not be only scriptural, the more particularly so as the present Venezuelan Government made known in their financial statement that they were holders of nearly one-third of the £1,500,000 bonds ? The registry was, I believe, subsequently made, owing to the notice given to you by General Guzman Blanco in February last. This necessity is new to me, as from the year 1823 to 1837 I was a resident merchant in Carácas, and had never known any proceeding for the fulfilment of the decrees of all the governments that existed during that period, than by "Bando," and inscribed in the *Registro Oficial* (equivalent to our *London Gazette*).

I send you a note of Mr. Carl Hahn, one of the liquidators of the Bank affairs ; No. 2, shewing the total liabilities of the Government ; and at foot, No. 3, shewing the sums paid thereon, and the balance left unpaid by General Paez's Government. I beg to refer you to the letter of H. E. Pedro José Rojas to your agents of 3rd October, 1862, confirming the conditions of the Loan. Also to my letter of 10th April, 1863, shewing that the proceeds of the Loan were ample for the requirements stipulated for. Señor Guzman states that no accounts were kept ; this appears impossible, as the Government nominated a commission consisting of Messrs. Ruete, Röhl, & Co., Santana Brothers, and H. L. Boulton & Co. ; and this Commission appointed the Bank of Hahn and Servadio to attend to the payments of the vales and notes presented ; these parties sent to the Commission entitled " Seccion de Credito Publico " a letter No. 4, and a note, of which you have a copy and translation, No. 5, shewing the amounts of the creditors and the settlement thereof, and the bills drawn for each creditor, under document No. 6. I also addressed a letter to the Commission, on the 22nd December, 1862, stating the amounts delivered by me to His Excellency the Secretary-General, and crossed by me, " Redeemed by the Government ;" this is shown in letter No. 7.

I addressed a letter to His Excellency Pedro José Rojas, relative to the payments of the Bank creditors by the commission, dated 27th November, 1862 ; copy herewith, No. 8. Also His Excellency's reply of the same date, No. 9. Prior to the settlement of the diplomatic claims, which were placed in the hands of G. Stürup, Esq., Danish Consul General, consisting of the British, Danish, United States, and Dutch claims, your agents received the authorization on the 17th November, 1862, as shewn in copy and translation of His Excellency

Pedro José Rojas' letter (accompanied by a long statement from the Foreign Office, too profuse to add, the totals being the exact sums paid to each), No. 10. The French and Spanish claims were not brought before your agents, who consequently could know nothing of them. The Collector of Customs of La Guayra, sent the list of inscribed creditors, as per copy with translation No. 11 ; the amounts thereof were paid by bills on you. To prove that the whole of the funds were faithfully applied, I send you under No. 12, copy and translation of the letter of His Excellency the Secretary of State, acknowledging receipt of all the vouchers I had presented.

Of the 23 signatures attached to the memorial, I find nine received their 20 and 10 per cent.; viz.:—Carl Hahn, D. B. Barrios, Santiago Vera, L. Sucre, J. B. Calcano, Eduardo Gathman, Modesto Urbaneja, Alexandro Viso, Manuel M. A. Aurrecoechea.

Considering that I have fully exonerated myself from the charge of neglect of duty, and that you are satisfied that due diligence has been observed by me,

I have the honour to be, Gentlemen,

Yours respectfully,

(Signed)          E. MOCATTA.

---

Republic of Venezuela.

CARÁCAS, November 17th, 1862.

Office of Secretary General, Finance Department.    Section Number.

MESSRS. E. MOCATTA AND F. D. ORME.

You are hereby authorised to pay to the representatives of the foreign Governments, which this Government owes for international claims, already acknowledged and liquidated, in conformity with the account which will be presented to you from the Department of Foreign Affairs.

I am, Sirs,

Your obedient servant,

(Signed)          PEDRO JOSÉ ROJAS.

Note.—The payments must be made at latest for the packet of 7th December.

(Signed)          ROJAS.

---

This Custom-house is indebted for orders which have been presented up to date.

| Owners. | Dates. | | Nos. | Amounts. |
|---|---|---|---|---|
| Cs. Geyler . . . . . . . | May 14, 1862 | 380 | $1008.94 |
| Jn. Boggio & Servadio Monsanto & Co. . . | June 17 | ,, | 428 | 10,737.26 |
| Owner of the Custom-house of Puerto Cabello | do. 30 | ,, | 233 | 6960.71 |
| Cipriano Morales . . . | July 22 | ,, | 31 | 1000 |
| Herrara Hermanos . . . | Aug. 20 | ,, | 70 | 8412.68 |
| Vicente Perez )    Endorsed to Messrs. | July 23 | ,, | 34 | 604 |
| do.    { Neckelmann, Roosen, & Co. | do. 23 | ,, | 35 | 2404 |
| G. Servadio )    Half of three orders<br>Alejo. Viso }    amounting to | Aug. 20 | ,, | 71/73 | 16,159.98 |
| Alejandro Viso, 2 orders . . . . | do. 20 | ,, | 89,90 | 4000 |
| Francisco Ramirez — Endorsed to Messrs.<br>   Marturet, Bros., & Co. . . . . | do. 21 | ,, | 80 | 2954.55 |
| Guillo. Stürup . . | do. 25 | ,, | 83 | 909.88 |
| Syers, Brasch, & Co. | Sept. 6 | ,, | 103 | 6621.44 |
| Do. | Oct. 3 | ,, | 149 | 149.85 |

$61,923.29

Lr Guayra, *October 13th*, 1862.

(Signed)     J. M. BADUEL.

---

[Copy.]

CARÁCAS. *November 27th*, 1862.

His Excellency Pedro José Rojas, Secretary General, &c., &c., &c.

EXCELLENT SIR,

My attention has been called to the 5th article of the resolution of the Government, relative to the execution of the decrees regarding "Billetes y Acciones del Banco de Venezuela," and published in the *Independiente* of the 21st inst.

I have now to state that all I have agreed to do, as agent for Messrs. Baring, Brothers, & Co., is to place bills in the hands of the Commission appointed by the Government, the 20 per cent for the "Billetes y Acciones de Preferencia," and 10 per cent. for the "Acciones Ordinarias."

It is absolutely necessary that the Commission should be informed that the Government will pay the 10 per cent. on the "Acciones Ordinarias" in February next, and that I am in no way concerned as agent for Messrs. Baring, Brothers, & Co. for the same.

I trust you will make this known at once, as the Commission should be informed of the actual position of the arrangement, prior to receiving the " Billetes y Acciones " from the holders thereof.

I have the honour to be,<br>Excellent Sir,<br>Your most obedient Servant.<br>(Signed)    E. MOCATTA.

*Republic of Venezuela.*

CARÁCAS, *November 27th*, 1862.

Finance Department, Section 1st, Number 1796.

SIR,

I have the honour to inform you that I have given proper instructions to the Director of the Section of Public Credit, and to the Commission appointed in conformity with the decrees issued by his Excellency the Supreme Chief, on the 15th instant, to attend to the indications of your note of this date, to which I reply.

Your most obedient Servant,<br>(Signed)    PEDRO JOSÉ ROJAS.

E. Mocatta, Esq.

[Copy.]

CARÁCAS, *December 22nd*, 1862.

Messrs. Ruete, Röhl, & Co.
    Santana, Brothers, & Co,
    H. L. Boulton & Co.

GENTLEMEN,

I beg to inform you that I have handed to his Excellency the Secretary-General the following Billetes, &c., crossed by me, " Redimidos por el Gobierno," and on which neither the 20 and 10 per cent., nor the 10 and 5 per cent. on the acciones ordinarias are payable :—

```
$141,680 Ruote presentados por Belletes, Röhl & Co.
  37,950 id.        id.      ,,  C. Hahn
 112,950 id.        id.      ,,  J. B. de Leon
  20,000 id.        id.      ,,        do.
 164,250 Acciones de preferencia por do.
 481,250 Acciones ordinarias por       do.
  20,000 id.        id.      ,,        do.
```

There is still to be arranged with you the Billetes, &c., handed in by Messrs. Marcano, Hos., & Co.

There are also $44,868.58
and    17,445.05 } Billetes in the hands of the Treasurer,

which were handed in by me by order of his Excellency ; the same were returned by Mr. Guillo. Stürup, and Mr. F. D. Orme, on the settlement of their diplomatic recognized claims.

For the balance of the 20 and 10 per cent. on the Billetes and Acciones, the Government held more than sufficient of the same to cover your claim, and I beg to refer you to his Excellency the Secretary-General to satisfy you thereon.

I am, Gentlemen,

Yours, respectfully,

(Signed)        E. MOCATTA.

CARÁCAS, November 6th, 1862.

I have received of Messrs. Baring, Brothers, & Co., of London, agents to the Government of Venezuela, by the hands of Messrs. E. Mocatta and F. D. Orme, up to this day, in bills and cash, on account of the Loan of the 31st July of the present year, the sum of one hundred and ninety-one thousand one hundred and twenty-five pounds sterling, which are placed to the credit of the said Messrs. Baring, Brothers, & Co., for account of the Government.

The Secretary-General,

(Signed)        PEDRO JOSÉ ROJAS.

CARÁCAS, November 22nd, 1862.

As Secretary-General, I have received of Mr. E. Mocatta, on account of the Loan contracted with Messrs. Baring, Brothers, & Co., fifty-two thousand one hundred pounds sterling, in bills on London.

(Signed)        PEDRO JOSÉ ROJAS.

CARÁCAS, December 6th, 1862.

As Secretary-General, I have received of Mr. E. Mocatta, on account of the Loan contracted with Messrs. Baring, Brothers, & Co., the sum of one hundred and fifty-five thousand seven hundred and ninety-two pounds sterling and fourteen shillings.

(Signed)        PEDRO JOSÉ ROJAS.

For £155,792 : 14s.

### Mr. Carl Hahn's Memorandum of Bank Affairs.

Cash for Vales of La Guayra Custom-house . . . $92,000
,, ,, Puerto Cabello ,, . . . . 700
Cash from the Government to make up part of claims of prefer-
ence credits . . . . . . . . . 78,387.19
————
$171,087.19

$2,961,373.13 debt of Government in account current, which
includes all Billetes (Notes at 30 per cent. after deduct-
ing $100,000) . . . . . . . . . 888,417.94
$3,181,459.71 Capital of the Bank, at 15 per cent. . 477,218.85
————
$1,536,723.98

Of the above the $171,087.19 was paid in full, in Bills and
Specie, thus leaving to be paid . . . . . . $1,365,636.19
Bills drawn and Specie—total paid for the Bank
accounts . . . . . . . . . £164,040
Deduct the sterling value of the $171,087.19, about 26,837
————
£137,203

At the Exchange of $6.50 to the £ sterling . . . 891,820

Balance which should have been paid by the Government in
February, 1863 . . . . . . $473,816.19
Equivalent in sterling to £72,900

———

[Copy.]
*Bank of Carácas.*

Messrs. Ruete, Röhl, & Co.
Santana, Brothers, & Co.
H. L. Boulton & Co.

Carácas, *December 4th*, 1862, A.M.

Gentlemen,

We have the honour to hand you a note of the bills of exchange,
which were applied for yesterday, and also a statement of the lists handed
in by the Section of Public Credit, another presented by the creditors,
and another of the amount of credits in bills and cash.

To-morrow we will hand in lists of the creditors who may come
to-day, and remain,

Your obedient Servants,

For the Bank of Carácas.

(Signed) Carl Hahn.
G. Servadio.

The Section of Public Credit handed in the following Lists :—

| | | | |
|---|---|---:|---:|
| 1st | In Notes of the Bank . | . $1,023,299.50 | |
| 2nd | ,, do. do. | . 202,946.06 | |
| | Titles . | 116,701.10 | |
| | | | $1,342,946.66 |
| 1st | ,, Preference Shares | $412,080 | |
| 2nd | ,, do. . | 7,750 | |
| | | | 419,830 |
| | | | $1,762,776.66 |
| 1st | ,, Ordinary Shares | $2,330,500 | |
| 2nd | ,, do. | 187,250 | |
| | | | 2,517,750 |
| | | | $4,280,526.66 |

Brought forward by Creditors up to December 3rd, 4 o'clock, P.M. :—

| | | Calculated at 20 & 10. |
|---|---:|---:|
| Bills and Titles . | $1,117,310 | $223,462.04 |
| Preference Shares . . | 420,580 | 84,116 |
| Ordinary do. . | 2,452,500 | 245,250 |
| | | $552,828.04 |
| Bills applied for . . . | £81,730 | $521,028.75 |
| Cash for small sums and balances . | | 31,799.29 |
| For the Bank of Carácas . . | | $552,828.04 |

(Signed)     CARL HAHN,<br>
G. SERVADIO.

[Copy.]

1st List of Amounts to be drawn on London :—

| | | | |
|---|---|---|---:|
| * | Carl Hahn . | . | £4410 |
| * | id. | . . | 1190 |
| 212 | id. | . . | 120 |
| 213 | id. | . . . | 190 |
| 214 | id. | . | 180 |
| 215 | id. . . | . . . | 150 |
| 216 | Rafael Martinez | . . | 120 |
| 217 | G. Ronzone . . | . . | 3410 |
| 218 | Oscar de Lanzieres | . . | 800 |
| 219 | Luis Elizondo . | . . | 120 |
| | Carry forward | | £10,690 |

* Drawn separately.

|  |  | Brought forward . | £10,690 |
|---|---|---|---|
| 220 | J. B. Calcaño | . . . . | 110 |
| 221 | Santiago, Vera, & Co. | | 1410 |
| 222 | H. G. Schimmel & Co. . | | 1100 |
| 223 | F. Garrido | . . | 240 |
| 224 | L. Weber & Co. | | 150 |
| 225 | Lindo & Co. | . | 210 |
| 226 | Octavio Pardo | . . . | 190 |
| 227 | Hermanos Delfino y Sobrino | | 2320 |
| 228 | Cipriano Morales | . . | 140 |
| 229 | Canuto Garcia | . | 840 |
| 230 | M. Tovar Galindo | . | 370 |
| 231 | Fortunato Corvaia | | 8080 |
| 232 | J. M. Martel | . . . . . . | 440 |
| 233 | G. Petit de Meurville, Chancelier de la Legation Francaise | . . . . . . . | 150 |
| 234 | A. M. Seixas & Co. | | 370 |
| 235 | J. Viso | . . . | 670 |
| 236 | Santana, Herms., y Ca. . | | 130 |
| 237 | Mauricio Poggi | . | 400 |
| 238 | Hernandez y Rivodó | | 180 |
| 239 | Lorenzo A. Mendoza | | 490 |
| 240 | C. Madriz | . . | 300 |
| 241 | Sosa, Duran, y Ca. . | | 260 |
| 242 | D. B. Barrios | . | 760 |
| 243 | Modesto Urbaneja | | 200 |
| 244 | id. | . | 100 |
| 245 | id. | | 100 |
| 246 | id. | | 600 |
| 247 | id. | | 1000 |
| 248 | id. | . | 1000 |
| 249 | id. | . | 1000 |
| 250 | H. L. Boulton & Co. | | 310 |
| 251 | M. Martel | . . | 130 |
| 252 | Alejandro Viso | | 230 |
| 253 | Guillo. Rivas | . | 110 |
| 254 | Santiago Vera | . | 950 |
| 255 | M. M. Rodriguez Sosa | | 150 |
| 256 | Juan Boggio | . | 260 |
| 257 | Juan D. Conell | . | 170 |
| 258 | J. B. de Leon (£3374) . | | *16,240 |
| 259 | C. Espino y Ca. en liquidn. | | 220 |
|  |  | Carry forward | £52,770 |

* Only £3374, the rest having been previously drawn.

|  | | £52,770 |
|---|---|---|
|  | Brought forward | £52,770 |
| 260 | Syers, Braasch, y Ca. | 1660 |
| 261 | Pedro Vegas | 250 |
| 262 | Agustina Perez de Garrotte | 200 |
| 263 | B. .Rivodó | 330 |
| * | J. B. de Leon | 940 |
| 264 | Ruete, Röhl, & Co. | 1360 |
| 265 | A. F. Carranza | 190 |
| 266 | Gutierrez y Guardia | 380 |
| 267 | Tomas Aquerrevere | 200 |
| 268 | Juan Dr. Perez é hijos | 450 |
| 269 | Eduardo Espino | 120 |
| 270 | Jose Reyes | 160 |
| 271 | Escobar, Herms., en liquidn. | 110 |
| 272 | F. Ramirez | 120 |
| 273 | T. S. Nevett | 360 |
| 274 | Hugo Valentiner | 100 |
| 275 | J. Jacinto Rivas | 360 |
| 276 | Hugo Valentiner | 490 |
| 277 | id. | 170 |
| 278 | T. Smith y Schroeder | 100 |
| † | Marcano, Brothers, y Ca. | 120 |
| † | id. | 480 |
| 279 | Sojo, Larralde, y Ca. | 1010 |
| 280 | Carl Hahn | 1400 |
| 281 | Luis Vallenilla | 840 |
| 282 | Carlos Soublette | 390 |
| 283 | Eduardo Gathmann | 110 |
| 284 | Andres Ma. Caballero | 530 |
| 285 | id. | 390 |
| 286 | id. | 390 |
| 287 | Marxen & Craso | 520 |
| 288 | Gullielmo Stürup | 140 |
| 289 | id. | 110 |
| 290 | Manuel Martel | 160 |
| 291 | id. | 310 |
| 292 | Aristides Calcasio | 300 |
| 293 | id. | 290 |
| 294 | Camilo Alfaro, Junr. | 2340 |
| 295 | Domingo Rodriguez | 120 |
| 296 | M. M. Aurrecoechea | 620 |
|  | Carry forward | £71,390 |

* Previously drawn.
† Subsequently arranged.

|  |  | Brought forward | £71,390 |
|---|---|---|---|
| 297 | Esteban Herrera | . . . . | 870 |
| 298 | Luis Sucre . | . | 950 |
| 299 | R. Mijares | . | 130 |
| 300 | M. Zarraga . . . | . . | 150 |
| * | Marcano, Brothers, & Co. | . | 1690 |
| 301 | J. Igno. Rodriguez . | . | 180 |
| 302 | G. Servadio . . | . | 2210 |
| 303 | J. M. Echeverria | . | 1400 |
| 304 | Martin J. Larralde | . | 340 |
| 305 | Gonell Hermanos | . . | 340 |
| 306 | A. Ma. Callabero | . . | 290 |
| 307 | Miguel Zaldarriaga | . . | 140 |
| 308 | Santiago Vera . | . | 110 |
| 309 | M. M. Aurrecoechea | . . | 100 |
| 310 | J. A. Mosquera hijo | . | 400 |
| 311 | Carl Hahn . | . . | 190 |
| 312 | id. . . | . | 850 |

|  |  |
|---|---|
| Por el banco de Carácas | £81,730 |

(Signed)    CARL HAHN,
G. SERVADIO.

[Copy.]

To the Bills as per private list of this morning, please to add :—

PAID IN SPECIE IN LIEU OF BILLS.

| 8 addition of this morning | . | £1600 |
|---|---|---|
| Ruete, Röhl, & Co. . . | . . | 4440 |
| Gabriel J. Machado . | . | 150 |
| Manuel Sanchez | . | 110 |
| José Perez Oropeza | . | 140 |
| Luis Felipe Garcia . | . . | 180 |
| Boggio & Debarbieri . | . | 150 |
| José Bottaro . . . | . | 120 |
| A. J. Carranza . | . | 230 |

|  |  |  |
|---|---|---|
| 16 Bills | . . . | £7120 |

(Signed)    C. HAHN.

*December 4th*, 1862.

---

* Subsequently arranged.

*Account of £45,000 remitted to the Bank of St. Thomas's for Negotiation.*

|  |  |  |  |
|---|---|---|---|
| | £45,000 at exchange $4.90 ℔ £ stg., Dollars | | $220,500 |
| | Less commission charged . . | | 3,307.50 |
| | | | $217,192.50 |
| 6th Oct. | Received ℔ "Isabel" . . $100,000 | | |
| 21st ,, | Do. do. . . 116,007.25 | | |
| | Insurance at St. Thomas' . 1,115.25 | | |
| | | | $217,122.50 |
| 9th Oct. | Paid by order of his Excellency the Secretary-General £2000 . . . . | | $13,000 |
| ,, ,, | Do. to the London Committee £1000 . | | 6,500 |
| ,, ,, | Do. to Sn. Eyzaguirre . . . . | | 32,550 |
| ,, ,, | Do. his Excellency the Secretary-General at La Guayra . . . . . | | 78,750 |
| 22nd ,, | Do. by order of his Excellency £2000 . | | 13,000 |
| ,, ,, | Do. do. do. at La Guayra 40,000 hard dollars . . . . | | 52,520 |
| ,, ,, | Do. do. to Sn. Eyzaguirre . . | | 53,355.50 |
| ,, ,, | Do. do. do. . . | | 17,293.62 |
| ,, ,, | Do. do. $2100, $10,000 (to the S. Government) . . . . . . | | 12,100 |
| | Taken by me for charges . . . $3250 | | |
| | Less freight charges on first remittance . . . $440 | | |
| | Do. second do. . 387.87 | | |
| | Carriage from La Guayra . 21 | | |
| | ———— 848.87 | | |
| | | | 2,401.13 |
| | Net proceeds . . . | | $281,470.25 |

Carácas, *November*, 1862.
    E. Mocatta.

*Bills drawn on Messrs. Baring, Brothers, & Co., and Money received from the London Loan, for account of the Government of Venezuela, viz. :—*

|  |  |  |  |  |
|---|---|---|---|---|
| Bills negotiated at St. Thomas', as per separate account | £45,000 | 0 |
| ,, by orders of his Excellency the Secretary-General £5000, £5000, £500 | 10,500 | 0 |
| ,, in favour of Messrs. J. H. Moron & Co. £5000, £6000, £6000, £10,000 | 27,000 | 0 |

|  |  |  |  |  |
|---|---|---|---|---|
| ,, ,, of Eggers & Echer-raguia . . £1750 | in account | | |
| ,, ,, of Ruete, Röhl, & Co. 7000 | of *Billetes* | | |
| ,, ,, of Pardo & Co. . 30,000 | and Shares | | |
| ,, ,, Paid to the Bank . 15,400 | of Bank. | | |
| ,, ,, Pardo & Co. . 3374 | | 57,524 | 0 |

| | | | |
|---|---|---|---|
| ,, ,, of sundries, in payment of debts, Custom House, La Guayra . . . . | 9175 | 0 |
| ,, ,, Hermanos, Pages, & Co., £3000, £3000, £1000 . . . . . . | 7000 | 0 |
| ,, ,, Eggers & Echenagueia, their contract $2272 . . . . . . | 350 | 0 |
| ,, ,, Chartier & Olavarria £2000, £3175 . | 5175 | 0 |
| ,, ,, Santana, Hermanos, & Co. $10,000 . | 1500 | 0 |
| ,, ,, Sr. M. Larda, Treasurer of Carácas, £1000, £1000, £1000 . . . . . | 3000 | 0 |
| ,, ,, Sold for cash and on credit . . . | 3760 | 0 |
| ,, ,, Fco. Michelena. . . . . . | 200 | 0 |
| ,, ,, Marcano, Hs., & Co. £2350, £2650 . | 5000 | 0 |
| ,, ,, Vicente Piccioni . . . . . | 1500 | 0 |
| ,, ,, Ruete, Röhl, & Co. . . . . | 1500 | 0 |
| ,, ,, Santana, Hermanos, & Co. (Isla de Aves) | 2000 | 0 |
| ,, ,, Blohm, Nolting, & Co. . . . | 2000 | 0 |
| ,, ,, G. Servadio & C. Hahn . | 10,000 | 0 |
| ,, ,, N. J. Jessurum . . . . | 500 | 0 |
| ,, ,, H. G. Schimmel & Co. . . . | 770 | 0 |
| ,, ,, Lyons, Brasch, & Co., £2000, £2500 . | 4500 | 0 |
| ,, ,, G. Stürup, Diplomatic claims . . . | 9300 | 0 |
| ,, ,, F. D. Orme do. . . | 13,103 | 0 |
| ,, ,, E. D. Culver do. . . | 15,378 | 0 |
| ,, ,, Rolandus do. . . | 1685 | 0 |
| ,, ,, Sundries for the conversion of *Billetes* and Bank Shares . . . . | 56,660 | 0 |
| ,, ,, M. Sanchez per Blohm & Co. . . | 1850 | 0 |

|  |  |  |  |
|---|---|---|---|
| First remittance from London . . £50,000 | 0 |
| Second do. do. . 50,000 | 0 |
| Insurance, freights, &c. . . 2,587 | 14 |
| | 102,587 | 14 |

Carácas, *December 10th,* 1862.

E. MOCATTA.

£398,517 14

*Account of the £100,000 stg. received from Messrs. Baring, Brothers, & Co.,
from London.*

| | | |
|---|---|---|
| 8 Boxes, each £5000, delivered to his Excellency the Secretary-General at La Guayra . . . . | £40,000 | 0 |
| 2 Boxes, each £5000, taken by me as per separate account | 10,000 | 0 |
| Delivered in La Guayra, to the order of the Commission of *Billetes*, for account of the Government . . | 40,000 | 0 |
| Do. in La Guayra, to his Excellency the Secretary-General . . . . . . . . | 10,000 | 0 |
| Charges at Debit of the Government in account with Messrs. Baring, Brothers, & Co. . . . . | 2,587 | 14 |
| Carácas, *December*, 1862. | | |
| E. Mocatta. | £102,587 | 14 |

*Republic of Venezuela.*

Carácas, *December 22nd*, 1862.

Finance Department.

E. Mocatta, Esq.

I have the honour to inform you, that I have laid before his Excellency the Supreme Chief of the State, the documents which you remitted to me for that purpose on the 20th inst., relative to various operations effected with the funds of the Loan obtained in London this year, and that his Excellency has directed that they be annexed to the documents having connection with this matter, detailing them in this dispatch, for your satisfaction, in the same order as in the statement you sent, as follows :—

No. 1 3rd of bill in favour of Consul F. Hemming for £500.

    2 Receipt of H. L. Boulton & Co. for freight of the money from St. Thomas, $351.87. The difference of $440 charged in the account, consists in the charges.

    3 Do. of Blohm, Nolting, & Co., freight of the " Isabel," $387.87.

    4 Do. of Mr. R. M. Landa (Treasurer) for £5000, the half of £10,000 drawn in favour of Servadio & Hahn.

    5 Do. Mr. A. Eyzaguirre (Cashier of the Treasury), November 27th, for $32,500.

    6 Do. Messrs. Blohm, Nolting, & Co., freight, $812.50.

    7 Do. do. do. $812.50.

    8 Do. Mr. A. Eyzaguirre, of Espina and Diaz (Cashier of the Treasury) $6350.

    9 Do. Mr. Eyzaguirre for $44,868.56 in Notes of the Bank, from Mr. G. Stürup.

10 Do. Mr. A. Eyzaguirre for $17,445.05 in Notes of the Bank, from
   Mr. Orme.
11 Do. of Mr. G. Stürup for $63,106.60 for Danish claims.
12 Do. of Mr. Rolandus, £1685, and $4241.16, equivalent to $15,193.66
   for Dutch claims.
13 Do. E. D. Culver for $100,000 for United States' claims.
14 Do. F. D. Orme, $97,278.43 for British claims.
15 Do. Messrs. Marcano, Brothers, & Co., £5000.
   Do. Eggers & Echenagucia by Carl Hahn, $11,383 for 30 per cent. on
   $37,950 Notes of the Bank.
16 Do. Notes of Hand of the Administrator of the Custom-house of La
   Guayra, for the Bank of Venezuela paid to Pardo & Co. $70,000, or
   be it $70,599.66.
17 Do. of the Bank of Venezuela for $99,600.34.
18 Note of receipt and egress of £45,000 negotiated in St. Thomas, proceeds $281,470.25.
19 Note of Bills drawn and cash received from Messrs. Baring, Brothers,
   & Co., £398,517 14s.
20 Do. of the Accounts of the Custom-house of La Guayra settled and
   paid.
21 Do. separately of the £100,000.
22 Account current balanced in $10,701.27.
23 Provincial receipts of the Bank of Carácas for Notes of the Bank
   redeemed by the Government for Ruete, Röhl, & Co., $141,680.
   $37,950 Eggers & Echenagucia.
   $20,000 ; $164,250 Preference Shares ; $112,950 Bank Notes ;
   $481,250 Ordinary Shares ; $20,000 Bank Notes for J. B. de
   Leon.


With feelings of distinguished consideration,

       I have the honour to subscribe myself,

            Your most obedient Servant,

              (Signed)      PEDRO JOSÉ ROJAS.

# E. MOCATTA IN ACCOUNT WITH THE GOVERNMENT OF VENEZUELA.



**Dr.**

| | | | | |
|---|---|---|---|---|
| Balance per separate account of £500 taken for charges | | | | $ 2,401.13 |
| Value of £3760 sold on credit | | | | 23,910 |
| £10,000 of the money from England | | | | 65,000 |
| Received balance of Bill of Pardo & Hutton | $100 | | | |
| ,, ,, Lyon, Brasch, &Co. | 250 | | | |
| ,, ,, Man & Sauchet | 25 | | | |
| ,, ,, Schimmel & Co. | 5 | | | |
| ,, ,, Chartier & Olavarria | 2.50 | 382.50 | | |
| | | | | $91,693.63 |

**Cr.**

| | | |
|---|---|---|
| Balances of Accounts of the Custom-house of La Guayra :— | | |
| Paid to Sen. Alejo Viso | $ 40 | |
| ,, ,, Wm. Stürup | 249.88 | |
| ,, ,, Lyons, Brasch, & Co. | 21.44 | |
| ,, Messrs. Neckelmann, Room, & Co. | 38 | |
| | $349.32 | |
| Received balance from Herrera Hs. $49.32 | | |
| ,, ,, Maturet & Co. 15.45 | 64.77 | |
| | $284.55 | |
| Paid balance of *billetes* of Röhl & Co. | 1,245 | |
| Freight, per "Isabel," of the first remittance from London | 812.50 | |
| Bringing the money from La Guayra | 27 | |
| Delivered to Sen. Eyzaguirre | 32,500 | |
| ,, ,, per Espino & Dict | 6,350 | |
| Balance paid upon 161,680 *billetes*, $56,500 Shares on account of the Government, less 4 per cent. interest, total or remainder with the *remanets* included | 19,911.12 | $61,130.17 |
| Paid balance of international claims :— | | |
| To Mr. F. D. Orme $12,108.93 | | |
| ,, Mr. Wm. Stürup 2,656.60 | | |
| ,, Mr. Culver 43 | | |
| ,, Mr. Rolandus 4,241.16 | 19,049.19 | |
| Freight of the second remittance from London by the "Isabel" | 812.50 | 19,862.19 |
| | | 80,992.36 |
| Balance in favour of the Government paid this day, 22nd December, 1862 | | 10,701.27 |
| | | $91,693.63 |

(Signed)  E. MOCATTA.

*Messrs. Baring, Brothers, & Co.'s Account of the Loan of 1862.*

| | £ | s. | d. |
|---|---|---|---|
| Venezuela Loan of 1862 . . . . | £630,000 | 0 | 0 |
| Brokerage not claimed, re-credited, &c. . . | 560 | 17 | 6 |
| Cr. | £630,560 | 17 | 6 |

| | £ | s. | d. |
|---|---|---|---|
| Amount paid to Government in Venezuela . . | £398,517 | 14 | 0 |
| Debt in London . . . . . . . | 14,719 | 1 | 3 |
| Seymour & Co. . . . . . . . | 6,300 | 0 | 0 |
| Commission and Brokerage . . . . | 12,500 | 0 | 0 |
| Agency . . . . . . . . | 3,647 | 5 | 3 |
| Dividend 1st July, 1862, on 3 per cent., 1½ per cent., and 6 per cent. Bonds . . | 41,755 | 9 | 3 |
| ,, November, on 6 per cent. . . . | 30,000 | 0 | 0 |
| ,, 1st January, 1863, on 3 per cent., &c. . | 41,755 | 9 | 4 |
| ,, 1st May, 1863, on 6 per cent. . . . | 30,300 | 0 | 0 |
| Commission on Coupons converted into 6 per cent. Bonds . . . . . . | 2,102 | 0 | 0 |
| 20 per cent. paid holders of Venezuela Coupons, due 1840 to 1847, converted into 3 per cents. . . . . . . . | 1,920 | 0 | 0 |
| Paid 24th March, 1863, by order of the Government, to Señor Don H. Nadal . . | 26,141 | 16 | 4 |
| Transferred 23rd October, 1863, to General A. Guzman Blanco . . . . . | 20,902 | 2 | 1 |
| | £630,560 | 17 | 6 |

THE END.